W9-AYR-312

ALSO BY GRANT GINDER

The People We Hate at the Wedding

Honestly, We Meant Well

Driver's Education

This Is How It Starts

LET'S
NOT
DO
THAT
AGAIN

LET'S NOT DO THAT AGAIN

A NOVEL

GRANT GINDER

 HENRY HOLT AND COMPANY   NEW YORK

Henry Holt and Company
Publishers since 1866
120 Broadway
New York, New York 10271
www.henryholt.com

Henry Holt® and Ⓗ® are registered trademarks of
Macmillan Publishing Group, LLC.

Copyright © 2022 by Grant Ginder
All rights reserved.
Distributed in Canada by Raincoast Book Distribution Limited

Library of Congress Cataloging-in-Publication Data

Names: Ginder, Grant, author.
Title: Let's not do that again : a novel / Grant Ginder.
Other titles: Let us not do that again
Description: First Edition. | New York : Henry Holt and Company, 2022.
Identifiers: LCCN 2021060804 (print) | LCCN 2021060805 (ebook) |
     ISBN 9781250243775 (hardcover) | ISBN 9781250243768 (ebook)
Classification: LCC PS3607.I4567 L48 2022 (print) | LCC PS3607.I4567
     (ebook) | DDC 813/.6—dc23
LC record available at https://lccn.loc.gov/2021060804
LC ebook record available at https://lccn.loc.gov/2021060805

Our books may be purchased in bulk for promotional, educational, or business use. Please contact
your local bookseller or the Macmillan Corporate and Premium Sales Department at (800) 221-7945,
extension 5442, or by e-mail at MacmillanSpecialMarkets@macmillan.com.

First Edition 2022

Illustrations on page xi © Thedafkish / Getty Images

Designed by Kelly S. Too

Printed in the United States of America

1   3   5   7   9   10   8   6   4   2

This is a work of fiction. All of the characters, organizations, and events portrayed in
this novel either are products of the author's imagination or are used fictitiously.

For Richard Pine

Non, rien de rien
Non, je ne regrette rien

—Édith Piaf

CONTENTS

Give Me a Smile   1

Act One: Crisis Communications   5

Act Two: La Misérable   73

Act Three: Paris Vous Aime   127

Act Four: October Surprises   181

Act Five: Elect Nancy Harrison!   263

Epilogue: Five Years Later   328

LET'S
NOT
DO
THAT
AGAIN

GIVE ME A SMILE

The champagne has gone to her head.

Also, there's the problem of the smoke. It's everywhere. The smell of burning wood and plastic assaulting her nostrils; the crisp static of smoldering embers. It's raining, but that hardly helps: fires spill from the storefronts along the avenue. Flames outside of Bulgari; singed mannequins at Hugo Boss and Lacoste. A bank with smashed windows, turned into an open-air theater. Shirts with their tags still on them strewn across the street.

She finds herself part of an organized and slow-moving chaos. Protesters creep up the Champs-Élysées, their jackets slick with rain, until the police, feeling as if they've been too generous, force them to relinquish ground. This is how it works, how it surges. Two steps forward, one step back. The sea as the tide rises, climbing over shells on a long stretch of beach. Some of them wear gas masks that make them appear alien, insectile, and those who do not wrap their faces with handkerchiefs and scarves. A strip of wool bearing the logo of Paris Saint-Germain, or—in her case—a square of silk from Hermès. Often, she sees the marchers—*patriots* to some, *terrorists* to others—stop to take selfies. *Here we are, and here France burns*, their smiles say, and when they are finished, they march on. They dodge giant hoses and sing. They balance their lit cigarettes behind their ears so they can use both their fists.

They inch closer toward the Arc de Triomphe and, from behind police barricades, tear gas cannons pop like so many corks. The mob's anatomy is the structure of an atom: at the center is a tight nucleus, around which orbits a wild tangle of electrons. She is one of those orbiters—she could be eighteen, but she could also be thirty; the smoke smudges out her years, adding lines where there shouldn't be lines while stealing others away. She wears a black Chanel dress and a pair of Adidas trainers, and in her right hand she holds a half-full bottle of champagne. Beneath her silk scarf she's smiling, but it's a different smile from the others; hers is not wild and tenacious but rather curious. The mild surprise of someone who's just woken up from a long summer nap. She reads some of the signs around her, and joins in some of the chants, but after a few minutes she gets restless, bored. She takes another swig of the champagne and drifts farther away.

Two people follow her—the first, a camera operator from a French news station, the second, a handsome man with full brown hair. They track her as she crosses avenue George V and stops—finally—beneath the bloodred awnings of Fouquet's. The girl looks at the man with the camera, then up at the iconic restaurant—*This*, she seems to be saying to him, *is the spot*. Bits of marble lie at her feet, the detritus of a facade that used to stand here or on the *grands boulevards*, scabs picked from the face of Paris. She crouches down to touch them, and for a pure, crystalline instant, the sounds of the avenue quiet and the world calms: here is a girl, her hair in her face, running her fingers along the smooth edge of a stone. But then, on rue de Bassano, there is the wail of a siren. Close and high and loud, like the screech of bombers grazing tops of trees.

The girl stands up and whips her head around. She waits for the siren to fade, and once it does she looks down at the champagne, as if she suddenly remembers she is holding it. With her head tilted back, she finishes what's left of the bottle. Then, she hurls it as hard as she can through the front window of Fouquet's.

Glass shatters; a waiter screams. Her hands now freed, the girl searches her pockets for a cigarette.

The camera coaxes her into focus and, beside it, the handsome man laughs.

"*Greta!*" he shouts. "*Give me a smile!*"

At first, the man with the camera worries that his friend has made a mistake. The girl stares at them blankly, her eyes wide and green and full. But a moment later—*aha*, there it is: the devilish curl of her lips. The glint of her perfect, American teeth.

ACT ONE

CRISIS COMMUNICATIONS

Morning Briefing

The phone rings three times, which for Nancy Harrison is two times too many.

"Good morning, Nancy."

"*Cate.*"

"I was about to call you."

"What the fuck is this email?"

"So, you've seen it. Are you sure it's her?"

Nancy presses the phone against her shoulder and brings her laptop within an inch of her nose.

"Oh, it's her, all right. I'd know those cheekbones anywhere."

"How? Or, why?"

"Because they're *my* cheekbones, Cate. I *gave* her those cheekbones."

A cup of coffee steams on the kitchen counter. On the table behind her, a banana languishes, peeled and utterly ignored. Nancy runs both hands through her hair and turns toward the television, where the *Today* show plays on mute. Cataclysmic fires in California and protests in Paris. The two hosts, smiling as they make sense of a senseless world.

From the hall outside the apartment comes an abominable crash: the sound of a wall being torn down.

"Jesus, what was that?" Cate says.

"They're installing the new trash-compacting system."

"They're actually doing it?"

"They're actually doing it. Ten years I've spent as president of this building's co-op board, and I've finally convinced these idiots that there's a more efficient way to get rid of their tampons and chicken bones than putting them in a bag and waiting for a porter to pick them up."

"Well, good for you, Nancy." Cate pauses. "I thought you said Greta was taking cooking classes."

"That's what she told me she was doing." Nancy rubs her palm against her cheek and stares at Greta's face. "That little brat. I loved Fouquet's."

Cate clears her throat.

"The good news is that the *Times* more or less buried it. I mean, it's on the home page, but you have to scroll down to see it. The other outlets . . . well, there's a gallery at the Met named after your mother-in-law, Nancy—"

"My *ex*-mother-in-law."

"—and this election is going to determine who controls the Senate. So, unfortunately, your daughter mugging for the camera as she destroys property in France is not exactly a story the *Post* is going to pass up. We need to decide how to respond."

Nancy ignores her. She moves the cursor over Greta's neck and Greta's thin arms. Greta's dusty, untied shoes.

"She's supposed to be learning how to separate egg whites. She's supposed to be making fucking coq au vin."

"It was a protest over the new EU trade deal. Has Greta ever expressed interest in international economics?"

"International economics? Cate, have you met my daughter? Why the hell would she be at that?"

"I have no idea, but the internet is coming up with some theories."

The *Today* show cuts to a commercial, and Nancy sips from her coffee. It's hot and nearly scalds her throat. *This was supposed to be easy*, she thinks. An open Senate seat, an endorsement from the president—*this was supposed to be easy*. She takes a bigger sip.

"Talk to me about polls," she says. "What are they telling us?"

"Gallup has Carmichael ahead by four points. He's still killing us with boomers."

"And I've got videos of my daughter throwing champagne bottles through windows on the other side of the Atlantic. *Shit*."

She returns to the laptop and the video of Greta. Cate had sent it to her this morning, attached to an email that had as its subject line *pls advise*. The quality is coarse, grainy; Cate said that it ran on a French news channel six hours ago. Since then, it's spread like wildfire. Fox, the *Post*, the *Daily News*, *New York*, *Vogue*. And despite the blurred focus, the sun's blanching glare, there's no doubt the woman in the picture is Greta. At first, Nancy wasn't able to speak, she simply stared at the image, the slow drip of the coffee machine breaking the silence. Seven floors below her, Central Park unfurled itself, the tops of trees poking through a blanket of October fog. On the other side of the East River, beyond Roosevelt Island and the rooftops of Queens, a plane descended toward LaGuardia Airport. She felt exposed, and angry, and above all else guilty. Walking to the window, she recalled a night three months ago, in July. A dinner, here in this apartment, not at the small table in the kitchen but in the dining room, on the other side of the wall. Waiters in stiff white coats; Greta drunk in gold heels; Nancy, grabbing her wrist and dragging her into the foyer.

Pushing her hair out of her face, she turned back to the image on the computer's screen. Her daughter looked fed, and healthy, her cheeks ruddy and her eyes clear. Her feet had shoes on them, and over a black dress that Nancy had bought her, she had remembered to put on a coat.

She thought, *Well, at least she's staying warm*, then picked up the phone to call Cate.

Now, shutting the laptop, Nancy takes another infernal gulp of coffee and redirects her attention toward the television. The commercials have ended; the hosts are back. They are joined by a guest, a political reporter from the *Washington Post*. With the volume still on mute, Nancy watches the conversation unfold, her breath caught in her throat. Then, finally, it happens. The screen cuts to the same video that Nancy has spent the last hour staring at: Greta the Destroyer; Greta with champagne; Greta, now broadcast live for 4.5 million people to see.

"Goddamn it," she says.

The sun tears through clouds in the sky above New York.

Nancy turns off the television and throws its controller on the floor.

"Cate," she says. "I've got to go."

"Where are you going?"

"Downtown. I need to talk to my son."

"Why?"

"Because I have to tell him he's flying to Paris."

Hello to All That!

It feels like spiders crawling around inside his head. Eight legs, multiplied by four, by six, by twelve, scratching against the backs of his eyes, building webs that trammel his thoughts. Spiders, tap dancing on his frontal lobe. Laying eggs that hatch in an explosion of incandescent sparks.

"Is there anything else?" the doctor asks.

Nausea. Yesterday, he vomited twice. Once before lunch, and then another time around four o'clock. He also gets tired—suddenly, cripplingly tired. The sort of tired he's always associated with running a marathon (which he's never done) or narcolepsy (which he doesn't have).

"Right. Okay. That's it?"

Yes—or, no. Not really. Because on top of the electric demon spiders and the twice-daily vomiting and the flashes of fatigue there are the mood swings. Manic fluctuations that whip him from euphoric to irritable to catatonically sad, and that leave him bewildered, as if a tornado has left a gash across his mind. They come swiftly, and without warning: yesterday, when he was at his neighborhood bodega, a Celine Dion ballad came over the radio and, with his fingers piercing an overripe avocado, he burst into tears.

"Which one?"

"The Garden of Eatin', on Fulton Street."

"No, I meant which song."

"Oh." Nick Harrison scratches the back of his knee. "'Taking Chances.'"

Dr. Franklin presses the chilly end of his stethoscope against Nick's chest and nods.

"That's a good one," he says. "Now, breathe."

"Do you think I should be worried?"

"About the avocado?"

"About the symptoms."

"Oh, ha. No. You were on Prozac—"

"Lexapro."

"—sorry, *Lexapro*—for ten years."

"Correct. And also Ativan and Ambien and Klonopin and occasionally—like, *very* occasionally, and honestly only when Congress was trying to pass the budget—a little Zyprexa. But, yes. At the end, it's just been the Lexapro."

The doctor shrugs.

"You're going through withdrawal."

Nick waits for him to say something else. A description of how neurons rediscover long-forgotten pathways, of how blunted synapses sharpen themselves anew. It would all be repetitive—since deciding to stop taking the pills two weeks ago he has spent minutes, hours, stretches of cold autumn nights on the internet, ferreting out explanations for the havoc in his brain. It doesn't matter; he wants to hear what the doctor has to say, anyway. An assurance that this won't last forever. A promise that at some point the spiders will abandon their webs and die.

Instead, Dr. Franklin pats the edge of the examination table and asks Nick to lie flat. Using two fingers, he taps at different spots on Nick's torso, his eyes narrowing as he listens to the soft thud of flesh against flesh. He instructs Nick to inhale, to exhale, to hold his breath. Outside, on Fourteenth Street, a truck blares its horn and a woman begins to yell, a string of *assholes* and *jerk-offs* that is only silenced by the sound of a second horn. Working his lower lip with his teeth, Nick stares up at a spot on the room's ceiling, a brown stain on the plaster the shape of a banana. He thinks: *New York Fucking City.*

Dr. Franklin moves his hands to the left of Nick's belly button.

"How's your mother's Senate campaign going?"

"Not great!"

"You're pleased about that?"

"No—I'm sorry. What you did with your thumb tickled." Nick wiggles his toes. "Chip Carmichael—who would have thought he'd give Nancy such a run for her money?"

"I used to love that television show he was on in the eighties, the one where he played the senator. What was it called again?"

"*Self-Evident*. And a lot of people did. I think that's part of the problem."

"There's still this scene that I remember from the episode with the secret fleet of Russian submarines in the Chesapeake. Carmichael walks up to the president—I think Tom Selleck played him?—anyway, he walks up to him and points his finger at him and says, 'Don't lecture *me* about liberty, sir.' Gives me chills every time."

The doctor moves his hands above Nick's appendix.

"I must have missed that one," he says.

"It was well before your time." The doctor gives a hearty chuckle. "Anyhoo, I bet she's glad she has you to get things back on track."

The office smells of vinyl and latex, beneath which lurks something else, something sweeter. *Peppermint*, Nick thinks. And sugar. The afterthought of Dr. Franklin's breath mint.

"I actually don't work for her anymore," Nick says. "I left a year ago."

Dr. Franklin drapes the stethoscope around his neck. He's thick, a bear of a man, with furry forearms and a bald, cratered scalp. When he sits, his thighs spill over the chair's edge.

"I don't think I knew that," he says.

"It was a big decision." Nick nods. "But there's only so many times that a person can see his mother's name on the bottom of his paycheck before going totally insane."

That's part of it—most of it, actually—but there are also other explanations that Nick keeps to himself, the simplest of which is this: he had had enough. Enough time spent shuttling himself between New York and Washington; enough time spent in the Rayburn cafeteria; enough time spent having the same steak dinner with the same obsequious lobbyists. In theory and title, he had been his mother's speechwriter, but in practice he was her fixer—along with telling her what to say, he planted her stories, patched her leaks, helped her win. Chuck Schumer knew his phone number by heart, and at the behest of his mother Nick had made not one but both Cuomo brothers cry. He was good at his job—great at it, in fact, which is another reason why he knew he needed to quit. Moral equivocations were becoming a bit too facile, and he was falling asleep a little too easily at night. As a boy, he had always liked stories that had clear heroes and clearer villains, and he worried that the more time he spent in politics, the more that line was becoming blurred. He worried that if he didn't get out soon, then What Was Good and What Was Bad would always be a matter for negotiation.

"So, what are you up to now?" Dr. Franklin asks.

"Teaching writing, over at NYU. I finally decided to put that English PhD to work." The doctor thuds two fingers on Nick's appendix. "My real passion though is this musical I'm writing."

"You're writing a musical?"

"Yes. Or, the lyrics. I'm writing the lyrics to a musical. Now I just need to find someone who will write the music."

"Details." *Thud.* "My wife loves musicals. What's it about?"

"Joan Didion."

Another horn on Fourteenth Street. Dr. Franklin purses his lips.

"Her early years, mostly," Nick adds. "Like, when she came to New York to work at *Vogue.* I'm thinking of calling it *Hello to All That!*"

"Say *ah.*"

Nick does as he's told. Light fills his mouth; a wooden depressor nestles into his tongue. When Dr. Franklin's finished, Nick sucks on the insides of his cheeks and tastes the chalky, disappointing end of a popsicle.

"How long do you think the brain zaps will last?" he asks.

"Hard to say. Three months? Six?"

"Six months!"

"Maybe? Who knows!" The doctor throws the tongue depressor at a trash can and misses. He removes his latex gloves. "Why'd you decide to go off it in the first place?"

Nick thinks. How does he describe what it feels like for the first time in two years to experience joy? Not pleasure. Not the fleeting ecstasy of a good meal, or the luck-rush of an expertly timed commute, but *joy*. The sturdy kind. The kind that's rooted and complex. A fire as it roars to life in winter; the sound of a bow as it's pulled across a cello's strings. It's not perpetual—it comes in flashes. Sunlight, glinting off the spire of the Chrysler Building; the light on someone's face the second before she laughs. Moments where Nick sinks into himself and thinks, *Well, hello, old friend.* He had known it was there, waiting for him, but the last ten years had distracted him from it. All those late-night phone calls from Chuck, all those early-morning trains with Nancy—it wasn't until he ditched them that he realized they were keeping him an inch away from happiness. And it's for this reason that he's weaning himself off the drugs, breaking little white pills into halves and fourths and eighths each morning on the wet edge of his sink. Simply put: he doesn't need them anymore. For the first time in a decade, Nick feels like he's living his own life.

He says, "Because I no longer work for my mother."

The doctor nods. As far as reasons go, this seems to be enough.

"Well, don't feel ashamed if it doesn't work out. These drugs save people's lives, you know."

"I know that."

"And you can always call me, Nick. I'm always here if you need some help."

"I appreciate that, Dr. Franklin."

"You can put your pants on now."

Nick pushes himself from the table. He's left his clothes in a heap on the examination room's floor, and now he untangles his underwear from his jeans. Down the hall, in the waiting room, a telephone rings. Dr. Franklin checks the clock. Turning to the room's sink, he begins washing his hands, working the lather between his knuckles and across the leathered planes of his palms.

"So, what's the verdict?" Nick asks. "Will I live to see next year?"

"You'll live to see a lot more than that. You're fit as a fiddle."

Nick slips his legs into his pants and pulls them up to his waist. Sucking in his breath, he buttons them and zips up his fly.

"I've always liked that saying," he says. "Never understood it, but always liked it. And hey—there's a black box theater I'm eyeing in Long Island City. For the musical, I mean. You and your wife should come, once it's up. I think I know a guy who can get you tickets."

Cinching his belt, Nick winks.

The doctor says nothing. He opens the door and leads Nick into the office's waiting room, which is empty, save a woman with two large Rite Aid bags, her head buried in a crossword. It's windowless, stuffy; in one corner is a rack of month-old magazines, and in another is a sign that says NO CELL PHONES OR ROLLER BLADES. An elevator opens directly into the office, groaning as it climbs up the building's spine and rattling the fifth-floor doors. Fixed to one of the walls is a framed poster of the city's skyline and then, next to it, a small, muted television. It's tuned to CNN—*Facts First*—and Nick watches as a report on a sinking island in Indonesia is replaced by a taped interview with his mother. The chyron: "Nancy Harrison: I'm Running for Our Lives."

Setting a hand on Nick's shoulder, Dr. Franklin gives him a good squeeze.

"Maria at the front desk will take care of your copay," he says. Then, before retreating to the examination room, he adds: "And hey, Nick?"

Nick glances up from his wallet. Spiders spin telephone wires across his brain. "Yeah?"

"Best of luck with Joan."

On Self-Respect

Nick chews a pen cap and reads the bits of dialogue he's spent the past hour writing. He's in his office in the Critical Thinking and Writing Department, which is housed on the second floor of a cast-iron building on Lafayette Street, four blocks east of Washington Square. Above him is NYU's Center for Residential Life, and below him is Me, Myself, and Thai, a pan-Asian restaurant that sells noodles by the pound. The office itself is small and square, and has a single window—a rectangle of drafty glass that lets in not only the chilly autumn air but also the scent of frying garlic and fish sauce, ginger and tamarind. His pen still lodged between his molars, Nick bites down. His physical with Dr. Franklin required blood work, which meant that he had to fast; instead of breakfast this morning, he got a needle prick and a Flintstones Band-Aid, stuck to the crux of his left arm. Now his stomach rumbles.

"I can't figure out how to end this thing," he says.

Lisa, his office mate, turns in her chair.

"End what?'"

"This musical. I've written everything but the last scene, and now I can't figure out how to end it."

Curling her lips in, Lisa thinks.

"I've got it," she says. "Joan holds up the Federal Reserve, robs it blind, and redistributes the cash to solve systemic wealth inequality."

From downstairs: oyster sauce, and the earthy smell of mushrooms. The relentless seduction of *pad see ew*.

Nick says, "It's not really that kind of show."

Lisa shakes her head.

"Then I don't know what to tell you," she says, and turns back to her computer. On the screen, Nick catches a glimpse of a layered stack of home pages: the *Washington Post* and the *New York Times*. CNN, MSNBC, and the Daily Beast. Lisa is a news junkie, a tragedy addict. She begins conversations with reports of explosions in the West Bank, droughts in South Sudan. One morning two weeks ago, Nick unlocked the office's door to find her sitting in the dark, watching a video on YouTube—a montage of walruses tumbling down a cliff, their dead bodies piling up among the gently lapping waves.

"It's in Russia," she said, her voice quiet and small. "They aren't supposed to be up that high, but the sea ice has melted. They've got nowhere to go."

A bull teetered over a precipice, its fins outstretched as if, in a fairer world, it might fly. Right before it collided with the rocks, Nick's brain went *zap* and he turned away. With his one hand he squeezed Lisa's shoulder, and with the other he turned on the light.

He does not blame her. He tells her he does not want to engage, but he does not blame her, he understands. There was a time, back when his life was measured in media cycles, that he acted the same way. He reached for his phone before he opened his eyes in the morning. He subsided on cycles of information and analysis; he traded in an economy of Knowing First, of Hot Takes. If something happened—a vote, a pandemic, a series finale—he sent messages to his friends and colleagues that were devoid of context. "Italy, geez," or "Who knew she had it in her." When, seconds later, his phone buzzed with their responses ("Lombardy!" and "I did") he felt comforted. He told himself that when The End finally came, at least they'd have these, their dress rehearsals for the apocalypse. At least they'd be able to say they saw it coming.

And then, when he left politics, he unplugged himself. Or—not entirely, but mostly. He downloaded an app that locked him out of all his favorite sites until eight o'clock each evening. At first it was difficult—not knowing what calamities were currently befalling humanity made him feel marooned—but quickly that changed. The world, he learned,

couldn't make sense of what it had endured that day until around dinner-
time, anyway, so all the stuff that came before it rarely amounted to anything more than hand-wringing. Meanwhile, in the elongating spaces
between articles—between the shrinking ice caps and the outbreaks
and the crashing markets—he began to notice things he hadn't realized
he'd missed. The pleasant daze of a wandering mind; the pricelessness
of boredom. The way that, instead of racing, his thoughts now settled,
blanketing his mind like silt.

And time! Good God, the time he has now. Time to open books and
actually read them, and start shows and actually finish them, and play
records and actually hear them. Time to write a musical! It was an idea
that came to him last fall when, in his Introduction to Thinking course,
he asked his students to read "On Self-Respect," the essay that Didion published in *Vogue* in 1961, the one that, as he explained to them, *really put
her on the map*. He remembers how, in the minutes before class started,
he rolled up his shirtsleeves and smelled the fresh ink on the stack of
copies he'd xeroxed. It was his first day on the job—his first day of life
free from the incessant demands of Washington, the country, and his
mother—and he was excited. Excited to see minds bloom! To help them
untangle the mysteries of the world! To *learn*! As the clock crept closer
to nine o'clock, he polished his glasses and checked his teeth; he sat in
his chair and then, thinking better of it, leaned on the edge of his desk
instead. One by one, the students filed in, unloading their backpacks and
taking seats around the seminar table. How young they looked! And how
eager! He greeted each of them with a hearty *hello*; when they asked him
if he was *Professor Harrison*, he laughed and waved the question away.
Professor Harrison was someone who wore tweed jackets and said things
like *indubitably*. They could call him Nick.

He didn't bother with the syllabus, the tedious parsing of due dates
and attendance policies, the arithmetic of final grades. Instead, he hit
them with a bang—he hit them with the Didion. For the first minute, they
approached the text timidly: a group of swimmers, using their toes to test
the temperature of the lake. And then slowly, they began to wade in.

"So, let's start with the big question," he said once the last student had
finished the essay. "What *is* self-respect?"

At first: crickets. The soft creak of weight being redistributed in chairs. And then—*bingo*: a hand. The girl across the table, who by now had tucked her pencil into a loose bun of raven hair. A freshman whose name, a quick glance at Nick's roll sheet revealed, was Vanessa.

"Yes." He clasped his hands together and pointed at her. "Take it away."

"I actually find this essay to be really problematic."

The class stared at Nick; Nick bit his lip.

"Oh. Well—huh."

"If you check out the fifth-to-last paragraph, for example." A flurry of turning pages; raindrops alighting on flat-faced leaves. "She says, 'People who respect themselves are willing to accept the risk that the Indians will be hostile.'"

"Right."

"Well, first of all, it's Native Americans."

"I, uh—okay, that's a fair point."

"And second of all, hostile from whose perspective? A bunch of smallpox-infested white guys who have come to steal their land?"

"Oh, I think she was using that as a callback to the paragraph before. Where she quotes from the diary of the young pioneer girl?"

"Okay. So, the *daughter* of a smallpox-infested white guy who has come to steal their land."

Nick scratched his head.

"It was 1961," he offered.

"Meaning . . ."

"Meaning that maybe they didn't have, uh, the same perspective on that word yet?"

"Or the same perspective on the brutalities of Manifest Destiny, evidently. Because I hardly think that being a foot soldier in the mass genocide of native peoples calls for a celebration of *self-respect*, even if you"—Vanessa scanned the page, narrowed in on a quote—"'have the courage of your own mistakes.'"

Someone coughed. Outside, a garbage man collected bags on West Eleventh Street, hurling them into the yawning rear of a truck.

"Okay," Nick said. "So, let's acknowledge that the use of 'Indians' in this paragraph is, uh, as Vanessa said, problematic. Beyond that, though, what is Didion really saying here? What does she mean when she says that 'We flatter ourselves by thinking this compulsion to please others an attractive trait: a gift for imaginative empathy, evidence of our willingness to give.' Why does this 'compulsion to please' stand in opposition to self-respect?"

Vanessa's hand shot up, but Nick pretended he didn't see it. Instead, he directed his attention to her right, where a boy with a nose ring was drawing circles in the margins of his paper.

"Amir," he said. "What do you think about this whole idea of a 'compulsion to please'?"

Setting his pen down, Amir glanced at Vanessa, and then at the rest of the class. He seemed nervous, skittish. His glasses slipped, and he reached up to straighten them.

"Um, you said this was published in *Vogue*?"

"That's right. In 1961."

"Oh."

"Oh?"

"Yeah." Amir blushed. "I guess I just find that a little weird."

Vanessa nodded; Nick scratched his neck.

"Why is that?"

"Well, *Vogue* is a fashion magazine, right?"

"Yes, primarily, but they've also published some of the best—"

"And isn't a fashion magazine mostly concerned with telling women— well, white women, really—how to make themselves appear pleasing to others? Like, isn't that basically why fashion magazines exist?"

"I—well, I think that the people who work at fashion magazines might say that's debatable."

Amir reached up and twisted his nose ring.

"I guess all I'm saying is that it seems a little hypocritical to be writing about self-respect for a magazine that I imagine makes a lot of women question their worth. That's all."

And so on, and so forth, and et cetera. For the next hour and fifteen minutes they discussed the essay's troubling allusions to Jordan Baker, and its misguided admiration of Chinese Gordon in Khartoum; they discussed the name Chinese Gordon. They discussed the intellectual privilege of

Phi Beta Kappa, and the shaming of Cathy in *Wuthering Heights*, and the essay's "presumptive" and "all-encompassing" use of *we*. They discussed Julian English and *Appointment in Samarra* and the nineteenth century and paper Food Fair bags. They never—not even once—discussed self-respect.

This was invigorating (the energy of young minds!) but also disappointing. Nick's lesson plan for the next three classes depended upon their reaching at least a vague consensus of what the essay meant. Beyond that, he was curious, and genuinely so: what was self-respect, and—a subquestion—how does a person know that he has it? Joan said that it was about "taking one's own measure" and "making one's own peace." Had Nick done that when he struck out on his own? Had Joan? Is that what she felt when she graduated from Berkeley? Or how about when she won the Prix de Paris and moved to New York?

He often imagined her boarding that plane, her ticket clutched with both hands, her heart going haywire in her chest. He imagined her walking into *Vogue* and getting homesick for the dry Sacramento summers and writing *Run River* and meeting John Gregory Dunne. He imagined her falling in love. And as Nick did so—as he relived these memories that were never really his—something else materialized for him. A rainbow, suddenly appearing across a swath of rain-scrubbed sky. An arc, the story of a life. A musical! Joan, singing a lament for California; Joan, belting in the heart of Herald Square. He didn't know any composers, at least not directly, but this was New York—the land of waiters with Juilliard degrees, the mecca of frustratingly underworked talent. After talking to two friends and sending three emails, he had connected with Celeste, a jazz pianist from the Peabody Institute who had abandoned a life of gigs to write jingles for car commercials.

They met at a pub near Union Square, a happy-hour spot with big, square windows through which Nick could see snow gathering on the hoods of cars. He wore a rumpled button-down and jeans; Celeste dressed in all black. She remained perfectly still as he explained the project, moving only to take slow, long sips from her Syrah. Around them, the bar began to fill: wool slacks and ironed shirts; black coats hanging from the backs of chairs.

"Joan Didion," she said.

"Yes, that's right."

"Like, *Slouching Toward Bethlehem* Joan Didion."

"That's the one. *SLOUCHING!* was actually my original title."

Celeste ran a finger around the rim of her glass.

"Yeah," she said. "I don't think so."

"What do you mean?"

"I mean it's not for me."

Nick took a sip of beer and licked the foam from his lips: this was an outcome for which he had not prepared.

"We could workshop it, of course," he said. "Share a creative vision, and all that. We could—"

"Listen." Celeste raised a hand to stop him. "I don't think it's the most compelling subject matter. No offense."

Nick looked down. Snow melted on the tips of his shoes.

"There was literally a musical called *Chess*," he said.

He reached out to other composers. A pianist from Oberlin who was tied up with a one-act about Gettysburg; a rocker with gray hair and a CBGB shirt who said she'd be more interested in the project if it were about Joan Jett. At the end of each of these meetings, as Nick ventured out alone into the frozen city, he forbade himself to get discouraged. He had a dream of his own—he couldn't remember the last time he was able to say that—and now he was committed to seeing it through. The songs would come, he told himself, it was only a matter of time, and as he waited he would continue to work feverishly, rereading Joan's essays and novels, trying to get a sense of the woman behind the page. His story— *Joan's story*—would be one of intimacy, and candor; a journey, as it were, *toward self-respect*. With it, Nick would finally—

"Nick." Lisa is speaking to her computer screen. Lisa is always speaking to her computer screen. "Have you seen this?"

"If it's the news, then no. It's not eight o'clock at night yet."

"I think you might want to."

"I think I probably don't." Nick drums a pen against his forehead. "How about a fade to black? For *Hello to All That!* I mean."

"Do they do that in musicals?"

"Sure, why not?"

Lisa turns, considers the idea, then shakes her head.

"You know, I think it's just really hard to write the ending for something as sentimental as a musical that's about someone famously unsentimental. Also, you're buzzing."

"I'm what?"

"You're buzzing. Like, you're vibrating. Someone's calling you."

Nick glances at the corner of his desk, where his iPhone dances next to a stack of ungraded essays. Picking it up, he says, "Huh."

"Who is it?"

"My mother."

He stares at the phone, feeling it rattle against his palm.

"*Oooooh*. The *senator*. Aren't you going to answer it?"

"She's not a senator yet. And no—I don't think so. I need to come up with an ending."

"I bet you'll answer it."

"Lisa, I won't."

"Ten bucks says you will."

"Lisa, I swear to God, I won't."

"Okay, fine. You won't."

"Hi, Mom."

Lisa holds up ten fingers; Nick sits back down and cradles the phone against his shoulder.

"Nick, we need to talk."

"I'm sort of busy right now."

Mouth agape, Lisa lifts an eyebrow. Nick shrugs and whispers, "What?"

"Well, whatever you're doing, put a pin in it," Nancy says. "Because I'm at the Thai place downstairs."

A Better Good

The walls of Me, Myself, and Thai are the color of radioactive egg yolks, a brilliant, unnatural yellow that, the longer Nick is confronted with it, seems to glow. Pictures of smiling noodles have been painted directly onto them, each one engaged in a very human task. Here is a noodle chopping an onion; here is a noodle walking a dachshund; here is a noodle eating a plate of other noodles. They have button noses and big round eyes that stare—with what one might assume is a certain amount of dread—at the lines of students, waiting to place their orders. And they're certainly there, the students, at least twenty of them, their faces buried in their phones, their backpacks dangling from single, drooped shoulders. They don't lift their heads as the line moves—their sneakers shuffle along by instinct. They wear jeans and NYU hoodies, and many of them have their school ID cards hanging from purple lanyards looped around their necks. The pictures on these cards bear very little resemblance to the faces that own them, and this is something that always surprises Nick. How quickly real life transforms them! The IDs act as relics of a more optimistic time. They remind everyone that given the right preparation, these faces can be fresh, and rosy. All it takes is a good comb and a toothbrush and their mothers, driving in from New Jersey to do their laundry.

On the subject of mothers: Nick scans their faces for his own, and when he doesn't see her he moves into the restaurant's only other room, which is filled with tables and chairs and napkin dispensers, and on whose walls are painted the same pictures of cannibalistic Pad Thai. There are fewer people here. Only three of the room's seven tables are occupied, and he spots Nancy at one of them immediately. She's wearing a white blouse and gray wool slacks, and her hair, which she has worn in the same crisp bob since time immemorial, frames her very studious face. Across from her sits a student, a girl with a head two sizes too big for her body, who is speaking and gesticulating wildly. A plate of untouched green curry sits between them, right alongside the girl's Monster Energy Zero Ultra drink, a red spiral-bound notebook, and a copy of Nancy's book.

It—the book—is called *A Better Good* and was released last year, in anticipation of Nancy's sprint for the Senate. In terms of its content, it adheres more or less to the rules of political memoir—a genre that, so far as Nick can tell, requires that each of its protagonists re-create the monomyth. The hero leaves the village, the hero sees that hardworking Americans deserve better social services, the hero returns to the village and endeavors to make it so. In Nancy's case the impetus for this journey was not a military tour in Afghanistan, but rather tragedy: namely, the death of her husband, Nick and Greta's father. Howard had represented New York's tenth congressional district before Nancy; he was also the son of the state's former governor. When he died—a single-car crash in Amagansett—Nancy stopped practicing law to take his place. She bore the duty humbly, or as humbly as Nancy Harrison is capable of bearing anything.

The truth, however, is that her understanding of politics—of the mechanisms of power and the ambition it takes to control them—was preternatural. Within two terms she had a seat on Appropriations, and within four she was chairing Intelligence. People started talking, and the DNC took notice. She could connect people, and inspire them to get things done. She stood up to Big Oil and fought for universal healthcare and, to date, has done more to protect the rights of undocumented immigrants than any sitting Democrat. No one outright admitted that it was a good thing that Howard died, no matter how much they might have thought it. Instead, they said that Nancy was better than Howard could have ever hoped to be; Nancy, they said, should have been The One all along. As for Nick, he is losing the few memories he has of his father. He was ten when all this happened, and Greta only four. Occasionally half-ghosts emerge. The baritone of Howard's voice, calling Nick's name in a field upstate; the spice of his aftershave in the morning. These fade, though, almost as quickly as they materialize. Really, Nick and Greta had Nancy, and only Nancy.

The girl is still talking, her head wobbling back and forth like a golf ball ready to roll off its tee. Nick smells tamarind and ginger, the same scents that linger in his office, but now ten times stronger. Glancing over, Nancy spots him, discreetly raises a finger—*one minute*—and then nods, earnestly, at whatever the girl is saying. It's an expression that Nick knows well, one that he has seen his mother perfect over the years: *I am listening and I hear you.* She practiced it on him whenever he had a complaint as a child, and now he finds himself mimicking it when he speaks to his students. A performative empathy meant to absorb the pain and frustrations of others. Lately, Greta has started to hate it. When Nick does it, but especially when Nancy does. She calls it phony, empty. The rhetorical equivalent of a one-armed hug.

Reaching into her purse, Nancy retrieves a pen, which she uses to sign the copy of *A Better Good* sitting on the table. The girl beams, accepts the gift with both hands, and—is this for real?—bows. Then she puts the book away, along with her spiral-bound notebook and Monster Energy drink, and heaves her backpack over her shoulder. When she leaves, it's with her head held high and her shoulders thrust back. She brushes past Nick without so much as a glance.

"I got you some green curry," Nancy says once Nick has sat down.

"Thanks, but I'm okay." He turns toward the door through which the girl left. "What was that all about?"

"*That* was a constituent. She registered in New York so she can vote for me. She also read my book."

"Lucky her."

"Nick, please have some of this food. You don't eat enough. You never have. You look so *thin*."

"Mom, I'm fine. And if I eat anything it's not going to be green curry. It's, like, ten o'clock in the morning."

Nancy is no longer listening to him, though. Nancy is staring at her phone and frowning.

"What's wrong?" Nick asks.

"It's fucking Mrs. Branovich, that old lady who lives down the hall in Seven D. She just sent me an email in all caps."

"What's she want?"

"She's worried that her dog is going to fall into the trash compactor."

"You finally got them installed? And I always liked that dog. Linda, its name is, right?"

"Its name is Helen and it's a terror. And yes, I did get them installed. Ten Cram-a-Lot X-treme One Thousands—it's the best large-scale compactor on the market. So help me God, Nick, when I die I want my tombstone to say that I was the woman who fixed American healthcare and who got a modern refuse system installed in the San Marino."

"That seems a little long for a tombstone."

"Then buy a bigger one."

Nancy closes her email and opens a new window, which she holds up for Nick to see. On it, a video shows the inner workings of a trash compactor, an arrangement of thick plates and spinning gears preparing to work. From the shaft above falls a steel box—a spec that grows bigger and bigger until it lands in a mess of springs and glass and broken vents.

"Is that an oven?" Nick asks.

"Watch—the Cram-a-Lot will crush it. Right down to the size of a bowling ball."

"I believe you. Mom—why are you here?"

Nancy picks up a fork and plants it into a mound of rice. Leaning back in her chair, she folds her arms across her chest.

"Your sister threw a champagne bottle through the window of Fouquet's. During that riot in Paris."

"She did *what*?"

"She. Threw. A. Champagne. Bottle. Through. The. Window—"

"No, no. I heard you. Why the hell would she do that?"

Nancy sighs, fiddles on her phone again, and slides it across the table like a hockey puck. There's a new video, and while it's grainy, Nick can still make out the details: a champagne bottle arcing through the air; glass strewn across the sidewalk like rose petals; Greta, smiling in a long, black dress.

"Fouquet's had the best steak tartare," he says.

"Well, now your sister's ruined it. Greta's ruined steak tartare at Fouquet's for everyone."

Nick runs his hands through his hair and shakes his head.

"Wow. She told me she was taking cooking classes."

"Yes, well, it seems that cooking classes were a lie, Nick."

At the table across from them, a student sits down holding a tray laden with grotesquely red noodles.

"I talked to her two days ago," he says. "She told me she cut her finger slicing eggplant for ratatouille."

"I tried calling her this morning."

"And?"

"And she didn't pick up. Her phone didn't even ring. She's turned it off."

"What about her Instagram? Twitter?"

"She deleted all that six months ago, when she broke up with Ethan. She said social media was for publicists and pedophiles."

"Right. *Fuck.*"

The student turns to stare at Nick. Nick stares back and the student shies away.

"She didn't get arrested, which is both a good thing and a bad thing—if she were in jail, at least I'd know how to find her." Nancy knocks her knuckles against the table. "Did she say anything to you?"

"What do you mean?"

"Just that: did she say anything to you? Greta . . . she tells you things that she doesn't tell me."

This is true, it has always been true. Of all the roles that Nick has played—fixer, professor, brother, lover, son—being the conduit between his mother and his sister is perhaps the one at which he has grown most adept. Greta is difficult; Nancy is difficult; Nick loves them both, which lands him squarely in the middle. He doesn't feel torn—Nick is not a martyr, and this isn't *Sophie's Choice*—so much as he feels as though he's fluent in three distinct languages: his sister's, his mother's, and the tongue that bridges the two.

Hunching over the phone, he zooms in on the picture.

"No," he says. "She didn't say anything to me. But maybe—"

"Maybe what?"

"Maybe she had her reasons."

Nick waits as his mother considers the possibility that, perhaps, Greta was motivated by something that she could not understand. Her lips curl inward and her eyes soften and—*no*. Congresswoman Harrison shakes her head.

"She didn't have reasons. Greta's given up on reasons. She saw a bunch of people breaking things, and she didn't want to feel left out. In any event, people are talking about this."

"Like who?"

"Carmichael's campaign. The *Daily News*. *Vogue*."

"Why does *Vogue* care?"

"They like her dress."

Nick nods. "It's a very nice dress."

"I bought her that dress, Nick. That's something that *Vogue* didn't mention. *I bought her that dress*."

His eyes still fixed on the phone, Nick leans back in his chair and crosses his arms.

"Who broke the story first?"

"A French news station ran the footage, and those vultures at Fox got their hands on it. From there—well, everyone has something to say. Goddamn it, Nick, she's fucking with me, I know it."

"I'm saying this from a place of love, Mom, but I think the two of you could really benefit from some couch time." Nick leans forward again. "What'd the *Post* write?"

"'French Twist! Nancy Harrison's Daughter Rocks Paris.'"

"'French Twist' is actually pretty good."

"Nick, they were talking about it on the *Today* show."

The curry makes Nick's stomach growl. With a single finger he pushes the plate to the other end of the table.

"The *Today* show?!"

"Yes. Along with CNN, MSNBC, BuzzFeed, and New York One. Like I said, it's everywhere, and Carmichael is polling four points ahead."

Nick tents his fingers and rests his chin on top.

"And what would you like me to do about it?" he asks.

"I need you to go to Paris. I need you to find your sister and bring her back here, ideally before she burns down the Arc de Triomphe and causes a bigger mess."

"Mom—"

"Cate is working on getting you a flight, and we've booked you a room at the Hôtel du Louvre. They have a good breakfast, lots of those little yogurts in fancy glass pots. You'll like it."

"*Mom*. When I left a year ago, you said you'd never do this. You said you'd never come to me with requests like this."

"It's for your sister."

"It's for you."

"It's for both of us. Nick, this will be the last time."

And there they are again, Nick thinks, *the spiders*. Playing hopscotch along his temporal lobe. Sending shocks to his nose and colluding with his past. Nick presses two knuckles against his temple and turns them against the soft flesh.

"I'm sorry, but I can't," he says. "I love you, Mom, but this is a problem you need to fix on your own. Besides, it's not like she's being held hostage. Greta will come back. She always does."

Nancy is quiet, an eerie silence that Nick worries will be followed by either a slap or a hug. Instead, she reaches out and takes hold of her son's wrist. Her fingers feel cold, and a little sweaty, and they press ever so slightly against his pulse.

She says: "Do you think I'm a bad mother?"

Startled, Nick opens his eyes. Her voice is raw, fragile—wounded skin, in the minutes before it scabs. He squeezes his mother's hand.

"I think you're a very good politician," he says.

Nancy swallows, and she doesn't blink, and for a moment Nick fears she'll begin to cry. He fears that here, among the restaurant's yellow walls and cruel fluorescent lights, he will need to hold his mother, the congresswoman, and tell her that despite Greta and Paris and the *Post* and Carmichael, everything will be fine. That the history of civilization is one of daughters throwing bottles and of windows breaking; of politicians scheming and journalists meddling; and yet someway, somehow, people have managed and survived. He prepares himself to do this; he readies the words. And yet, before he takes in the necessary air to say them, Nancy releases him and stands.

"A good politician and a bad mother," she says, straightening out her blouse. "One out of two ain't bad."

Again she tells him to think about Paris—"the flight's at ten," she says, "should you come to your senses."

Then she puts on her sunglasses, slings her purse over her shoulder, and leaves.

The Management

Can I eat beef Stroganoff for breakfast? This is the question that Cate Alvarez is actually asking herself. She can, can't she? It's not like there's a law prohibiting it. After all, food is food—it's convention that has delineated it into certain categories, relegating eggs and Lucky Charms to the waking hours of the morning. When you take away those norms, when you *free yourself from culinary despotism*, you're left with the basics: carbs (the noodles), protein (the beef), vitamins (the . . . cream of mushroom soup?); the foundations for a nutritious start to the day. And besides, she's an adult—she's thirty-two!—and that means she can eat whatever she wants whenever she wants it. Cookies before lunch, just because she can; pancakes for dinner, because why the hell not? Cate Alvarez has agency, Cate Alvarez has power. Cate Alvarez is in control.

Or: there aren't any other options. When she left her apartment at five forty-five this morning it was in a rush. News of Greta's video from Paris had recently broken, and her only concern was getting from her apartment in Cobble Hill to the campaign's headquarters, on Varick Street. She wasn't thinking about food—she wasn't even thinking about coffee. As she hustled down the subway stairs, her mind was already racing through what she needed to do today. Get Nancy on the phone and bring her up to speed. Call the biggest donors and walk them back from the ledge. Talking points for surrogates, some statements for the press, a quick brush-up on the politics of French gas prices. Swim, swim, swim, Cate, lest you stop and die. It wasn't until five minutes ago that she realized that (1) it was suddenly ten thirty, and (2) the only thing she'd consumed today was water and a few errant drips of toothpaste. Her mind was fuzzy and her stomach growled; she needed something to eat. She checked her email one more time, then went to the kitchen to see what she could scavenge.

Enter the Stroganoff. It's nestled in a tin takeout container, and it's the only thing in the office refrigerator. She peels open the plastic top and sees that the sour cream has congealed on the tops of the noodles, giving them an orangish crust. It's been picked apart; there are only four pieces of actual beef left, each one the size and shape of a slug. Peeling back the plastic a few more inches, she investigates further: it smells earthy, and a little tart. Bits of mushrooms sit in a beige sauce, marinating alongside a few soggy onions. *Beef Stroganoff.* Who the fuck ordered this? She definitely didn't. Whoever it was left it in the fridge, though, and that means it's fair game. She finds a fork in the sink, wipes it against her pants, and pokes a mound of noodles. *What a strange, schizophrenic dish.* Ramen that wandered into a Burger King. Fettucine in the hands of a drunk, hungry czar.

"What, you didn't eat leftovers when you worked at Google?"

Cate turns and sees Tom Cooper, the campaign's press man, standing in the kitchen's doorway. *No,* she thinks, turning back to the Stroganoff, *I sure as fuck didn't.* If she were still at Google, a chef in a clean white toque would be making her an omelet. Tomatoes, pancetta, and basil, with a generous sprinkling of Parmigiano-Reggiano, because why not? Or, no—wait. On second thought, she'd skip the omelet station and go to the yogurt bar instead. Holy *hell* does she miss the yogurt bar. Bucket after bucket of berries, granola, and honey squeezed from the asses of genetically engineered bees. Lunch would be grilled salmon (sensible), and if she got hungry in the afternoon she'd head up to the ninth floor to get an éclair with her coffee. At no point, and under precisely zero circumstances, would she be eating someone else's leftover beef Stroganoff.

"Seriously, though." Tom is still standing in the doorway. "I wouldn't do that."

"Why?"

"Because it's been in there for, like, a week and a half."

The refrigerator door swings farther open, knocking against Cate's knee.

"Well, I'm starving."

Tom shrugs. "Suit yourself."

He's a few years older than Cate is—pushing forty, she'd bet—and he has a thing for expensive, elaborate sneakers. The sort of man, she reasons, who complains about twenty-year-olds, but only when he's not too busy trying to be one of them. If he were ever to find the right light, she also imagines he might be attractive. He's got a full head of hair and the face of a character actor—one of those guys whose name Cate can never remember when she spots him on *Law & Order*, but whom she's nonetheless sort of pleased to see. This is his third campaign with Harrison, and he regards Cate the same way she senses the rest of the staff does: with curiosity, reverence, and a little bit of contempt. She is an intruder, Nancy's shiny new toy. The tech mercenary who's getting paid way too much to dirty her hands for democracy.

Tom grins and leans against the door, his arms folded high across his chest.

Outside the kitchen, a telephone rings, and an intern answers it, fumbling over his words. Cate gazes down into the chaos of the Stroganoff. Then she grabs a fork, which she loads with as many noodles as she can, and shoves it into her mouth. She chews, moving her jaw in wide, deliberate circles. Tom stares at her and she stares back. She loads up another bite and, his grin gone, he walks away.

Nancy arrives at eleven and, without slowing her stride, calls Tom and Cate into an open office for a meeting.

"You two, with me," she says, her purse swinging like an ax. "*Now.*"

As she passes their desks, the campaign's interns and junior staffers glance up and then immediately back to their computers. Cate watches as they lean forward, like they're hoping to disappear into their screens.

The office that she leads them to is small and windowless—a storage closet into which has been shoehorned a desk, two chairs, and leftover campaign paraphernalia. Cardboard boxes overflowing with T-shirts bearing Nancy's name. Stacks of pamphlets outlining Nancy's platform. Posters of Nancy speaking in front of the Capitol, of Nancy on Ellis

Island, of Nancy in Albany. A five-gallon bucket—the sort that's drummed in subway stations throughout the city—filled with pins the size of black-and-white cookies. HARRISON ♥ NY. HARRISON FOR SENATE. And then, on top of them all: ELECT NANCY HARRISON!

Tom sits and, seeing that no one else has done so, promptly stands again. Nancy slams the door.

"Okay," she says. "What the fuck are we going to do."

THE CALL TO JOIN THE campaign came two months ago, in August. Cate was massaging some talking points about data security when the phone rang and there she was, Nancy Harrison, her old boss, inviting her to lunch in SoHo.

"Get the rotisserie chicken salad," she said once they'd sat down. "It'll change your world."

Cate took in the space around her. The restaurant was big and airy, with high ceilings and arched windows. An étagère lined with wineglasses bifurcated the room, and in the spaces between their stems Cate could see a table of women ignoring a basket of bread. There was music, but it was hardly noticeable—the sort of toothless jazz that a person wouldn't miss until she realized it was gone. The trill of a piano to fill the space between a question and an answer; an alto sax giving you time to think. Cate noticed that Nancy was watching her, and so she took a sip of water. Then she opened her menu and spread her napkin on her lap.

"That salad costs thirty-two dollars," she said.

"I don't care, it's worth it. In a town of overpriced salads, this one is king." Nancy cleared her throat. She was wearing a herringbone blazer, an American flag pinned cockeyed to its lapel. "I was sorry to hear about your mother."

"Oh. Yes." Cate swallowed—it had been five years, and still *mother* was a word she could hardly stand to hear. "I never properly got a chance to thank you for—"

"There's no need to thank me." Nancy batted her hand in front of her face as a new song began: the first wobbly notes of "Cheek to Cheek." "How long ago did you work for me, Cate?"

Crossing her legs, Cate did a little math.

"Nine years ago," she said. "I was in your DC office for three years after I graduated from Michigan."

"*Michigan*—that's where you went. I couldn't remember." Nancy sipped from her water. "And then Google swooped in and stole you away with promises of being able to bring your dog to work."

Cate tried to suppress a smile. She failed.

"Still don't have that dog, but yes, I suppose they did."

Half a baguette filled a basket between them, and now Nancy reached to tear a chunk off its heel.

"What if I told you I wanted you to come back and run my campaign?"

Cate's cheeks began to flush and she willed them to stop. Her water was in front of her, and she reached for it, trying to play it cool. The glass was sweaty, though, and slipped from her fingers to the floor, where it shattered. The women on the other side of the étagère turned their heads and Nancy grinned. For the first time in her life, cool was something that Cate Alvarez was not.

"*Shit*," she whispered, and pulled herself together. "What makes you think that I'd want to?"

"Because I've been around for a long time, Cate." Nancy smeared butter across her bread. "And I know that someone with your talents doesn't want to spend her life shilling for a company that's counting all the grains of sand in the world just because it can—"

"Incidentally, I don't think that project's moving forward."

"—and because for the past three months you've been emailing my campaign your unsolicited advice."

Once again Cate felt her face go red, though this time there was no turning back. Nancy was right. Cate felt stifled at Google, purposeless. Yes, there were the perks, but the longer she worked there, the more she sensed that the free yoga workshops and stock options and yogurt bars were only there to distract her from an uncomfortable truth—namely, that her job was to create solutions for problems that didn't actually exist. Every morning when she read the paper, she learned that another glacier had melted, or that another racist cop had gotten away with murder, and then she would go off to craft arguments for why it was acceptable to harvest housewives' private data. The realization ate away at her: the world was in crisis, and *this* is what she was doing about it. It's why she began sending the emails—Nancy was right about that, too. She couldn't stand to see the campaign lose. Not to an actor whose most impressive accomplishment was hiding his Botox. Not when there was so much at stake, and Nancy had done so much for her.

She said, "You stopped responding. I figured they were going to your spam."

"They weren't." Nancy straightened out her lapel pin and picked a piece of lint from her shoulder. "So, what do you say?"

Outside, rain began to dot the sidewalks of SoHo. Slowly, Cate nodded.

"So we're clear, I'm a lot more expensive than I was when I was twenty-five," she said.

Nancy laughed.

"Good thing I've got the cash."

A waiter arrived to bring a fresh glass, and to take their orders. Nancy asked for the salad. Cate got a burger, medium rare.

"Wow," Nancy said once the waiter had left. "Big mistake."

"I'm willing to take my chances."

The rain worsened, battering the restaurant's awnings. Pedestrians sought cover, and clouds gathered over Manhattan, their undersides the color of week-old bruises.

Cate said, "I hate watching this country not live up to its promises, Nancy."

Crumbs were scattered across the table, small clusters of them next to the saltshaker and between the flat bases of wineglasses. For a moment Nancy stared at them. Then she sent them to the floor with a decisive brush of her hand.

"So do I," she said. "It's the only thing worse than losing."

Tom's the first to speak.

"Carmichael just released a new spot," he says. "Thirty seconds of Greta throwing the bottle on a loop, and a window with 'Democracy' written across it shattering as a woman screams. It's playing everywhere."

Nancy kicks a cardboard box. "*Fuck.*"

"He also called into *Fox and Friends* this morning, and my bet is that he'll be back on tonight. He's calling you a communist, and Greta a menace, and he's claiming that any mother who can't control her own daughter doesn't deserve to represent New York. It's a matter of family values—that's what he's saying. Americans want them, and you don't have them."

"And people are buying this shit?"

"We won't know for sure until we hear back from the pollsters, but anecdotally I'm getting the sense it's resonating with older voters. We should get you out speaking to them. Plan some events at retirement homes."

Nancy shakes her head. "Those fucking boomers."

Tom steals a glance at Cate. He says, "They like him, ma'am. They all loved him on *Self-Evident*, and they think that he'd signal a return to decency and moderation in Washington."

"He's been married three times. When his second wife got lymphoma he cheated on her with her sister."

"That still counts as family values in America," Tom offers.

"And he's not moderate—he's an opportunist. The son of a bitch was a speaker at the DNC a decade ago, back when he *first* tried for the Senate. He switched parties so he could run against me. He'd call himself a fucking Whig if it meant getting back in the spotlight."

"Yeah . . ." Tom rubs the back of his head. "My sense is that he's just someone they'd want to grab a beer with."

Nancy stares at Tom, leaning against a desk. A stapler sits next to her left hand, and for a split second Cate worries she might pick it up and throw it.

Instead, she says, "So what are we going to do about it?"

Tom clears his throat.

"We have a statement ready to go," he says. "You're proud that Greta is engaged in political activism while abroad, because being active is what's going to help make real, substantive change for the people of New York."

"And then what?"

"We leave it," he says. "Look, most Americans couldn't pick out France on a map. So, we keep talking about the issues that resonate with voters.

Sensible gun laws. The work you've done on healthcare. Getting billionaires to pay their fucking taxes. The more attention we give this thing the more likely it is to get blown out of proportion. Let the story run its cycle. In two days, someone else'll throw a champagne bottle and everyone will forget who Greta is. Carmichael will have to blow another million dollars on a new ad."

Nancy thinks, her lips pressed together. Then she turns to Cate.

"And you?"

What does Cate think? That they need to get in front of this thing. Greta's face is a known quantity—she's from one of the most prominent political families in New York—and now that face is popping up on computer screens in cubicles from Staten Island to Saratoga; Greta is fucking trending. Of course, no one actually cares to understand what's going on in the picture. Understanding is arduous, slow; knowing—being able to parrot back a headline—is easy, and happens in an instant. All it takes is a clip, a sound bite, a meme. The new protocols of information demand not accuracy but speed. Take a picture and add four words. Click send and wait as a million lies are launched. That's what they're racing against: the moment when fact becomes inextricable from fiction. When they lose control over what Truth is because two hundred million people have already dictated it for them. *Everyone will forget who Greta is.* No, Tom, they won't. The internet won't let them.

"It's a bad idea," Cate says.

"What do you mean, 'it's a bad idea'?"

"I mean it's not enough. We need to do more. We're going to get fucking swiftboated by this thing if we don't act fast."

Tom scoffs. "Weren't you, like, a fetus when people were talking about swiftboaters?"

"Shut up, Tom." Nancy holds up a hand. "What are you proposing, Cate? What's your plan?"

Shaking his head, Tom sits down and takes one of the campaign pins from the open box. He passes it back and forth between his hands, then tosses it to the ground.

"We add some muscle to the statement Tom wrote, and then we get you on TV this afternoon. Somewhere friendly, like CNN. The booker for Jodi Washington has been calling me all morning. We use it as an opportunity to distance yourself from Greta's actions, but also to accuse Carmichael of misogyny for calling you an unfit mother. We change the conversation, and we buy ourselves some time. We shoot down all the insane rumors that are already out there until we can figure out what's actually going on. We don't have a choice. If we don't do this, then by tomorrow Twitter is going to declare Greta the next Patty Fucking Hearst. It'll tank us."

Nancy turns around to pace, but there is nowhere to go: they are contained, trapped by the room's walls, the boxes, the pins, the heat of their own exhausted bodies. What do people imagine when they decide to work in politics? Long, stately halls lined with statues? The sound of heels clicking on a polished marble floor? History changed beneath a Corinthian colonnade? Cate can't remember. What she knows now is that decisions—important ones—are often made in places not befitting them. Treaties may be signed in Versailles, but they're written on the hoods of cars by overcaffeinated lawyers. Breakfast is someone else's beef Stroganoff and lunch is yesterday's sandwich. Politics is a scavenger hunt. Between decisions and their consequences, you're scrambling for a pen that works and something safe to eat.

Within the bowels of the building an angry radiator clanks, and Nancy turns back around.

"Tom—get me in front of some geriatrics," she says. "And Cate, call Jodi Washington's people. But listen to me closely—make *sure* it's Jodi. I'm not going to go on CNN to have Jake Tapper tell me what it takes to be a fucking mother."

Maybe Love Isn't for You

When Nick returns to his office, Lisa is still there, clicking around on her computer. A stack of ungraded essays sits to her right, and next to it is a fresh cup of coffee, steam wafting from its lip.

"So," she says. "What was that all about?"

Nick shuts the door and collapses in his chair.

"My sister threw a bottle through a window in Paris—"

"I know."

"—and now, apparently, everyone is talking about it."

"I know! I was trying to tell you about it before you went downstairs. I've been reading about it all morning. It's everywhere! Jezebel, Politico, the *New Yorker*—"

"Wait, the *New Yorker*!?"

"You betcha. Hold on—I'll find it." Lisa clicks one of the twenty tabs she has open on her browser and then, clearing her throat, begins to read aloud. "'If Greta Harrison throwing a bottle through a window reveals anything, it's the sheer fragility of our current moment, and that the values that for centuries we have taken for granted are nothing but panes of glass. Beyond them may lie the promise of steak au poivre and a glass of Cabernet Franc, but that promise is transparent and brittle, susceptible to the whims of a naïve ingénue, equipped with nothing but rage and champagne.'"

"Jesus Christ."

"I know. 'Equipped with nothing but rage and champagne' got me a little tingly, too." Lisa takes a sip of coffee. "What's Nancy saying about it?"

"She's apoplectic. She wants me to fly to Paris and bring Greta back."

"*Whoa.*"

"I know."

Kicking her shoes off, Lisa pulls her feet beneath her, sitting cross-legged in her chair.

"I mean, you're going to, right?"

Nick picks up a pen and taps it against his forehead.

"No," he says. "I'm not."

"Nick! Aren't you worried about your sister? Don't you want your mom to win?"

Lisa leans forward. The coffee cup tilts, and a few drops splash to the floor.

It's an obvious question, with obvious answers. Yes, of course he is worried about his sister. He also knows that in moments of crisis, the first thing everyone needs to do is breathe. Is it unfortunate that Greta Harrison threw a champagne bottle through a window during a lugubriously slow news cycle? Yes. Does that mean that Greta Harrison is an anarchist revolutionary who is capitalizing on—what did the *New Yorker* call it?—"the fragility of our current moment"? No. If Nick's time in Washington taught him anything, it's that conspiracies only grow legs if you let them, and that the most obvious explanation is, more often than not, the truth. And in the case of his sister, that obvious explanation is this: Greta, who is naturally prone to whimsy (see: majoring in French), also happens to be experiencing a state of heightened whimsicality. She's gone to Paris to, in her words, "get her shit back on track," and between learning how to chop onions and brown beef, she has decided to partake in a little political tourism. It's too bad that Fouquet's was her target—the steak tartare there really was delicious—but, in Greta's defense, the place was extortionately overpriced.

As for Nancy, she has dealt with worse. Rumors that she sucks children's blood, envelopes filled with suspicious white powders, attacks—bloody, treasonous, absurd—on the Capitol. While Nick's immediate response is to fix things, experience has shown him that playing the hero isn't all that it's cracked up to be. You plug one hole on a ship that's sinking only to find five more, and five more after that. You run everywhere; you twist your body into impossible positions to use your toes, your fingers, your nose, your elbows. The hull creaks from the pressure, and fish stare through portholes, mildly bemused. But then the ship levels itself and rises to the surface. Its passengers strut down the gangplank and wave for the cameras; you, meanwhile, are soaking wet and wondering what, exactly, you saved when, out of the corner of your eye, you spot another leak.

He says, "I think I had better sit this one out."

From downstairs comes a waft of frying onions. Behind Lisa, on her computer, Nick catches another glimpse of the photograph that ran alongside the story from the *New Yorker*. Greta alone. Greta in Paris. A blur of lights and flesh and glass.

Lisa shrugs. "Well, good for you," she says. "What are you going to do tonight instead?"

"I don't know. Grade these essays about Thoreau? Heat up some leftovers? Rewatch season two of *The Crown*?"

"Your life is very depressing."

"I was kidding, Lisa. I have plans."

"Another meeting with a composer?"

"No. Actually, I have a date."

Lisa frowns.

"Oh, Nick," she says.

"What's that supposed to mean? Also, you're going to spill that fucking coffee."

"It's just—do you think that's best? The last few dates you've been on haven't exactly gone swimmingly."

Splashes of red color Lisa's pale cheeks, and her tangle of brown-gray hair is held precariously together by a disposable chopstick. The sweater she's wearing is thick, and seems like it would be itchy. It's been stretched to the point of shapelessness and manages to cover both her knees and her feet, which are still folded beneath her. *Take away the chair*, Nick thinks, *and you'd swear she was levitating*. She has, in other words, perfected the appearance that Nick has found to be common in academia, a dedication to an aesthetic that falls between not caring and caring very much; between philosopher-queen and loon-on-the-street.

He says, "Thank you for your concern, Lisa."

"It's weird. You're good-looking, you're smart, you don't particularly smell bad, and yet still you end up on dates with guys who, like, use old MetroCards to floss at the table. Maybe love isn't for you?"

"*I said thank you for your concern, Lisa.*"

She unfolds her legs and Nick hears her knees crack. Above them, the office's air conditioner whirs.

"I'll always be here for you, Nick," she says. "Anyway, who's tonight's contender?"

Spinning back toward his desk, Nick picks up an essay and uncaps a red pen. He loves Lisa, dearly. He also wants her to shut up.

"His name is Charlie," he says, circling a misplaced comma. "Charlie Liu."

Hunting Sword with Scabbard

The elevator's doors slide closed and, for a moment, there is silence. Then, using her knuckle, Nancy punches the button for the lobby. Gears turn, cables tighten, Cate shifts her weight from heel to heel. The doors are silver, and in them Nancy considers her own reflection: foundation is caked on her forehead, and her lips are the color of chilies—a rush job, courtesy of Jodi Washington's makeup girl. She finds her eyes and stares into them. She dares herself to blink.

"Well," Cate says. "That didn't go as planned."

Nancy doesn't say anything. She feels the floor fall beneath her and curls her fingers into fists.

Tom is waiting for them in a car on Fifty-Ninth Street, and when Nancy gets in its driver, Bruce, switches the radio from soft rock to Fox News. *Know thine enemy and know thy self*—that's a rule of Nancy's. You can't change what they're saying about you until you know what lies they're telling. Tonight, they're talking about her already. Guy Benson and his guest, Chip Carmichael, salivating over the last twenty-four hours of Nancy's life.

"And did you see her on CNN half an hour ago?" Nancy hears Benson say.

"You know," Carmichael says, "I did, Guy."

"So you saw her lose it."

"Unfortunately, yes."

"You saw Nancy Harrison *totally freakin' lose it*."

"You know, it was . . . well, it was disappointing, Guy. I'm not sure if you remember, but there was an episode of *Self-Evident* where I had to comfort a grieving mother who had just lost her son to a swarm of murderous bees from Mexico. I got my second Emmy for that one. Anyway, the lesson I learned from that is—"

Nancy glances over at Cate; Cate stares at her phone.

"What are you talking about, Chip?" Benson laughs. "It was spectacular! To be clear, I'm no fan of CNN. I think CNN is about as fake as it gets. But this Jodi Washington—she was doing her job! She was asking simple questions—softball questions, really. Stuff like 'I know what I would say to Greta if she were my daughter and here in the studio with me right now. But I'd love to hear what you would say. If Greta were here now what would you tell her?' *If Greta were here now what would you tell her?* I mean, that's some Oprah-Winfrey's-couch-level bull crap, you know? Apparently, Nancy didn't think so, though, because it looked like her goddamned head was about to explode. Jodi, though, she's a pro. She does her job, and she keeps pushing. Nancy doesn't like this. Nancy doesn't like anything, but Nancy especially doesn't like this. So—and this is when it gets *really* good—Nancy rips off her mic and stands up, and as she's leaving she says, 'And what the hell are you, Jodi, Mother of the Year?' Which is a problem, because Jodi Washington *was* Mother of the Year!"

"According to *Elle* magazine, if I'm not mistaken, Guy?" Carmichael says.

"*Bingo*, Chip. They gave her an award and everything. A big ol' crystal plate that says, clear as day, 'Mother of the Year.' They liked all the work she was doing with autistic kids."

"I said it early on, but I've got to reiterate it now: it's disappointing. I know my opponent is known for this kind of . . . well, *unhinged* behavior, but you still hate to see it in an elected official."

"She'd be a hard woman to live with, that's for sure. It makes you wonder if her husband's death was really an accident."

There is, for the first time since Nancy has entered the car, a brief silence.

Then Carmichael says, "Well, now, Guy, I'm a Lutheran. I don't gossip about people—I pray for them. What I do know is that marriage takes work. It's something that people don't seem to understand these days. Regardless, it's an unequivocal tragedy that Howard Harrison died."

"*Died?!* Nancy probably drove him over the edge, Chip! America's Worst Mother wants to be in the Senate! She doesn't know a *thing* about family values, and here she is, trying to tell us how to live our lives. You know, if I'm being honest, if I were her husband, I'd lose my marbles, too! It's enough to make you go—"

"Turn that crap off," Nancy says.

Tom's eyes shift in the rearview mirror. Cate looks up from her phone.

"But Nancy, it's important that we—"

Nancy raises her hand to silence Cate. She clears her throat, repeats herself. "Tom, turn that crap off."

A moment later, the car is quiet.

"Traffic's pretty light," Cate says, clearing her throat. "It should only take us a few minutes to get you back home to the San Marino. We can drop you off first, then Bruce can drive us home."

She has a map open on her phone and when Nancy glances over, she can see a bright blue dot, squeezing its way up Central Park West. Turning away, she begins to chew on her cuticles, peeling flecks of skin away from the deep crescents of her nails. She does it when she's nervous—and only when she's nervous—and with each small tear, she can hear her mother-in-law's voice, high and sharp, haranguing her: *Keep your fingers out of your mouth, Nancy. Try, for once, to be a lady.*

"That was a disaster," she says, rolling down the window. "A god-damned disaster."

They're stopped at a light at Seventy-Second Street, and Nancy watches as a woman in black leggings walks her Labrador into the park. An evening mist obscures the tops of trees, the upper halves of buildings: this is New York abbreviated, curtailed.

"I think . . ."

"You're mumbling, Cate. Speak up."

"I think you should have answered Jodi's question."

"Oh, really? Is that what you think?"

"Yes."

"Interesting. Because I think I never should have gone on that fucking show in the first place."

Cate faces Nancy. The glare of headlights flashes across her cheeks.

"What would you like me to do?"

"Fix it," Nancy says. "I want you to find my daughter, and I want you to fix it."

Cate says nothing, and suddenly Nancy can't bear to look at her. When she turns away, though, she is faced with her own reflection in the window, and she can't bear to look at that, either. She is exhausted; this is exhausting. Having her maternal bona fides questioned on national television; trying to find out in which arrondissement Greta is currently squatting; listening to Chip Carmichael on the radio. Christ: *Chip Carmichael on the radio.* That hearty chuckle, that wholesome lilt. A treatise on family values, delivered by a philandering Jimmy Stewart. The mist swells, and she gets back to work on her cuticles, running her fingers across her lips like she was eating a cob of corn. Bite, tear, *pull.* Bite, tear, *pull.* When they stop in front of the San Marino the car jolts, and her jaw slips, driving her incisors into her thumb. She winces and closes her lips around her finger.

"You fucked up, Cate," she says, tasting the bitter alkalinity of blood. "You really fucked up."

DIED?! NANCY PROBABLY DROVE HIM TO THE EDGE!

She had heard that before. When Howard died, Nancy's mother-in-law told Nancy it was her fault. It happened during the wake, which was at Eugenia's town house on East Seventy-Fourth Street. The memorial was crowded, an *event.* When he was alive, Howard's father had been governor and then attorney general; Eugenia's family had buildings named after it, entire city blocks. Nancy had married into a clan who knew people, and who wanted to be known. The house was enormous, and still she felt suffocated. Searching for a place to be alone, she wandered between rooms of well-wishers in dark suits and tight black dresses, their fingers clutching flutes of overpriced champagne. She found somewhere to breathe, finally, in the foyer. There, on an antique trunk, she discovered a small framed photograph that she'd taken of Howard right after they'd met, on the Dukakis campaign. She was reaching out to pick it up when Eugenia took hold of her arm, led her into the massive salon, and brought her lips to Nancy's ear.

"You killed him," she whispered. Her tone was soft, sweet; it was the same voice Nancy often heard singing lullabies to her children.

"No." Nancy wrested her arm back. "A car accident did that."

Eugenia clicked her tongue and shook her head. Nancy's throat went dry and she fought back tears; Nick was ten and Greta was four, and she refused to let them see her cry. She wondered if this was the moment when she'd actually grow old—not her marriage, or two pregnancies, or passing the bar, but this: the realization that the worst could, and would, happen to her, that tragedy wasn't only meant for someone else.

"You know what you did, Nancy." Eugenia kissed a woman in black on the cheek, said *Thank you for the ham.* Nancy felt fingers loop around hers: Greta, nuzzling against her thigh.

Kneeling, Eugenia wiped something from her granddaughter's face and smoothed down her hair.

"Your mother's greedy, Greta," she said. "And now we all have to pay the price."

She got rid of Howard's belongings a week later. She told herself that she wouldn't be one of those widows she'd read about, one who sleeps in her dead husband's shirt and waits for him to come home and open his mail. She filled cardboard boxes, which she set out on Seventy-Fourth Street—she didn't want to sell his things or give them away; she wanted strangers to take them. A leather briefcase and a pair of running shoes, freed forever of their context. At first she watched with a set of old opera glasses from her bedroom window: she wanted to see who took what, and how long they needed to decide. After an hour she stopped; she found herself getting angry when someone passed something over, which was the opposite of the point. She went back to work, reading depositions in the kitchen. Around lunchtime she checked to see if everything was gone and, seeing that it was, brought another box down.

In the end, she kept only one item: an eighteenth-century German hunting sword, which now sits on a credenza in her living room. It was made in Bavaria—Munich—and it looks as one would expect a sword to look: long and sharp, with a blade made of steel. All that's remarkable about the weapon is its hilt, which is carved of ivory and shows two laughing monkeys, clutching a crescent moon between their hands. It had belonged to Howard, and when he died Eugenia asked for it back. It was expensive, she told Nancy, and a family heirloom; Eugenia had plans to donate it to the Met. *Hunting Sword with Scabbard.* That's what the placard would say. *Generously donated by Eugenia Harrison.* Nancy listened patiently to her entreaties, and then said no. The sword was ugly and graceless, but it reminded her of her husband, and she knew this was exactly why Eugenia wanted it; she'd never let her son love Nancy, not fully, and now she intended to steal back what little Nancy possessed of him, even in death. Nancy wouldn't have it—she wouldn't give up. She figured that if Eugenia thought she was a greedy girl, then she'd show Eugenia how greedy she could be. The tug-of-war was protracted and expensive: Eugenia hired a lawyer and fought, but Nancy fought harder. When she won, she had the sword polished and sharpened. She placed it, along with its scabbard, right next to Howard's ashes and the picture from the Dukakis campaign. She'd stolen it when she left the wake.

THE ELEVATOR'S DOORS SLIDE OPEN on the seventh floor of the San Marino, the building on Central Park West where Nancy lives. Her heels sinking into the carpet, she walks down the hall to her apartment and unlocks the door. She's hungry, so she heats up a plate of leftover linguine and fills a glass with water, both of which she consumes standing up, her back pressed against the cold steel of the refrigerator. When the dirty dishes are piled in the sink, she gathers the ingredients to make herself a boulevardier. Bourbon, Campari, some sweet red vermouth: shake, pour, sip, and sip, and sip, and sip. Her hand is shaking, but she doesn't realize it until she hears the ice trembling against the tumbler. She puts on some music, *Let It All Out*, a little Nina Simone. It doesn't work; the ice still dances.

You fucked up, Cate. You really fucked up. She hadn't meant to say that. What she'd meant to say was *I'm sorry.*

IT WAS HER IDEA TO run for her husband's seat, and no one else's. A month had passed since the funeral—Nancy was finally beginning to distinguish between night and day—when she rang up Howard's chief of staff, Edward, and asked him to meet her for a walk in Central Park.

"I'm doing it," she told Edward, leading him to a bench. "It's nonnegotiable."

Nancy lit a cigarette. It would be one of the last times she smoked.

"But what about everything that's happened?" Edward said. "What about—"

Nancy waved smoke away from her face.

"I don't care about all that. This is something that I have to do."

Slinging an arm over the back of the bench, Edward crossed his legs. He looked out toward the lake.

"You don't need the money, Nancy. Everything that Howard had already inherited from Eugenia is now legally yours."

"I'm not doing it for the money. And don't talk about inheritance—it's crass."

"Then why? Why subject yourself to all the public scrutiny? All the bullshit?"

Couples paddled rented wooden boats, dipping their oars unevenly into the water. Nancy watched them and twirled her cigarette.

"Because of Greta," she said. "And because of Nick. Because I'm not going to spend the rest of my life planning luncheons—not when those idiots in Washington are running my kids' futures into the ground."

Edward ran a hand over his cheek, thinking. Above them, wind shook free two browning leaves.

"It's not a preposterous idea," he said. "You had a successful law practice, you're a known entity among the constituents, and everything that's happened gives you . . . well, it makes you a compelling candidate."

"I'm a widow, is what you mean to say. I'm a widow and that makes me sympathetic."

She thought of the last time she saw her husband, the last night he was alive. They had fought viciously, pouring drinks and screaming at each other for hours until Howard grabbed his keys from the table and announced that he was leaving. Nancy didn't stop him—even though they could both barely stand. She told him to get the hell out. Instantly she regretted it. It was the summer; the children were with Eugenia on Martha's Vineyard, and Howard and Nancy had rented a house for the week in Amagansett, a big empty place where rooms were only ever half-lit and every sound was thunder. She sat on the sofa and listened to the door slam, the car start, the wheels screech. When a police officer phoned her an hour later, she hardly let her speak. She heard her say, "Is this Nancy Harrison?" and then she dropped the phone.

"It won't be hard to get the leadership on board with the idea," Edward said. "Though you should be prepared for Eugenia to throw a very public fit."

Nancy stubbed out her cigarette on the park bench and brushed some ash from her slacks.

She said, "I'll take care of my mother-in-law."

"No. It's absolutely out of the question." Eugenia shook her head, clicked her tongue. "Congresswoman Nancy Harrison. *Honestly.*"

Above them, a giant blue whale was suspended from the ceiling. Three days earlier, at breakfast, Nick had announced that he intended to be a marine biologist when he grew up, so now they were here, in the Museum of Natural History, to learn about baleen; it was also raining outside, an abysmal downpour, and they needed something to do. Nancy had called Eugenia and invited her to join them—the children hadn't seen their grandmother in nearly a month, she said, and they had been asking about her. Mostly, though, Nancy wanted her on neutral ground.

Nick led Greta to a diorama on the far side of the room. He reached down and gently took hold of his sister with one hand, and with the other he pointed to three stuffed walruses, staring at one another.

She said, "I'm not asking your permission, Eugenia. I'm telling you I'm doing this. What I was hoping for was your blessing."

A security guard passed two feet in front of the bench where they were sitting. Eugenia reached for her purse and set it on her lap.

"Well, don't hold your breath, dear," she said. "Or, do."

Folding her hands on her knees, Nancy turned her attention back to the whale: she had expected this. She had hoped against it, but had expected it. The first time that Nancy came to the house on East Seventy-Fourth to meet her, Eugenia told Nancy to take her shoes off at the door—not anyone else, only her, lest Nancy should track whatever shit she stood in across the floor. She loathed that Nancy earned her money, instead of inheriting it, that both her parents had worked two jobs. Nancy did everything she could to change her mother-in-law's opinion, to show Eugenia that she deserved the life she was living. She wasted her earnings on new clothes and wasted her time at silent auctions; she sat through an entire season at the Met. None of it worked or seemed to matter. Eugenia would always think of her as a fraud, an intruder, gauche, bourgeois. A piece of Midwest trash in heels who had somehow blown east. If her husband's death had a silver lining, it was this: finally, Nancy could stop caring what her mother-in-law thought.

A docent herded a school group in front of a dolphin display; Nancy turned toward the walruses, though Nick and Greta were no longer there. She stood, her heart racing, and scanned the room: blue walls, wet jackets, a flock of seabirds suspended in flight. The bright voices of children and the haggard eyes of their parents, as they allowed themselves to be dragged from ecosystem to ecosystem. And then—thank God—two bodies she knew, standing next to Eugenia. Greta had taken her hand; Nick lingered three feet away.

"And what will happen to them?" Eugenia asked Nancy once she had gathered her coat and joined them. She stroked Greta's hair, and Nancy gently pulled her daughter away.

"They're why I'm doing this," she said.

"Don't be ridiculous, Nancy. *You're* why you're doing this. What will you do when you lose?"

"I don't intend to lose."

Eugenia sucked in her cheeks and smirked. She wrapped a scarf around her neck.

"Don't ever expect me to make this easy for you."

Nancy scooped Greta up in her arms.

"How surprising," she said. "Given all those times you've made it easy before."

WINNING WAS SIMPLE; THE JOB was not. Howard had been gregarious and handsome. Thick hair, an earnest smile, a pedigree: when voters saw his photograph in papers he reminded them of who they imagined their politicians to be. He had not been particularly effective—Nancy found this out early—though this had also not mattered; he spoke often enough, and loudly enough, to convince people he was getting things done.

During her first year on the job, Nancy changed nothing in the office that she inherited from him. She kept the same desk, the same chair, the same pictures of New York City hanging on the Longworth Building's walls. She had expected—naively—that she would be treated to the same fawning admiration that her husband received; the Golden Boy is dead, people would say, and now here's his Golden Girl. She was wrong—of course she was wrong. No doors were magically unlocked for her, no favors granted; after she was sworn in, she got a few pitiful glances on the east front of the Capitol, and that was it. *Fine*, she remembers thinking to herself as she lined up for a portrait with twenty-two other freshmen members, *so be it*. If Howard got to be charming, then Nancy would have to be tough. She had no qualms with that—she knew how things worked. Besides, tough was something Nancy knew how to be.

Now she returns to the living room, where she sits on the sofa with her feet folded beneath her, her toes and arches aching. When her first term was up, she ran again and she won; for nearly twenty years, she's kept on winning. It drew her away from her children, though, and this was hell. At night, she would call them from the studio apartment that she kept—that she still keeps—on Capitol Hill, a five-hundred-square-foot box with a bed, a television, a microwave, and a row of picture frames with their price tags still on. She would speak to the series of nannies that she hired and then, when he was old enough to watch Greta on his own, to Nick. With the phone pinned against her shoulder, she would try as hard as she could to re-create their days—the dinners they refused to eat, the baths they refused to take, the tired smiles that crept across their faces as they drifted off to sleep. Hearing them clamor for her filled her with an agonizing joy. Their voices reminded her that she belonged to them, but also of the missed birthdays, the skipped meals, the late-night shuttles from National to LaGuardia. Perhaps the cruelest irony of fighting for her children was that she could not also be there for them, at least not in the way she had always intended to be.

Sinking deeper into the couch, she finishes her drink, leans her head against a pillow, closes her eyes. She needs to find her daughter; she's terrified of what could happen to her. Not a single phone call since she left and this is how she resurfaces: standing in front of a window she broke, smiling like she's posing for a senior class photo. It's a smile Nancy knows, one that emerged a little over a year ago and has refused to go away—a provocation that asks *What now, Mom?* and then refutes whatever Nancy has to say. She reaches for her drink, remembers that she's finished it, and—disappointed—checks her watch. It's six thirty, which means that it's after midnight in Paris, and that with any luck Greta is sleeping, curled up wherever it is that Greta sleeps.

Her throat relaxes, and she forgets her empty glass.

She thinks: *Please, baby, just come home.*

Singled Out

The last person Nick Harrison went on a date with was an investment banker named Jonathan. He was tall and chiseled, and wore a silver watch; Nick didn't know what kind it was—he himself didn't wear a watch—but the way that Jonathan kept playing with it led him to believe that he wanted Nick to see it, that it was the sort of watch that other investment bankers would recognize as expensive. They had a few drinks, and then, because they couldn't agree on a place to get dinner, went back to Jonathan's apartment in Tribeca. It—the apartment—was a large loft with a beautiful television and exactly two books: the first, a glossy collection of black-and-white male nudes by Herb Ritts; the second, a glossy collection of full-color male nudes on Fire Island. The furniture all matched, had clean lines, and was, in most cases, the same items that Nick had seen in other apartments owned by men who had gone to business school. A coffee table composed of hexagonal tiles; an L-shaped sofa with sleek wooden legs. They had sex, because it seemed like a suitable alternative to dinner, and afterward, while Nick was washing off in a shower with exquisite Hudson views, he mulled over the nicest way to tell Jonathan that, perhaps, they were after different things.

"So!" he said ten minutes later, when he emerged from the bathroom smelling of eucalyptus. "That's some water pressure."

Jonathan, who hadn't gotten around to putting on his underwear, was staring at his phone.

"Wait a second," he said. "Are you Nancy Harrison's son?"

Only two of the buttons on Nick's shirt were fastened, and now he hurried to finish the rest.

"I—uh, maybe?"

"I fucking *love* Nancy Harrison!" Jonathan jumped; his testicles shook. "I mean, I'm voting for Carmichael, obviously, because of, like, the market, but oh my God—Nancy Harrison! *So* fucking fierce."

"Yes, I get that from gay men a lot. I think it's the blazers she wears."

"And that hair! It's always so perfect and, like, *coiffed*. What did she say when she was a judge on *Drag Race* again? To that one queen who dressed up like Eleanor Roosevelt in a thong?"

"That it looked like the last time she waxed her upper lip was during the Great Depression."

"Yes! Fuck, that is *so* good." He reached for his phone again. "I can't wait to tell my friends about this."

"You know, I wish you wouldn't?"

"I mean, I *never* sleep with guys who are under six feet, but this time, it was worth it."

Nick tucked in his shirt, looped his belt.

"The door's that way, right?"

"Don't get me wrong—I had a good time!" He smiled. "You're funny."

"Well . . . thanks?"

The television had a screen saver on it—a picture of Jonathan in a bathing suit on a sparkling Mexican beach.

"You want to stick around for some fries?" he asked. "I just ordered some."

"I, um." The picture floated around the giant frame, lightly bouncing off its edges. "That's very generous, but I think I better go."

Since then, the highlights of his dating life have included but have not been limited to: a man who only ate cold food; a man who, as far as Nick could ascertain, ate *no* food; a man who only ate food soaked in organic bone broth. A mouth breather, a close talker, a loud laugher; a fashion model who asked if he could suck Nick's nose. Someone who had never voted, someone who was obsessed with voting, someone who had only voted once, and for Donald Trump. A blond who had never seen *When Harry Met Sally*; a brunet who hated *The Princess Bride*. Men who kissed

with their teeth, men whose breath smelled like oysters, men who very earnestly tried to swallow Nick's tongue. Evangelists, anarchists, vegans; Californians, Texans, and—*oops*—a Republican.

And yet, he persists. He sets up online profiles, and collects flattering pictures of himself, and allows well-meaning friends to arrange blind dates, and puts himself out there perhaps a little more than he should. To be clear: he does not do these things because he is lonely—he is, in fact, very good at being alone—so much as he does them because he is ready. Up until a year ago, his free time was spent on trains between New York and Washington, where he kept himself company with old paperbacks and bottles of Amtrak Chardonnay. That is not to say that there were no men in his life, because there were. One-offs and hookups and people from the gym. Frenetic evenings of unbuckling belts and untying shoes. Of rolling over to check his email before the lights turned back on. But the anxious anticipation of a phone call? The indecisiveness over what to wear? These are things that he suspects he once felt, and that—now—he is prepared to feel again.

"You want to wait until he gets here, or you want a glass to get loose?"

He is in a bar on Hudson Street, one where Nick has found that the music isn't too loud, the wine isn't too expensive, and the bartender, Eileen, who has just asked him if he "wants to get loose," is the right amount of surly. It also has to recommend it an ideal location: five minutes away is a restaurant with low lighting and good food, should the date prove promising; eight minutes away is Nick's apartment, should things turn south.

Now Eileen wipes her hands on a dish towel and Nick thinks of his sister, breaking windows in France.

"It's been a day," he says. "Let's have one now."

A glass is set in front of Nick, and wine climbs toward its rim. It's a good pour.

"Why don't we date, Eileen?" he asks.

"Because I like redheads. And because you like men." She corks the bottle and sets it down behind her. "Pretty soon you're going to have to expand your dating radius to Connecticut—I think you've hit all the guys in New York."

Nick swirls his glass—he knows nothing about wine.

He says: "I shall never admit that kind of defeat."

The observation does raise an interesting question: How long is too long to live in New York? Is it when you've eaten at all the restaurants, snuck out early from every party, dated all the men? Joan left after eight years. When she turned twenty-eight she discovered that *everything that was said she seemed to have heard before,* and that it was *distinctly possible to stay too long at the fair.* All places have their stories, their peculiar mythologies that make them tolerable. But one day a person begins to see past those myths, and instead recognizes the buildings and the streets and the tired faces that populate them for what they really are. New York is no different. It's something that Nick has been thinking about with increasing regularity; lying in bed after a bad date, he often imagines himself elsewhere. He tells himself that all it takes to live in this city is to move here, which means that all it takes not to live here is to leave. He could go somewhere quiet, like Vermont or Sonoma. A place where subway lines won't conspire against him, and where breakfast isn't a bacon, egg, and cheese from the bodega on the corner; a place that isn't so miserable in the rain. The problem with those alternatives is that while they do not have the bodegas and the subways, they also *do not have the bodegas and the subways.* He'd be trading one set of myths for another, and, frankly, he's perfectly content with the one that he's got. Put another way: the allure of Everywhere Else is very attractive until he realizes that Everywhere Else can never surprise him like New York.

There's a rush of sound from the street outside and, turning on his stool, Nick sees a handsome if slightly frazzled man.

Eileen tops him off with another splash of wine and raises an eyebrow. "Okay, Romeo," she says. "Showtime."

WHEN CHARLIE LIU LAUGHS, HE tilts his head back at an angle that, while barely perceptible, causes Nick to believe, at least for a second, that he's the funniest person on earth. He has a strong, trapezoidal chin, and his ears, one of which he is now absently tugging on, are shaped like perfect little shells. He's wearing jeans, a blazer, and an ironed white oxford, which he's unbuttoned nearly to his sternum, revealing a single red mole, set like a ruby in the center of his chest. A glass of bourbon

sits in front of him—his second (big; on the house; *thank you, Eileen*)—
and every so often when he drinks from it he'll give its ice a gentle shake.
The younger of two brothers, he grew up—"depending on which freeway you take"—forty-five minutes south of Los Angeles. And sometimes
when he speaks, Nick can hear it—the lengthening of certain vowels,
a casual sunniness; traces of a childhood spent at land's end. He lives,
now, in Chelsea, with his dog, Frank, and a collection of plants that, no
matter how much love he gives them, he can't seem to keep alive. He
hasn't mentioned Nancy Harrison, he's read Joan Didion, and—Nick is
learning now—he works for the FBI.

"The FBI!"

"That's right." Charlie winks. "So, hide your drugs."

Eileen cuts limes next to a container of cherries; on the other side of
the bar, another first date sputters.

"What drew you to the job?" Nick asks.

Charlie lifts his eyebrows half an inch. He gives his glass another shake.

"My dad disappeared when I was a kid," he says. "He went to work
one day and never came home. People—my mom—they said he deserted
us, but I never believed it. Something happened to him, and I told myself
that when I grew up I'd find out what it was."

For a moment Nick is quiet and watches Charlie's face. Then he sets
a hand on his knee.

"I'm so sorry," he says.

Charlie looks up. Flecks of gold flash in his chestnut eyes.

"I'm kidding." He gives a penitent grin, and Nick exhales. "That's so
awful—God, I apologize. My dad never left. There were a few times when
I *wish* he had, mostly when I was a teenager, but he didn't. It's just—people
are always asking me why I do what I do, and the answers that I come up
with never seem to be enough. It's funny to me: here I am, someone who
has gone through training for interrogation, and the question I find myself
stumbling over most is why *I* decided to join the bureau."

Music swells from hidden speakers; Eileen gives a martini a lazy
shake.

"Well, why did you?" Nick asks.

"When I tell you, you'll think I'm nuts."

"I promise I won't."

"I promise you *will.*"

Raising his right hand, Nick clears his throat. His words slip, his lips twitch: he is having a very good time.

"I swear on this glass of free Chenin Blanc," he says, "that I will not think you're nuts when you tell me why you decided to work for the FBI."

Charlie considers the offer and, shaking his head, chuckles.

"Okay, fine," he says. "I was obsessed with Nancy Drew."

Slowly, Nick nods. "Nancy Drew," he says, and does his best to keep his teeth on his tongue.

"Yes! I wanted to be like her—solving all those mysteries, putting together puzzles. I can tell you're trying not to laugh, by the way."

"That's not true at all."

"It is true—your face is turning red."

Nick says nothing. His shoulders convulse, his legs shake; ducking his chin to his neck, he begins to giggle.

"I can't believe it!" Charlie tosses up his hands. "Laughter, coming from a man who's writing a musical about Joan Didion!"

"Hey, have you been to Times Square recently? People have written musicals about much weirder shit."

"I guess you've got a point," Charlie says, smiling. "But regardless, I'm not going to apologize for Nancy Drew."

"Nor should you."

"She's much better than the fucking Hardy Boys."

"Absolutely. Little pricks, those two."

"You never saw her asking some sibling to help her out. Nancy got shit *done.*"

A candle flickers on the bar between them, and Charlie runs his palm an inch above its flame.

Glancing up, Nick catches Eileen's eye. He signals for the check.

"How about we get some dinner," he says. "I know a place nearby."

In Search of Lost Time

SoHo, Manhattan, the corner of West Broadway and Prince. Fog—thin now, but growing thicker—hovers an inch above the borough's roofs. Farther downtown, One World Trade is a sheath of hazy light. Cate Alvarez steps out of the car that brought her here and considers the neighborhood. On one side of the street: a lingerie store, a jewelry designer, a boutique selling overpriced purses. On the other: shoes, coffee, Technicolor macarons.

The interview started out promising, hadn't it? A few softballs from Jodi about the gridlock in Washington and the prospects of holding on to the Senate. Then some macrolevel, state-of-the-world stuff. What was with all the polarization? How is it possible that the world has managed to cleave itself into an even starker divide? After having our differences obliterated by disease and war, recession and famine, how had we emerged even more torn than before? Nancy juggled the questions nimbly; she bemoaned the demise of unity, and then blamed its death on The Other Side. From where Cate was watching, next to the show's producer, she nodded along, each answer solidifying her belief that getting Nancy on air was the right call. When the conversation inevitably looped around to Greta, Nancy fared equally well. She wove her way through the talking points Cate had written for her and was—or at least appeared to be—genuinely concerned. But then that question came—*What would you want to tell Greta if she were here now?*—and, suddenly, a switch flipped. Cate didn't understand it; Cate still doesn't understand it. It was, on its face, one of the easier questions of the night. All Nancy had to do was say something innocuous, and boring, and empty; something like *I love you*, and move on. That isn't what happened, though. Instead, Nancy heard an attack. A dog whistle that shrieked across whatever hidden frequency mothers use to lob their offenses at each other. Her calves clenched, followed by her knees, her knuckles, her teeth. She ripped the microphone from her lapel and, after asking Jodi Washington if she was "mother of the goddamned year," stormed out of the interview.

She hears a car door slam and turns to see Tom, thanking Bruce for the ride.

"Well, that didn't go well," he says once he's standing next to her.

"Give it a rest, Tom."

"But Jodi *was* Mother of the Year, you know."

"I know that, okay? And I told Nancy that. I fucking *told* Nancy that."

"Well, apparently, she wasn't listening."

No, apparently, she wasn't. And now, in the words of Nancy, Cate had fucked up. Cate had *really fucked up.* The clip would be edited and aired on a loop for the next forty-eight hours; Nancy, along with her daughter, would be a meme; Jodi Washington would write twelve hundred words for *Elle* on what it meant to be a mother, and, unless Cate did something to change the narrative, it would all be her fault.

Tom checks his email, then turns toward the building in front of them—seven stories of cast-iron architecture with a heavy steel door.

"Whoa," he says. "This is where you live?"

"No."

Cate finds the intercom and locates a name: Rashad Davis, apartment 6C. She presses the button next to it.

"Then what are we doing here?"

"Greta's not the only person in that video, Tom." The door buzzes; Cate pushes it open. "There's someone else, and we're going to find out who it is."

RASHAD DAVIS IS SMALL, FIVE-FOOT-TWO, with hands that belong to a much larger man. Watching his fingers float across the keyboard, Cate imagines a pianist or a surgeon. *Scalpel, please, Alvarez, let's cut this mother-fucker open.*

"There." She points to the laptop's screen, where Greta stands, the wreckage of Fouquet's in the background. "Stop right there."

Rashad stops the video, presses rewind, and cranks up the computer's volume. When he hits play again, Cate hears it—a voice behind the camera, telling Greta to smile. Its timbre is deep, and far too inviting—the sort of man Cate knows not to trust when he asks to buy her a drink at the bar.

"That guy speaking," she says. "I want to know his name."

Swiveling in his chair, Rashad frees a piece of gum from a pack of Dentyne Ice.

"You got the three hundred bucks?"

"We said two hundred."

"Nice try, Alvarez."

Cate shakes her head. She opens her wallet and counts out the cash.

"I can't guarantee this is going to work." Rashad folds the bills in half and sticks them in his pocket. "If there isn't audio of this guy floating around out there already, then the search won't pick any matches."

"And what happens then?"

Rashad shrugs. "I keep the cash and buy myself a new pair of jeans."

Glancing behind her, Cate sees Tom, inspecting an acrylic chair.

"I'm willing to bet on the internet," she says.

"Probably a good bet. Make yourself at home—this will take a few minutes."

He leaves, walking into an office on the north side of the loft with his laptop under his arm. His footsteps echo—the walls are white and bare, and Rashad has hardly any furniture, only the acrylic chair, an L-shaped sofa, an inflatable pink donut with no apparent use, and a bookcase, set flush against the wall. Wandering over to it, Cate inspects its contents: programming stuff, mostly, and some cerebral sci-fi. Scattered among the spines she finds George Eliot and Joyce. Proust's *In Search of Lost Time.*

"Did he recently move in?"

Tom is still standing near the chair, hovering around it like he doesn't know if he's allowed to sit.

"No." Cate pulls *Swann's Way* from the shelf and flips through its pages. "He just likes things sparse."

"He your boyfriend or something?"

"We worked together. He was an engineer on the voice recognition team. He left a year before me."

Tom has given up on the chair. Now he circles the sofa.

"What's he do now?"

"He doesn't tell me and I don't ask. Whatever it is, it pays him enough to afford a place like this."

Tom scratches his ear.

"I need a new fucking job," he says. "Anyway. You got one?"

"One of what?"

"A boyfriend. Or a husband. Or a whatever."

Cate closes the book and returns it to its spot on the shelf.

She says, "Tom, don't be weird."

The sun is setting, and it's starting to rain; the loft is cast in a dove-gray light. Three windows are aligned on the far side of the room. Through them, Cate sees water towers, crowning the roofs of SoHo.

"You're loyal to her," Tom says. "Nancy, I mean. Coming down here, forking out three hundred bucks of your own money for something you don't even know will work—no one wants to win more than I do, and I'm not sure I'd even do that."

Two birds circle each other in the twilight, their wings smudges against the darkening sky.

"I owe it to her," Cate says.

"Sure." Tom shrugs and picks something from his teeth. "She signs our paychecks. We all *owe it to her*, but—"

"She bought me another year with my mom. She helped keep her alive so I had time to say goodbye."

Tom's eyes soften, his gaze drifting down to his shoes.

"I—sorry, I didn't know that," he says.

"Why would you? And there's no reason to make that face—it's just what happened."

Cate turns her back to him and again faces the window. She wants to move on, to evade a story that for over half a decade she's choreographed her way out of telling. The problem is that, presently, there's nowhere to go; she's standing in a room that's so emptied of distractions that the only thing she can focus on is Tom's breath, echoing as he waits for her to speak.

"It was lung cancer, if that's what you're wondering," she says eventually. "She kept getting these awful cases of bronchitis. Like, these heavy, wet coughs that would basically shake the house and wake my dad up at night. She wasn't a smoker—she'd never had a cigarette—so her doctor didn't think about ordering a biopsy until it was too late."

She explains how she was in Nancy's office in Washington when she got the news. An intern told her that her father was on the line, and Cate told the kid to take a message—she was late for an interview at Google, and she'd have to call him back. When she did, three hours later, his voice was haggard, the ends of his sentences frayed like rope. He told her that her mother was dying, and in the same breath apologized for calling so many times. Cate's knees stiffened and her throat dried up; she reached into her purse and saw twelve missed calls on her cell phone.

"He teaches high school civics, back in Denver," she tells Tom. "He's got good insurance, but the treatments my mom needed . . . well, I don't think I have to tell you how fucked up healthcare is in this country."

Slowly, Tom nods. Cate scratches the back of her neck, chews the inside of her cheek. "When Nancy found out what was happening, she had my mom moved to Memorial Sloan Kettering, here in New York. They had some trial under way, this experimental treatment for the specific kind of mutation my mom had, and Nancy wanted her to be part it. I wasn't even working for her anymore—in the middle of it all, I left for Google—but she didn't care, and never once did we see a hospital bill. In any event, the treatment didn't work. Not on my mom, at least, but that's hardly Nancy's fault, is it? In the end, she bought my mom—she bought us—fourteen more months together. There's no sufficient way to thank a person for something like that."

The sun disappears behind New Jersey, and streetlamps flicker to life. Tom crosses his arms across his chest.

"Jesus, Cate," he says. "I'm so sorry."

She looks at him, then quietly laughs. "That's the fucked-up thing about time, isn't it? You don't start counting seconds until you know they're almost gone."

Down the hall, in Rashad's office, there comes the muffled sound of a drawer shutting and hinges swinging open. A moment later, Cate hears the heels of his shoes, hitting the hardwood floor.

"I found him."

Cate uses a single knuckle to wipe at the sides of her eyes.

"Who is he?"

"His name's Xavier de la Marinière." In one hand, Rashad is holding the open laptop, and in the other, a half-finished Corona. "I don't think you're going to like the rest."

"Tom?" She turns to face him, but he's already got his phone an inch from his nose.

"I'm on it."

Cate takes the laptop from Rashad and, sitting in the acrylic chair, begins reading what's on the screen. She's hardly a sentence deep when her eyes go wide and she starts feeling her heart thumping against her throat.

From two feet behind her, she hears Tom say, "Oh, shit."

Love, Deferred

"I'm sorry." Charlie sounds concerned—his voice dips below the music. "Was that too much?"

Nick tastes peppermint. The vestiges of Charlie's lip balm.

He says, "Nope. In fact, it wasn't enough."

Charlie grins and kisses Nick again.

"You want another drink?"

At the bar, someone orders a round of tequila shots, and a shirtless bartender prepares them, pouring too much liquor into the tumblers, kissing their rims with slices of lime.

"Sure," he says. "Why not?"

Weaving through the crowd, Charlie squeezes past waists and taps on shoulders to get to where he needs to go. From where he's standing in the corner, Nick considers checking his watch but stops himself—he doesn't want to know what time it is, doesn't want to hear his bed beckoning him home. It's been at least an hour since they finished dinner, and they walked for thirty minutes after that. They moved at a snail's pace, stopping at crosswalks with no cars coming and lingering to stare into empty store windows. When they spoke (they are always speaking), their breaths formed clouds that occasionally touched, their borders dissolving into each other before they disintegrated into the night. Neither of them wanted to go home—why would they?—and so, at last, they decided to come here.

It's a bar, in the purest sense of the word: a few high-top tables up front, a single bathroom with an empty soap dispenser, and two hundred square feet in the back where people can dance. It smells like this kind of bar usually does: of beer, of boys, of sweat. The lights are low, and tinted red, and reflect in occasional bursts off a punch-bowl-sized disco ball. Half the time it turns and half the time it doesn't, though when it does it paints the room a prism, making kaleidoscopes of unshaven cheeks. You can't stare at it for too long—this is something Nick has learned—because if you do, you risk slipping into a haze, one in which you promise yourself that this night will be memorable, even though all the other nights ended up being the same. Nights of cheap vodka and pop queens and not being able to find your coat. Nights where you wait in line to order the drink you've been ordering for the past ten years, wondering what sort of collective lack of imagination dictates that in a city flooded with an incogitable excess of possibilities, everyone always ends up at the exact same place.

Except tonight is different—actually, provably different—and if Nick needs evidence of that, then here it is: a kiss. When he felt Charlie's mouth press against his he worried, at least for a second, that he had forgotten how to do this. Not to kiss, per se, but to kiss with actual meaning. To let someone know, via the pressure of lips and the movements of tongues, that this kiss was not the stuff of dance floors, those transient flirtations that if nothing else are made to be forgotten, but rather was meant to be cataloged, remembered. Five years from now: *This* is where they kissed for the first time. While Whitney Houston blared on a speaker and a man in a crop top spilled a beer, this is where Charlie let Nick's fingers entwine with his, where Nick tasted the balm on Charlie's lips. In reality it did not last long—as far as kisses go, it was on the shorter side—though now Nick allows himself to imagine that when they talk about it in the future they will say it lasted an eternity. They'll laugh, and tell friends how, their mouths still touching, they had to move aside so people could walk past them; how a drag queen in sequins told them to get a room. What a gift, they'll say, to never want something to end.

The Whitney Houston song finishes and, on the wings of its last breath, another one begins. Charlie leans over a stack of paper napkins to call out his order to the bartender while, in the depths of Nick's pocket, he feels his phone, buzzing against his thigh.

"Cate," he says once he's fished it out and answered it, "I'm a little busy right now."

"Nick, you're there. Thank God."

"Are you in love, Cate? And if so, when did you know? Actually, I'm drunk—don't answer that."

"I need to talk to you."

"Is it about my mother? And if so, can it wait until, I don't know, never?"

"Nick, *stop*. I know where Greta is."

"So do I," he says. "She's drinking champagne in Paris and throwing away the bottles. Ha, ha."

"No, goddamn it. Listen, have you ever heard of someone called Xavier de la Marinière?"

"That sounds like a cologne I can't afford."

"It's not a cologne—it's a person. Are you near a computer?"

Someone knocks him from behind. He waits for an apology, but it never comes. Two seconds later, he feels something cold and sticky seeping through his shirt.

He sighs.

"No, but I've got my phone."

"Okay, google Xavier de la Marinière."

"I don't know how to spell that."

"It's x-a-v-i-e-r, then *de* and *la*, then m-a-r-i-n-i-e-r-e. Oh, and there's an accent over the first *e* in the last name."

"Which way is it pointing?"

"Down."

"Down toward the *r* or down toward the *i*? You're going to have to be more specific, Cate."

"I'm going to be honest: I don't think the accent matters."

She's right. Nick googles the name and is quickly rewarded with pictures of a very handsome man.

"Wow," he says. "This guy is hot."

"The hottest. Now read."

He does. He clicks on a series of links until he finds an English article, which with one eye closed he scans.

"Shit," he says.

"Exactly."

"Oh my God."

"*Exactly.*"

"Does Nancy know?"

"Tom's on the phone with her now. Nick, your sister is in trouble, and so are we. Carmichael just gained two more points. If this gets out, we're fucked. It's over."

Whatever was spilled on Nick's shirt is now sticking to his back. He looks around him: the prismatic trance of the disco ball, and boys dancing in the shifting light. Charlie, walking toward him with two drinks and a smile.

The spiders awaken; the spiders wrestle.

Nick reaches for his coat.

"Cate," he says, "call Nancy. Tell her I'm getting on that flight to Paris. Tell her I'm bringing Greta back."

LA MISÉRABLE

I've always had a hard time telling the difference between being lonely and being bored. Loneliness, I've always thought, is existential and literary. An ugly black bird perched on your shoulder, or walking around in a long coat on a rainy night. Something like that. Boredom, meanwhile, is something small. Ordinary. Basically, you're bored because you can't figure out something else to do. Where it gets tricky is that the flip side can also be true. Doing nothing can feel so all-consuming that, sometimes, you forget that what you really are is alone.

I think I was lonely, or bored, or maybe both, when I met Xavier de la Marinière.

It was the end of July. August? No, definitely July. I know that because six months earlier I had broken up with Ethan. For two years—ever since I finished undergrad—we had been sharing a place in the West Village. When I dumped him, I abandoned it for a room in an apartment above a doggy day care called BowHaus in Bushwick, north of Irving Avenue. I found the room on Craigslist, and when I first went to see it one of the people who already lived in the apartment—this antique dealer named Carl—promised me that I'd never even know it was there. Apparently, a special kind of insulation had been installed between the floors, a mixture of foam and some other, multisyllabic synthetic that I thought sounded toxic but was nonetheless meant to trap the noise. *Peaceful* was the word Carl used. *Like you've crawled back into the womb.* I understood what he was trying to say, but also I didn't, because honestly who could possibly remember what it was like to not be born? Still, I took the apartment, and realized pretty quickly that Carl had either lied or that wombs are really fucking loud, because in the mornings I could hear all these terriers yapping as their owners dropped them off, and then at night the same little yaps as their owners picked them up to leave.

Aside from Carl, I shared the apartment with two other people. A bartender named Rosie whom I only met twice, and a Hungarian model named Zsófia, who was Carl's girlfriend. She—Zsófia—was tall and had a face that looked like a pigeon's. Dark eyes, beakish mouth, and this shaved head that was so perfectly round that you couldn't help thinking of it in a bowling alley, smashing chin-first into a row of pins. I don't think I ever saw her work, not even once, but she still managed to have money to do things that people with money in the city do. Take Ubers and hang out at restaurants in Tribeca and travel to beaches where you need a passport. Her English was very good, until I asked her to do something, like wash her dishes, at which point she would stare at me, her little pigeon eyes pinched together, and say *mit*? It means *what* in Hungarian, and I heard it often enough that, sometimes, I'd wonder whether Zsófia actually hadn't understood me. But then an hour later I'd overhear her talking to Carl, who was originally from Chicago. They'd be speaking English, because that was the only language that Carl sort of knew, and *what* was a word that they used very, very often.

None of them were there on the afternoon that I met Xavier. I remember I had just come back from the Apple Store, where I work. I bought an iced coffee and Sour Patch Kids at the bodega on the corner, and when I got to the apartment it was empty. In the living room was a pile of mail, which I ignored, and two bags from Barney's, which I went through. I don't know what I was expecting to find, but what I did wasn't exactly interesting: underwear, a leather belt, and four different versions of a plain white T-shirt. After that I put the clothes and tissue paper back as best I could and set the bags down where I found them, which was on the floor between a coffee table and Zsófia's enormous cat, Attila. Then I threw my keys on the couch, went to my room, and shut the door.

It was the smallest room in the apartment, which was sort of bullshit because I was still paying a thousand dollars in rent. Basically, there was space for a twin bed and a dresser—or, in my case, a full bed and nothing else. I hadn't put anything on the walls except for this black-and-white poster of Jane Jacobs, and I stacked my books in the corner by the door: *L'étranger*, Sontag, Zola's *J'accuse* . . . *!* I opened my Sour Patch Kids, then took out a shoebox where I kept all these ancient iPhones. I'd just gotten the latest model, so I tossed the old one I'd been using inside the box and slipped it back beneath my bed. Then I started flipping through a *New Yorker* from about a year earlier. Ethan's name was printed on its address label, and its cover had a drawing of this sad, pensive polar bear staring at an ice cube. I made it through one of the Talk of the Towns before I got bored and climbed onto my duvet.

Once I got comfortable, I stripped off my pants and my shirt because I was sweating, and then put on some Juliette Gréco. I didn't have air-conditioning—having no air-conditioning seemed, at least at that moment, to be a condition of my life. So, to cool down I pressed the iced coffee against the side of my neck and opened my window. A woman in this giant sun hat carried a trash bag filled with empty cans down the street, and outside of BowHaus a beagle tried to mount a mastiff. I watched it, but before long I turned away; there's nothing quite as embarrassing, I don't think, as watching two dogs hump. I listened to Juliette plead for love for a little longer, and then I put on my gaming headset and opened Nostalgeum.

I want to make something clear here: I was not—am not—a *gamer*. I didn't have some chair with a permanent indent of my ass in it, I changed my underwear every day, and I always brushed my teeth. At the time, though, I wasn't doing much of anything else. Also, Nostalgeum was different from those other games. It wasn't about slaughtering aliens or invading Iraq—it was about teaming up with other people around the world to rebuild lost things. B. Dalton's and Musicland stores and all those other places that Amazon and Netflix have pushed the way of the dinosaurs. You could get lost in it—a lot of times, I did. I'd find myself playing the game and not remembering when I had started. Entire nights would go by without my sleeping; I'd look out my window and see that it was morning and I'd suddenly become anxious. And not because I'd spent so much time playing, but because I knew that soon I'd have to stop. The world—the real one—was a much uglier place.

I was building a Blockbuster Video the afternoon I met Xavier. It was me and a pile of bricks on this street I'd created called Mulberry Lane when his avatar walked up to mine and I heard his voice in my headset saying: "Hi, I'm Xavier."

I spun myself around to face him. I was holding a sledgehammer.

"Oh." I adjusted my mic. "I'm Greta."

That was it—we didn't even tell each other our last names.

"What are you making, Greta?"

He had an accent that I recognized.

I said, in French, "Um, a video store."

I instantly felt foolish, saying it out loud, and in a different language. No one could see me, and still I blushed.

But then he said, "Ah! I can stop embarrassing myself in English, how wonderful. Do you mind if I help?"

I ate a few Sour Patch Kids. I had never really spoken to anyone else on Nostalgeum before. Lately I wasn't speaking to anyone at all.

I smiled.

"Sure."

We worked together for three hours, erecting walls and filling shelves with VHS tapes. His avatar wore a blue suit, and mine a pair of denim overalls, and once in a while they would run into each other and I'd hear him laugh in my headset. It was a smooth, songlike laugh; it reminded me of my father's. He asked me why I studied French in school, and I told him that it was because I liked the country's capacity for revolutions. Also, I thought there was something romantic about a language where the words for *love* and *death* sound so much alike. He had never been to New York before—he told me that while we were stocking the candy display by the cash registers—though he was dying to go. He wanted to see the Statue of Liberty ("it's French, you know"), and he had heard that New York girls were pretty.

I blushed again.

"Some of us are, I guess."

Then I checked the clock on my bedroom wall. It was almost one o'clock.

"Shit," I said. "I'm going to be late for my shift."

THE APPLE STORE WHERE I worked is at the corner of Flatbush and Lafayette, on the first floor of this super-thin luxury apartment building that I'm sure everyone thought was interesting and different at the time it was built but that now, a few years later, sort of looked like a tacky Cubist Pac-Man. I'd been working there ever since I left Ethan, which coincided with when I walked out of my paralegal job at my mother's old law firm. I had wanted once to be a lawyer, or to work at the United Nations, though not anymore. Every other day my mother would email me to say that she could help me find someplace else to work, a position where I could use my degree, but I always told her no; while she was right that I didn't read Baudelaire to end up hawking iPads, I also wasn't about to be in debt to her, not after what my grandmother Eugenia had told me. Besides, I liked knowing that my refusals—and the fact that she couldn't under stand them—pissed Nancy off. Giving up on my ambitions was worth it to be the one thing she couldn't control.

My official title at the store was a *specialist*, which basically meant that I answered people's questions about gigabytes and tried to get them to buy the more expensive version of whatever tablet they happened to pick up. I actually didn't mind it. I was on my feet all day, which was better than sitting at a desk, and I got to spy on all the weird apps people had downloaded on their phones. Also, while I didn't really care about things like wireless earphones, when you convinced someone to buy them they were legitimately thankful, like by getting them to spend two hundred dollars you'd made their life a little bit better. And the feeling of making someone's life a little bit better was always a good one to have.

I showed up five minutes late to my shift, but the only person who noticed was this white guy with dreadlocks named Neil. He was standing by the Genius Bar, helping a woman set up her new phone, and he glanced over at me. I was sweating—the train that I had taken from

Bushwick suddenly went out of service, so I had to sprint to the store from Clinton Hill. Before hitting the floor, I had gone to the staff bathroom to wipe down my forehead and armpits and try to do something with my hair, and now I could feel my blue polo shirt sticking to my back. Neil winked at me. He thought it looked charming, I'm sure, but it didn't. It looked like he'd gotten jizz in his eye.

He was annoying, the sort of person who couldn't pick up on a hint if it had its hands around his balls. We'd been hired around the same time, and did our training together, and no matter how hard I tried to get away from him, he was always there, breathing down my neck.

"You're Greta Harrison"—that's what he said to me the first day he saw me, before I'd even introduced myself.

"Who?" I said.

"Your mother's Nancy Harrison—she's represented the tenth district of New York for almost twenty years. Your father was Howard Harrison, and your grandfather was governor. When you were five, you modeled in a Polo catalog."

He told me these things like I didn't know them, like I was meeting my family for the first time. Neil was obsessed with politics. This didn't make me like him more—only less.

"I have no idea what you're talking about," I said, because how are you supposed to tell a guy like Neil that all you want to be is someone else?

"I've seen pictures of you in the newspaper with your mother. Page Six and stuff. I mean, *I* don't read the *Post*, but my MAGA sister gets it and—"

"Dude," I said. "Give it a fucking rest."

WHEN I GOT HOME, MY living room was full of Zsófia's friends. Most of them were tall, and most of them were beautiful. The sort of people you sometimes see on the subway and think, *Who on earth do these people hang out with?* The answer, FYI, is *with each other*. Living with a bald Hungarian model will teach you this: New York is filled with pockets of beautiful people who, through an unequitable doling out of genetics and fate, aren't subject to the same rules as the rest of us. They don't have to wait at restaurants or pay their rent, and when they want to have parties they go ahead and have them, even if it's in the living room of an apartment they share with three other people, and it's a Wednesday night.

I felt something brush against my ankle and looked down to see this Pomeranian chewing on my shoelaces. It was the shape and color of an apricot, and when I picked it up the dog stared dumbly at me, its tongue lolling out from the side of its mouth.

"Zsófia," I said, "whose dog is this?"

"I don't know, but I like how you're carrying it. Like a furry little handbag."

"Is it from downstairs?"

"No. Yes? I think so. Milo thought it would be funny: 'I did not bring you the drugs you asked for, but here is a dog instead!' Milo is a very strange boy."

"You can't just go around stealing other people's dogs."

"I didn't—Milo did."

"I'm going to bring it back downstairs."

"But Greta, he is so happy." Zsófia reached out and pinched the dog's tongue. "He would like I think very much to stay."

I tucked the Pomeranian under my arm and brought it back down to the night manager at BowHaus, pushing past a scrum of sharp elbows and long necks and smooth, ropy biceps. On the way back up to the apartment, I ran into Rosie, the bartender whom I'd met precisely twice before, and whose existence I often questioned. She was dressed in a black sweatshirt and sunglasses, and she was moving so fast that when she passed me she almost knocked me down the stairs.

"Whoa," I said. "It's you."

"It's me."

"You're not sticking around for the party?"

Rosie looked up the stairwell, and then back at me.

"With those mutants? I'd rather put a hole in my head."

She jogged down the rest of the steps two at a time, and I stood still and listened to the door close behind her. It was the longest conversation we'd ever had.

A FEW MINUTES LATER I opened the window to feel the breeze, and then booted up Nostalgeum. The Blockbuster Video wasn't finished—it still needed to be painted—and I figured I'd do that and then check out what other people were up to.

I didn't expect to see Xavier again, but he was already there, waiting for me.

"Hi," he said.

"Wow." I brought the mic closer to my mouth. "You're here."

"I was thinking about you, and what we built together. I wanted to see you again."

My heart went light, and I couldn't feel my feet.

I said, "I wanted to see you again, too."

WE TALKED FOR SIX OR seven hours that night, and every other night that week. On the other side of my door, I would hear little signs that the world was fumbling on without me. Milo's music thumping, the voices of demonically beautiful people, Rosie coming and leaving and coming again, Zsófia and Carl starting and ending a fight. Outside, the streetlamps turned on, gnats swarming beneath them, and then, as dawn approached, they faded into the purple light.

Together, Xavier and I finished painting the Blockbuster Video, and then started digging the foundations for a Tower Records down the street. Mostly, though, we talked, our avatars facing each other on a wide, pixelated sidewalk beneath the shadow of an elm tree I had planted a month ago. Occasionally other people would wander onto the screen, little figures wearing dresses and hats and, sometimes, peacoats, but they never stuck around for longer than a few minutes. I imagine that from the outside, it didn't seem like much was going on.

We talked about nothing, and everything—what we ate for breakfast that day, and whether we were afraid of death. I couldn't remember the last time I had spoken to someone like this, the last time I had talked and talked without worrying that I was being boring. Where I felt like my words were permeating the space between us, instead of bouncing back at me. The realization was like watching the tide roll back after months of barely keeping my chin an inch above water—without knowing it I had been drowning, and now, finally, I could feel the sand beneath my feet.

I gave him my phone number and we started talking there, away from the game, in the real world. He asked me about where I lived and I told him about Zsófia and the barking terriers downstairs, and then I asked him where he lived and he described for me his apartment in Paris. It was in the seventh arrondissement, near the quai Voltaire. His aunt who raised him had left it for him when she moved to the family's estate in Avignon. It had four bedrooms, and a salon with an antique sofa, but he lived there all by himself—when he woke up each morning, he would see the sun creep over the Seine, alone.

"It would be so much more beautiful," he said. "If you were here with me."

THE NEXT WEEKEND, MY BROTHER, Nick, called and asked me if I wanted to go to some fitness class in Chelsea. It had an alliterative, militant name, and when I asked him what, exactly, I'd have to do when I got there, Nick paused and stuttered and avoided getting into the details.

"I promise you'll like it. It's fun," he said. "Besides, I'm worried your hands are going to meld to your computer if you don't stop playing that dumb game."

Attila was circling around my feet and after kicking him away I agreed. I hadn't seen Nick in a while, and I missed him; he practically raised me, after all, what with my mother abandoning us for Washington. Also, he told me that when we were done he'd buy me lunch.

The room where the class took place was about the size of a CVS, and was filled with weights, trampolines, and ropes as thick as my thighs. There was loud music, and the lighting was low and red—the color that I imagine when I think about the insides of Russian submarines. The instructor was this prodigiously muscular man named Robbie B, and when I asked him what the *B* stood for he gave me a big, toothy grin and said "my last name." Because it was my first time, and because I made the dumb mistake of telling him as much, he led me into the room five minutes before the class started so he could, as he explained, "show me the ropes."

"Ha," I laughed. "That's a good one."

"What is?"

"Just that you're going to 'show me the ropes' and there are literally ropes over there."

Robbie B stared down at me, and in the room's Slavic glow his nostrils looked like stoplights.

"Forget it," I said. "It wasn't funny."

The class was divided into three stations, and Robbie B explained each of them to me with a *g*-less version of its corresponding gerund: *trampin'*, *liftin'*, *whippin'*. At the first one, *trampin'*, he told me to bounce as high as I could or to run in place or to hop on one foot on the trampoline—"no matter what it is, the most important thing is that you don't stop." In *liftin'* I'd be doing things with weights: curling them, pressing them over my head—the sort of shit that I'm sure people consider manual labor elsewhere, but that in New York you pay fifty-two dollars to do. At the third and final station—*whippin'*—Robbie told me to thrash the ropes, which were as long as school buses and looped through giant metal hooks.

"Just throw them around?" I asked. I was wearing the pair of gym shorts and the old Yale shirt that I'd slept in, and I used its sleeve to wipe my nose.

"As hard as you can. I want to see you crush it." Robbie B slapped me hard on the back. "Do you think you can crush it, Greta?"

I yawned.

"Sure. Why not."

The class was not fun, as Nick had promised. *Fun* was not the word that came to my mind to describe it. Once, Robbie B yelled at me over his microphone, *by name*, to "whip" harder, so I did. I whipped so fucking hard that as he was walking by, the rope sprang up and hit him in the face.

"Holy shit," I said.

His nose was red and blood was pouring down to his shirt. He started clapping.

"Greta!" he said. "Keep it up!"

"You don't need help? You don't want me to stop?"

"Don't stop! Never stop!"

Robbie B picked up the rope and shoved it back into my hands. Then he waited for me to start whipping again, and when I had he moved on and started screaming things at people bouncing on trampolines.

When the hour was over he led us through a bunch of ten-second stretches. I waited for the rest of the class to leave and then went up to him to apologize.

"I'm sorry," I said. "I guess I don't know my own strength."

"What are you talking about—that was awesome!" The bridge of his nose was all puffy and swollen and his left eye was starting to bruise. "In fact, I'm going to tell the front desk to give you a free class."

He high-fived me and jogged out of the room.

Once he was gone I turned and stared at Nick, who was so sweaty you'd have thought he'd jumped in the Hudson.

"I don't know what to tell you," he said. "We live in very strange times."

AFTERWARD WE DRANK SMOOTHIES THAT tasted like mulch, then ate salads at a place on Seventeenth Street. It all seemed like a routine to Nick, like he walked on autopilot from the workout studio to the restaurant, his feet landing on the sidewalk with a steady, mindless cadence. He hardly raised his head when we crossed the street, and when our waitress offered him a menu he thanked her but told her no—he already knew what he wanted.

"How often do you do this?" I asked him once our food arrived.

"Honestly? Pretty much every weekend."

"But why?"

"I don't know," he said. "Because someone at some point told me that this is what it means to be gay."

I watched him stab a tomato. We don't look that much alike—Nick has my mom's sharp face, while I've got my dad's round one. Nick's skin is smooth, like flawless windswept marble, whereas I'm nothing but freckles.

"Being gay sounds awful," I said.

"I'm kidding, Greta. I do it because I hate myself."

His gym bag was open at his feet, and peeking into it I saw an orange pill bottle. My brother used to take a lot of medication, stuff that any sane person would need if they had to work for my mother. He'd been off most of them for a while, ever since he got a new job, but from what I could gather there were still artifacts from that period scattered around his life. Lone white tablets disintegrating in his bathroom. Bottles with faded instructions in various suitcases and bags.

Nodding at it, I said, "What's that?"

Nick glanced down, toward the bag, and pulled the bottle out.

"Oh, geez." He squinted and read the label. "Lorazepam, it looks like."

"Can I have it?"

"What? No. It's probably expired, anyway."

"Well, then can I have *some*?"

He thought for a second, and then, taking my hand in his, shook three of the pills out into my palm.

"Don't take them all at once," he said. "And *don't* drink on them. That will really fuck you up."

I promised him I wouldn't and slipped the pills into my pocket.

"Oh, I meant to tell you," he said once he'd put the bottle back, "I saw Ethan the other day."

I knew exactly who he was talking about, but still I asked, "Ethan who?"

"Ethan Kahn? You might remember him. He was the delightful, handsome man you dated for four years and whose heart you inexplicably broke."

I picked up my fork. "Doesn't ring any bells."

"*Right.*" Nick rolled his eyes so far back that for a second I thought they were stuck. "Anyway, I was getting off the subway at Columbus Circle, and there he was, locking up his bike outside the Time Warner Center. We chatted for a little bit—don't give me that face, I didn't say anything about *you*, I just asked what he was up to. He mentioned he's moving to Chicago in a week. Did you know that?"

"This may come as a surprise to you, but I don't really speak to Ethan Kahn anymore."

"I figured that was the case." Nick sighed grievously, like I'd recited death statistics from a tsunami in Indonesia. "He got a job at the Obama Foundation, something that he said he couldn't pass up. Jesus, Greta, he was *such* a nice guy."

I briefly considered throwing my salad in my brother's face—just letting him have it, spinach and all—but then figured that would be rude, considering I wasn't the one who had paid for it, and so I opted instead simply not to respond. I knew what he thought about Ethan—I had known what everyone thought about Ethan since we had started dating, during the fall of my junior year at Yale. He was three years older than I was—a second-year law student—and we met after I spilled a beer on him at Gryphon's Pub. He didn't get mad, because he never got mad; instead he bought me another IPA and asked me out on a date. I said yes, because he was smart, and funny, and his dimples were so perfect they looked like they'd been created in a laboratory—this is what people told me, it seemed nearly every day. He was also effortlessly *good.* He rarely got drunk or wasted money on frivolous things, and his weekends he spent volunteering at an organization in downtown New Haven that provided legal aid for undocumented immigrants. It goes without saying, I think, that my mother adored him. For years this made me proud, the fact that I was with someone like Ethan, that someone like Ethan would be with someone like me. I wanted to impress him, to show him that I cared about important things, too. I changed my schedule and routines and started volunteering, showing up hungover to dig holes for trees and teach Yemeni kids English. I stopped taking Ubers everywhere and started riding a secondhand bike. I wanted him—I wanted everyone—to see that I could be just as good.

None of it mattered—or if it did, then it wasn't enough. After graduation, once Ethan and I had both found jobs in the city and were living together, the goodness—the effort to be good—became exhausting, a Sisyphean task. I didn't recognize it at the time—rather, I told myself that I needed to try harder. I would watch as Ethan moved from the trash an empty carton of yogurt that I should have placed in the recycling bin, and I would silently chastise myself for being so selfish, so careless. When we went to my mother's house, which we did very often, I would listen from the couch in the living room as she lavished praises on him in the kitchen; it was Ethan, always, who cooked everyone dinner. Her voice would slip into a terrible trill, and in the space between her compliments I would hear unspoken rebukes of myself, these tacit acknowledgments that when it came to Ethan and me, I was the one who had better hang on tight. Which I suppose is one of the many reasons why, six months later, I finally decided to let go.

"Let's change the subject," I said.

"Fine." Nick held up both of his palms. "Have you given any more thought to Mom's dinner?" He waited for me to acknowledge what he'd said, and when I didn't he added: "Please? It's with her biggest donors, Greta. She really needs this. Carmichael's polling well and—"

"I don't care."

I poked around at my salad, a nest of greens, chicken, and feta cheese.

He stopped eating and set down his fork. He sighed.

"What?" I asked.

"I'm worried about you. That's all."

"What's that supposed to mean?"

"It means that over the past six months you've flung yourself into this fucking self-imposed exile in Brooklyn, Greta, and I don't understand why."

"I think 'self-imposed exile' is being *a little dramatic*. And it's Brooklyn—not Siberia."

"Is it dramatic, though? You've got your face glued to your computer all day. You hardly see your friends or me. You don't talk to anyone—"

"—that's not true."

"—you've got a job that's taking you nowhere."

"Oh, and what, teaching college freshmen how to use semicolons while writing a Joan Didion musical is going to win you the Nobel?"

Nick hit the table with his fist and pointed at me.

"*Hey*," he said. "That musical is going to be *big*."

He lowered his finger, and we were both quiet. I felt terrible, like I'd kicked a giant bruise on his heart. Picking up his fork again, he shook his head in this way that told me he wasn't angry, that his patience was still at least partially intact. I loved my brother, and I knew he loved me. The problem was that we had different ways of showing it: he thought loving me meant fixing me, whereas I thought it meant knowing we were always on each other's team.

He ate another tomato, and my heart broke a little.

"Okay, fine," I said. "I'll think about Nancy's dinner."

I HAD A SHIFT AFTER lunch, and when I got to the store, Neil was waiting for me by a display of iPhone cases. He had this crazed look in his eyes, like if he didn't get to talk to me his nostrils would consume his entire face, so I ignored him and walked to the opposite end of the store, where I saw a customer eyeing some AirPods Pro.

"So, are these worth it, or what?" he asked me.

"Excuse me?"

He held the white box a few inches from my nose, like he wanted me to smell it.

"I asked if these are worth it. Like, are they really that much better?"

"Oh, absolutely." I didn't know. "They're the best."

"They're two hundred forty dollars."

"Well, sir, this is Apple."

"So?"

"So, two hundred forty dollars is actually pretty cheap."

He flicked the box with his finger.

"What makes them so much better?"

From next to the iPhone display case, Neil was still staring at me. He held up his phone, but I couldn't see what was on the screen. I turned away.

"Have you ever been to Machu Picchu?" I asked the customer.

"Like, in Peru?"

"Yeah, in Peru."

"No, I haven't."

"Then let me put it like this. Trying to describe what makes the Air-Pods Pro so much better than normal AirPods would be like trying to tell you how beautiful the sunrise is at Machu Picchu. It's impossible to convey the magic—you've got to experience it for yourself."

The guy puffed his cheeks.

"Machu Picchu, huh?"

"You've got to go." I'd never been. "It'll blow your mind."

He bought them, and after I'd swiped his card and given him his bag I started frantically searching for someone else to help. I wasn't fast enough, though. Thirty seconds later, I could sense Neil, hovering behind me. He was breathing through his mouth, loudly, and he smelled like a ham sandwich.

"Did you see this?" he asked me.

"No."

"How can you know if you've seen it or not if you won't even turn around?"

I rolled my eyes. Outside, on Flatbush Avenue, a dog pulled a man on a skateboard across the street.

"All right," I said, turning to face Neil. "*What.*"

He was still holding his phone, and now he handed it to me so I could see what was on the screen. It was the *Daily News* website—an article about my mother's Senate campaign. I saw her name—*Nancy Harrison*—and then something about the guy she was running against, the actor Chip Carmichael. I looked at it for about two seconds before I handed it back to him.

"No, thanks," I said.

"Carmichael's doing better than expected." Neil seemed distraught. "It's all those fucking boomers, you know? They loved him on a TV show, and now they're willing to risk their healthcare because of it. He's convinced everyone that he's one of the last compassionate moderates, but I don't believe a fucking word of it. He's taking money from the NRA—I read about it on *Vice.*"

"Maybe the show was really good."

"Greta, if Carmichael wins this election, then we lose control of the Senate."

"Poor us."

"None of this bothers you? You're not worried whether your mother is going to win *at all*?"

His cheeks were red and I could see veins in his neck. A dirty rubber band kept his dreads pulled back from his face.

I put my hands on his shoulders.

"Neil," I said, as nicely as I could. "I don't know how else to tell you that I couldn't give two shits."

WHEN I GOT HOME, I was tired from work, and also from all the trampin', liftin', and whippin', so I turned off the lights in my room and lay on top of my sheets. For whatever reason, I couldn't sleep; every time I was about to doze off, a thought would jolt me awake again. I stared at the ceiling for a while, reciting my Social Security number in my head because it was palindromic and meditative, and when that didn't work, I reached for my journal and began to write.

I never expected to be someone who kept a journal. The whole ordeal struck me as performative and self-conscious, like staring in the mirror and practicing to look sad, or happy, or surprised. It was another way to control the shape of a memory, I figured, instead of letting it have a life of its own. But then for graduation my brother got me this nice leather notebook. One day I got bored and started writing, and I found I couldn't stop. The words kept appearing, like they'd been balled up in my fingertips and could now finally escape. And contrary to what I'd thought before, I didn't care who read it. Me in five years, me in ten years, God, Oprah, whoever—it was immaterial. My ideas were there, they had taken shape, which meant that now they were a little more real. And to me, that was all that mattered.

On that night, I didn't get very far. After a page and a half, my phone started ringing, and when I glanced down at its screen, my heart skipped a beat.

"Hi," I said.

"Well, hello, my little rabbit."

I propped myself up on my elbow.

"What are you up to?" I asked.

"Thinking of you. And yourself?"

I glanced at my journal.

"Oh, reading," I said.

"What are you reading?"

Tossing my journal to the floor, I hauled my knees up to my chest. I said, "Stendhal."

"Ah! One of my beloved countrymen. *Armance?*"

"No." I thought: *What else did Stendhal write? What would sound the most impressive?* "*Le rouge et le noir.*"

"Of course. A classic. Julien Sorel was a boyhood hero of mine."

"Really? I've always thought he was kind of a hypocrite."

Xavier was quiet. I worried that I'd said something wrong.

"Maybe," he finally said. "But so are many people."

Outside I heard a door slam, followed by aggressive footsteps: Rosie, fleeing the apartment for work.

"How was your day?" he asked me.

"It was fine." I scratched my arm and reached over to close the window. "I saw my brother. We went to a workout class where you pay fifty-two dollars to jump on trampolines and throw things around."

"I will never understand Americans."

"I hit the instructor with a rope." The pills Nick gave me were still in my pocket, and now I fished them out and set them on the floor next to my journal. "I think I broke his nose."

"Spectacular!"

"I know. Nuts, right? I guess I didn't do it right."

"No! That is not the case at all, my little doe."

"What do you mean?"

"I mean that it seems to me that you have done everything right. You were given a rope, and you broke someone's nose. You are a motherfucking ninja."

A motherfucking ninja.

I smiled.

"Sure," I said. "Something like that. Anyway, after I broke the guy's nose, we went and got lunch, and my brother told me that he ran into my ex."

"Ah, there is an ex. Of course."

"Isn't there always?"

"I suppose so, especially with a woman like you. Tell me, my shrimp—did he break your heart? Because if he did, I will have to find him."

I curled my toes, heard them crack.

"I think it was the other way around," I said.

Falling back against my pillow, I began telling him about Ethan—how, for the first few years, he inspired me, but by the end I felt as though I was in a race I would never, ever win. I told him about how my efforts to be righteous always came out flawed, or inadequate, and how when I screwed up, Ethan's refusal to get angry at me—his ability to not judge, and forgive—only made my anger worse. I told him about the empty yogurt cups.

"My mother wanted me to marry him," I said. "When she found out I'd broken up with Ethan, she looked at me like I was throwing away the only thing I had."

"Your mother is wrong. People like that—people like Ethan—are hiding something, Greta. They use their goodness as a shield from the world."

He said he wanted to see what I looked like. At first, I hesitated to say yes. I think I was worried that seeing each other would break something, that it would instantly pervert the pureness of what we shared online. This fear, though, was only half as strong as my fear of telling him no, so I agreed and said that we could FaceTime.

He was unnervingly beautiful. I don't know what I was expecting, but it definitely wasn't that. He was in bed—I could see the white pillows next to him, the way his back was propped up against the dark oak of a headboard. His eyes matched the blue of his shirt, and his hair was full and dark. The thing that I really couldn't stop staring at was his mouth. It was so delicate and feminine, and as I watched his lips curl at their edges I kept imagining myself leaning in and waiting for him to kiss me.

Immediately, I hung up.

"Sorry!" I texted him. "My roommate's fucking cat knocked my phone over and spilled a glass of water. 2 secs."

I tore off the old hoodie that I was wearing and ran to Zsófia's room, where I changed into one of her overpriced white T-shirts from Barney's. Then I went through her drawers until I found some makeup—lipstick, eyeliner, a little mascara. I pulled my hair out of the ponytail it had been in for the past eight hours and used one of her brushes to smooth out the knots. Then, back in my bedroom, I fucked with the lighting so I didn't look like a goblin, and slapped a little life into my cheeks.

He was still there, resting against the headboard, when I called him back. He appraised me for a moment, his face blank, but then his smile returned, and when it did it felt like a hole had opened in the ceiling and sucked me straight up to the sky.

"Just as I suspected," he said.

"What?"

"Don't play coy, my little *ninjette*. You're gorgeous."

TWO DAYS LATER, MY MOTHER texted me and asked if I'd meet her for a drink that evening. I was suspicious, so before I agreed, I called my brother to see what he knew.

"It feels like a setup," I said.

"A setup? You mean like a *trap*?"

"Yes, that."

"What do you think she's going to do? Buy you a martini and then club you over the head? This is our mother we're talking about, Greta. Not a Bond villain."

"I haven't spoken to her in nearly a month."

"Well, maybe that has something to do with it?"

I was in Carl and Zsófia's room because they were both gone and I knew Carl had a little bit of weed. He kept it in an old Altoids tin, along with his coke and a handful of tiny orange pills that—now, at least—sort of smelled like peppermint.

"You know more than you're letting on," I said.

The line was quiet for a second, and I thought Nick had hung up on me or that I'd lost him.

But then he said, "I told her you were coming to dinner. I think it's probably about that."

"I never said I was coming to dinner, Nick. I said I would *think* about it."

"Yes, well, I might have embellished for the sake of family harmony. Look, where does she want you to meet her?"

I rolled a joint with some of Carl's weed.

"The King Cole Bar."

"At the St. Regis?"

"Yes."

"Oh, for God's sake, *go*. The last time I was there I got some whiskey thing that cost thirty-seven dollars and I drank it next to Whoopi Goldberg. *Whoopi Goldberg*, Greta. That alone is worth it."

Nick kept talking, listing off other reasons why I should go uptown, but he was giving me a headache, so I stopped him. I told him I would meet our mother, but that I was doing it for him, and not for her.

"Fine, whatever," he said. "But text me if you see Whoopi."

The weather, I remember, was beautiful. In the morning it had rained, but now the sky was a crystalline blue. I took the train to Columbus Circle and walked around in Central Park for a bit, listening to the pedicab drivers bait tourists for rides, the sounds of the street fade into the trees. I had smoked a little more of Carl's weed before I left the apartment, and now colors were taking on a dull brilliance. Reds asking to be dived into; greens you could wrap around your shoulders like a towel.

My mother was already at a table when I got to the bar, reading a stack of papers over the top of her glasses. There was a boulevardier in front of her, along with a glass of water. She was wearing a gray suit, and whenever she flipped over a page she reached up to twirl one of her pearl earrings. A brown bag from Bloomingdale's sat at her feet.

"Hi, sweetie," she said when I sat down across from her, and then: "Just ignore all these papers."

They were set in a neat pile, their corners perfectly aligned. Between us was a bowl of nuts. I took a few and sucked the salt from their skins.

"What are they?" I asked.

"They're a speech."

"A speech for what?"

Nancy took a sip of her boulevardier.

"I'm speaking at a senior center on Riverside Drive. As part of the campaign." She cleared her throat. "It's for that."

"Because old people aren't voting for you."

"Well, now, I think that's a pretty big generalization, but—"

"That's not what I've read. I read they like Carmichael more. I read they don't trust you."

For a minute or two neither of us said anything, and in the background I heard forgettable music—an algorithmic mix of drums and bass and inoffensive synthesizers. I looked around me: wood walls; low lights; a mural of King Cole, smirking like an idiot between two grimacing guards. It was the sort of place people got gift certificates to for their wedding and then never got around to using them. The sort of place Zsófia would come in a tight dress and ask men her father's age to buy her drinks.

Nancy cleared her throat again and brushed some air from the table. She forced a bit of good cheer.

"It's so nice to see you, Greta," she said. "How are things in Brooklyn?"

"Why don't you go ahead and tell me why I'm here."

A man at the other end of the bar laughed. I watched him toss his head back, his Adam's apple bulging like a walnut trapped inside a condom. Nancy closed her eyes and took a breath.

She smiled, her cheeks pulled taut.

"Nick mentioned that he saw Ethan!"

"I'm not talking about Ethan Kahn with you."

"I'm only telling you what your brother said." She couldn't fucking help herself. "I just thought he was so *good* for you."

"I'm leaving."

I began to stand up, but Nancy set her hand on my wrist.

"Please don't," she said, and gently pulled me down. "I'm—well, let's talk about something else."

"Okay." I stared at her. "What?"

My mother's face went blank for a moment, before tightening again into her Washington smile.

She said, "I hear you'll be joining us for dinner next week—"

"I said that I would *think* about it."

"—and I thought you might like to wear this."

Nancy reached beneath the table for the Bloomingdale's bag and handed it to me. In it was a black charmeuse dress from Chanel and a pair of gold heels.

"What, you're worried I'm going to wear my Apple shirt? You're worried I'm going to embarrass you?"

"That's not what I said. I . . . well, I thought it would look nice on you."

"Well, I don't want it." I gave her back the bag. "*If* I come to dinner, I'll wear whatever I want."

A waiter who had a face like a young Daniel Day-Lewis showed up to take my order. I got a vodka gimlet that was called something else because it had ginger in it, and asked if he also wouldn't mind bringing us more nuts.

Across the table, my mother shook her head: her plan wasn't working.

"I don't know what I did to you, Greta—"

"Who said you did anything to me?"

"—but I need you to start acting like an adult again. This dinner needs to go well—we need that money. Things are tense right now. The polls aren't where they should be—you're right about that." She moved one of the papers in front of her so the stack was askew, and then she straightened things out again. "Greta, we're so close. Do you understand that? We're *so close*."

"Close to what? Making more empty promises? Being another Washington hypocrite?"

"I resent that, and you know I resent that. I've worked fucking hard. If it weren't for me, we'd still have a third-world healthcare system. I—"

"Yes, please continue to recite your progressive résumé to me while you sip your forty-dollar glass of bourbon."

"You didn't seem to have a problem with my forty-dollar glasses of bourbon when I was paying your tuition at Yale."

Daniel Day-Lewis swept back in with my gimlet and my bowl of nuts. I thanked him and turned toward the bar's entrance. I wanted to throw my mother out of it. I wanted to pick her up by the collar of her St. John Knits and toss her all the way down Fifth Avenue.

"That was before I knew any better," I said.

"Oh, and I suspect you think that bucking *the establishment* amounts to knowing better now?" Nancy twirled an earring and crossed her legs. "I hate to break it to you, but being angry and difficult isn't a substitute for a personality, Greta. It just means you're angry and difficult."

I didn't say anything, because I was difficult, and I was angry. I was also very stoned.

Still, Nancy seemed disappointed that I didn't snap back, because after a minute or so she shook her head and reached into her purse.

"Looking for your gun?" I asked.

"The NRA has given me an *F* for fifteen years, Greta, and I *literally* wrote the bill on expanding background checks. So, no—I'm not looking for my *gun*. I'm looking for my credit card."

She waved Daniel Day-Lewis over and asked him for the bill.

"Where are you going?" I asked.

"To fight for your fucking future." The check came, and when she signed her name she dotted the *i* in Harrison like she was stabbing someone's heart.

Then she stood up, leaving the Bloomingdale's bag beside me.

"You *will* come to dinner, do you understand me? You will be polite, you will act like you want to be there, and you will wear that dress."

Her cheeks were shaking, and she was white-knuckling her purse: I could tell that she was scared.

"We'll see," I said, and reached for some more nuts.

"I KNOW EXACTLY WHY SHE wants me to go," I told Xavier.

"And why is that, my little flea?"

"Because she wants to show all these donors that on top of being a politician, she's also a single mother who has raised two well-adjusted children. She wants them to think that she's fucking Superwoman."

"And are you well adjusted?"

"That's beside the point." I set my computer on a pillow and folded my feet beneath me. "God, she's so transparent, I don't know how other people don't see this."

"But will you go? Will you help her?"

I ripped one of my fingernails away with my teeth.

"I don't know," I said. "My brother's begging me to go, and it seems like Nancy really wants me there."

"I don't understand."

"What don't you understand?"

"You resent her, but you also care what she thinks?"

"Yes, exactly. Christ, Xavier, haven't you ever had a mother?"

I had decided to walk back to Bushwick from the St. Regis—I wasn't working that day, and I didn't have anything else to do. By the time I got downtown, to the Lower East Side, it was beginning to get dark. I passed by all the usual sights: bodegas, head shops, ice cream stores; ex–frat boys smoking cigarettes outside bars. The night was warm and sticky, and in the light of the streetlamps the neighborhood, what with its graffiti and monosyllabically named clothing boutiques, seemed to me to be less of a place and more of a set, a stage where people were able to act out some imagined, New York–ified version of their lives. I used to know what my place was in that illusion, but now I felt apart from it, like I'd been kicked offstage and told to wait in the wings.

Now, on my bed, my feet ached.

"She bought me this dress she wants me to wear. It's black, and from Chanel. I'm sure it was expensive."

I reached into the Bloomingdale's bag and held the dress up so Xavier could see it.

"It's beautiful," he said.

"It's not bad."

"Can I see it on you?"

"What?"

"I said I'd like to see it on you."

I thought, and then a second later reached a hand over to the window to shut the blinds.

"Okay," I said. "Give me a second, and I'll call you back."

"*No.*" Xavier's voice was firm. "I want to see you undress."

The dress was draped over my crossed arms, and I held it there as I faced the computer screen.

"Okay," I said. "But you first."

He adjusted his camera and the lamp on his desk: suddenly, the room lit up. I could see a sofa, a marble coffee table, and two sketches of bridges hanging on the wall. Between them was Xavier, wearing jeans, a belt, and a white dress shirt, which he was now frantically beginning to remove.

"No." I shook my head. "Go slowly."

Pausing, he bit his lip, contritely. Then, at half the speed as before, he returned to the business of unfastening the buttons, sliding them off one by one until his torso was bare and glowing on my screen.

"Your pants now. The underwear, too."

Again, I had to slow him down, and again he listened to me, following my instructions to deliberately remove each leg from his jeans and his briefs until he was completely nude. I told him to turn, first to the right, and then to the left, so I could see all of him: the hair on his thighs, his cock, the long curve of his spine. When I was finished, I told him to stay still, and then I took off my clothes.

There wasn't a ton of space in my room, but I worked with what I had. Occasionally, Xavier would give me instructions—a directive to show him a particular part of me, or to touch myself in a certain way, and I would oblige; mostly, though, I made him watch. Every action that I made carried with it a reaction on the other side of the screen: I brushed my hand across my breasts, and he reached for his dick; I showed him my ass, and his nostrils flared. The dress, once it was on my skin, felt like stepping into a cloud. The fabric was light, airy, and it hugged my waist perfectly. There are a lot of terrible things I could say about my mother, and they would all be true; none of them, however, would change the fact that she knows what looks good on me. I couldn't remember the last time I felt this beautiful.

"You're gorgeous," Xavier said. He had cleaned himself up and put on a pair of sweatpants.

"I'm *fine.*"

"Your mother the senator will be very pleased when she sees you."

"She's a congresswoman—not a senator yet." I thought of the story that Neil had shown me, the one from the *Daily News*. I added: "And from how things are going, she might never be one."

"And this makes you happy?"

"It doesn't make me anything. I don't care what happens ⸺ ."

An ambulance sped by outside, and I listened to its siren ricochet throughout Bushwick. When it was gone, and it was quiet again, I didn't say anything. I ran my free hand through my hair and listened to myself breathe.

"Greta," Xavier said, "tell me why you hate your mother."

I looked down the dress and at my bare feet on the floor.

I said, "Because she killed my father."

MY GRANDMOTHER EUGENIA TOLD ME what happened—this is what I explained to Xavier. She lives on the Upper East Side, in a town house on Seventy-Fourth Street that's half a block away from Fifth Avenue and Central Park. From the outside it's plain, unassuming, five floors of white limestone with a few bay windows and Juliet balconies. Inside, though, it's grand, and absurdly expansive—one of those New York houses that make you feel like you've passed through the looking glass, the kind where you wander into one room only to find another, where you climb stairs and wonder if they're ever going to stop. In the back, through a pair of antique French doors, is a garden with high walls that, in the spring, explodes with purple and blue wisteria blossoms. They shade a small fountain in the shape of a woman crying and, on either side of her, two wooden benches.

Also: there's art everywhere. Paintings, sculptures, swords. A hallway on the second floor lined with nineteenth-century vases. My grandmother is a collector, as was her husband—I never met my grandfather, he was dead by the time I was born, but there's a gallery named after them both at the Met. I remember one time I asked her why she did it, why she spent so much time and so much money amassing old canvases. Instead of giving me a direct answer, she peered at me over her glasses and turned the question back on me: why do *you* think I do it, Greta? I thought for a moment and then said, "Beauty." The world was ugly, and getting uglier by the day, against which art provided our only shield. She shook her head and told me that wasn't it at all. Rather, she said, it was about having a say in history. These objects, every last one of them, had a story. A tale that began with war, or famine, or lust, or wine, and ended—now and until she decided otherwise—with her.

I started going to see her during my sophomore year of high school. I was walking back to the West Side one day when I found myself outside her house and, on a whim, decided to knock on her door. The housekeeper, Cora, led me into the foyer, where I straightened out my school uniform and fixed my hair in a mirror with a gilded gold frame. I hadn't seen my grandmother in years. When we were younger, Nancy used to take Nick and me to see her in the park every Sunday afternoon; Eugenia would come from the East Side, and we could come from the West Side, and my mother would sit with her arms folded and a strained smile on her face as we climbed on Eugenia's lap. After a few years, though, Nick stopped wanting to come—he was a teenager, and the idea of spending his weekend with an old woman who smelled, in his words, "like asparagus" became suddenly unthinkable. Nancy used the opportunity to cancel one meeting, and then another one; before long—by the time I was ten, I'd say—we were hardly seeing Eugenia at all. This, I think, was partly the reason that I knocked on her door. I felt bad for her, sitting there all alone with her art. I also knew what it was like to feel discarded, a disappointment: at home, I was beginning to sense that I didn't belong. Nick had a natural intuition of how to please my mother, of being what Nancy wanted him to be. A speechwriter, her fixer, even gay. I remember when he came out how happy she was—like his sexuality was somehow another feather in her cap, another bona fide on her progressive résumé. Suddenly she started marching in pride parades and mentioning her "gay son" in her speeches—it was like she'd won the lottery. A few years later I asked Nick if it bothered him, and he sort of shrugged. He took a Klonopin and said that he was just happy to help.

I, on the other hand, was an intrusion. If Nick was the child Nancy *wanted*, then I was the child Nancy *had*. A delicate balance had existed, but my arrival had thrown it off. That's not to say that I didn't try—in fact, I tried very hard. I let Nancy trot me around in little dresses like some show pony, and I smiled so much my cheeks ached. I turned down cigarettes when everyone started smoking them in the eighth grade, and

I dutifully thanked the ambassador to Chile when, at a dinner at the United Nations, he stepped on my foot. None of it was ever enough, and all of it was exhausting. Living up to my mother's impossible expectations, knowing that whatever I did would always only be halfway to good.

"It must have angered you," Xavier said. He had opened a beer, and now he brought the bottle to his lips.

"It did."

I told him how when Eugenia saw me that first time in the foyer, she hugged me, pulling me in with her thin arms and holding me for so long that, for a second, I worried I would never escape. She smelled like lilac, and her sweater was soft against my cheek; once she had let me go, she told Cora to make us some coffee, and led me to a table in the kitchen. We talked for an hour or two—about school, about life, about Nancy—and then, seeing how the light outside was turning golden, I told her I'd better go. She seemed sad—I still remember the way her hand shook when she set her coffee cup on its saucer—and she asked me if I'd come see her again. Kissing her cheek, I promised her yes, I'd be back next week. I kept my word, too. I saw her then, and every week thereafter.

"And it was during one of these visits that she told you about your father?"

"Yes." My left leg had fallen asleep, and now I tried to move it. Pins and needles shot up through my thigh. "On a Saturday last July."

We were eating lunch—Caesar salads—beneath a Degas painting on the second floor. It was of a group of ballerinas dancing, their arms long and outstretched, their faces obscured by smears of brown and white. My grandmother loved Degas, was obsessed with him, really, particularly the works he did of the ballet. She was a dancer herself when she was younger, and from everything that I've heard she was very good. She trained at the Joffrey, and also the ABT, and had every intention of making it her career. When she was twenty-three, though, which was two years before she gave birth to my father, her left leg got crushed by a horse—she was out riding with her sister when the animal tripped and fell, pinning her beneath its flank. Her tibia was shattered, and doctors had to reconstruct her ankle with metal plates. Needless to say, she never danced again. And while she's never told me this explicitly, that's part of the reason why my father meant so much to her, I think. He was her child, obviously, but he was also something more—one love that was able to replace another. Something precious to fill an empty void.

I loved the painting, too—not because of the composition or the colors, but because according to Eugenia, it had been my father's favorite piece in the house. One of the girls reminded him of me, she said; he liked to call me his little star. I don't remember him saying this—I hardly remember him at all—though Eugenia had told me the story enough times that it was beginning to feel like my own. The same was true of the rest of my memories of him—I couldn't tell if they were hers, or mine, or fantasies that I had constructed from pieces of the two. I also didn't care. I was just glad that I had them.

"I miss him," I said, staring up at the girl's face. She didn't look anything like me. She had dark hair and clear, pale cheeks. She didn't have all these goddamned freckles.

I speared a piece of romaine and, chomping down on it, noticed that Eugenia had gotten very quiet.

"What's wrong?" I asked her once I'd swallowed.

"Greta," she said. "There's something I'd like you to know."

My mother didn't kill my father with a bullet, or knife; instead, she broke his heart. She was sleeping with his campaign manager, a man named Edward—Eugenia saw them together, at a restaurant on Lexington Avenue. Edward was reaching across the table to hold Nancy's hand, and Nancy wasn't doing anything to stop him. At first, my grandmother didn't do anything—she just kept walking. But then, a few days later, she resolved that she had to tell my father. It was her duty as a mother, she explained to me; she didn't have any choice. My father confronted Nancy, and they got into a fight. A knockdown, drag-out brawl that ended with my father driving his car, drunk, into an oak tree in Sagaponack. Eugenia knew, because Eugenia was on the phone with him when he crashed.

"Your mother is greedy and wants what she doesn't deserve," Eugenia said. "And we all have to pay the price."

She was stoic as she explained this all to me, her spine rigid and her eyes fixed forward. Not knowing what else to do, I set my plate on the floor and reached for her hand.

"What did you say to her?" Xavier asked me.

"I thanked her for telling me," I said. "Then I finished my salad, and I left."

For a month after I learned what had happened, I did nothing. I kept going to work at my mother's old law firm, shuffling around papers for lawyers who treated me like royalty. On weekends when Ethan was gone, I went out to expensive bars with discerning doormen—places that used to be old pharmacies but where you now paid twenty-eight dollars for a glass of bad gin. I got drunk and woke up hungover in our West Village apartment; I went to fucking brunch. I figured that my parents' problems had been their problems—that affairs were ordinary, another part of marriage, and that people were allowed to make mistakes. But then, at work, I would hear my mother speaking on one of the TVs that lorded over the cubicles where the firm corralled the paralegals. She'd be on CNN, talking to a well-lit anchor, and I'd hear her say something about fairness, or truth. It would be a hackneyed political Mad Libs that I'd heard her rattle off a thousand times before, but this time, it would stick with me. I'd play it over in my head, alongside the story Eugenia had told me, and I'd ask: *What right does Nancy Harrison have to talk about truth?*

That, I think, was the first crack in the dam, the tiny fissure from which everything else sprang forth. I couldn't listen to my mother on television—I could hardly stand to look at her. When Ethan forced me to join her and Nick for dinner at an uptown restaurant—something that we'd previously done often—I would stay quiet, reserved. Afterward, she would ask me what was wrong (Nancy, I'll admit, has a nose for trouble), and in response all I'd offer would be a tight smile, a clipped *nothing*. I suppose I could have confronted her, or told Nick or Ethan about it, but I didn't; the new understanding that Eugenia had given me felt too fragile, too needing of nourishment, and besides, I wasn't interested in hearing anyone's excuses. Instead, what I wanted was to unbind myself from Nancy and to live free of her hypocrisy. And so, I erased myself. I quit the job that she had got me, deleted all my social media accounts, and abandoned the apartment for which she was the guarantor. I walked away from Ethan, and the friends who idolized her, and those dumb, over-priced bars where we used to meet. I never went to brunch again.

I told Xavier all of this, and when I was finished, he set his beer down and folded his hands on the table.

"This all must be so terrible for you, my doe," he said.

"You know, it actually is."

"You feel as though you have worked your entire life to impress someone, only to find out that she is a hypocrite and a liar. The only true thing you know is that because you refuse to play her game, she no longer has any use for you, and you are alone. She has betrayed you."

"Yes. Exactly."

Outside, the streetlamps flickered off, and a ribbon of orange appeared over Bushwick.

Xavier said, "I would never do that, Greta. I would never betray you. Do you know that?"

"I do."

"Say it to me, then. Say that you trust me."

"I trust you." I had been crying, and upon realizing it, I started to laugh. "I trust you, and I don't even know your last name."

"It's de la Marinière."

I thought about his name, and then recited it back to him.

"Xavier de la Marinière—that's pretty." I smiled and saw my reflection in the window. I said, "I can't believe I'm still wearing this stupid dress."

I SHOULD HAVE IMMEDIATELY GOOGLED him, or found him on Instagram or something, but I didn't. Instead, I slept for three hours, took a shower, and went to work, where I sold a seventy-year-old woman her first laptop and dodged conversations with Neil. There was a part of me, I think, that thought the less I knew about Xavier in the real world, the happier I would be. I didn't want to be disappointed when I found out that he regularly posted selfies from the gym, or that he had some beautiful ex-girlfriend; I wanted to keep him exactly as I had found him.

That didn't last for long. When I got home that afternoon, Zsófia, Carl, and their friend Milo were cutting lines of cocaine on Carl's copy of *Profiles in Courage*. Zsófia asked me if I wanted some, and I told her no; even after everything that had happened, I refused to allow myself to become the sort of person who did blow off John F. Kennedy's forehead, and besides, it was only three o'clock in the afternoon. Instead, I went to my room and googled Xavier's name. The first thing that popped up was a YouTube clip of him speaking that had nearly fifty thousand views. He was dressed formally and standing in front of a giant French flag, though I recognized him immediately—his blue eyes, his full hair, his soft, girlish mouth. The speaker on my laptop was broken, so I pulled my headphones from my backpack and plugged them into my computer. I started the video over, and this is what I heard:

"The narratives that you have been fed are there to enslave you, and yet for your entire life you have been too entranced to realize it. In school, you were no doubt taught to question authority, and yet you never stopped long enough to realize that it was authority itself who was telling you this. You may think that you are revolutionary and open-minded, but really you have accepted what they want you to believe. Black people and brown people and white people smiling together in cereal commercials; politicians insisting Islam is a religion of peace, even though two days earlier a man screamed *Allahu Akbar* before blowing up a café in Cologne. It is polite, bourgeois society, propped up by cowards who apologize for the success of European civilization.

"And because of this, France currently is in a state of cultural, economic, and social free fall. We are a country that is occupied. Our occupiers today are not the Germans nor the collaborators—they are the ones who have made a mockery of our values and our freedoms and our heritage. I am speaking of the intellectuals in Paris, who would rather fatten the purses in Brussels than put bread on the table in Provence. They are the immigrants whom those intellectuals aid and abet, who invade our borders and steal our jobs and turn our countryside into a savage land. They are the radical Islamists who, in the name of tolerance and multiculturalism, have allowed Sharia law to creep into our schools and our libraries and our very government. They are the violent feminists who tell us that women are better off breaking their backs at work than caring for a family at home. They are the—"

There was a knock on my bedroom door. I gasped and pressed pause. "Yes?"

"Hello, Greta?"

"What is it, Zsófia."

"We're going to play some music now."

"You can open the door."

"Oh." The door opened. "I did not know if you were *decent*."

I was still sitting on my bed, and now I pulled my earphones out.

"I am," I said. "I think."

Zsófia frowned.

"Are you all right?"

"I think my boyfriend is a French nationalist troll."

She thought, and then shrugged.

"We're going to play some music now, so I thought I would give you these." Zsófia handed me a pair of headphones. "A man in a suit gave me them last week."

"Who?"

"A man in a suit."

"Oh." The headphones were huge, and white, and weighed as much as a motorcycle helmet. The ones that I had been using were little red pellets that I'd bought at CVS. "You're really going to be that loud?"

"Milo says he needs the volume to be extremely high for him to feel it."

"Right. Okay."

"Anyway, I thought with those you could still watch your videos."

"My videos?"

Zsófia pointed to my laptop, where the screen was frozen on the clip of Xavier.

"If your boyfriend is a troll," she said, "then at least he is very good-looking."

MILO'S BASS WAS TYRANNICAL AND made the apartment shake. I held my phone in one hand, and with the other, I plugged my free ear.

"Hello, my little shrimp," Xavier said.

"You fucking lied to me."

"What's this?"

"I said you fucking *lied*."

"About what? Greta, you sound very angry."

Standing up, I walked to the window. He was right: I was furious. I couldn't stop trembling.

"You're a xenophobe and a misogynist. You're a goddamned nationalist troll."

Xavier was silent for a moment.

Then, he said, "I think that *troll* is a very cruel thing to call a man, particularly when he is as beautiful as me."

There was a pack of Parliament Lights on the windowsill, and I struggled to light one with a flimsy match. Out in the living room, Zsófia's laughter pierced through the music, a sharp cackle that made my eyelids ache.

"I'm such an idiot." I sucked in as much smoke as my lungs would allow. "I'm such a *fucking* idiot."

"Greta, I think you are being too hard on yourself."

"*You* shut up." I pointed the cigarette at my phone's screen. "I'm not listening to someone who has twenty-seven videos of himself online spouting off some racist theories about how Arabs are the reason for all of France's problems."

"There are twenty-seven?"

"Christ, I showed you my fucking *tits*."

"Greta." His voice was calm, even. "Have you considered that perhaps you are the racist one?"

"Knock it off."

"I have said nothing at all of Arabs, but rather speak of Islamists, who are radicals that seek to occupy Europe, turn our churches into mosques, and cover beautiful faces like yours with mandatory foulards. It is you who has assumed that these individuals are Arabs and only Arabs. Perhaps that's something you'd like to consider?"

Ash fell from my cigarette, and I used my toe to grind it into the floor.

"I'm not getting into semantics with you," I said. "I told you everything—about me, about my mother, about my life—and you fucking sat there and lied."

Xavier ran a hand over his cheek and closed his eyes. An overhead lamp cast his kitchen in yellow light.

"I never lied to you, Greta. I never told you I was something that I wasn't. And besides, a man is more than what he believes."

"You're as bad as she is."

"Please don't say that. Greta, what if you came here? You think that I am a monster—what if you came to Paris and saw what I was really like? Would you allow me to change your mind?"

"You're fucking nuts."

"Your mother would be furious. I am the anti-Ethan! Is that not appealing to you?"

The cigarette was almost done. I used its butt to light another one.

"I'm not going to Paris," I said. "And we're never going to talk again."

"We could be like Romeo and Juliet. We could—"

"Romeo and Juliet! *Listen* to yourself, Xavier. And I'll remind you that the Montagues *only* hated the Capulets—you, on the other hand, hate *everyone*."

"No. No, that's not true." He shook his head furiously. "I love you."

The words hung in the air for a little too long.

I heard Zsófia laugh again, and I said, "I have to go."

HE TRIED CALLING ME AGAIN, right after I hung up, and then in the days that followed. I never answered. A few times I thought about it—I would see his number flash on my screen and I would think of all the things I could say to him, all of the reasons why I was angry and hurt. I always stopped myself, though; I couldn't see the point of speaking to someone only to tell him I wanted him to disappear. I didn't have social media anymore—I got rid of all of it already—so there was no need to block him on Instagram or Twitter or anything. On Nostalgeum, however, I detonated the Blockbuster Video and everything else that we made together—I just wanted it gone. None of it mattered. He kept calling, leaving me voicemails and sending me texts. "Can we talk?" and "Think of your mother" and "I love you."

I deleted the first two. The last one I kept.

TEMPERATURES SPIKED OVER THE NEXT six days. High atmospheric pressure from Mexico or something crept north and made itself comfortable over New York. A *heat tsunami*, the newspapers called it, because they needed something to call it. Cooling stations popped up everywhere. In Bed-Stuy, a couple of kids got themselves on NY1 for turning a dumpster into a swimming pool. Reports said that it had been five years since the city was this hot, which actually wasn't that long ago, but everyone acted like it was. That was easier, I think, than admitting that things like this were happening all the time now. Moving your body was sticky and miserable, so no one wanted to do much of anything. People said *fuck* when they stepped outside, so they mostly stayed in, and bodegas ran out of bottles of water. I tried to find a routine. In the mornings I lay in bed awake, basically smelling the sweat on my body from the night before. I'd stay there for an hour or two, however long it took for me to decide that not moving was hotter than moving—that at least when I was walking, I could feel the inklings of a breeze. If I left the apartment I'd usually go to the deli on the corner, where I'd use twelve quarters from Zsófia's laundry money to buy an iced coffee. I'd try to spread it out over a few hours, though the ice itself would melt in a matter of minutes. In the afternoons I read, and wrote, and played Nostalgeum—I did anything that would distract me from the void that Xavier had left, anything that would keep me from answering his calls.

I signed up for extra shifts at work, because somehow I was broke, and also because the store had Apple-grade air-conditioning. It was impossible not to show up drenched in sweat; the subway was a sauna and the sidewalks infernal, so usually for the first hour I was there I would stand in one place where I could cool off and dry. Customers would approach me, their iPhones held out like offerings, and I would answer their questions about gigabytes like I knew what I was talking about. My voice felt detached from my body during these conversations. I could feel the words coming out of my mouth, and I could hear myself saying them, but if someone would have told me that it was another person speaking, I would have believed her.

During my breaks, I would either get a seltzer at the empanada cart parked outside the store or go out to the loading dock to smoke. There was shade there—not enough to make a huge difference, but enough to make it seem less counterintuitive, the act of having a cigarette during a heat tsunami, of filling my body with yet more warmth. Occasionally, Neil would follow me on these outings. He didn't smoke, but he liked to eat sunflower seeds, and often he would bring a little plastic bag with him.

"I saw in the *Daily News* that your mother got a new campaign manager," I remember he'd said to me.

On the other side of Flatbush, a guy in a Nike T-shirt poured water over his head.

"Oh yeah?" I said.

"Cate Alvarez. She used to do public affairs at Google."

"Cool."

There wasn't any wind. Smoke drifted from my nostrils in ribbons that gathered in a stubborn cloud above my head.

"New blood can't be a bad thing, you know? At this point, with Carmichael polling where he is, and with it already being August, I feel like the strategy should be to fucking clean house and get this shit back on track. Rallies at senior centers, take control of the conversation about prescription drug prices, remind people that *moderate* doesn't mean *better*, just really . . . hey, are you okay?"

I tapped a little ash from the end of my Parliament and it fluttered to the ground.

"What do you mean?" I said.

"I'm talking about politics, and you haven't told me to fuck off, or shut up, or go to hell."

A shell from a sunflower seed was stuck to his face, to the left of his mouth, and reaching up, I gently flicked it away.

"You're sweet for asking, Neil," I said. "But I'm fine."

I DON'T THINK I REALIZED how much I would miss him. I hated it—I reminded myself of the terrible things I had heard him say—but it was the truth: I missed knowing that he was always there. In the evenings, when I got home from work, I would sometimes take lukewarm baths and think about what Xavier had told me during our last conversation, how he said a man was more than what he believed. The water would turn gray around me, and as I sank back against the porcelain I would wonder if this was true: whether it was possible to pick the parts of someone you wanted to keep and simply ignore the rest; whether it was okay to forgive the unforgivable in order to be loved.

One day, Zsófia came to me. It was sometime in the early evening—I had already taken my bath—and I heard a knock on my bedroom door. Juliette Gréco was playing and I was staring at a new text from Xavier, deciding if, this time, I would finally read it and respond.

"Hello?" I said.

"Greta? Are you there? It's me. It's Zsófia."

"Okay."

"Can I come in?"

"I guess?"

The knob turned and the door opened and there Zsófia was. She was wearing a torn black tank top that seemed expensive and frayed jean shorts, and leaning against the door's frame, she had a particularly avian appearance. Like a crane, or a disappointed heron, with its wings folded across its chest.

"Les feuilles mortes" played on my laptop and I had no plans to shut it off.

"What is it?" I asked.

Zsófia reached up and scratched her head. She wasn't wearing a bra, and I could see her nipples through her shirt.

"It is nothing important! I just have not seen you in a while and I wanted to make sure you were not dead."

"Well, thanks, but I'm not. I'm here, alive."

I reached forward and turned up the volume on my laptop.

Tu vois, je n'ai pas oublié / Les feuilles mortes se ramassent à la pelle.

Zsófia didn't leave. She nodded and took a step into the room. There was music on the street—a saxophone—and she went to the window and searched for whoever was playing it.

"We are going out. Milo is here, and he is taking us to a new bar on top of a hotel in Williamsburg. It is supposed to be very cool, very chic. Milo knows the bouncer." The saxophone player stopped. "Would you like to come?"

"To a bar on top of a hotel in Williamsburg where Milo knows the bouncer?"

I heard the sentence coming out of my mouth and felt immediately allergic to it.

"Yes." Zsófia smiled. She sat on the edge of my bed and closed my laptop. "I can give you something to wear."

My phone was next to me, and on its screen a notification for Xavier's unopened text. I didn't want to leave. I wanted to keep staring at it.

I said, "Sure. Why not."

THE BAR WAS CALLED VÜ and from it you could see all of Manhattan. It was about eleven o'clock when we arrived, and outside was a scrum of people, waiting to get in. We bypassed it—Milo really did know the bouncer—and once we were inside I peeled myself away from the group and walked to one of the windows. To the south were the spires of Midtown, and beyond them, the glass faces of Lower Manhattan. The city shimmered, like it had been dipped in glitter and was now sticking through the scrim of some duller, lifeless world. I remembered Xavier's text and wondered what it said.

Then I felt Zsófia tapping my shoulder.

"I would like to buy you a drink!" she said.

"Oh." Lights twinkled on the Williamsburg Bridge. "A vodka, neat, thanks."

Ten minutes later, she came back holding two martini glasses filled with something called a How the Fuck Did You Get This Number, which as far as I could tell was mostly rose water and chartreuse. I drank it anyway, and by the time I was done Zsófia had abandoned me, and a man named Greg was complimenting my shirt. It was plain, and the color of dishwater if you'd just washed a plate of beets, though given that Zsófia had lent it to me, I assumed it cost more than it should.

"So, what do you do?" he asked me.

"I work at Apple," I said.

"Nice!" The music got louder, and he raised his voice so I could hear him. "Marketing?"

I shrugged. "Sure."

He kept talking. He told me about the nonprofit he had started, which was focused on getting kids in war-torn places like Sudan or Myanmar to express themselves through ceramics. He bought me three more drinks and then led me to a corner, where we snuck bumps of coke next to a giant fake fern. Watching him fumble with the bag, I was reminded of the guys I slept with in college, before I met Ethan. They were sensitive types. Writers and art history majors and readers of critical theory. Boys who carried around copies of Knausgaard, and who liked to remind me that Philip Roth hated women. They looked the same; they were all, pretty much, the same. Pale, hairy bellies covered in free-trade cotton T-shirts. Beards and thick glasses they didn't technically need, canvas bags from Radiolab and Penguin Press.

I handed him back his drugs and his keys, and he asked me if I wanted another drink. A faint ring of white crowned his right nostril, and I considered telling him to wipe it away. I didn't. Instead, I started thinking about the triangle of perfect, bronzed skin formed by the open collar of Xavier's shirt. How his hair was always combed, and styled, and slick.

"Maybe in a little bit," I told him. Then, glancing over my shoulder, I said, "I'll be right back."

The bathrooms were unisex and smelled like sandalwood and hand soap. I waited in line behind two girls talking about Montauk, and when a stall opened up without them noticing, I slipped into it and closed the door. My vision was blurry—I was more fucked-up than I thought—and I had to squint to punch in my pass code and unlock my phone.

"It's a beautiful sunrise," the text said. "I wish you were here in my arms to see it."

I read it again, and then again. I thought about sunlight spilling over the Bois de Vincennes and the Seine. Shops unlocking their doors. Florists and Franprixs and those perfect little French pharmacies. A boulangerie turned golden by the scent of croissants. Effortlessly cool teenagers, cigarettes balanced on their lips, leaning against Lutetian limestone walls, waiting for their schools to open; street cleaners flooding a thousand kilometers of gutters. Just another day beginning, and Xavier and I watching as Paris wrested itself awake.

Outside the walls of the stall, urinals flushed and sinks turned on. Music thumped at my feet.

I typed "show me" and pressed send.

WHEN I WOKE UP THE next day I was wearing Zsófia's beet-red shirt and no pants and there was makeup smeared on my pillow. My head hurt, my lungs burned, and my mouth tasted like someone had shat in it. On the floor was a half-finished Rolling Rock, and my laptop sat on the corner of my bed. Skype was open, and the camera was on—according to my chat log, Xavier and I had spoken until eight o'clock in the morning. I tried to remember what I had said, or what he had said, or what either of us had done. It was impossible—I couldn't even remember leaving the bar. Voices were outside my door—Zsófia and Carl and Milo, all sounding hellishly chipper. I listened to them for a moment and then collapsed back onto my pillows. Bunching my bedsheets up in my fists, I pulled them over my head and shut my eyes. I committed to staying there for as long as I could.

Thirty seconds later, my cell phone rang. I reached an arm out from beneath the sheets, found it, and opened one eye to see my brother's name on its screen.

"Make it snappy," I said.

"So, you *are* alive."

"That's debatable." The bedsheet settled on my nose, and I blew it away. "What time is it?"

"It's three o'clock in the afternoon. I've been trying to get ahold of you for the past four hours."

"Well, now you've finally got me. What do you want?"

"To tell you to get up and get dressed. I'll be there in forty-five minutes."

"What are you talking about?"

"Tonight is Mom's dinner. She wants us at her place at five." I could hear the hiss of an espresso machine on the other end of the line. "I'm ordering an Uber, and I'm coming to pick you up."

The Chanel dress was hanging from the doorknob of my closet. I tried to conjure the energy to fight him.

"Nick, that's so far out of the way—"

"It'll give me a chance to see scenic East Williamsburg."

"—and there's no guarantee that I won't vomit on someone."

The espresso machine stopped, and I heard a loud *clunk*: my brother, knocking the grounds into the sink.

"I guess we'll have to take our chances, won't we," he said. "Now get up and brush your teeth."

I LOOKED OUT THE CAR'S window. We were crossing the bridge, leaving Brooklyn for Manhattan. To the left I could see Governors Island, and then beyond it the faint outline of the Statue of Liberty.

Crossing my legs, I smoothed out the dress over my knees.

"Remind me who's going to be there?" I said.

Nick was wearing a light gray suit with no tie, and sunglasses. Thinking, he took them off and glanced up from his phone.

"A movie producer, I think? And also, some woman from Goldman Sachs. Those are the big ones. Aside from that, the usual crew—some friends, her new campaign manager, a few DC types with bad haircuts. Folks who worked with Dad and are now lobbyists for the Sierra Club. You know the drill."

The bridge deposited us onto Delancey Street, where a snarl of traffic was waiting; at Essex, a truck pulled in front of us and the driver abruptly swerved to the right. Nick sat up straighter and then returned to his phone, where he scrolled, and scrolled, and swiped his finger like he was cutting off a gopher's head.

I watched him. Then I shook out from my purse the three Lorazepams that he'd given me a few weeks earlier and swallowed them, dry. They tasted chalky and sweet—sort of like a Smartie—and once they were down, I ran my tongue over the back sides of my teeth.

Sighing, Nick leaned back against the headrest and slipped his phone into the inside pocket of his blazer. We were nearly to the West Side.

"How would you end a musical loosely based on Joan Didion's early life in New York?" he asked.

The car went over a pothole, and we rocked in our seats. I didn't have the heart to tell him that I didn't know, because who in their right mind would write a musical like that to begin with?

I said, "How about, on the way to some bullshit dinner for their mother, Joan and her brother decide to make a run for it in a silver Toyota Camry driven by a man they've never met."

Nick smiled and squeezed my knee.

"You look pretty, Greta," he said. "You look really pretty."

My mother didn't think so. She didn't say as much—she's smarter than that—but the second Nick and I walked through the front door, she pulled me into the bathroom and started fussing with my hair. I'd pulled it back in a ponytail, but now she let it down and started teasing it out with a brush. When she was finished, she put a little rouge on my cheeks and told me to look up while she lined both my eyes. I let her—I figured at this point resistance was futile, and besides, the Lorazepam had started kicking in, I could hardly feel my toes. I was on the edge of the bathtub, and I remembered how when I was a little girl, I would sit in this same place to watch my mother get ready for work; it surprised me how, after so many years, a place could still feel so familiar, so totally unchanged.

"You smell like a deli." Her voice was creaky, on edge. "Are you feeling all right?"

I stood up. The edges of my vision were soft, and the floor felt two degrees off-center.

I said, "I'm perfectly fine."

She left me to go scream at some caterers, and once she did I immediately started going through her drawers. I didn't find much—a vial of Chanel No. 5, which I pocketed, and a white jar filled with skin cream. It was small, and on its top there was a name that was Swedish, and when I googled it on my phone I saw that it sold for five hundred dollars an ounce. I unscrewed the jar's lid and put my nose about half an inch from the cream's surface. It smelled like fish eggs and formaldehyde and something sweet—Cracker Jacks, maybe. With two fingers, I scooped up about a shot glass's worth and slathered it across the top of my other hand. I rubbed it until my skin was smooth and glistening, until the floor had shifted another degree to the left.

WHEN I GOT TO THE living room, my brother was standing next to the mantel where my mother kept an old German hunting sword that once belonged to my father's family, and that she had stolen after his death. In one hand, Nick was holding a glass of wine, and in the other a paper napkin, which he used to wipe some dust away from the sword's scabbard. Seeing me, he smiled and gave me a little thumbs-up. I sort of smiled back, and then took a champagne flute off a caterer's tray. I walked toward the windows and saw, on the way, my mother's new campaign manager, Cate. She was on her phone and drinking a seltzer and—I think—flirting with the campaign's press secretary, Tom. Scanning the room, I counted six other people: a theater critic from the New Yorker whom I'd only ever seen wearing smocks; a black poet who'd won a MacArthur grant; an older stage actress who was revered and a nonthreatening lesbian; a history professor from Columbia who wrote eight-hundred-page biographies of First Ladies; a man in a gray cashmere sweater and jeans who I assumed to be the movie producer; and a woman in a white pantsuit and don't-fuck-with-me heels who was—very clearly—the executive from Goldman Sachs.

I will hand it to Nancy: the living room looked good, better than I'd seen it in a while. The manila envelopes that were usually stacked on the coffee table were gone, and my mother had filled the place with fresh-cut flowers. Gladioluses on the side table next to the sofa, and a bunch of lilies on the credenza by the front door. The shades were pulled up and from the windows on the east side of the room you could see the park, all lush and buzzing with summer, the last bit of the day's light turning everything gold.

The kitchen door swung open and two cater-waiters appeared, each one holding a little silver tray topped with hors d'oeuvres. My mother trailed them. She had changed since I'd last seen her—now she wore nice jeans and an oversized oxford shirt with an open collar. On her feet were ballet flats and around her neck she'd looped a string of pearls. I knew this outfit—it was all over the West Side. It was the outfit of the kind of lady who wears sweaters in July and has a son at Amherst. The sort who doesn't see the irony of hanging a portrait of Mao Zedong in the living room of her classic-six on the park. For my mother, it was her *You are a friend and welcome in my humble home* outfit, her way of saying *We're going to relax and drink some wine before I ask you for money.*

She had put on a Bill Evans playlist, and between the chords I heard someone knocking. Nancy hissed a few orders at the cater-waiters—stuff along the lines of "No, you stand *there*," and "Are those *pigs in a blanket*?"—and then she left them to open the door. A man walked into the apartment and, after hugging my mother, kissed her on the cheek. He was tall, about six-foot-two, with graying hair and sloped shoulders; as Nancy led him into the living room I heard him say something about delays at DCA.

I stumbled a little, and some champagne fell from my glass. Taking hold of my shoulder, Nick righted me. Over the past five minutes I had drifted over to him and now my eyes fell to my father's old sword, to the weird, laughing monkeys engraved on its scabbard.

"Are you okay?" Nick asked.

"It's these dumb heels." I nodded to the man who had just walked in. "Who's that guy?"

Nick followed my gaze.

"Edward Barrett. He used to work for Dad, then moved over to the State Department. I'm pretty sure he's been there ever since?" A tray of *gougères* passed by, and Nick plucked one off. "Getting stuck in the bureau-cracy, man—what a slow, mindless death."

I thought, though not well; the Lorazepam was getting busy, and my brain was not cooperating.

"He was Dad's chief of staff," I said finally.

"Yes, correct. Wow—I'm surprised you remembered that. You must have been like seven years old the last time you saw him."

"What's he doing *here*?"

"Getting a free meal? Escaping the bad restaurants in Washington? I don't know—he helps Mom once in a while on policy stuff. She always invites him to these things, but he very rarely shows up." Nick glanced over his shoulder. "Where the fuck did those *gougères* go? Hey, what's wrong?"

I was staring at Edward. Nancy had cornered him near a vase of lilies, and together they were laughing at something the movie producer had said.

My mother caught my eye and smiled. Then she fixed her pearls.

"Nothing's wrong." I finished what was left of my champagne. "I just need another drink."

I ESCAPED TO THE KITCHEN and saw myself in the glass of the oven's door. My cheeks were red and my nose was blurry; my eyes were two black slits.

"*Edward*," I said, though the name came out wet and squishy—I tripped a little over the *d*'s, which pissed me off even more.

On the counter were the rest of the *gougères* that Nick wanted, and then next to them an opened bottle of Chenin Blanc. I took down my first glass in two big swigs.

"What are you going to do, drink the whole bottle?"

I heard my mother but I didn't look at her.

"If I want to," I said. I picked up the Chenin Blanc and filled my glass again.

Nancy edged her way to the counter so she could face me. I tried to turn away, but she grabbed my shoulders, squaring me to her.

"You're drunk," she said. "I've been watching you wobble around for the last hour."

"You're a liar. I have done no such wobbling."

She snatched the glass from my hand and emptied it into the sink. The bottle went next; she shook out what was left in it, then threw it in the trash.

"Shouldn't you be *recycling* that?" I said.

Her cheeks filled with air like she was getting ready to duck under-water, and I could tell she was clenching her teeth. But then she shook her head. Her eyes softened.

"Fix your hair and get yourself together," she said. "We're sitting down to eat."

I COULDN'T BELIEVE HER—OR, ACTUALLY, I could, which was worse. Noth-ing about my mother's actions surprised me—not the way she swanned around the living room like she was in the Ice Capades, or the fact that she invited the man with whom she broke my father's heart (and cranium) to dinner. It was the sort of person she was.

That said, I will admit that I should not have had all the Chenin Blanc. I'm not saying that I regret what happened next, but I will admit that drinking an entire bottle of wine in the time it typically takes me to drink half a glass was imprudent, particularly because I had already taken three Lorazepams, and because when I sat down at the dinner table there was a martini waiting for me, which I drank very quickly, too. I was nervous—that much was clear—and tired of having my brain pulled in so many directions. I remember how a salad was set in front of me and, reaching for my fork, I accidentally knocked the plate to the floor. Scallions, toma-toes, and clumps of frisée scattered around my heels.

"Fuck," I said. One of the servers was already on his hands and knees, sweeping the mess into a napkin. "I'm sorry."

Everyone smiled politely and began picking at their own plates. Even without looking at her I could feel my mother staring at me.

About five seconds later, I heard a knife, tapping against crystal.

"If I may, I'd like to say a few words," a man's voice announced. It was

Edward, standing up to make a toast. I lifted my napkin to my face and covered my mouth.

"Almost twenty years ago," he went on, "Nancy invited me for a walk in Central Park to tell me that she planned to run for her late husband's seat. Howard had passed away not a month earlier, and I was heartbroken—he wasn't a perfect man, but he was my boss, and my best friend. I was devastated. Suddenly, nothing seemed possible, least of all what Nancy was proposing. I tried to dissuade her, but . . . well, I'm sure you all know how easy it is to dissuade Nancy Harrison."

Everyone laughed, and I saw red. Edward raised his glass.

"I'm glad I failed, Nancy, for the sake of New York, and the country. You're going to be a hell of a senator."

Around me, cups clinked against each other, and someone muttered *Here, here.*

Dropping my napkin, I looked at Edward and said, "You're a fucking hypocrite."

He lowered his glass.

"Excuse me?"

"I said you're a fucking hypocrite."

The poet's eyebrows lifted and he said, very quietly, "Oh, shit."

Across the table, I watched as Nick hid his face behind his hands, but I wasn't about to stop myself, not when everyone was listening, not when I'd drunk an entire bottle of Chenin Blanc.

"You never cared about my father, and neither did Nancy. The two of you were—"

My mother stood up. She excused herself and smiled apologetically at her guests, and then dragged me back into the foyer, where—without saying anything first—she slapped me. Good, and hard, and across my left cheek. Initially I felt nothing, save the tears welling up and spilling over. But then—there it was. Something between a sting and a sunburn, radiating up from my chin. She'd never slapped me before, no matter how many times I imagine she'd wanted to, and now I looked at her and I slapped her right back. Her head barely moved. I think I expected her to recoil, to be stunned by what we had both done, but if she was then she certainly didn't show it. Her neck muscles clenched, and she glared.

"Get out of my house," she said.

I brought my hand to my cheek.

"What?"

Reaching forward, she cupped my chin in her right hand and turned my head so she could press her lips against my ear.

She said: "*Get. Out.*"

I LEFT THE SAN MARINO and crossed the street to get into Central Park. I was furious. My cheek still stung, and when I got to the reservoir, I let out a ragged scream that scared two joggers half to death. I wanted a cigarette, but I was worried that if I stopped long enough to light one, then the anger that I was feeling would overcome me, swallow me whole. So I walked, first east, and then a little south, following the park's trails until I reached Fifth Avenue and the Met. I walked faster and faster until I was practically jogging, until I had to lift the hem of my dress up to keep it from getting tangled between my knees.

"Greta, what on earth—"

Cora, my grandmother's housekeeper, stared at me as if I'd grown a second set of eyes. The lamp in the entryway was on, and the light formed a faint halo around her white hair. Stepping aside, she let me in.

"Sorry, I should've called." Walking over, I had managed to forget how drunk I was, but now, listening to myself, I remembered again. "Is she here?"

Cora shut the door, locked it, folded her arms.

"She's sitting down to dinner."

"The salon?"

"The dining room. Were you planning on—"

"No need to make me a plate." I stumbled toward the stairs. "I'm not here to eat."

On the second floor, I found Eugenia sitting at the far end of a long oak table, grinding pepper into a bowl of soup. Behind her were two windows through which I could see the garden, a tangle of vines bathed in silver light.

"My word," my grandmother said when she saw me. "What is that horrendous dress you're wearing?"

"I'm broke and I need money to fly to Paris." My breathing was heavy and I could feel my heart pounding against my chest: I had taken the stairs at a sprint.

Eugenia set down the pepper grinder.

"And why do you need to go to Paris?"

"Because there's a man there who loves me and who can help me ruin my mother's life."

Dipping her spoon into her bowl, my grandmother nodded, sipped some soup, and—I think—smiled.

"My purse is in the kitchen," she said, "go write yourself a check."

PARIS VOUS AIME

Rive Droite

Morning on the second Thursday of October: clear, crisp, the world's colors exceedingly defined. An autumn wind blows from the east, causing hats to flee from heads and flags to slap the air. In the Tuileries, rows of chestnut trees cling to their last golden leaves; on the other side of the Seine, the Eiffel Tower skewers a cloudless sky. At half past nine, a Citroën negotiates the traffic in the city's first arrondissement, its driver maintaining steadfast pressure on its horn as the car hurls past a Foot Locker and a Sephora and the curved glass windows of La Samaritaine. It's a business of close calls, of just-misses: in the shadow of the Tour Saint-Jacques, a man on a Vespa swerves and cusses; at the corner of place du Châtelet, the Citroën's front wheels graze a woman's skirt. The driver is unfazed. He keeps his hand on the horn as he bobs and weaves, ducks and dodges, scorching the earth beneath rue de Rivoli until he stops, with a screech, the car's tires brushing against the curb. In the backseat, Nick Harrison, jetlagged and yawning, shakes himself awake. He sees a sign—HÔTEL DU LOUVRE—and, after retrieving his wallet, counts out euros for the fare. Satisfied, the Citröen leaves with the fury with which it came; alone on the curb, Nick shakes some life into his cheeks. He steps into the hotel's lobby, locates the reception, and wipes the sleep from his eyes.

"*Bonjour, monsieur. Bienvenue à l'Hôtel du Louvre.*"

"Uh, *bonjour.*"

A calculation: immediate, imperceptible. The receptionist downshifts to English and smiles.

"Checking in?" she asks.

"Yes, that's right."

"A name for the reservation?"

"Harrison. Nicholas."

Fingers fly across a keyboard. The air is heavy with patchouli and sandalwood. Music—Chopin's "Waltz de l'adieu"—floats from hidden speakers. On the opposite side of the lobby, a revolving door coughs up two women in fur.

"I have you with us for three nights—is that correct?"

Nick adjusts his backpack. Behind him, heels clack across a marble floor. *Three nights*. Is that how long it takes to find a wayward sister? To knock some sense into her and bring her home?

"Three nights should be fine."

"*Très bien*." The receptionist nods. Her lips turn purple in the light of a computer's screen. "And tell me, Monsieur Harrison, what brings you to Paris? The art, perhaps? The Degas exhibit at the d'Orsay?"

Outside, an errant cloud eclipses the sun high above Montmartre and a sudden gust of wind depletes the chestnut trees of their last stubborn leaves.

In the lobby of the Hôtel, the Chopin waltz ends, and Nick forces a smile. *What a pity*, he thinks. His father loved Degas.

"Sure," he says, and takes his key. "Something like that."

In his room: a desk, a chair, a painting of the Gare du Nord, a bed with obscenely plush sheets. Across from him, a window frames the sturdy resplendence of the Opéra Garnier. Harmony and Poetry in gilt copper; bronze busts of Beethoven and Auber and Halévy. Walking to it, he pushes apart the curtains, letting the morning muscle its way into the room. He searches all around him and—*thank God*, there it is: coffee. A Lavazza single-serving machine that hiccups as Nick brings it to life. He conjures an espresso, blows some steam from the cup, throws it back, and begins brewing a second one before he's got time to swallow. The caffeine hits him quickly, but the rush is empty and leaves him jittery; when his mother calls him moments later, he jumps an inch from the ground. Nick Harrison is alert, but that's hardly the same as awake.

"*Salut*," he says. "Also, don't you ever sleep?"

"No—I'm a vampire." There is an ambient purring: Nancy's white noise machine. She must be propped up in bed. "Also, I really appreciate you going over there."

On the street below his window, a child uses her scooter to play chicken with pedestrians. Two meters away, an old man fusses over today's *Le Monde*, turning each page like he's plucking teeth.

"Oh, it's no problem," Nick says. "It's been a while since I've been to Paris—I'm excited to see the sights. Maybe I'll catch a show at the Moulin Rouge."

"Don't be cute. For all we know, Greta's firebombing the Eiffel Tower as we speak. I don't understand, Nick. Greta is a *woman*. She's supposed to *internalize* her pain and suffering, not act out on it."

"I understand the urgency, but I'd imagine firebombs are hard to come by, Mom."

"You say that, but do you know how bad this de la Marinière guy is?"

"My sense is very."

"I had an intern translate some of his YouTube videos—he's got twenty-seven of them, a whole fucking channel. The gist of it is that he thinks there's some grand conspiracy between liberal elites and immigrants to replace the white European population via birth rates and mass migration. He thinks the only way to protect against it is to close France's borders and send everyone who isn't white back to the country of their ancestors. Two years ago, he got together with some of his buddies and funded an antimigrant boat to troll the Mediterranean and fuck with NGOs and humanitarian groups who were trying to help refugees making the crossing. He's a monster, Nick, and I say that as someone who works in Washington. Even Marine Le Pen has disavowed him. My God, how could she go from Ethan Kahn to this asshole? Since when does your sister have such abysmal taste in men?"

On the street, the child's mother spots her and, a lit cigarette in her right hand, scoops the little girl and the scooter up with her left; the old man bores of *Le Monde* and throws it away in a nearby trash can.

"How about we forget Ethan Kahn for the moment," Nick says. "Tell me what else we know for sure."

"She got to Paris on August eleventh."

"And we're sure she's been with this Xavier guy since then?"

"Yes. She's been living with him in an apartment somewhere on the Left Bank that his aunt pays for."

"Okay, the Left Bank. That's a start. Do we know where, exactly?"

"You think if I knew that I'd be sitting here in New York? You think I wouldn't be over there, dragging her out by the ear?"

Booting up the Lavazza machine, Nick cranks out another espresso, his fourth.

"I'm going to head over there now and start asking around. Someone must have seen her." He grabs his coat, his room key, his wallet. He walks toward the room's door and stops a moment before opening it. "Mom, did something happen between you two? Like, something more than usual, I mean."

For a moment Nancy is quiet. Nick hears horns, sirens, voices. Outside the door, a housekeeper pushes a cart with a squeaky wheel down the hall.

"Just bring her home, Nick. And please—be safe."

Rive Gauche

Less than a mile away, beneath two sketches of nude women, Greta Harrison reclines on a sofa and props an iPad on her knees. Enlarged on its screen: a picture of herself, hair a mess and smile askew, the hem of a black dress, blowing in the wind. There is glass on the street in the photograph and now, her feet bare, she can remember what it felt like as her heels crushed it. The snap of something precious breaking; the power of her own weight. She can still feel the bottle, flinging from her fingertips; she can still smell the gas from the gendarmes' cannons. Vinegar is what Xavier told her it would remind her of—vinegar, mixed with hellish black pepper. He was right. They could smell it as she marched up the Champs-Élysées, and it followed them onto the smaller streets that branched off the avenue. Rue Marbeuf and rue Galilée. Finally: rue de Bassano, where she stopped and wiped her eyes with her sleeve. Where she saw the red awning of her mother's favorite restaurant, finished what was left of the champagne, and said to the cameraman they'd picked up along the way: *Make sure you zoom in.*

"You'll never believe this," she calls out now. "But I'm in *Vogue*."

The kitchen door opens and Xavier emerges, a cookbook open in his hand.

"Really?"

"Yes! Like, I knew the *Post* and the *Daily News* and whatever would pick it up, but *Vogue*, Xavier! Fucking *Vogue*!"

He kisses her. His cheek is smooth and smells of aftershave and garlic. Pulling him closer, Greta feels a shiver work its way down her spine.

"Thank God you wore the Chanel," he says.

"They loved it. They said that I managed to turn couture into revolutionary chic."

In the kitchen, a teakettle whines and Xavier rushes to tend to it. Standing, Greta sets down the iPad. She takes a cigarette from a pack on the coffee table, crosses to the other side of the living room, and strikes a match.

The refrigerator door opens and closes. Louder than before she says, "I bet she wishes she never bought me that dress!"

Xavier appears in the doorway again, though this time his hands are free and he's frowning.

"What's wrong?" Greta asks.

"I wanted to make coq au vin," he says. "But I need a bottle of Burgundy."

Bald branches claw against the apartment's windows.

On the Seine, a *bateau mouche* cuts through the water, painting the river with ribbons of green and white.

"I'll go get one." Greta retrieves her heels from beneath the sofa. "I could use a walk."

"You don't mind?"

"Not at all."

Smiling, Xavier takes Greta into his arms and kisses her again. She feels his mouth move from her lips, to her chin, to her ear. He lingers there for a second, and then bites the lobe, holding it between his teeth. Greta smiles, but then he clenches down harder and she wiggles to get free. When he doesn't immediately release her, she pushes him away.

"I bet she's so pissed. Because I threw the bottle, obviously, but also because I'm in *Vogue* and she's not." She rubs the spot where his teeth had pressed into her. "I'm never going back there. I'm never going back to New York."

Xavier steals her cigarette and takes a drag. He laughs.

"Of course not," he says. "Now, off you go."

En Attendant

Greta plucks the cigarette from Xavier's lips and, giving him one last kiss, prances out of the living room. Xavier waits to hear the front door close, and once he does, he goes to the bedroom window. Looking down, he sees Greta step out onto the sidewalk. Across the river are the mansard roofs of the Louvre; to her left, the belfry of Notre-Dame. The wind tousles her hair, and she turns her back to it to light another cigarette. It takes her a few tries, but once it's lit, she takes a long drag, faces east, and begins walking down the quay. She's in a new pair of heels, and every tenth step or so, she wobbles. His nose pressed against the glass, Xavier watches Greta follow the road around a corner until—going, going, *gone*—she finally disappears.

Reaching down, he yanks his phone from his pocket.

He types, "She's gone," and then hits send.

In his closet he finds his shirts: white, pressed, tailored to hug his shoulders by a man on rue de Richelieu. He selects one and, buttoning it from the bottom, thinks of pictures he's seen of Italy under Mussolini. Rows of boys in their neat black shirts. Fastening a set of ivory cuff links, he remembers his aunt Céline's old adage: "Anything looks good in the right shoes and suit."

Five minutes pass, and then ten; Xavier goes to the kitchen and peers down the empty street. Frowning, he texts Greta to tell her that, along with the wine, he needs some carrots and onions, and oh—oops!—a chicken, too. She answers him immediately and, with a string of smiling faces and cloying red hearts, tells him that it's not a problem—she'll pass by the supermarket; in fact, she's already on the way home.

"*Merde*," Xavier says.

He drums his knuckles on the counter, thinks, and then types: "Actually, would you mind going to the butcher on rue Royer-Collard? A bit farther away, but the best poultry in Paris! ;)"

This time, Greta takes a moment to respond, and when she does, there are no unicorns or happy little mouths. Instead, all she says is: "Sure."

Relieved, Xavier tosses his phone next to the sink, pours water from the kettle into his cup of tea, and goes to the living room to turn on the television. The news is playing: an interview with the minister of the interior, his face caught somewhere between constipated and concerned, followed by B-roll footage from the weekend's protests. Gendarmes in gas masks on boulevard Saint-Denis; a message—*France pour les français!*—spray-painted on the place de la Bastille. There are also fights. An Arab shoving a man in a Generation Identity shirt; students throwing punches next to the Porte Saint-Martin. And then, finally, the image that he has been waiting for: Greta, hurling an empty bottle through the gleaming windows of Fouquet's.

The news cuts back to the constipated minister as, at last, Xavier hears a knock. Setting his tea down, he wets two fingers and uses them to slick down his hair. Then he rushes to the door.

Boulevard Saint-Germain

On the corner of rue de Verneuil, a woman in a red coat knocks Greta's shoulder.

"*Pardon*," she says, and, smiling, continues north.

Greta watches her—the coat is beautiful, the color of ripe strawberries, or blood.

Moments later, her phone buzzes in her hand: a second text from Xavier.

"Actually, would you mind going to the butcher on rue Royer-Collard?" it says. "A bit farther away, but the best poultry in Paris! ;)"

Greta searches for *rue Royer-Collard* on her phone, sees that it's nearly a twenty-minute walk and frowns. She is only three blocks from the apartment, and besides, she's staring at a perfectly good grocery store. Maybe she could pretend that she didn't see the message. She could slip her phone into her pocket, walk through the market's sliding-glass doors, and grab the first shrink-wrapped bird she sees on its shelves. It would take five minutes, and in ten she'd be back in Xavier's arms.

A stroller careens toward her, its pusher oblivious. Stepping out of its path, Greta puffs her cheeks.

"Sure," she types, and presses send.

Turning around, she heads back east, to boulevard Saint-Germain, taking long, slow strides beneath the half-bare trees. She passes perfumeries, dogs in knit sweaters, a slew of famous cafés. Les Deux Magots and Café de Flore, their terraces filled with tourists, slapping mustard on chunks of bread, timidly examining plates of raw steak. At a florist she stops and buys—on a whim—a bouquet of tall, white lilies. Whatever mild annoyance she was feeling fades, because how could anyone—especially Greta Harrison—be angry in Paris? Two months ago she was hawking iPhones on Flatbush Avenue and doing bumps of someone else's cocaine behind giant fake ferns; now she is strolling to buy a beautiful chicken for a beautiful man in the most beautiful city in the world. She is neither lonely nor bored, and—this, for Greta, is the clincher—she has ruined her mother's life.

She still can't quite believe how easy it had been. One minute she had been lying naked, next to a handsome Frenchman, and the next an empty champagne bottle was fleeing her fingertips. To be sure, Greta didn't wholly understand what the protests were about—a trade deal? Unions? Petrol prices? It all struck her, like the majority of French politics and certain French verb tenses, as intentionally convoluted. Still, she liked that they were happening, how she and Xavier could hear the distant pop of tear-gas cannons from across the river. There was a romance to the smell of smoke, the foreign shouts; in addition to the *pain au chocolats* and the sex on Louis XV beds, they proved to her how far she was from her old life.

Xavier must have sensed this, the grip the city had on her, because before too long, he was reaching over and slipping a hand between her thighs.

"I've got an idea," he said. "Let's go have a little fun."

She hardly needed to be convinced—when Greta heard what Xavier was proposing, and that he knew a cameraman who'd be game to film it, she agreed to the plan straightaway. The riots growing louder, they got out of bed, quickly got dressed, and polished off a first bottle of champagne. Only once, as Xavier was unwrapping the foil from a second bottle, did Greta pause, and even then, it wasn't to stop what had been set in motion, but rather because she felt the urgent need to make something clear.

"I'm doing this because I hate my mother," she said.

"And rightfully so, my little duck."

"What I mean is that I haven't turned into some crazy xenophobe or something. Like, I grew up in Manhattan, for God's sake. I understand that without immigration we wouldn't have good Italian food. Do you understand what I'm saying?"

Xavier smiled and popped the champagne's cork.

"I don't need you to believe those things. I need you to believe in *me*."

Greta stared at his alarmingly blue eyes, his girlish lips, and then nodded.

"Cool." She took a swig from the bottle. "Then let's hit the road."

Now, at carrefour de l'Odéon, she walks past someone failing to get her waiter's attention at Les Éditeurs. The woman shouts and puffs her cheeks and tosses her hands in the air; Greta continues south toward rue Royer-Collard and Xavier's far-flung chicken. The sidewalk is narrow, precarious; it cuts a jagged path between high stone buildings, against which Greta presses herself to allow others to pass. Things open up again once she crosses boulevard Saint-Michel, and, after dodging a pile of dog shit, she stops to check her phone and get her bearings. A bank is on one side of her, and on the other, a hair salon; rue Royer-Collard is three blocks away. Putting her phone away, she turns and glances inside the salon. There are five chairs—four of which are taken. In the fifth one sits a stylist, a woman with a brown bob who lazily twists the chair back and forth as she flips through a magazine. Greta watches her—long enough to catch sight of her own reflection in the window—and then checks the time. It's only one o'clock—the chicken, she decides, can wait. She takes a final drag of her cigarette, extinguishes what's left of it beneath her heel, and walks inside.

La Copine

Colette Legard shimmies out of her bloodred coat and tosses it to Xavier.

Eyeing him up and down, she grins and says, "Why do you always wear such nice clothes when you know I'm going to rip them off?"

A cloud passes before the sun and wind shakes the windows. Grabbing the back of Colette's neck, Xavier kisses her.

"I sent her off to rue Royer-Collard," he says. "We've only got thirty minutes."

"Plenty of time." A hat is removed, and then a blouse: copper hair falls to Colette's breasts. "I've never known you to last longer than ten."

Reaching out, she pinches his lower lip and uses it to drag Xavier through the living room to the sofa. There, she unzips his trousers, yanks down his underwear, and pushes him onto the cushions. She's wearing white panties, and she nudges them aside as she climbs on top of Xavier, using his shoulders for balance, then leverage. Straining his neck, he tries to kiss her, but it's a wasted effort: when he's six inches away from her mouth, she presses the palm of her hand against his face, forcing his head against the sofa and holding it there as she grinds harder and harder into him. On the wall behind them, picture frames are knocked askew; on the ground at their feet, a glass of water left by Greta spills. Xavier's thighs tense and his breathing becomes ragged: he announces that he's close. Colette slaps him across the face—"No, you're not," she says—but it's a lost cause, and they both know it; the slap has sent Xavier over the edge. He spasms, sighs, shrinks. Rolling off him, Colette reaches for a tissue.

"Ten minutes was generous," she says. "Because that was hardly four."

She slips her blouse back over her head but doesn't bother with her pants. From the couch, where he's still splayed out, naked, Xavier watches as she walks to the liquor cabinet—an étagère that, if he's to believe his aunt, once belonged to the Duke of Orléans. There, she fills a tumbler with two—no, three—fingers of cognac before heading into the bedroom. He hears the opening of closets, the thud of drawers slamming shut. A few moments later, Colette emerges again, this time in a gray cashmere sweater.

"She bought that yesterday." Xavier reaches for his underwear. "On rue des Francs-Bourgeois."

Colette walks to a mirror.

"Who wears it better?" she asks.

Xavier yawns.

He says, "You, of course."

Turning, Colette inspects her profile. She straightens her spine and sucks in her stomach; with one hand, she smooths the cashmere over her chest.

"These dumb American girls," she says. "They think they can come to Paris, throw on a beret and a nice sweater, and—poof—suddenly they're French. Someone should tell them what they really look like."

"And what do they really look like?"

"Isn't it obvious? Fat little mice with crepes on their heads." She turns toward the television. A pundit has replaced the footage of the riots—a man with a neck nearly as thin as his tie. "How's it going with your new girlfriend, anyway."

"She's not my girlfriend, Colette."

"Oh, is that so?" Bringing the cognac to her nose, Colette sniffs, takes a sip, winces. "So, what are we calling her, then?"

"I don't know—what do you call Jean-Luc?"

She stares at him.

"My husband, Xavier."

Xavier nods.

He says, "I guess that makes sense."

What *does* he call Greta Harrison? Is she a tool? A distraction? A joke?

"An experiment," he tells Colette. "She's an experiment."

He had been talking to a few of them when he met her—sad, lonely girls, wandering around the back alleys of the internet. He found them on any number of places. Reddit, Twitter, 4Chan, Nostalgeum. Anywhere that was filled with people who wanted to be told that they mattered, who were searching for something to believe. The problem was that he got bored easily; he would convince them that they needed him, and then he would ask for a picture of their tits, and then, antsy, he would move on. They would call, and write, and beg, and plead, but he would ignore them: he had riots to incite, mosques to deface; he was a busy man. Greta, though, was different—it was why instead of letting her go he chased her back, pinned her down, drew her to Paris. She had a famous mother whom she hated—one who was against everything Xavier believed. With Greta, he would be patient. He wanted to see how far he could push her, how wholly corrosive love could be.

Running her hand through his hair, Colette takes another sip of cognac. Greta's sweater is soft against Xavier's cheek.

"Well then, how is your *experiment* going?" she asks.

"Have you seen the news lately? I'd say it's going pretty well."

"Yes." Colette purses her lips. "For someone so small, she has a very strong arm."

She adjusts herself on Xavier's lap and, together, they both turn toward the muted television, where the pundit is still running his mouth.

"What do you think he's saying?" she asks.

"What they always say. He's calling us racists and nationalists. He's saying that we're a menace to the republic. In about two minutes he'll start comparing what's happening now to what happened in 2018—all those yellow vests—and he'll say that the right is back to its bullshit again. We're using social unrest like we use everything else: as a vehicle to decry a pluralistic Europe, to call for a return to a white and Catholic France."

"You always say it's because they're afraid."

"Of course he's afraid—he's a coward. He knows that the greatest threat to the republic is the replacement of its people—he sees it in spiking unemployment numbers, in the proliferation of dark faces in headscarves dotting the streets—but to say so out loud would be blasphemy!

Just imagine what they'd call him at their universities and on their news programs. His editorials would stop being published in their bourgeois journals, and—*quelle horreur*—he would not be invited to their bourgeois dinner parties."

Colette stands, and feeling returns to Xavier's thighs. She walks to the étagère and pours herself another drink.

"And you think you should be up there?" she says. "You think you should be on that television, poking holes in his argument?"

"Don't be dumb, Colette—of course I should be. The camera loves me. They won't have me, though." Xavier watches the man's mouth move. "No one will have me, not after what Marine Le Pen said about my work in the Mediterranean."

"*A nasty little troll*, she called you."

Xavier winces. His entire childhood he had spent as no one—the orphaned charge of a widowed aunt, who insisted that if he lived with her he take her noble name. Of course, he was happy to, he needed no convincing. His mother had run off with an Arab, and his father, the pussy, had killed himself rather than sustain the melancholy of heartbreak. Best to rid himself of that legacy, Xavier wagered, lest it follow him around like a mangy, spiteful dog. At school it didn't much matter; he was still mocked for being too small, too slight, too feminine. But oh, if those same brats could see him fifteen years on! After years of shaking the right hands and kissing the right asses, he was, at last, poised to become a household name; he was *so close*. Weekly his phone was ringing with requests for him to appear on television. People stopped him in the streets and gawked at him on the Métro; *Le Monde* ran a headline, "Le Petit Provacateur." No longer would he be posting homemade videos on YouTube, or replying to illegible messages from hicks in Béarn. Instead, he would be respected, reviled, and—the thing he wanted, that he *still* wants most of all—famous. But then—*poof!* It was gone. A hired boat off the coast of Marseille, a raft of wet, trembling bodies, stopped dead in its tracks: he did the thing that politicians only dared to speak about, and for that he was scorned, his meteoric rise turned to humiliation and exile.

"I wasn't asking you to remind me," he says. "And please don't say *troll*—it's gauche."

"*A nasty little troll who needs to be spanked by his mother.* And on live TV! Jean-Luc still talks about it." She tries, barely, to hide her smirk. "He said Le Pen was right."

"That doesn't surprise me. Your husband is just like the rest of them."

"The rest of what?"

"All those spineless pussies in cheap, skinny ties."

The news cuts to a commercial: an ice cream bar, advertised on a frigid fall day. Sipping from her cognac, Colette walks to the window. The sleeves of Greta's sweater bunch at her wrists.

The ice cream commercial ends and—a little angry—she turns to Xavier.

"If you want fat ties and men with guns, then why don't you run off to America with your little whore with the good arm."

Xavier smiles.

He says, "That, my dear, is the plan."

Châtelet–Les Halles

The Métro station at Châtelet–Les Halles is an experiment in mayhem for which there were never any controls: this, at least, is Nick Harrison's assessment of it. And the result, as far as he can tell, is an outrageously large rat maze—a mess of corridors and escalators and Zara bags that lacks any discernible logic. He's been here for fifteen minutes, though it seems like fifteen hours, and no matter which crowded tunnel he ventures down, he manages to end up in the exact same place: a central, circular depository where he is surrounded by ticket machines and tourists, wandering around with the same glazed-over expression of the hopelessly lost.

His phone rings and, without checking to see who's calling, he answers.

"Mom." He is staring up at two signs, both promising him the 4 line: one points left, the other points right. "I might die in a Métro station."

"Uh, yes." The man on the other end of the line clears his throat. "I'm calling to report a missing date?"

Nick grins, and then—remembering last night—feels his cheeks go red: it's Charlie.

He picks the sign directing him to the left. "Could you, uh, describe this missing date of yours?"

"Sure. Brown hair, cute nose, ears a little uneven. An obsession with Joan Didion that falls somewhere between adorable and unhealthy. In any event, it was the weirdest thing. I was having the time of my life with him, and I went to go buy us two shitty vodka-sodas from a bartender who was definitely on steroids, and when I come back he tells me that he actually can't *have* the shitty vodka-soda because—get this—*he has to catch a plane to Paris."*

The sign leads Nick to a staircase, and then a moving walkway, slicing through another tunnel. Finally, he sees it: the platform that he's been searching for. Line 4, south, *direction Mairie de Montrouge.*

"I hope you drank both the drinks—it's so hard to find a good shitty vodka-soda in Chelsea these days." Nick walks faster. "About this missing date of yours: Have you tried calling the FBI?"

Charlie laughs.

"Very funny," he says. "How's it going over there?"

Nick tries to remember what he told Charlie, the shoddy explanation that he gave him as he scrambled to get on his coat and raced out of the bar. He was drunk, and frazzled; he was trying to recall where he'd put his passport. Did he mention the mess that Greta had gotten herself into? The troublesome associations she had made? No—he doesn't think so. Instead, he had painted a vague picture of a sister who needed him; a well-intentioned trip to Europe that had gone, suddenly, awry. Charlie understood—well-intentioned trips to Europe gone awry were, after all, the stuff of American mythology. And even if they weren't, it wouldn't have mattered: Charlie is someone who reads the news.

"Good! I'm on my way to meet Greta now."

"I'd tell you to give her my best," Charlie says. "But she sort of ruined my date."

A gush of air hits Nick's cheek and he hears a distant roar: the train, barreling into the station.

"How about I make it up to you when I get back?" he says.

"I might consider it." The wind gets stronger, the roaring gets louder. To hear Charlie, Nick plugs his other ear. "But only if shitty vodka-sodas are in the offering."

"The shittiest in all of New York."

"Okay then, Nick Harrison." Gliding into the station, the train opens its doors. "You're on."

Chez la Coiffeuse

"Do whatever you want," Greta says. "Surprise me."

The stylist, a reed-thin woman named Yvette, lifts an eyebrow. She runs her hands through Greta's hair, inspecting its split ends, letting it fall through her fingers.

"Whatever I want?" she asks.

"That's right—whatever. Just give me something new."

Yvette purses her lips, tilts her head an inch to the right, and narrows her eyes: her wrists smell like Dior Diorissimo and smoke.

"Okay." She sets both hands on Greta's shoulders. "Follow me."

She leads her to a basin in the back of the salon, where she cradles her neck and begins washing out her hair. The water is hot—too hot—and Greta winces a little as it hits her scalp.

"Those are nice shoes," Yvette says. She pumps some shampoo into her palms.

Her head still tilted back, Greta peers down as best she can, past the gray smock Yvette has given her, past her thighs and her knees, to her pair of heels. They're black sling-back pumps, with steel toes, and she'd bought them a week ago at the Louis Vuitton store on rue Saint-Honoré. They had also cost her over a thousand dollars. She had the money, finally, and it wasn't from selling extra iPhones on Flatbush Avenue—the check she'd written herself at her grandmother's town house had been for fifteen grand. Or, no, that's not entirely true. Originally, it had been for twenty-five hundred, which was enough, she figured, to get her to Paris, and then back to New York, if things with Xavier went south. Upon seeing it, though, Eugenia had laughed and torn it up. She said that if Greta was going to ruin her mother's life, then she deserved to fly first class. She uncapped a pen with her brittle teeth and cut her a new check herself.

Now the world goes dark: Yvette has draped her head with a towel. She begins rubbing vigorously, and then wipes some conditioner away from Greta's forehead.

"Okay," she says. "Let's go."

They return to the chair, where Yvette pours Greta a glass of Sancerre, and then a larger one for herself. She yells something at one of her colleagues—a bit of argot that Greta can't quite decipher—and then picks up her scissors and slices a huge chunk away. In the mirror's reflection, Greta watches as her hair flutters helplessly to the ground.

"Do you have a plan?" she asks.

Yvette snips again, this time from the left side of Greta's head.

"What do you mean, a plan?"

Greta thinks and considers her glass of Sancerre, sitting on the counter next to a purple comb. She's here because she feels like a different person, which means she should look like one, too.

"Never mind," she says. "You can keep going."

Yvette nods and drinks her wine, and returns to attacking Greta's hair with a wild, savage abandon.

Five minutes later, when the floor is littered with blond shrapnel, she says: "You look familiar."

Greta sits up a little straighter and crosses her legs.

"I do?"

"Yes. You look like the woman who slept with my husband."

Slouching again, Greta says: "Oh."

Yvette twirls Greta so her back is to the mirror and snips some strands away from Greta's temple. She can hear the blades kissing.

"You are American, no?"

"Yes. Or, sort of. I'm from New York."

"Your French is very good."

"Thank you." Greta smiles. "I live here now."

"Oh? Where is home?"

"Not far. Near where rue de Beaune hits quai Voltaire. I live there with my boyfriend."

Hearing herself say this out loud startles Greta: she can't remember the last time she identified where home was so easily. She hasn't been in Paris for long, and already New York feels like a dream. Or, not a dream but a nightmare, one from which she has finally awakened. Cramped apartments in Bushwick, lonely nights on hotel rooftops, her mother slapping her at dinner—these are shapes that are drifting farther and farther away. In their place, she has the Eiffel Tower, and the Seine, and Xavier. He picked her up at the airport—when, she wonders, was the last time someone did that? Unlike her family, Xavier does not think that Greta needs to be fixed.

A blow-dryer hums, and a gush of hot air hits Greta's eyes. She closes them, feeling the tug of a brush against her scalp. In the chair next to her, a woman complains about her deadbeat husband. The stylist responds in intervals. *Merde* and *Quel dommage*. Once in a while a lazy *Hum*.

"Okay." Yvette turns the blow-dryer off and spins the chair around. "All done."

Greta inspects herself in the mirror. She can see her shoulders, her neck, the sides of her face. She has a bob, she realizes, and bangs—messy ones that hang above her eyes. She glances up at Yvette, who is standing behind her, smiling: she has given Greta her haircut.

"So?" Yvette claps her hands together. "What do you think?"

"It's great." Greta takes off the frock. "Thanks."

At the register, she gathers her things—Xavier's Burgundy, her impulse lilies—and then waits while Yvette runs her credit card. It's midday, lunchtime, and across boulevard Saint-Michel people gather outside the sushi bars and takeout joints on rue Monsieur-le-Prince.

"I'm sorry for the wait." Yvette wipes Greta's card on her pants. "This dumb machine."

Greta shrugs. She says "no problem" and picks up the salon's copy of *Madame Figaro*. Its pages are damp, sticky—someone had spilled their Sancerre—and as she turns them she occasionally has to peel them apart. There's an article about how to lose two kilos that she flips past, and then a profile of a French Instagram star, which she sort of reads. By the time

Yvette manages to finally run her card—a process that took blowing, more wiping, and a little spit—Greta has reached the horoscopes. She searches for Scorpio but sees an advertisement next to Aries that makes her say, "Fuck."

"What?"

Yvette sets a receipt on the counter, and its ends curl toward each other.

"This Degas exhibit at the d'Orsay." Greta points to the magazine. "My grandmother loves Degas. I should really go see it."

Yvette rolls her eyes.

"Grandmothers," she says. "They always love Degas."

Bonjour Fox News

A car honks furiously on quai Voltaire.

Inside Xavier's apartment, Colette Legard sets down her glass and pouts.

"You're going to the United States?" she says.

Xavier strikes a match for a cigarette. He imagines his face on television screens in westward American states. Kansas and Nebraska—places whose borders are carved from soil and grass, and where he will never, ever deign to go. He sees himself eating brash American meals in brash American restaurants. Traveling to universities to speak to fawning coeds while liberals protest him on the quad.

He says, "Yes."

"But *why*?"

"Because I was meant to be famous, and filthy fucking rich. And because we live in a castrated country, Colette, it's a fact." He waves his cigarette in front of him, smoke trailing his hand. "This place—the only thing it cares about are its bureaucracy and its *grandes écoles*. Men here won't *die* without first getting permission from their government. Christ, it's no wonder I'm underappreciated! What I need is somewhere that understands what I'm capable of, don't you see? A place where you can say anything, do anything, and someone will always be there with a camera at the ready."

"And that's the United States?"

"*Are you kidding me?* Think about all those thick necks and big, white teeth! Think of all those idiots in costumes driving their big-wheeled trucks! Colette, darling, *there* is a country that prioritizes showmanship over facts. All you have to do is bark the loudest and they'll give you your own television show."

Reaching for her own cigarette, Colette furrows her brow, confused. On the surface of her cognac, a lamp reflects its yellow light.

"But why will anyone pay attention to you there?"

Xavier smiles—Colette is stupid. He is reminded—again—that he isn't fucking her for her brains.

"You think I'm letting this American girl take up space in my bed because I get cold at night?" he says. "Her mother's a politician, Colette, and if she loses her election, her party will lose control of the Senate."

"Oh." Colette shakes her head. "I don't follow politics. All those ugly men and bad suits."

Xavier closes his eyes: this is getting frustrating.

"Okay, then how about this: when Greta and I are done with her mother, you will have a very famous boyfriend—"

"I don't think Jean-Luc would like you referring to yourself as my *boyfriend*."

"—I'll have book deals, television shows, cash, you name it. And Marine Fucking Le Pen sure as hell won't be calling me a troll anymore."

Colette exhales a thin ribbon of smoke.

"And you think this American girl will go along with it?"

"She was more than willing to throw a bottle through Fouquet's. If I tell her to, she'll say yes."

"And if she doesn't?"

Xavier stands up. "Then I guess I'll have to take care of it."

He begins to get dressed: first the trousers, and then the white shirt. A smudge of pink is on its collar—a trace of Colette's lipstick. He'll toss it in the wash and put on another one before Greta gets home.

"Give me that sweater," he says. "She'll want it back."

"I'll miss you," Colette says, pulling the sweater over her head. For a moment Xavier is worried she's going to start to cry.

"You'll have your husband."

"Don't you see? That's the problem."

Glancing at his watch, Xavier tosses Colette her pants, then ushers her toward the door.

"Whenever you want to see me," he says, "turn on Fox News."

Boulevard Saint-Michel

"Have you seen her? I've got another picture, if that helps."

A less-than-industrious waiter wipes his hands against his apron. Taking Nick's phone, he squints and enlarges the image with his thumb and forefinger. Behind him, at the outdoor tables of a restaurant called Les Éditeurs, water glasses sit half-empty and lunch orders remain untaken. A Peugeot screeches around the corner and nearly collides with a woman on a scooter. Nick gasps; the waiter doesn't blink.

"The police have not arrested her?" he says.

"Not that I know of, no."

The man exhales and hands Nick's phone back to him.

He says, "No, I have not seen her."

Another waiter—this one more committed to the steady functioning of lunchtime—spirals around Nick with an armful of plates. Half-eaten hamburgers and an empty pint glass. The last green shreds of a *salade Chinoise*. Nick thanks the man, then leaves him, giving him the space to continue ignoring his work. Turning north, he sees a woman with short hair and a bouquet of lilies crossing the street, and then doubling back southward, he finds himself facing three small roads. They're not perpendicular to any other street or avenue; rather, they sprout haphazardly from the square, trailing off at narrow, inconsistent angles. In appearance, they are nearly identical: limestone facades and sloped zinc roofs; awnings that provide shade for florists and bookstores and cafés carved out of the sidewalk. They could also lead him anywhere. To more forked roads; to dead ends; to Greta. If New York is a grid, Paris is a handful of spaghetti, dropped on the floor by a toddler.

He picks one of the streets and follows it, peering into shop windows and scrutinizing faces until the road dead-ends at the Luxembourg Gardens. He enters its gates, near a large pond at the gardens' north end. The morning's bluster has calmed to a gentle breeze, which smears the water's surface, blurring the reflections of trees and clouds. Toy boats float on the edges of the pool, tiny vessels with taut canvas sails that have been dyed red and blue and green. A few yards away, a boy who appears to be about five tracks one of them, manipulating its direction with a long wooden stick. He cajoles the boat left, then right, straightening its bow before he pushes it out farther from the basin's edge. Nick scans the chairs that line the pond's perimeter. Greta is not sitting in any of them.

No one has seen his sister. For the last two hours, he has scoured the left bank, stepping into clothing stores, bakeries, and cheese shops to show Greta's picture and ask in his pigeon French if she'd been around. The answer has always been the same—a swift, if mildly perturbed, *non*. Only once did someone respond with something different; after carefully scrutinizing Greta's face, a clerk at a small hotel asked for her number. He said that Fouquet's was overpriced and regularly fucked up its croque monsieur, and that any woman who threw a champagne bottle through its window deserved to be taken to dinner.

Nick runs a hand over his face, takes a breath, tries to think. Greta has always been good at hide-and-seek. When they were children, she would squirrel herself away for hours, ignoring his calls that the game was up, that it was time to come out and eat something. Once, at their grandmother's town house on Seventy-Fourth Street, she spent half a day in a dumbwaiter, having fallen asleep while Nick was searching for her. She was eight at the time, which made Nick fourteen. For three hours, he ran up and down the stairs shouting her name, and when she didn't appear, he begged his grandmother to call the police. She acquiesced—she had a thing for Greta—and before long two cops showed up in a flurry of flashing lights and sharp blue hats. Five minutes was all it took to find her. Stirred by the sirens, she lowered herself into the kitchen, where one of the officers was standing. Rubbing her eyes, she squinted up at him and said, "What in the *hell* is going on?"

But this time Greta isn't asleep in a dumbwaiter at their grandmother's house. She's in Paris with a despicable man who believes in despicable things, and from what Nick can gather, she doesn't want to be found. What will become of her? What happens if he fails, or if, worse, he's failed already? Until now, he has not allowed himself to imagine that his sister has fundamentally changed. He knows her, which is to say that he has devised a digestible narrative to explain what has happened: Greta got drunk; Greta got angry; Greta threw a bottle of champagne. However, that logic is founded on the assumption that he still understands how she thinks. They share the same heroes and the same villains, and when they say they *want to make the world a better place*, they're talking about the same thing. What if he's wrong? Will he still be able to love his sister—to speak to her, even—if she's committed herself to something monstrous?

He shakes his head, quells the spiders—he's not yet willing to think that the worst has happened to Greta, at least not yet. Turning away from the pond, he sees an exit to the gardens and begins jogging toward it, past two lovers getting acquainted with each other's tongues, and a statue of an ecstatic faun. Moments later, he emerges onto boulevard Saint-Michel, where he faces a gentle hill and the dome of the Panthéon. He steps off the curb—he doesn't bother checking for cars—and narrowly escapes getting squashed by the wheels of a bus. Horns blare, and Nick jumps back; the doors swing open, and as passengers funnel out, the driver yells. Nick doesn't stop to listen and instead crosses the boulevard. Once he's on the sidewalk, he stops to catch his breath and orient himself. On the other side of the street is a sushi restaurant; behind him is a hair salon and a bank. Turning, he looks into both of their windows and decides which one to try first. The line at the bank is long, and filled with angry faces, and besides, Greta has never been particularly interested in money.

He unbuttons his coat and walks into the hair salon instead.

Coq au Vin

"You cut your hair."

"Do you like it?"

Xavier takes the groceries from Greta and puts the lilies in a vase with water.

"Yes, my little duck," he says, kissing her cheek. "It's very chic."

A mirror hangs next to the apartment's front door and, slipping her coat from her shoulders, Greta inspects herself in it.

"I was a little worried that I looked like my mother, or a lollipop. I guess I never realized I had so much *neck*." She turns her head left, then right. "It's starting to grow on me, though. Oh, and by the way, there's a Degas exhibit at the d'Orsay. Tomorrow's the last day—I thought we could go."

"Of course. Anything you'd like."

There is music playing. Françoise Hardy, singing about all the girls and boys. Late afternoon light bathes the apartment, turning the floor the color of caramel. Across the river, Greta sees the tip of the obelisk in place de la Concorde and the tops of trees in the Tuileries. Paris is a city a person feels in her bones. All the bridges and rooftops and wild, erratic scooters; the boulevards that have buried beneath them whispers of bloodshed and war. She hopes she never gets tired of this view.

An ambulance passes beneath the window. Glancing down, Greta sees on the sill a half-finished glass of cognac.

"Getting started early, are we?" she calls out.

A *thud* comes from the kitchen. The sound of Xavier's knife, slicing through a carrot.

"What was that, my love?"

The cognac tastes like toffee and burns the back of Greta's throat. She carries the glass into the kitchen.

"I asked if we're starting drinking early." A pot bubbles on the stove and Greta peers into it. She sees onions, softening in rendered chicken fat. "That smells delicious."

Gently directing her by the hips, Xavier moves Greta away from the stove. The browned limbs of a butchered chicken sit on a nearby cutting board and, using the blunt edge of his knife, he returns them to the pot. Then he uncorks the bottle of Burgundy and, after taking a swig, adds that, as well.

"Yes, I suppose I did have some early cognac. I'm sorry, Greta. My heart is hurting, if I'm being honest with you."

Plunging a wooden spoon into the pot, he gives it a stir and sighs.

Greta feels her mouth go dry. She drinks more cognac.

"Did I do something wrong?" she asks.

"You?" Xavier laughs wanly. "No, you could never do anything wrong, my duck. It's your mother."

A weight lifts from Greta's chest.

"Oh, her," she says. "Well, she's a bitch."

His hand still wrapped around the wooden spoon, Xavier stirs with increasing vigor.

"She's worse than that. She's a monster. A murderer."

"Well, now she's a murderous monster who has a big fucking problem on her hands." Greta holds out her glass. "Do you want some of this?"

Steam wafts from the pot. Greta smells garlic, the earthy scent of thyme.

Xavier takes the cognac and finishes what's left.

"It makes me sick how she lied to you. How she manipulated you. Think about it, Greta—if it weren't for your mother, you would have had a father."

Leaning against the counter, Greta folds her arms against her chest and her eyes drift down. The window behind her is cracked open, and now she can feel the breeze, prickling the back of her neck.

"Okay," she says quietly, "but I'm here now."

Xavier takes Greta's chin in his hand, and she raises her eyes. His fingers feel warm against her skin.

"It's not enough, my duck. Do you see that? You are entitled to justice. Your father is entitled to justice. We must do more."

"Like what?"

Another bottle of wine sits next to her on the counter. Xavier opens it, using his teeth to remove the last stubborn inches of cork. Without asking if Greta wants any, he fills her cognac glass to its rim.

"We must go to New York," he says.

"What do you mean, go to New York?" Greta gulps down a mouthful of Burgundy. "I just fucking got here."

Xavier hangs his head.

"You are unwanted, Greta. That is the truth. Your mother promised the world to everyone but you, her own daughter, whom she has been happy to cast aside. It's her fault that you were so lonely, so miserable. You do not deserve this! You must understand me when I say that. You deserve to be loved."

Greta realizes that she's crying, though she doesn't know when that began. All she feels are hot tears that are running down her face and that she can't seem to stop. Using the back of her fist, she wipes furiously at her cheeks.

When she has found her voice again, she asks, "Do you love me?"

The pot's lid rattles. Xavier kisses both of Greta's eyes.

"I do," he says. "And that is why I am telling you that we must go to New York. Can you do that, Greta? Can you do that for me?"

She takes a deep breath and tries to stop her chest from shuddering. The Françoise Hardy song ends and, a moment later, Joe Dassin replaces her—the happy first chords of "Les Champs-Élysées."

She says, "Okay, I'll do it for you."

Chez la Coiffeuse, Partie Deux

A blow-dryer makes waves of straight black hair. At a sink at the rear of the salon, a woman leans back as water gushes over her wrinkled forehead.

"She's blond, and short." Nick points to his cheeks. "Also, she's got freckles, here, and here, and here."

The receptionist stares at him as if he's farted through his nostrils, her face scrunched up in fascinated disgust.

"*J'parle pas anglais*," she says, and turns back to her magazine.

"Hold on." A phone is produced. "I've got a picture."

Scrolling his thumb across the screen, Nick finds the image that at this point he feels as if he's shown to nearly half of the Left Bank. In it, Greta is standing on the Brooklyn Bridge, the wind tousling her hair. She's wearing a red shirt and her arms are tan; behind her New York Harbor is a blur of sun and silver. It was taken in June. She and Nick were on their way to get hamburgers in Red Hook when Greta had to pee so badly ("really, Nick, I'm about to *burst*") that she made him buy a slice of pizza from a place in Dumbo so she could use the bathroom. Aside from the press shot of Greta throwing a champagne bottle, it is the most recent picture Nick has.

The receptionist glances down, and Nick prepares himself to hear yet another curt *non*. Instead, her eyes narrow. She gives the picture a second look.

Then she holds up a finger, its nail sharp and manicured. With the other hand, she takes Nick's phone.

"*Attendez*," she says, and walks to the salon's fifth and final chair. There, she taps on the back of a tall brunette with a thin neck and bony arms, who hardly glances at the photo and nods. A conversation follows, a flurry of lips moving and shoulders shrugging that ends with the receptionist pointing another sharp finger at Nick. The brunette stares at him and purses her lips; when a minute later she walks toward him and the salon's reception, it's with a pair of scissors twirling around her finger.

"I am Yvette. You are searching for this woman?"

She extends her arm to hand Nick his phone. The cuff of her sleeve lifts an inch, revealing a small half-moon tattooed on her wrist.

"Have you seen her?"

"Maybe." Yvette's arms fold across her chest. "I am not in the habit of talking to strange men about my clients."

Nick's knees buckle.

"Please, I'm her brother," he says. "She's in trouble."

"Trouble? She did not seem in trouble. She was smiling and drinking Sancerre. Your sister's French, it is very good."

"My mother paid a lot of money for that French."

"I thought Americans only paid money for cars and wars."

Nick frowns: the observation is astute.

"Did she say anything else?" he asks.

Yvette leans a slim hip against the receptionist's desk.

"She seemed very happy. She spoke of her handsome boyfriend and his big apartment."

On the boulevard behind Nick, an ambulance sounds. He fumbles, again, for his phone.

"The boyfriend," he says, holding up an image of Xavier. "Was it this man?"

Now mildly annoyed, Yvette looks at the phone again. This time, however, her expression is different. Her eyebrows lift and her cheeks fill with air, and when, finally, she exhales, her face settles somewhere between astonishment, boredom, exhaustion, and disgust.

"*Putain*," she says.

"Pardon?"

"This is the boyfriend?"

"Yes."

"This man." She points at Nick's phone. "He is the scraping of a bidet."

"The what now?"

"He is an asshole."

"Ah. Yes. That's the sense I'm getting."

"She should not be with him." Her arms uncross. "I heard he pushed a woman down a flight of stairs."

"*What?*"

"The Cours Julien, in Marseille. He did not like that she was wearing a foulard over her head, and *oop!* Down she went. Rumors, *bien sûr*, but I am telling you, this asshole, he would do such a thing. Your sister, she does not know how to pick a man."

"You have to help me," Nick says. "Did she say where this man lives?"

"*Non . . .*" Trailing off, Yvette shakes her head and frowns. A moment later, though, her head perks up. "But—"

"Yes?"

"There was an exhibit."

Magazines are piled next to the salon's register, and one by one, Yvette begins flipping through them: *Time Out Paris, Elle, Vogue*. The pages fly by until, three-quarters of the way through *Madame Figaro*, she stops.

"*There*," she says, pointing to a small image in the magazine. "She said she wanted to see this, at the Musée d'Orsay."

The image is of a painting by Edgar Degas: a girl dancing in the center of a stage, her tulle skirt a smear of white and red. Reorienting the magazine to get a better view, Nick has visions of suffocating afternoons in his grandmother's living room. Endless hours that were spent among chairs that weren't meant to be sat in, and books that weren't meant to be touched. Similar ballerinas haunted that room's walls, their lithe bodies trapped within thick gold frames.

Scanning the advertisement, his eyes lands on tomorrow's date.

"What's this mean?" he asks.

Yvette brings her head an inch closer to Nick's so she, too, can read the advertisement. She smells like hair spray and perfume; outside, and two blocks north, the sun sets over the Sorbonne.

"It says that it's closing tomorrow." She straightens her spine and raises an eyebrow. "And that means you're in luck."

Le Musée d'Orsay

A ten-year-old knocks her fists on the *Gates of Hell* and, pressing her ear against them, strains to listen.

Next to her, a boy stands. He has small shoulders and big feet, and when he steps closer to the girl he trips, knocking her in the shoulder.

"What do you hear?" he asks.

"Nothing." The girl pushes him away. "Because you can't shut your big mouth."

His cheeks go red, and his eyes drift down. From a few feet to his left, Greta watches as he picks at a scab on his elbow.

The girl tries again, slamming her knuckles on the plaster head of Count Ugolino.

Five seconds pass, and then ten. The doors stay shut and she says, "Maybe there's nobody home."

Shaking his head, the boy shoves past her.

"You're not doing it hard enough." He wipes his nose with the back of his hand. "If you want the devil to hear you, you've got to *pound*."

Raising his fist, he prepares to pummel Paolo and Francesca, Dante's doomed lovers. The instant before he lets his hand fly, though, he is stopped, his wrist clenched in the air by the long fingers of his teacher.

"Étienne!" The woman gives the little arm a good shake. "I do not think Auguste Rodin would appreciate you treating his masterpiece like a punching bag."

Lifting her chin an inch, the girl clasps her hands behind her back.

"That's what I told him, too, madame. I said, 'Étienne, that is a *masterpiece* and not a punching bag.' He wouldn't listen, though. He never does."

"Thank you, Sophie." The teacher checks over her shoulder to where the rest of her class is gathered. Students mill around a bust of Beethoven. "That is very helpful."

The girl smiles; the boy gawks.

He says, "She's a goddamned liar," and the teacher whips her head around.

"Watch your mouth, Étienne!" she says. "Or I'll show you what Hell is really about."

A bit of squabbling follows—fingers are pointed and accusations denied—though before too long the children are being ushered back to their group, their chins dropped to their chests. From where she stands, Greta watches the scene unfold. Then, when space allows, she continues on, passing a bronze archer and two fallen angels as she follows the signs to Degas.

They lead her to the first floor, where light from the glass ceiling spills over a central hall of sculptures, brightening marble cheeks and slick, bare thighs. The exhibit is to the museum's north end—a collection of galleries featuring dancers and singers and ballet rehearsals, rendered in pastel and oil. It is also sparsely attended; as Greta wanders among the frames, she finds that she is often the only person in any given room. There are voices outside, and footsteps echoing in that great, sun-filled hall, but when she sits on a bench before a ballerina in a white dress, she has only her own breath to keep her company.

Ten minutes ago, Xavier left her—that, on top of it being Wednesday morning and the exhibit's final day, is why she is alone. As they were checking their coats, his cell phone began ringing and, apologizing, he ducked into the museum's gift shop to answer it. She searches for him now—how long until he finds her?—but sees instead an old man in a gray wool cap, inspecting a dancer with a bouquet. Turning back around, she rubs her eyes and yawns; she had difficulty sleeping last night, and now she can feel exhaustion slowly creeping up on her. She remembers how, as Xavier breathed steadily next to her, she stared at the ceiling for hours, watching shadows chase each other across the plaster. The apartment smelled like coq au vin, and the bedsheets like sex, and although she was tired, no matter how hard she tried she couldn't stop her mind from working. She thought, repeatedly, of what she had agreed to—the promise of returning to New York, and why—and each time she did she felt her throat close in on itself. Twice she thought of waking him, of begging him to stay, but both times she stopped herself and instead rolled on her side to face him. His neck was silver in the moonlight, and below his chin she could make out the faint pulse of his heart beating. Reaching out a hand, she gently ran two fingers through his hair and plucked a strand from his head. He shifted, and murmured something she couldn't quite make out before his breath settled back to its predictable rhythm. Greta wrapped the hair around her finger, tightening it until she could feel it cut into her skin. Until now she hadn't known how perfectly this could feel—to have someone care for her more than she had ever cared for herself. She hadn't known the happiness of being seen so clearly, heard so loudly, and loved so fiercely. And who was she—who was anyone—to ask for anything else?

The man in the wool cap leaves—Greta hears his cough, echoing as he shuffles into another room. Once she's alone again she stands, stretches her legs, and takes a step closer to the painting. She's never been good about art. This is not for lack of trying; she's taken all the classes and read all the books, but rarely has anything ever stuck. Her problem is that she can't get past one fundamental question—namely, what makes something remarkable, aside from all the right people saying that it's so? What makes something worth discussing, worth remembering, worth traipsing to the d'Orsay on a cold fall day to see?

Greta doesn't know—she doesn't think anyone does, really—but she figures that she's here, so she might as well take a few pictures and send them to her grandmother; it is, after all, the reason that she came. Reaching into the pocket of her coat, she retrieves her phone and zooms in on the painting. The girl's ecstatic face, the black ribbon around her neck, the specks of red on her skirt: she centers it all on the screen as, from somewhere near the back of the gallery, she hears the steady fall of footsteps. She ignores them at first, but soon they become louder, and nearer, and faster. Heel, toe, heel, toe, heel *toe*. Their pace grows to a frantic staccato until—an inch behind her spine—they stop.

Degas à l'Opéra

"Did I surprise you?"

Xavier wraps himself around Greta's waist and feels her body melt.

"A little." She kisses him. "What took you so long?"

"I'm sorry. My aunt Céline called, and then on the way here I got stopped by a fan."

"A fan?"

"Someone who likes my videos."

"Oh." Greta frowns. "That's nice."

The collar of her shirt is askew, and now Xavier reaches out to straighten it. He kisses her again and pulls her closer, and marvels at how easy love makes it to tell a lie. Or, in this case, a half-lie—which, in Xavier's defense, is also a half-truth. Céline didn't call—that was the part that he fibbed. In fact, as far as Xavier knows, she's forgotten his face, his name, and how to operate a telephone. Dementia is the reason—that thief of memory, that destroyer of grandparents, that angel who bestows upon doting only nephews the gift of six-bedroom flats. Every few months he'll consider ringing her—the apartment really is something special—though the prospect of a conversation always leaves him queasy. An hour he would have to spend, answering the same three questions—*I'm your nephew. You raised me. Your sister is dead.* Who has that kind of time? Even if Xavier did, and even if his aunt managed, for a moment, to break through the mental cloud that entraps her, there is simply too much to catch up on. YouTube channels, rafts in the Mediterranean, a rise to national infamy—it's hard to explain all that to someone, particularly when (a) she thinks a computer is a shoebox, and (b) you haven't spoken in five years.

The other part, though—the fan who stopped him—that actually happened; that was not a lie. He was leaving the gift shop when a man, dressed in a brown coat and a pair of wrinkled trousers, tapped Xavier's shoulder and asked if he could have a word.

"Yes?" Discreetly, Xavier brushed at the spot where the man had touched him—his shirt was agnès b. "What is it?"

Small craters pocked the man's cheeks—remnants of a lost battle with acne.

"I know you," he said, and his voice trembled. "I watch your videos. All the time."

Xavier stopped himself from beaming.

"Is that so?" he asked. "And what do you think of them?"

Removing his hat, the man raised his eyebrows.

"The things you say—they are exactly what I am thinking. We don't know how to be proud anymore. France is changing. Our jobs are being stolen out from beneath us. We are under assault."

Xavier set his hand on his shoulder and gave it a good squeeze.

"Keep watching." He signed his autograph on a postcard of Monet's water lilies that he hadn't paid for and handed it to the man. "I have some very big things in store."

Now, in the gallery's dim light, he releases Greta.

"You were taking a photograph of this?" he asks, nodding toward the painting before her.

"What? Oh, yeah." Her hair falls in her face, and she tucks it behind her ears. "It's one of my grandmother's favorite pieces."

Xavier assesses the canvas: a vapid, predictable choice. Positioning Greta in front of it, he takes her phone.

"Then you should be in it, as well, my dear. A beauty with a beauty." He taps open the camera and zooms in: an awkward smile fills the phone's screen. "Degas said that he enjoyed painting women in intimate scenarios because it was like watching them through a peephole. Would you like that, my flea? If I watched you through a peephole?"

Blushing, Greta rolls her eyes. She opens her mouth to admonish Xavier when, from behind him, an American voice says: "Now *that* is a great picture."

La Réunion

The color drains from Greta's face, first from her forehead, and then from her thin, freckled cheeks.

"Nick," she says. "What are you—"

"This is positively *wild*. Here I am, in gay Paree for a few days, and I decide to poke my head into the d'Orsay because I've got a free morning, and who do I find? My sister! Of all the places I could have wandered into!"

Greta's eyes are steel.

"Yes," she says. "Of all the places."

Next to her, Xavier clears his throat. Not waiting for an introduction, Nick walks across the gallery, taking hold of Xavier's hand and gripping it until he feels two knuckles crack. He gives it a vigorous shake.

"Nick Harrison," he says. "Real pleased to meet you."

"I—uh. Xavier de la Marinière." He turns to Greta, his wrist limp in Nick's hand. "Do you know this man?"

Greta curls her lips inward, her mouth a tight, angry line.

"He's my brother," she says.

"Your brother! How nice." Xavier's voice is cold, empty—ice on a newly frozen lake. Breaking free, he rubs his wrist and takes a step back. "You didn't tell me you had family coming to Paris, my little duck."

"That's because I didn't know he was."

Nick knocks Greta with his elbow.

"Surprise!" he says, and no one laughs.

At the other end of the gallery, a man pushes a stroller toward a bench, its wheels creaking. Muffled voices float in from an adjoining room.

"And what brings you to Paris?" Xavier asks.

"Oh, you know, work."

Greta lifts her eyebrows.

"What," she says, "did you find out that Joan Didion once took a shit in Sacré-Coeur?"

Nick smiles. "Different kind of work."

For a moment the three of them are quiet, their tense bodies forming a triangle among the gallery's frames.

"And you are a fan of Degas, as well?" Xavier says finally.

"Actually, no. My grandmother is, but I've always found him a bit tedious." Nick turns toward the painting. "He was a terrible anti-Semite, you know. Kicked out a model when he found out she was Jewish. Not a good guy, as it turns out."

Greta clasps her hands behind her back.

"Well," she says, "surely a man is more than his beliefs."

Nick takes a step closer to his sister. He brings his mouth closer to her ear.

He says, "Actually, Greta, I don't think that's true."

The man with the stroller leaves, and once Nick can no longer hear its broken wheel, the gallery descends into another fragile silence. From the corner of his eye he sees Xavier, glancing over both his shoulders, shifting back and forth on his heels. Nick thinks of the articles he's read about him, the videos that, in the past twenty-four hours, he has seen. Many of them he watched last night on his phone, squinting to decipher their subtitles as he drank whiskey after whiskey at the hotel bar. It was a mistake—or, if not a mistake, then unnecessary. The speeches Xavier made were the same speeches that Nick—that the world—had heard too many times before. Inevitably there would be a complaint about dark faces, moving around neighborhoods where they didn't belong, and then another about gay teachers, making queers of their students. A world turned on its head! Tradition being destroyed! A way of life at stake! It didn't matter if it was about headscarves in the Marais, or a fight about bathrooms in North Carolina—the complaint was always the same. *Toxic nostalgia porn*, is how

Nancy likes to describe it. Men who get off by sticking their heads in the sand. Who swear the future is destroying their country, as they pick its bones from their teeth.

A shrill ringing shatters the quiet. Jolted, Xavier reaches for his phone.

"I'm sorry—it's my aunt again," he says. "I'll be right back."

Nick watches him jog out of the gallery.

"He's much shorter than I expected," he says. "Online he looks so *big*."

"He's not that short."

"Greta, come on. He can't be more than—what?—five-foot-four? He's a regular Napoleon."

"How the fuck did you find me, Nick?"

"It turns out Mom's new campaign manager is very good at her job. Or, knows the right people, at least."

"I mean here, Nick. How did you know I would be *here*."

She's surprised, Nick thinks. *Angry still, but also surprised.* He wonders how long that will last.

"It was easy, really," he says. "I only had to talk to every single person on the Left Bank. A waiter who didn't do much waiting, a hotel clerk who asked for your number. A hairstylist named Yvette who, from the looks of your new do, isn't particularly creative."

Greta fusses with her bangs.

She says, "Of all the hair salons in all the towns in all the world—"

"—and I walked into yours. Anyway, she was nice. Yvette, I mean. And helpful, too." Nick leans an inch closer to her. "She wasn't a big fan of your boyfriend, though, and frankly, neither am I."

"You don't know him."

"You're right, I don't. But I've seen enough to know that he's dangerous. Come home, Greta. Whatever's going on here, we can fix it."

Glancing over her shoulder, Greta stands up straighter.

"No, I don't think so. Besides, not everything needs to be fixed. I love him, Nick, and you swooping into Paris isn't going to change that."

A baby cries in the gallery next door. Nick clears his throat.

He says, "Do you love him, or are you angry at Mom? Because from where I'm standing, those two things look very similar."

Her knuckles curved to sharp points, Greta punches Nick in the shoulder twice, and in quick secession—two machine-gun jabs that radiate pain down his arm.

"Ow," he says. "Jesus, Greta, that *really* hurt."

"Fuck you for thinking I don't know what love is."

She begins to leave and Nick reaches out, stopping her.

"Meet me later," he says. "We don't have to finish this now, and I'm not telling you that you have to come home. Just meet me later."

Her jaw clenched, she pulls her arm away.

"I don't think that's a good idea."

"Please"—Nick changes his tone; he decides to try begging—"I'm your brother."

The baby cries louder; the father tells him to *hush*.

Greta pauses. Her eyes are still fixed on Nick, though now they soften at their edges. Without warning, she reaches out her arms and he flinches.

"Fine." There are no more punches—now she hugs him. "The Tuileries. Six o'clock. Near the pond in the center of the garden, there's this statue. *Le bon Samaritain*. I'll be there."

L'Allée Centrale des Sculptures

No good, Xavier thinks, pinching his eyes shut. *This brother is no fucking good.*

Something shakes in his palm—his phone; he had nearly forgotten about it, and now it rings again with furor. He crouches behind a statue of Sappho—stone legs crossed; a lyre propped up against her thigh—and pins it to his ear.

"For God's sake, Colette," he says, "I told you I couldn't talk right now."

A wet sneeze explodes on the other end of the line, trailed by sniffles. Across the hall, a woman sits at the feet of Virgil, sneaking bites from a croissant.

"I can't take this, Xavier." Colette sneezes again. "I can't take you leaving me."

"I imagine it's difficult, but you'll survive."

"Why can't I go with you? I can be an American, if that's what you want." She coughs and pinches her voice into a nasal, Californian whine. *"Hey, dude, everything's awesome!* Do you see? I can be an American!"

Raising half a foot from his crouch, Xavier peeks into the Degas exhibit. There, standing right where he left them, Greta listens to her brother, her chin tilted down. What if, right now, he is trying to get her to leave Xavier? Certainly that is what Nick came here to do—he saw the videos, he flew to France, and now he is trying to take what Xavier has rightfully stolen. And what if he is successful? What if he manages to change Greta's mind, unraveling Xavier's hard work? The thought lodges itself in his brain, planting its stake, and he feels his pulse quicken. There will be no fame, no book deals, no dinners with Ivanka, *no Fox News*. Instead he will find himself in the exact position in which he has languished for the past year: exiled in his dying aunt's apartment, Marine Le Pen's nasty little troll. *This is the danger in betting on sad, lonely girls*, he thinks: *you never know who else is out there, trying to convince them that they matter.*

"I can't take you with me, Colette," he says.

"You are ruining my life."

"Then you should be happy that I'm leaving."

"Happy! You are abandoning me with Jean-Luc. His dick smells like Camembert and his breath tastes like boiled cabbage. How am I supposed to live with that?"

"You speak very highly of your husband."

Xavier rises on his tiptoes, craning his neck to see over Sappho's shoulders. Should he walk back to the gallery? Smile widely and say hello and break up the siblings' little *reunion* before any more damage is done? It's not as if he is without weapons of his own. Nick may have a brother's love on his side, but Xavier has a daughter's hatred of her mother. *And surely*, he thinks, *there's no power greater than that.*

He hears the sound of a glass breaking, and then Colette saying *shit*.

"You've made me so angry that I've dropped my fucking beer," she says.

"Then open another one, Colette."

"Call me every day that you're gone. Promise me."

"Sure, whatever."

Yes, he decides, he will go back to the gallery. Momentarily he was thrown off course—he has never been good with surprises—but now he has found his footing again. He is Xavier de la fucking Marinière. And Xavier de la fucking Marinière is not someone who stands idly by as an American homosexual challenges his fate.

"Say that you *promise me!*"

"Goddamn it, Colette, *I promise you!* Are you happy now?"

He doesn't wait for an answer—he simply hangs up the phone. Checking his breath and slicking back his hair, he begins walking across the hall. Halfway to the gallery, however, Xavier sees something that causes him to stop: Greta, embracing her brother, her nose buried against his chest. She keeps it there for a second or two, after which she looks up at him and says something that Xavier can't quite make out. Nick nods, kisses her forehead, and they release each other. Then, spinning around, Greta sees Xavier. Her eyes are glossy and her cheeks are red; smiling, she raises a hand to wave.

Thirty thousand feet above Paris, a cloud passes before the sun, causing shadows to pool on the museum's mud-slicked floor.

An inch from Virgil's toes, the woman finishes her clandestine croissant and, standing, licks its butter from her fingers.

Xavier stares at Greta. His eyes narrow, and he does not wave back.

Le Jardin des Tuileries

The Tuileries, five minutes before sunset. It rained all afternoon, from the time Nick left the museum until an hour ago, and now shrinking puddles reflect a cloudless, rose-red sky. He stands in front of Greta's statue— *Le bon Samaritain*, lifting a broken, beaten traveler in his arms—and turns his gaze west, away from the Louvre and toward place de la Concorde. There, traffic circles around a pair of fountains and the Luxor obelisk, its tip plated with gold. Is this where, nearly three hundred years ago, they set up the guillotine? Nick isn't sure—a person can only be expected to remember so many revolutions.

He doesn't know what he's going to say to her when she arrives. After leaving the d'Orsay, he had walked east, traversing the seventh arrondissement beneath a cheap umbrella until, an hour later, he found a small café where he could get a drink. It was the sort of place that he suspected existed everywhere in Paris—red lamps over flimsy wooden tables; a menu with things like *confit de canard* and carafes of Beaujolais. He asked the waiter for a whiskey, a pen, and a stack of napkins: he was going to compose an argument, a Treatise on Why Greta Should Listen to Him. He was a writer—a teacher of rhetoric—and he assumed that if he could find the right words, the perfect sentence, then Greta would blink, as if shaken from a bad dream, take his hand, and come home. An hour passed, and then another, and Nick wrote nothing. A task that had once seemed easy now struck him as impossible: how do you convince someone to believe you when you tell her she is loved?

The sun sinks, dipping behind the skyscrapers of La Défense. A few feet away, a woman wipes down a chair with a handful of paper napkins, then sits and opens a book. Throughout the garden, and in the shadow of the Louvre, vendors sell bottles of water, cans of sodas, cheap trinkets. Tiny gold Eiffel Towers and the Mona Lisa on a key chain; birds that, when their tails are wound, furiously flap their plastic wings. Nick watches one of these birds fly—up, then down, its nose crashing into the wet dirt. He wonders if Greta will even show up. He waits five minutes more, and then ten; he wipes down his own chair and sinks into it, despairing.

But then, once the sun has nearly vanished, he sees her, wearing a camel hair coat, along with a blue baseball cap. She has entered the gardens from the south, near the Musée de l'Orangerie, and having spotted Nick, she walks toward him. Her steps are quick, and every so often she checks over her shoulder, as if she suspects she's being followed.

"Hey," Nick says when she reaches him. She doesn't look up. Her hands are trembling, and once she sees that Nick has noticed, she curls her fingers into fists and shoves them into the coat's deep pockets.

"Hey."

"Nice hat."

"Oh. Thanks."

"Can you look at me?"

"I am looking at you."

"No, you're not, you're staring at your shoes."

"What is it that you wanted to say?"

"Greta, goddamn it, your haircut isn't that bad. I'm not going to have this conversation until you take off that hat and—"

She does, and then—slowly—she lifts her chin. Her nose is swollen at its bridge. A red gash begins at her right temple and curves downward, where it joins a mottled, darkening bruise. Tears well and spill over; Greta drops her phone, and its screen shatters in the dirt.

"Please, Nick," she says. "I just want to go home."

OCTOBER SURPRISES

Prodigal Daughters

Steam floats up from Cate's third cup of coffee, curling around itself before dissolving into the kitchen's light. Next to it, on a small plate, is half an onion bagel, a heap of ersatz white cream cheese smeared across its face. From the living room of Nancy's apartment—down the hall, past the bathroom—Cate hears the controlled hysteria of this morning's news. The market opened low and the MTA's in shambles; in Washington, Congress readies itself to vote on an infrastructure bill. She listens, waiting for some crumbs about the campaign, but hears nothing; the hysteria cuts to a commercial for antacids, and Cate breathes a sigh of relief.

She flips the page in today's *Post* and sees, from the corner of her eye, five fingers with chewed-off nails slowly reaching out for the bagel.

"Don't even fucking think about it, Tom," she says, and bats his hand away.

"Why? You're not going to eat it. It's been sitting there for ten minutes, getting lonely."

"I might want it later. Besides, you've had like eight bagels already."

"*Two* bagels, Catalina. I've had *two* bagels already."

Standing, he cracks his neck to the left and walks to the window. Beyond him, and across Central Park, the East Side is a wall of gray and white, set against a pale-blue sky.

"When's your train?" he asks.

Cate folds the paper in quarters and tosses it on the table. She checks her watch.

"In an hour," she says. "It should get us to DC forty-five minutes before the vote."

"And then you and Nancy are off on your grand, weeklong tour of western New York?"

"Our grand tour, Tom. You're meeting us in Buffalo." She taps her nails on the side of her mug—a chipped, porcelain thing that says WORLD'S BEST MOM in a disingenuous pink font. "By the way, do you have everything you need for that?"

"She's speaking at the opening of a new visitors center for the Erie Canal, Cate—I think I can handle it."

"You've called the *Buffalo News*?"

"Yesterday."

"How about the *Democrat and Chronicle*?"

"Just this morning."

His body framed by the window, Tom grins. *He smells different today,* Cate thinks. *Fresher.* Tom, she realizes, is wearing cologne.

She says, "Good."

Glancing over his shoulder, Tom looks in the direction of Greta's old room. For the past hour Nancy has been in there, the door locked, the voices behind it hushed.

"Do you think she's going to ask Greta to do it?" he whispers.

Cate rips off a piece of the bagel and chews it, slowly, sesame seeds lodging themselves in her gums. Nancy's reactions are about as reliable as the weather, though overall Cate would like to think that she's gotten better at anticipating them. She can tell, for example, that a twitching nose almost always presages a meltdown, or that carbs at lunch means the day's going well. When it comes to her daughter, though, all bets are off—it's like trying to predict snow in Kansas City.

Swallowing, she says, "I have no clue."

Tom sits down again and leans across the table. Moving her coffee so he doesn't knock it with his elbow, Cate leans back and crosses her legs. She takes a clandestine sniff and thinks: *it's a very nice cologne.*

"Okay," he says, "but you have to admit it's a good idea. Like, at least give me that."

The idea that he is talking about—the one that he's asking Cate to admit is good—is this: In a week and a half, after Cate and Nancy have tried to convince the western half of New York that a retired actor does not a senator make, Tom has arranged for Nancy to speak at the opening of a new retirement home in Manhattan. Or, no—not a new *retirement home*, because that's a phrase that brings to mind images of exhausted nurses and creaking mechanical beds, but rather *an active adult community*. Boom Town, the project is called, and it takes up an entire block on the island's West Side. A cleaner, safer city within a cleanish and mostly safe city, tailored to the needs of a generation that, after having endured very little hardship, now refuses to grow old: that is how Cate has come to understand it. Two hundred luxury apartments, sitting on top of an Olympic-sized swimming pool, five clay tennis courts, and a hall of virtual driving ranges. There is also, she has read, a dry cleaner, a grocery store, and two pharmacies; art studios for life-drawing classes; four private karaoke rooms; a tunnel that leads directly to Lincoln Center; and three gelato shops—all the necessary accoutrements to distract from nearing death.

Tom's genius is not arranging for Nancy to appear at the ribbon cutting—any idiot intern could have thought of that—but rather to have Greta speak alongside her. Combed hair, scrubbed cheeks, no champagne; a speech—one for the ages—that Cate herself would write. The picture, Tom swore, would paint itself: a family is reunited, America is healed. The prodigal daughter smiles at her mother before she steps up to the mic.

"It will be the Friday before the election," Tom told Cate when he first proposed the plan. "And besides, old people love that shit. I'm telling you—give them a good sob story that ends with a cute kid saying she loves her mom, and they'll be lining up their walkers to kiss Nancy's ass."

"Thanks for that visual, Tom."

They were in a bar on West Broadway, around the corner from the campaign's headquarters. It was midafternoon, around three o'clock, and already they were two beers deep. A few hours earlier, word had come through that Greta was back—Nick had called from the airport—and within five seconds, Nancy was sprinting out the door. She sent her staff home and canceled her meetings; any urgent calls, she said, were not as urgent as her child's return. From her desk, Cate watched as interns glanced at each other, and then began filing toward the elevator, their computers and desk lights darkened. She wasn't about to leave—there was still a heap of work to do for the trip to western New York—and soon, once the Interns' Exodus was over, she was the only one in the office. Or, rather, she *thought* she was the only one in the office. She was proven wrong, however, when, as she was booking a rental car in Rochester, Tom materialized next to her. He rocked back and forth on his heels, whistled a Pearl Jam song off-key, and said, "Well, Catalina, I guess we should go get drunk."

Now, in Nancy's kitchen, Cate searches for a distraction—she can feel Tom's eyes boring into her, waiting for her to tell him he's a genius. He's leaning farther forward, his face practically under her chin, his gaze straight up into her nostrils.

"You love it," he says. "I can tell."

To stop herself from smiling, Cate reaches for the bagel and chomps down on a second bite.

"Of course I love it, Tom," she says, her mouth a mess of cream cheese. "Why else would I be this irritated?"

"I KNOW SOMEONE IN THE police commissioner's office in Paris. I'm going to give her a call."

"Please don't, Mom."

"Your face, Greta. Think about what that monster did to your *face*. I'm not going to let him get away with that."

Greta's chin trembles. Burying her nose into Nancy's shoulder, she lets out an uneven cry. "Mom," she says, "I just want this all to be *over*."

As Nancy strokes her daughter's head, her gaze drifts toward the ceiling. They are in Greta's old room, seated on Greta's old bed. Surrounding them are vestiges of the girl she used to be, alongside glimpses at the woman she would eventually become. Posters of teen idols and field hockey trophies; a Simone de Beauvoir book with a well-worn spine. Her daughter's bruised cheek still pressed against her, Nancy considers how fragile Greta seems, but also, in her childhood room, how safe. If only she could keep her here, cocooned, she could protect her. If only she could stop her from growing up.

With drenched cheeks, Greta pulls her head away. Her nose is running, and now she wipes at it with the back of a clenched fist.

"All of this for some lousy French douchebag," she says. "I'm such a goddamned idiot."

"Oh, stop it." Nancy kisses the part in Greta's hair. "Before I met your father I dated a bassist in a jam band. We all make mistakes."

Between two ragged breaths Greta laughs, then winces at the way it stretches her scabs.

With moist eyes, she says, "Do you really have to go?"

She does, and soon—Nancy's train leaves Moynihan Station in forty-five minutes. The party needs her vote on the infrastructure bill, and if she isn't there to cast it, she'll be clobbered by not only the leadership but also the press. And as for western New York, she's got to find a way to swing those counties away from Carmichael and in her favor. The polling data that came in this morning was promising; the race is tightening, with Nancy nipping at Chip's heels. Without Buffalo and Rochester and the slew of towns between them, though, the Harrison campaign is as good as dead.

"I don't," she says, and kisses her daughter again. "I'll stay right here."

Greta's feet are crossed beneath her. She's wearing an old T-shirt from high school and pulls at a loose thread on its hem.

She says, "No, go. I know you need to—I'm being a baby. I'll be fine. Besides, I've fucked things up enough for you already."

"I don't have to, Greta. If you want me to stay, I'll stay."

"Please go. I'll feel worse if you don't."

Late-morning light falls across the bedroom's floor. On a desk in the corner, a collection of pens forms a bouquet in a tall tin cup.

"Nick will be here," Nancy says. "And I'll call every hour."

Nodding, Greta unfolds herself; when she rises a moment later, Nancy hears her knees crack. She stretches, lifting her thin arms high above her head, and then walks to the window, where she opens the curtains an inch further to peer down at the park. The room brightens; shadows shorten. From outside the bedroom door, a pair of voices conspire, just above a whisper.

Greta listens. After a long pause she says, "They want me to speak at that rally of yours, don't they. The one at the old folks' home the Friday before the election. I heard them talking to you about it this morning."

A bit of fuzz from the bed's duvet clings to Nancy's blazer. Standing, she picks it away.

"Tom suggested it."

"Do you want me to?"

Yes.

"I want you to do whatever you're comfortable doing."

"Do you think it's a good idea?"

I think it's brilliant. It reminds me why I keep Tom around.

"It's not your job to win this election for me."

Outside, a sparrow alights on the window's sill, a twig clenched in its beak. Greta watches it, then unloops an old necklace from the neck of a lamp, bowing over the pens on her desk. It's cheap—a gold chain turned green—and slowly she pools it in her palm.

"Do I have to decide now?" she asks.

From the foyer comes the loud *click* of a lock being opened, the rustle of a coat being removed—*it's Nick*, Nancy thinks, *back from NYU.*

Reaching out, she pulls Greta to her, wrapping her arms around her daughter's shoulders, and breathing in her scent—a mix of soap and shampoo and coffee and linens that, to Nancy, is home.

"Of course not," she says, and presses her eyes shut. "Oh, Greta. I'm so glad you're back."

"Begins to Unravel"

Five days later, Greta drinks a glass of water while, on the couch across the living room, Nick emits a defeated sigh. He is grading essays. Or, he is *sort of* grading essays, flipping through the pages without really reading them until something offensive catches his eye and he circles it furiously with a pen. He is also easily distracted. Every five minutes he'll set the essay down and pick up today's crossword puzzle, which he'll frown at for two minutes before becoming frustrated and diverting his attention again, this time to an old Agatha Christie paperback that their mother had lying around. They are in her apartment. They have been in her apartment since they returned from Paris a week ago, because Nancy has—"out of an abundance of caution and no lack of trust or love"— forbidden them to leave. Or—no. She has forbidden Greta to leave. Nick, meanwhile, is free to come and go as he pleases, so long as he can ensure, beyond the smallest shadow of the smallest doubt, that Greta stays at home. And because Nick is serious and believes in following rules, this means that, aside from taking the subway to NYU to teach his classes, he stays home, too. Greta understands. She destroyed property in France and had a brief flirtation (physically, emotionally, ideologically) with a right-wing troll: these are legitimate reasons for both Nancy and her brother to be wary of her, and for her to be in hiding.

"'Begins to unravel,'" Nick says from the couch.

Greta peeps at the crossword, balanced on his knees.

"How many letters?" she asks.

"Four."

She thinks, letting her eyes drift to the ceiling.

"Fray," she says a few seconds later. "Begins to unravel: fray."

Using a blue Bic with a gnawed-off top, Nick writes the letters into their squares and nods.

"Bingo."

Greta tips an imaginary hat and leaves him, walking to the nearest bathroom to inspect her bruises in the mirror. They are blue now, with faint green borders, and the gash next to her nose is a crusty scab. She touches it gently with her fingers and winces. It's getting better—she has to keep telling herself that. When she left Paris, her left eye was nearly swollen shut and sticky with blood.

On the couch, Nick has begun his cycle anew with another essay. Greta watches him, then walks to the window, where she can see the treetops in Central Park. The leaves have started to change, and now among the green are patches of gold and red. She misses the taste of fresh air and the bite of wind on her cheeks. After they had cleared customs at JFK, Nick had ushered her directly into a cab, which took them here, to the San Marino. All that she got of New York was what she could see out the window: the first two floors of buildings, and a snippet of the skyline as they crossed the Queensboro Bridge. She misses the city.

She says, "I need to run an errand."

NICK SETS DOWN THE PAPER he's grading—an essay that's endeavoring to compare ice hockey to imperialism, and on which he's written *WHAT????*

"An errand?" he asks.

Greta sits on one of the sofa's arms, her legs crossed at the ankles.

"Yes," she says. "People run errands. It's something people do."

"Okay, fine, but *what is the errand?*"

"I need to go back to my old apartment and get a few things."

"Oh." Nick rolls his pen in his palm. "What kind of things?"

"A toothbrush? Tampons? New clothes? I've been here for, like, almost a week, Nick, and I've been wearing the same two Chapin shirts the entire time."

"You could always borrow some of Mom's old clothes."

Greta stands up, aghast. Her head shakes, a flurry of blond hair.

"I am *not* wearing Eileen fucking Fisher."

He doesn't know what else to say. He and Nancy had quietly agreed that it was best for Greta to stay at the apartment, a decision that Nick suspects is as much about protecting his sister as it is about keeping her face out of the papers. He thought that enforcing this decision would be difficult—in many ways, he wanted it to be difficult. Greta arguing with him and, by extension, with Nancy, would at least feel like a return to the normalcy of a month ago, a time when things like family dinners did not result in someone absconding with a French nationalist, but rather followed a predictable pattern for which Nick has become nostalgic: cocktails and ruthless criticism, followed by a nice Pinot Blanc and someone in tears.

Instead, Greta has been acquiescent, withdrawn. She often spends hours of each day secluded in Nancy's study, where, through a crack in the door, Nick can see her staring blankly at one of the novels she's pulled from the bookshelf. When he asks her what happened (in France, but also, right before; he is genuinely curious how a person could experience such a radical change) she demurs, telling him that she'll explain one day, but that she is exhausted, and—"Please, Nick, not now." *It's as if*, he thinks, *she has awoken after a particularly disastrous night out, one during which she allowed herself to get wildly out of control. The lights are too bright and the sounds are too loud and every so often she'll wince, remembering something she shouldn't have said or done.*

This morning, though, she has shown signs of life. She ate the toast that he set out for her and asked for a second cup of coffee. Her face may still be a mess, but she's talking about how nice the weather is and she's looking at the city like she actually recognizes it. She wants to go outside. She wants *to run an errand.* It is not, Nick concedes, an unreasonable request. When they flew back from Paris, Greta had with her only the clothes that she was wearing, and that was it. Holding her close in the darkening gardens of the Louvre, Nick told her that he would go back for her suitcases, her bags, whatever she needed; he wanted to deal with Xavier.

"We have to call the police," he said, inspecting her face. "No one touches my sister."

Greta was insistent that he didn't, though—she begged him to let it all be done.

"All I left is a bunch of dumb shoes," she said, wiping her nose on his coat. "Please, Nick, let's get the fuck out of France."

Now, aside from the two Chapin shirts she's been cycling through, all Greta has at her disposal are the bits of childhood that have been left to fossilize in her old bedroom. A collection of artifacts and relics that, as far as Nick can tell, includes a pair of green sweatpants, a few stray Adderalls, a poster from a Ryan Adams concert, and a dog-eared copy of *Madame Bovary*.

"I've got class at three forty-five," he says, checking his watch. "If we leave now, I won't have time to come back here. I'll need to go straight to campus."

Greta tries to pull her hair back into a ponytail, then realizes that she can't—it's too short.

"I'll go with you."

"You don't mind sitting through my class?"

Shrugging, she says, "It can't be worse than what I've been doing here."

Nick looks out the window, at a hippopotamus-shaped cloud, and then back to the crossword. His eyes hurt and his brain is pudding. He wouldn't mind getting out of the house.

"Okay." He stuffs the essays and the crossword into his bag and grabs his jacket. "Let's go."

THEY TAKE THE C TRAIN south to Fourteenth Street, and then transfer to the L and head east to Brooklyn. Although it's the middle of the day, the subway is still crowded: Greta stands, wedged between a man in a Yankees hat and her brother, whose arm she takes hold of as the train tilts and sways. She's thankful for this—both for Nick's arm and to be back in her hometown's rhythm. The lurches and sudden stops; the wondering what will happen next.

"Do you remember when we did mushrooms and took the F to Coney Island?" she asks Nick, stepping aside to let someone shove past her as the train pulls into Bedford Avenue.

"How could I forget." He adjusts his bag's strap on his shoulder. "You barfed on the Cyclone."

The doors slide shut; the train hurtles forward. Greta frowns: that's not how she remembers things.

"We should do it again," she says.

"Ha!" Nick laughs, and the woman standing on the other side of him glances up from a magazine. "I think I'm a little too old for hallucinogens."

"I meant go to Coney Island."

"Oh—well, sure. I'd love that." Nick ruffles Greta's hair. "Are those new earrings?"

"These? No, they're Mom's."

"Well, they look nice on you."

Greta touches them—two small silver squares, pinned to her lobes. She shrugs.

"I guess I wanted to dress like an actual person."

When they arrive at Greta's building north of Irving Avenue, it's nearly two thirty. Dead leaves are piled high in the gutters, and outside the entrance to the doggy day care, a walker pulls a Yorkie off a black bag of trash. Stepping over its leash, Greta slides her key into the door and unlocks it, and together she and Nick climb the stairs. Inside the apartment, all of the lights are on and Attila, the cat, is rolling a lone battery across the uneven floorboards. Greta scratches his head and calls out *hello*; a second later she hears a familiar voice, beckoning her into the living room. There, she and Nick find Carl, the antique dealer, shaving Zsófia's head. Three dish towels cover her shoulders, and the stubble of her blond hair forms a ring around her feet.

"Greta!" Her eyes brighten. "You have returned."

"I have. Or—only for a second, really. I need to grab some things from my room."

Attila bores of his battery and runs his fat body against Carl's leg.

"It's nice to see you," Carl says, kicking the cat away.

"Yeah, you too. Anyway—" Greta looks around the apartment: nothing has changed. "I won't be long."

"But who is your friend!" Zsófia points her pinkie finger at Nick. "Introduce me!"

"Oh, this is my brother, Nick."

"The homosexual?"

"Yes," Nick says, and offers a small wave. "Among other things."

Zsófia is unimpressed.

"But where have you been staying?" she says, turning her attention back to Greta. "Where have you been *living*?"

Opening her purse, Greta begins searching for the key to her room—she had locked it before leaving for Paris.

"Uptown," she says. "At my mother's apartment."

"But I thought you hated your mother?"

"She can be kind of a bitch." Greta finds the key and tucks it in her palm. "But what mother isn't?"

Hearing this observation, Zsófia touches the bald half of her head and pushes out her lips, as if Greta has said something profound and she needs time to turn it over.

"Yes, mothers are bitches," she says finally. "Mine was a big one before she got decapitated by the Communists."

Nick stares at her—the half-shaved head, the sad, birdlike eyes.

"Uh," he says.

Dipping the razor into a salad bowl filled with water, Carl shakes his head and sighs.

"She's joking," Greta says before unlocking her bedroom. "Her mom runs an Olive Garden in Houston."

Promising Nick that she'll be fast, she closes the door behind her. Everything appears exactly as she left it: the sheets unmade, the pillows flattened, her journal lying facedown on the floor. She takes a second to straighten things up and then goes to her closet, where she digs out an old JanSport backpack and begins filling it with clothes. Some more shirts, two pairs of jeans, a few bras—it's a haphazard process that ends when Greta thinks the bag appears sufficiently full, at which point she tosses it aside and drops to her knees. There, on the ground, she glances behind her to make sure the door's still shut, and then retrieves an orange shoebox from beneath her bed. In it, alongside two old joints, is a nest of discarded technology: wires and chargers that have become inextricably tangled; headphones tied by fate into tight bowline knots. She digs through them until she finds, finally, what she came here for: her old iPhone, enclosed in a dusty black case. Slipping it into the pocket of her coat, she stands, grins, and brushes off her knees. Then, grabbing the backpack off the bed, she opens the bedroom door.

In the living room, Zsófia's head is nearly bald again, its crown reflecting the overhead light. Nick eyes Greta, then points to his watch. He's cringing like he wants a shower.

"Right," she says, slinging the backpack over her shoulder. "Let's get you to school."

"Interesting friends," Nick says.

"Not friends," Greta corrects him. "Former roommates."

They are back on the subway, this time westbound, toward Washington Square and NYU. It's emptier than it was an hour ago, and now they sit on one of the train's orange benches, their knees gently knocking. Across from them, a woman with a scarf draped over her hair dutifully clips her nails, flicking bits away and filing them to dull, rounded curves. Nick watches her, grimaces, and flexes his toes. He's happy to be off his feet.

"What should we do for dinner tonight?" he asks. "Charlie's going to join us again, if that's okay."

"Of course it's okay. You seem to really like him."

Tilting his head down to hide his blushing cheeks, Nick says: "I do."

Ten feet from Union Square, the train stops, starts, stops, inches forward.

The woman with the scarf extends her fingers, inspecting them.

"Then why don't you go out?" Greta says.

"Like, to a restaurant?"

"Or a movie, or a bar, or the zoo, or a shooting range. What I mean, Nick, is why don't you go on an actual *date*."

Steadying his bag on his lap, Nick considers the option. For the past five nights he has seen Charlie—each time at Nancy's apartment, each time with Greta alongside them. Mostly, these dates—if one could call them that—have included some combination of television and takeout, or, when she's feeling particularly repentant, television and Greta's cooking: pad thai and *Mad Men* on one occasion, overbaked ziti and *The Crown* on the next. Never once has Charlie asked for anything else, and never once has Charlie complained. Rather, he has told Nick what Nick already knows: that families are complicated (Nick: "some more than others")—and that, in the meantime, he's just happy to be around. For his part, Nick is as thankful as he is embarrassed: while he's happy to spend every free instant with Charlie, he'd prefer them to be outside of his mother's apartment. After all, it's hard to fall in love with someone when your sister's there, giggling on the couch next to you. It's hard to have the kind of sex that Nick would like to have, when she's sleeping right next door.

"You're sure you'd be okay on your own?" he asks.

Greta pats Nick on the knee.

"I'm sure."

"I want you to stay home. No wandering around or getting drunk at Dublin House. Order yourself some dinner and watch a movie."

"You got it."

"Do you promise?"

Greta holds up two fingers.

She says, "Scout's honor."

Two minutes later, the train arrives at West Fourth Street and, gathering their belongings, the Harrisons stand up. Feet shuffle, brakes squeak; the woman with the scarf, Nick notices, is watching them. She has pulled her lips into a tight, disapproving slit, and her green eyes dart between Nick and Greta's bruised eye.

Greta has noticed it, too—she must have—because as the doors slide open, Nick hears her say: "Don't worry, lady—it was some other jerk."

IN THE HOURS SINCE THEY left their mother's apartment the perfect day has become improbably more perfect. When they exit the subway, the sidewalks are crowded with people who have taken off their sweaters, and as they walk along the edge of Washington Square Park, Greta watches a group of teenagers huddle around a joint. At Fifth Avenue they head

north, passing a florist and NYU's Irish Studies Department until arriv-
ing, at last, at the building where her brother teaches.

"Do you have your ID?" Nick asks her. "They need it to let you in."

They are standing at a security desk, and behind it a woman who's
dressed up like a police officer is reaching out her hand.

"Oh." Greta takes out her driver's license. "Sure."

The woman holds the little plastic card up to the light.

"You cut your hair," she says.

"I did."

"And this is two years expired."

Greta glances at Nick.

She says, "Guilty."

The guard hands the license back to Greta.

"You can go ahead in."

The classroom Nick leads her to is in a windowless corner of the building's third floor. There's a large, rectangular table around which are
seventeen seats, and a wooden podium where Nick deposits his things.
Three of the four walls have whiteboards on them, and the fourth is covered with a projector screen with a tear in its lower left corner.

"It's hot in here." Greta fans herself with her hand.

"They turn on the heat on October fifteenth and then leave it on until
June." Nick reaches into his backpack, takes out his laptop and a book,
and then rolls up his shirtsleeves. "It's a facilities thing."

"Do you ever complain?"

"No."

"Why not?"

"Because the only thing that's worse than dealing with a classroom
that's ninety-four degrees is dealing with a university's bureaucracy."

Greta nods: this is sufficient.

"What should I do while you're teaching?" she asks.

"Read? Sleep? Participate? Actually, no—don't do that." Nick scratches
his neck, thinks, and then reaches into his bag for the newspaper. "How
about you help me with the crossword?"

Greta takes it from him, all those empty little squares, and tucks it
under her arm.

"Aye-aye, Captain."

As they speak, the door swings open and the first students enter: a pair of sophomores who stare at Greta bewilderedly, like they've encountered on Park Avenue a giraffe who's escaped from the zoo. She stares back at them until they look away, and then watches as, one by one, the rest of the students file in, colonizing sections of the table with their laptops, draping their jackets over the backs of chairs. Nick greets each of them by name and with private little jokes and then, once they have all settled, he begins his lesson. *It's weird, watching him teach*, Greta thinks; *he might as well start speaking with a German accent, or be dressed up as Shirley Temple.* There are parts of his personality that she recognizes, but also parts that she feels she was never meant to see. He uses extended metaphors to describe other even more extended metaphors, and when he walks around the room he seems—at least to her—to pose, resting his elbow on his wooden podium, leaning back against the whiteboard with his arms professorially crossed. It makes Greta uncomfortable—she would be embarrassed for him if he did not seem, for the first time since she can remember, truly, genuinely happy.

Sitting in a folding chair in the room's southeast corner, Greta unfolds the crossword across her knees and reads the first unanswered *down* clue: "Kidman's husband Urban." She thinks for a minute, writes in *Keith*, and then moves on. "Me and I": *pronouns.* "On a trip?" *High.* She is making good time—it is only Tuesday; the crossword is less of a puzzle and more of an ego hand job—and she keeps at it for five more minutes before glancing up. When she does, the room is silent. The students have been given an assignment, and now the only sound that Greta can hear is the occasional groan of the radiator and the scratching of fifteen pens on fifteen sheets of paper. Nick, too, has busied himself; a weathered copy of *The White Album* is propped up on the podium. Greta watches him for a minute or two, his eyes boring into the book's pages. Then, when she is convinced he is sufficiently distracted, she reaches into her pocket for her phones.

Phones, plural. There are two of them. The one she retrieved an hour ago, from the shoebox beneath her bed in Bushwick, and the one whose screen she shattered in Paris. That—dropping the device in the Tuileries—had been a real bitch. She remembers how it felt, slipping from her fingers, the silent *fuck!* she screamed as she saw its fragmented face. Now, her hand hidden by the crossword, she runs a finger over its back. There's a spiderweb of cracks on it—long, jagged lines that mark where the phone collided with ground. Once more she tries to turn it on, but again her efforts are met with a useless black screen. Puffing her cheeks, Greta tucks her hair out of the way and discreetly removes one of her mother's earrings, which she uses to release the phone's SIM card. Then, still under cover of Tuesday's crossword, she carefully places the chip in the old phone and turns it on.

Her eyes fixed to the screen, she waits.

The Obliterator

LeRoy, New York, just shy of noon: Cate stands in the kitchen of the Prospector Diner, a greasy spoon on Route 5 that's owned by the man standing in front of her. She's already forgotten his name—she's almost forgotten her own. She has been on the road for five days—first it was DC for the infrastructure vote, and now she's playing connect the dots in the western pocket of New York with Nancy in a rented Chevrolet. Mel—was it *Mel*? Cate looks at him: pewter curls, sagging jowls, a happy, placid smile. Sure, he could be a Mel. She tucks her chin to her chest, stifles a yawn. She slept through her alarm this morning, the first time she's done that in years. Woke up fifteen minutes late (still: twenty minutes before Nancy) and sprinted to her hotel room's shower, where she tore open plastic-wrapped soap with her teeth. Black coffee, green banana, the other half of yesterday's granola bar, and she was out the door. The yawn passes; her neck relaxes. It *has* to be Mel, right? He told her literally three minutes ago and now—*poof*—it's gone. She doesn't know how Nancy does it—some Jedi mind trick they must teach you in Congress. She could meet an intern at the field office in Elmira and two months later remember her mother's maiden name. It's not only listening, it's *absorbing*, cataloging facts and figures and stories in these little cerebral file cabinets. It's what she's been doing for the past hour, rotating among the red vinyl booths of the Prospector, where the residents of LeRoy have gathered, waiting for a piece of her ear. Cate will watch her. She'll learn.

"You picked out a sandwich yet?"

"What was that, Mel?"

"Oh, ha, it's Dave." *Damn.* "I asked if you picked out a sandwich yet."

Cate looks down—she has forgotten that she is holding a menu. A big, laminated placard that's got everything from poutine to cottage cheese and melon. The font is small—a bunch of ants pinned to the page—and she scans it until she finds a box that says SANDWICHES. She's come back here, to the diner's kitchen, to pick one out for Nancy to eat. This was part of the arrangement. Nancy sits, Nancy shakes hands, Nancy thoughtfully considers a sliced dill pickle for the cameras that have gathered.

Her phone chimes: the arrival of a new email.

"How about that one," she says, pointing to a bunch of words without reading them. "I think she'll like that one."

Dave takes the menu—he assures Cate it's an excellent choice.

"So, where you from?"

"I live in Brooklyn."

"How about before that?"

"Colorado. Denver."

She listens to the sizzle of the grill and reads her email. Polling results, she sees, from Quinnipiac. Carmichael's still ahead, but the margin has shrunk—instead of a four-point lead, they've knocked him down to one.

"Whaddya reading?" Dave is still there. Behind him, Cate sees a burger flip.

"Sorry—an email."

"Must be busy, this close to the Big Day."

"Like you wouldn't believe."

"How long have you worked for her?"

"Since August."

Cate's phone chimes again, this time with a text from Tom. "Miss me?" She smiles, rolls her eyes. The text unanswered, she puts the phone away.

"So how about that daughter with the champagne bottle?"

"What about her?"

"What was *that* all about?"

Cate flexes her toes. Her feet throb. "She's back. She's fine. One of her cooking classes got out of hand. An aggressive exercise in crème brûlée."

"The French, am I right?"

"*C'est vrai.*"

The burger flips again. Rings of onions plunge into a fryer.

"What happened to the other guy?" Dave asks.

"What other guy?"

"The person who had your job before you? Nancy was up here in the spring with someone else, another campaign manager. The other guy? What happened to him?"

"He got sacked."

"Why?"

Cate stares at Dave until he blinks.

She says, "Because he asked too many questions."

A SANDWICH, ONE OF THE biggest that Nancy has ever seen, towers high on a plate above french fries, crinkle-cut pickles, and a plastic cup of cole-slaw. It—the sandwich—is called the Obliterator, and according to the Prospector's menu, it holds between its two slices of marble rye a collective two pounds of pastrami, salami, corned beef, shredded lettuce, a whole tomato, half an onion, crushed potato chips ("for crunch"), maple syrup ("for sweetness"), and Russian dressing ("fresh and homemade"). Dave, the pear-shaped owner of the diner, sets the plate down in front of Nancy; across from her, Beth Hubbard, the woman with whom Nancy has been talking for the past ten minutes, joins the diners' other patrons to offer her applause. Nancy thanks Dave and smiles at the television cameras next to the soft-serve machine. Cate appears next to her, and through still-bared teeth Nancy whispers: "What the fuck am I supposed to do with this thing?"

"You're supposed to eat it," Cate says.

"With what? A forklift?"

Cate doesn't answer—she takes a picture of Nancy with her phone—and in the silence Nancy assesses her options: this is an issue of optics she had not considered. If she eats it as sandwiches are intended to be eaten, gripped in both hands, her fingers squishing into bread and all species of cured meat, the picture that will be published in tomorrow's papers will inevitably be of her wide-open mouth, a photo exposé of Nancy's tonsils, the Obliterator careening toward them like a 747 preparing to land. Her in-box will be filled with emails from vegans. Also: she will ruin her blouse. On the other hand, if she tries to do the civilized thing, which is to say eat the sandwich's discrete components with a knife and fork, then she will be written off as elitist, *out of touch*. Someone who's afraid to get her hands a little dirty out of fear that she will, well, *actually ruin her blouse*. Right-wing websites—the same ones that went rabid over the video of Greta with the champagne bottle in Paris—will now have a new meme for their circle jerks: Nancy dissecting a sandwich as if it were a fetal kitten and she a timid anatomy student. It won't play well, especially here, in western New York. And that's a problem, because western New York is precisely where she needs things to play well if she's going to have a shot at winning.

The pickles shimmer beneath the diner's lights and, on the other side of the booth, Beth nods, encouragingly. Nancy picks up the sandwich. She holds it there, letting the Russian dressing drip from the bread's crust. Then, once she's certain the papers have their picture, she decides the vegans will vote for her anyway and takes a bite.

"WHEN I'M SENATOR," NANCY SAYS, "I'm going to make that sandwich illegal."

"For the record," Cate says, buckling her seat belt and starting the car, "I told them to bring you turkey on rye." She pulls out of the parking lot and onto Route 5. "Also, just a heads-up: our next stop is Buffalo. Tom's there—he's been handling the advance team. We've got your speech celebrating the Erie Canal."

"What are we celebrating about it?"

"It's two hundred and one years old, and they're breaking ground on a new visitors center for it. You'll talk for a few minutes about the economy and then swing a sledgehammer at a wall before a bulldozer tears it down. Also, I can't believe you ate the whole thing."

"You'd be surprised by the calories you'll consume when you want something as badly as I do."

They head east, toward Buffalo. Outside are browning fields and leaf-less trees; a house with a bike left on its side in the driveway. Thumbs, drumming on the steering wheel; a turn signal flickering on and off. Cate checks the rearview mirror.

"Any word from Greta about Boom Town?" she asks.

"Nothing yet." Nancy raps her knuckles against the window. "And I'm not going to push it. If she wants to talk, she'll talk. She's been through enough. It's not her job to win this election for us, too."

Thinking, Nancy reaches for her phone. In the distance, New York dis-appears into the horizon.

"That woman Beth Hubbard," she says. "Get someone to find out where she lives, and then send her a turkey for Thanksgiving—she said she didn't know if she was going to be able to afford one this year."

"Thanksgiving is after the election, though."

"It doesn't matter. I want someone to send her a turkey. A big one." And then: "Oh, shit."

Cate glances at her over the tops of her sunglasses. "What?"

"Carmichael released his latest ad." Nancy holds up her phone. "Here, pull over and let's watch this thing."

The car hits a pothole and the whole world jerks. On the north side of Route 5, a dog pisses on the side of a bright blue house. A road sign flies by: they are twenty miles from Buffalo. Guiding the Chevrolet onto the shoulder, Cate puts the car in park and kills the engine. She holds up her phone and, after a few seconds of buffering, the ad begins to play. It opens with a shot of Carmichael, standing in an apple orchard upstate. He's a speck among the trees, but as the camera zooms in you get a better view of him: broad shoulders and that famous cloven chin; sleeves rolled up to reveal capable, American hands, one of which is wrapped around the hilt of an ax. The sun is shining and there's music—bright major chords that fade only slightly as Carmichael begins to speak. *My grandfather had me clear this space when I was a boy so he could plant his apple orchard*, he says, and Nancy snorts, *Ha.*

"What?" Cate asks.

"Carmichael grew up in Rye. And there's no way in hell that clown has ever swung an *ax.*"

"Because he's from Rye?"

"Because if he did he'd chop off his own head—he's the least coordinated person alive. There was this episode of *Self-Evident* where he was supposed to throw the first pitch at a baseball game in Houston, and they had to bring in a body double to do it because this idiot couldn't even *roll* the ball across home plate."

"You think you could?"

Nancy gives a single, decisive nod.

She says, "The Harrisons have very good arms."

A litany of buzzwords follows: *prosperity* and *freedom* and *hard work. Making lives better for all Americans.* It's the same vocabulary that Nancy uses, though when she says those words she means something different. For as long as she's been at this game, this fact never fails to surprise her—how at its heart politics is actually just a very expensive matter of semantics. Shadows have fallen over the orchard, and the music has taken on an ominous tone. Suddenly there is a storm; sheets of rain beat down on the orchard and, by way of a CGI flourish that couldn't have been cheap, the trees become the US Capitol Building. An image of Nancy's face appears, her eyes colored red to make her appear bloodthirsty, vampiric. Carmichael's voice shifts from Your Folksy Cousin to Doomsday Soothsayer. He calls Nancy a *communist* and a *hypocrite.* She wants to *raise your taxes*; she raised an *anarchist daughter* and she is a *radical danger to democracy.* In the commercial's final moments lightning strikes the Capitol and its storied dome erupts in flames. "Is this the future you want?" Carmichael asks. "Because with Nancy Harrison, this is the future you'll get."

Nancy puts her phone away and says, "Oh, for Christ's sake."

Cate stares out the window. Far away, Buffalo's skyline rises—a blur on the shores of Lake Erie.

She says, "It's got to be disappointing, being called all those things."

Nancy thinks: *How long has she been doing this?* Nearly twenty years—she can pin it to the month. The answer to that question can never untie itself from her husband's death: when Howard was killed, Nancy ran. Since then she has been called, among other things, a bitch, a cunt, a slut. Hysterical, emotional, irrational. Too fat, too thin, too tall, too short. Murderer of a husband, mother of a faggot, destroyer of liberty. A harpy, a ballbuster, a snowflake, a traitor. But also: a fighter. A role model. Sunglasses on, coat collar popped, walking down the Capitol steps. A hope, and probably just as often, a threat. The reason that the republic might ultimately prevail, but also the source of its ultimate demise.

She says: "America is disappointing, Cate. That's why we do what we do."

The Demolition Team

At half past three Cate maneuvers the car into a parking spot. Above them is the Buffalo Skyway, the overpass that connects the city's downtown to its outer harbor, and then extends southward on an embankment of slag. They are a hundred yards from the Buffalo River, and in that space is a waterfront park dotted with brightly colored Adirondack chairs. A bit farther away, and closer to the metal railings that separate the boardwalk from the water, a small stage has been erected, on each side of which stand New York State flags. There is also red, white, and blue bunting, along with a banner wishing a happy 201st birthday to the Erie Canal. Cate lifts her sunglasses and appraises it. Then she shuts off the car.

"Oh, good," Nancy says, "there's Tom."

She has stepped out of the car and is pointing to the opposite end of the park, where Tom, dressed in a white dress shirt and a pair of wool slacks, is jogging toward them, his jacket bunched up in his right hand.

"He seems sweaty, doesn't he?" Nancy shuts the car door. "I mean, he seems really sweaty."

Cate looks to where Nancy is pointing. Large patches of sweat dot the front of Tom's shirt, and through them Cate can see thick mats of chest hair and the pink buttons of his nipples. His sleeves are rolled up, and as he approaches them he uses his forearm to wipe his forehead dry.

"Jesus, Tom," Nancy says, "you look like a whore in church."

He smiles uneasily. "Well, it's hot out here!"

"It's forty-two degrees."

"Then it's the humidity, I guess."

Nancy takes off her sunglasses.

"Tom," she says. "Are you having a stroke?"

"A stroke!" Tom laughs—ha, ha, *ha*. No, he is not having a stroke. He drank two more cups of coffee than he typically does but, so far as he knows (and can one ever *really* know?), his brain is free of any meddlesome clots. The sweat—all this perspiration that's turned his shirt into, well, *gosh*, it looks like a veritable stretch-cotton Rorschach test, doesn't it?—is because, to be honest, Nancy, he's been running around. You see, things here in Buffalo have gone—how shall he put this delicately?—*not as expected*. But then, when does anything ever go as expected in politics? If they wanted expected they would have become accountants, hunkering down in their little cubes with a predictable stack of W-4s. That's not why they got into this mess, though, is it? No, people like Nancy and Tom and—oh, hi, Cate—live for the curveball, the plot twist. Why, does Nancy remember four (or maybe it was six?) years ago when they did that meet-and-greet at the Hargrave Senior Center on Columbus and *everyone* who went got norovirus? Who could have seen that one coming! What they're dealing with now—well, trust Tom on this one, it's nowhere near as bad as that. It'll take some *rearranging*, maybe, but so far as Tom can foresee no one's going to puke and they certainly won't need, like, extra rolls of toilet paper. In fact, if he can just—

"What the fuck is happening, Tom?"

A plane cuts across the blue-gray sky; Tom unfastens the shirt's second button, freeing another inch of soggy skin.

"Chip Carmichael is here," he says. "He's decided to crash the event."

"Excuse me?"

"No." Cate doesn't let Tom answer. "He's at a spaghetti lunch for the Rotary Club in Corinth. I checked his schedule this morning."

"Apparently, his schedule has changed. That's what Doug told me."

"Who the fuck is Doug?" Nancy asks.

"He's from the Erie Canal Economic Development Corporation—he'll be introducing you before you swing the hammer." Tom's shirt is now entirely translucent, save a small, half-dollar-sized spot beneath his first two ribs. "Small guy. Weird, egg-shaped head."

"And did Doug give you an explanation as to *why* Carmichael's schedule suddenly changed?"

Tom looks at Cate and swallows.

"He told me that Carmichael said you invited him."

Another plane flies overhead, this one leaving a milky contrail in its wake. Cate's phone buzzes, and Tom stands there, dripping. Nancy stares at them, then snaps her sunglasses in half.

TOM SWEATS, AND NANCY YELLS. A drop of spit lands on Cate's nose and, squatting down, she picks up the two halves of the broken sunglasses and sets them on the hood of the car.

She says, "Everyone shut up."

"What?"

Nancy's face is the color of cranberries.

"I said everyone shut up. Tom—where's the speech?"

His hands trembling, Tom reaches into his shirt pocket and pulls out four damp pages, held together with a paper clip and folded into thirds. Cate takes them and then opens her purse, sifting past melting packets of gum and hand sanitizer and empty Tylenol bottles to find a pen. With the papers pressed against the car's windshield, she uncaps the pen with her teeth and uses it to slash through a few words.

"What are you doing?" Nancy asks.

"I'm editing this speech," she says. "You're going to invite Carmichael to swing the hammer first."

"Like hell I am."

Cate finishes her last sentence—*now please, Chip, take it away*—then shuffles the pages back into their correct order.

She says, "An hour ago you told me he's the least coordinated person alive. You told me they had to bring in a body double on his show because he couldn't throw a *baseball*. What makes you think he's going to do any better with a sledgehammer? He'll swing it around like an idiot, and then you'll step in to get the job done."

"What if she can't swing it, either?" Tom asks.

"She can." Cate nods. "The Harrisons have very good arms."

On the Buffalo River, a barge sounds its horn, a disgruntled bellow that echoes off the underside of the Skyway. Tom jumps and says *shit*. Nancy grins.

"Tom," she says. "Tell that egghead Chip's taking the first crack at the wall."

At the northwest corner of the park, a crowd of twenty-some-odd people have gathered. They are all vying to shake someone's hand, and when their bodies momentarily part Cate sees Chip Carmichael. Thick neck, full gray hair: *he looks*, Cate thinks, *exactly like he does on TV*. A woman has asked him to pose for a selfie, and as she positions her phone Chip's fingers work their way toward the top of her ass.

Nancy sees it, too. She says, "Someone tell an intern to get me a fucking latte."

Tom coughs—a small, timid clearing of his throat that is not wholly indistinguishable from a death rattle.

"We actually don't do that anymore," he says.

"Don't do what?"

"Ask interns to get us coffee."

"That is *why* we have interns, Tom."

"Well, uh." A second death rattle. "I'm not sure if you remember but back in March you signed a pledge that we wouldn't do that anymore. Some of the interns found it triggering."

"Getting *coffee* was *triggering*."

"When they weren't being paid to do it, yes."

Nancy reaches for her sunglasses, realizes that they're sitting, functionless, on the hood of the car, and then stamps her left foot, piercing the grass with the heel of her shoe.

"When I was twenty-two I *thanked* Dick Gephardt for letting me get him a *ham fucking sandwich* from the *Rayburn* cafeteria. I—"

"Save it for the sledgehammer, Nancy," Cate says. "You're on in twenty."

TEN MINUTES LATER, AT THE Tim Hortons on Scott Street, Tom points to a shaker marked *cinnamon*. His shirt, Cate notes, is beginning to dry.

"Give me that, will you?" he asks. "Nancy likes a little spice in her lattes."

Cate obliges and watches as brown flecks rain down on a bed of foam. A song is playing—something by the Barenaked Ladies—and trying as hard as she can to ignore it, she checks her watch.

"How long do we have?" Tom asks.

"Nine minutes. Let's get some caffeine in her, shall we?"

Securing the lid to the latte, Tom nods and follows Cate to the stage, where a giant glass sign hangs, welcoming visitors to the Erie Canal. There, next to an old concrete wall, Nancy is smiling, making light conversation with the event's organizers and a small pool of reporters. Cate hands her the latte, and together with Tom slips away.

"You want some of this?" she hears Tom say.

Looking down, Cate sees a small, airplane-sized bottle of whiskey.

From two nearby speakers, a microphone squeals and, collectively, the crowd winces: the event is about to begin.

"I nipped two of them off the flight attendant's cart on the plane up— they were sitting there, winking at me from behind a pile of pretzels."

Nancy and Carmichael walk to the center of the stage, where they're joined by a small, impish man with blue pants and an egg-shaped head— Doug, Cate assumes, based on Tom's description. He taps the mic once, twice, three times, and then, after stumbling over a few introductions, launches into a wholly forgettable speech about the canal's former majesty. As he drones on, Cate watches as Carmichael's hands choke up on the handle of a blue sledgehammer. Her pulse kicks into high gear.

"Okay," she says. "Give me some of that."

Tom hands her the bottle, and Cate takes a swig.

"How strong are these Harrison arms?" he asks.

The microphone screeches again, and Cate sees flashes of the immediate future: Nancy, struggling to lift the hammer with her frail arms; Carmichael stepping in to show her how it's done.

She takes a bigger sip and says, "We're about to find out."

A minute later, Doug finishes droning and Nancy steps up to the mic. From where Cate is standing at the rear of the gathered crowd, she lifts up slightly on her toes to get a better view. Suddenly, Nancy seems even smaller than Cate remembers her to be; it's as if since Cate handed her the latte, she's shrunk another inch. A second mallet is at her side—a red one—and its handle reaches nearly to her waist. This was a terrible idea, a Hail Mary of disastrous proportions. What the *hell* was Cate thinking? They were on the rebound, and now *this*. Her eyes shut, Cate imagines tomorrow's headlines: "Harrison Leaves Heavy Lifting to Carmichael." "Gracious Chip Lends Nancy a Hand." Defeat is imminent; the options to describe it are endless. How pliable language is, how annoyingly elastic. A picture might be worth a thousand words, but with those same words you can tell at least a million stories.

Nancy says, "Take it away, Chip," and, responding with a shallow bow of thanks, Carmichael white-knuckles his mallet.

Her eyes wide with fear, Cate watches as, on all sides of her, photographers raise their cameras and focus their lenses. Soon she will hear the swoosh of the hammer through air, the snap of stone breaking, the electric millisecond of silence before a collective gasp or a rapturous applause.

Steeling herself, she finishes what's left of the whiskey.

Then she reaches down and finds Tom's hand.

A Tale of Two Dates

The bar—according to Greta, one of her favorites—is tucked away on Seventh Street, between First and Second Avenues. It's dark, and half-underground, and it smells of beer and ammonia. There are no windows, only a broken ATM and a sign that says CASH ONLY where two windows should be. Up front are three seating booths, but only one of them is occupied: a man, alone, scrolls through his phone, an almost empty glass of bourbon sitting next to him. Music is playing—classic rock—but the volume's low, and you have to strain to hear it. Also: there's a pool table in back, and the constant clack of balls colliding drowns about everything—and that includes Bon Jovi—out. The bartender, a brunette who barely clears five feet, has an old voice but a young face and throws people out on a whim. It's happened twice in the last hour alone: men were sitting there, halfway through their beers, when suddenly the bartender decided she didn't like the way they'd slurped off the foam and—*bam*—they were gone. It's for this reason, a man in a stained white shirt tells Xavier, that the four stools that surround the bar are usually empty.

"It's safer to be in the back," he says, "where the worst thing that'll happen to a guy is a jab in the eye from a pool cue."

Xavier thanks him but stays where he is, on a stool directly in front of the cash register, which he has wiped down with a napkin.

He flips a gold lighter open, closes it, and says, "I assure you, monsieur, I am not someone who gets 'thrown out.'"

The man in the white shirt raises his hands so Xavier can see the deep creases of his palms, which, despite his hard demeanor, are soft and pink.

"Suit yourself, bro," he says, and walks away.

Watching him go, Xavier thinks: *New Yorkers are pathologically friendly.* He noticed it when he arrived two days ago. After checking into his hotel in Times Square, he went to a nearby Starbucks, where he queued up to order a coffee. The line crept along slowly, and after an enraging five minutes of wondering *why* he looked toward the cashier and found his answer: the barista, a woman with a handwritten name tag that said JENN, was asking each of the customers *how they were doing*. It was appalling. What right did she have, and why did she care? Was she going to develop individual relationships with these people? Check in on them afterward to see if their moods had perhaps changed? Even more appalling was the way in which the other customers were answering, which was not with an honest response of how their days were going, but rather with the same question: *How are* you *doing?* The exchange, Xavier realized, was entirely decorative, a fun house mirror of a repeated greeting that required an answer but never actually got one. His pulse began to race, and as it did he tried his best to calm down. He reminded himself that he was dealing with Americans, and that if Americans are good at one thing it is uninvited and pointless intervention, even if it comes at the expense of a prolonged war in the Middle East, or—worse—a slow-moving Starbucks line.

"What do you want?" the bartender asks him, tossing a cardboard coaster down in front of him as if it were a grenade.

"One vodka, no ice."

Xavier smiles and the bartender does not. She reaches beneath the bar for the vodka bottle, wrapping her fingers around it like she's throttling a baby's neck. On the pool table, someone scratches and the cue ball goes flying, slicing through the stale air until it crashes against a wall. Everyone stares, save Xavier: he has felt the chill from outside, has heard the front door whooshing open and shut.

He turns to see who's there and then says: "Actually, you had better make that two."

CHARLIE'S DOG, FRANK, IS THE size of a carry-on suitcase and the color of charcoal—a black so light it borders on gray, with traces of white around the snout. He's either two or five or maybe, at the oldest, seven, and while he's got the frame of a Lab, the shape of his ears and the quickness of his eyes suggest a healthy dash of something less bovine, and more mischievous. Some sort of terrier, maybe, or a papillon—one of those breeds attracted to trouble and rats. That is not to say that he's a bad dog—on the contrary, Nick, who has never owned a plant, let alone an animal, finds him to be exemplary. In addition to sitting and shaking and (sometimes) rolling over, Frank pees where he's supposed to and hardly ever barks. He also—and this, to Nick, is the most important thing—knows to politely excuse himself when he and Charlie have sex.

"It was one of the first things I taught him after I adopted him," Charlie tells Nick, propping himself up on an elbow. They have, incidentally, just had sex. "See, I once dated a guy who had a vizsla that insisted on sitting at the edge of the bed whenever we were hooking up. You'd try to move him off, or whatever, but it was useless—he'd jump right back on."

"What'd he do?" Nick asks.

"Nothing, which was sort of the weirdest part. He'd sit there and *stare*."

Nick tries to imagine it: two canine eyes, scrutinizing his chest, his waist, his ass; a discerning nose, judging the top notes of his scent. A picture comes into focus, and as it does, Nick pulls a face.

"Yeah, exactly." Charlie sits up and, laughing, leans his back against a pillow. "Which is why I taught Frank that when the bedroom door is closed, he's on his own."

"You're not worried he'll get into trouble?"

"Trouble doing what?"

"I don't know." A streetlamp flickers outside of Charlie's window. "Eat a pillow, or something."

"Ha! No. He watches TV, mostly."

"He watches TV?"

"Sure. The news. Bravo. He can get into whatever's on." Swinging his legs over the side of the mattress, Charlie searches for his jeans. "Lately he's been really into reruns of *Seinfeld*."

Two hours ago, they went to dinner—an Italian restaurant on Twentieth Street that they both knew well, and appreciated for its handsome waiters and consistent mediocrity. The plan afterward was to go to a movie, though on the way to the cinema Charlie asked if they could swing by his apartment to grab a jacket; it was the Californian in him, he explained to Nick—he always thought theaters to be ten degrees too cold. Once they were inside, they never left—instead of putting a coat on, Nick took Charlie's shirt off. Lights were lowered, and hands sought hungrily for zippers. The film, which neither of them had any interest in seeing, was missed.

Reaching down in the half dark, Nick feels for his shirt, his underwear, his balled-up socks. He hears the plucky bass of *Seinfeld*'s theme song from the television in the living room, followed by a quick yelp from Frank, and he smiles. Idiosyncratic dogs and skipped movies—*so this is what it feels like*, he thinks, *to imagine a future with someone else.*

In the kitchen he finds Charlie rummaging around in the refrigerator. Light reflects off his bare shoulders, and when he turns to face Nick, he's holding two beers.

"After all that, I figured you might be thirsty," he says, and hands one of the bottles to Nick. "You think Greta's burned down the San Marino yet?"

Pilsner—cool and refreshing—froths over Nick's tongue. He thinks of earlier this evening, before he left to meet Charlie. He had put on a splash of aftershave and was preparing to leave his mother's apartment when his sister, sprawled out on the couch in her green sweatpants, sat up and stopped him.

"Is that what you're going to wear?" she said, setting down the book she'd been reading.

Nick glanced at himself in the mirror.

"I mean, yes, technically."

Greta adjusted her glasses and pulled her mouth to one side. Then she leapt from the couch and returned, a few minutes later, holding an ironed blue shirt.

"Try this one instead," she said, wetting two fingers to tame Nick's cowlick. "It brings out your eyes."

Now, in Charlie's kitchen, Nick takes a second swig of beer and smacks his lips.

"I don't think so," he says. "Champagne bottles aside, she's a pretty good kid."

Splayed across the counter is a collection of envelopes and magazines—neglected bits of Charlie's mail, Nick figures, the useless replicas of what he's already received online. Moving aside a J.Crew catalog, Nick sees an offer for a new credit card, along with a single-leaf advertisement—a glossy, cardboard rectangle on which there is a picture of a blond woman in a sequin dress, smashing a vintage convertible with a baseball bat. Beneath the image is written, in a soft, coquettish font: COMING TO BROADWAY THIS SPRING: *LOVE STORY*, A NEW MUSICAL FEATURING THE SONGS OF TAYLOR SWIFT.

"Oh my God," Nick says. "I want to see this."

His head craned to the right, Charlie reads the advertisement.

"You do?" he asks.

"Yes! It's supposed to be good. Or, not, like, *good* good, but have-a-few-drinks-at-intermission-and-wonder-what-you-just-saw good." Nick glances up at Charlie. He decides to take a chance. "I'm getting us tickets."

On the television, Elaine Benes bitches about her boss, and Frank growls.

Finishing his beer, Charlie shrugs.

"I'm game," he says. "When's it open?"

Nick scans the flyer for a date, which he finds directly beneath the drawing of a house, set on the rocky New England coast.

"Previews begin January sixteenth. So, you'll need to keep me around until then."

"Oh." Charlie's brow folds and he sets the empty bottle on the counter. He says, in a voice that is not at all joking, "That actually might be a problem."

GRETA TAKES DOWN THE VODKA in one Herculean gulp.

"I needed that," she says. "The B train was being a real cunt."

"I was worried when I didn't hear from you until this afternoon."

"Yeah, sorry about that." With Xavier's help, Greta slithers out of her coat. "I had to get my hands on my old phone."

"I'd forgotten you broke your old one."

She nods. "Like some clumsy idiot."

"Well, we're here now. How'd you manage to get away?"

"I convinced my brother to go on a date."

Xavier purses his lips. He says "*logique*," and then reaches out to stroke Greta's cheek.

"How bad does it look?" she asks. "And be honest."

"It is healing."

Shaking her head, Greta flags down the bartender and orders another vodka.

"Maybe you should have just hit me," she says.

"I know." Xavier kisses her cheek. "Next time."

The drink arrives and now Greta takes her time, letting the alcohol numb her lips. She thinks back to a little over a week ago. They had returned from the Musée d'Orsay, and Xavier was furious. He had gotten it in his head that Greta was suddenly going to desert him—that Nick was there to steal her away—and now he paced the apartment, smoking. For an hour Greta worked to convince Xavier otherwise, assuring him that, despite Nick's heroic intentions, she still belonged to him. Eventually, after much begging and one broken vase, she succeeded, and Xavier calmed down. He emptied two cups of their last dregs of coffee and filled them again with an inky Cabernet.

"You know," he said, swirling the wine in his mug, "this actually presents us with an opportunity."

From the ground, where she was sweeping up shards of broken ceramic into a small trash bin, Greta glanced up and raised her eyebrows: she was relieved he'd finally stopped yelling.

"Oh?"

Lighting a new cigarette, Xavier lifted her from the floor and led her to the sofa.

"You could make your brother believe that he has saved you. You could be our horse of Troy."

"You mean our Trojan Horse."

"So smart, my little duck. Yes, our *Trojan horse*. You say your mother is a liar—a *hypocrite*—so, surely, she is hiding something, no? You shall return as her doting daughter, find out what it is that she is hiding, and then together we shall reveal it."

Greta thought of the way her brother hugged her, the familiar, earnest timbre of his voice. She tried to swallow but could not. Something—guilt?—was lodged in her throat.

"Together?" she said.

"I told you that we should go to New York, did I not? To avenge your father, to find you the justice to which you are entitled? Yes, Greta, we will be together. You'll go with your brother, and to be safe, I'll come a few days behind you. And that will be the last time we'll ever be apart."

Xavier kissed Greta, letting his tongue linger on her lips. Once he pulled his head away, he smiled, and he tucked Greta's hair behind her ear. His eyes shone sapphire, their edges ringed with traces of post-rain light. Sinking into them, Greta felt her limbs, her lungs relax—whatever had been blocking her throat evaporated and, easily, she swallowed.

"Let's do it," she said. "Let's fuck Nancy up."

They knocked their mugs together and threw back the Cabernet. Then, as he reached for the bottle, Xavier's brow darkened. He began to frown.

"What is it?" Greta asked.

"Will your brother believe you? You were not exactly warm to him at the museum. Will he be suspicious if—*poof!*—you are now ready to return and make amends with your mother?"

Sediment clung to the sides of Greta's mug, gritty bits of sugar the color of blackberries. She hadn't considered that Nick would see through her, but hearing Xavier articulate it she suddenly began to. Nick was smart and perceptive; he had spent ten years working in Washington, where every fifth word is a lie. The notion that he wouldn't buy what Greta was selling now struck her as not only possible but likely.

"What should we do?"

Xavier stood, cupping his chin in his right hand. He walked in a slow circle.

"If only there were a way to make him think that you are fleeing from me," he said.

"Fleeing from you?"

"Yes. If he thought I had turned violent—that I had *hurt* you—then he would absolutely believe that you would return with him."

"What are you saying, that I should have, like, a black eye?"

Xavier's lips pursed. He tilted his head from side to side, thinking.

"It's not a bad idea, no?"

Instinctively, Greta lifted two fingers to touch her cheek. Her skin felt thin, hardly any protection at all; never before had she considered how close the bones were to its surface.

"So, what, you would hit me?" she asked.

"It would be out of love, my duck."

Greta didn't say anything, and in the silence Xavier's face took on an anguished expression, the corners of his mouth drooping down.

"No." His voice quivered. "I could never. Forgive me for even saying so. We will find another solution . . ."

His voice trailing off, Xavier began circling again, his feet shuffling on the floor. Watching him mope, Greta sank back against the sofa—it was stiff, and uncomfortable; an antique Louis XIV piece that was meant to be admired, not touched. Relief washed over her, but then, on its heels, a profound disappointment. She'd escaped getting slugged, yes, but also, she wanted to help.

Outside, the afternoon sun peeked through the last of the clouds and reflected in bursts off the Pyramide du Louvre. Greta stared at it for a moment, willing herself not to squint. She poured herself another mugful of Cabernet, drank it, and, rising, handed the mug to Xavier.

"Hold this," she said, and took a drag of his cigarette. Then she walked back to the sofa, where she threw her face against its sturdy walnut arm.

Now, in the bar, there is a small commotion: the bartender is tossing a man in a white shirt out.

"How was your flight?" Greta asks.

"Long. I sat next to a woman who smelled like garlic and would not stop farting. What did you find out about your mother?"

Greta takes another sip of vodka and taps her fingers against the glass. For the past week she has been going through her mother's affairs, secluding herself in Nancy's office with a novel cracked open on the floor in case

Nick walks in. She has read her emails and perused old bank statements and, on one desperate occasion, gone through the trash in the bathroom. The search has yielded nothing. Her mother has taken no bribes, broken no promises, buried no bodies. It maddened her: Nancy was a bitch, but worse than that, Nancy was good.

"Nothing," she says. "I found absolutely nothing."

Xavier curls his lips against his teeth and, his voice tinged with panic, says, "*Merde*. What are we going to do?"

His cheeks rouged, he takes a small sip from his drink. Greta studies him—the way the bar's low light dulls the sheen of his hair, the fragile manner in which he brings the glass to his lips. In Paris she had considered him part of the architecture, perfectly at home—necessary, even—among all those beaux arts facades. Here in New York, it is different; he is at odds with his surroundings. It's as if she's wandered into an airport bathroom and found Monet's haystacks hanging above the toilet. The feeling only makes her love him more.

"Don't worry," she says, with a widening grin. "I think I have an idea."

KRAMER BARGES INTO JERRY'S APARTMENT, his body vibrating like a guitar string. The audience erupts in applause.

"So, you're moving to California," Nick hears himself say. "That's what you're telling me—you're moving to California."

Charlie runs a hand through his hair. His cheeks, Nick notes, have gone red.

"I put in for a transfer to the LA bureau eight months ago, and when I didn't hear anything I honestly forgot about it. But then today Lawrence comes to me and tells me it's a go for January."

"Who's Lawrence?"

"Sorry. My boss."

The flyer for the musical is still in Nick's hand. In need of something to do, the desire to distract his churning brain, he folds it in half and sets it back on the counter.

"And you're going to do it? You're definitely going to go?"

The refrigerator door swings open, and Charlie pries the top off a second bottle of beer.

"I . . . I think so? My folks are getting old, you know? My dad can hardly get himself to the grocery store, and I'm all the way out here."

Pressing his lips together, Nick nods—he wants to seem understanding, empathetic; he wants to hide how he's upset. While Frank barks at the laugh track on the television, he tells himself that he has dealt with worse—that, in fact, *worse* is currently happening. Wars and famines and hurricanes, plucking lives from their roots, tragedies next to which Nick's disappointment is childish and inconsequential. Besides, he has dated people for longer, and broken up with them over less. Yes, Charlie was different—Charlie was *special*—but everything, even that which is different and special, has built within its DNA an inevitable death. Milk turns sour, fruit goes rotten, wine puckers to vinegar. *To this end*, Nick thinks, *what's happening isn't a big deal*—which is funny, really, considering how small it makes him feel.

"You're a good son," he manages to say. "You're doing the right thing."

In the apartment upstairs, footsteps race across the floor. Charlie glances up, then back at Nick.

"Where are you going?" he asks.

Without realizing it, Nick has taken hold of his jacket—it's right there, clutched like a lifesaver in his hand.

"Oh." He shakes the coat out and sticks one arm through a sleeve. "I should probably get back to Greta. I told her I'd be back by ten."

From the couch, Frank looks up at him. Nick reaches over and scratches his head.

"But I haven't finished what I wanted to tell you," Charlie says.

Flipping up his collar, Nick shrugs. "What else is there?"

"I want you to come with me."

THE BARTENDER KICKS ANOTHER PATRON out, but this time they do not turn to watch.

Instead, Xavier says, "So, you will take her to lunch and record her saying something terrible?"

"Yes, with this." Greta holds up her phone, the one from which she texted Xavier this afternoon. Her eyes are bright; her voice quickens. "She's asked me if I'll speak at this rally that's happening in a few days. She thinks it'll look good, having her reformed daughter going on and on about how fucking wonderful she is in front of all these baby boomers—she thinks it will help her win their votes. So, I'll agree. And then, when I'm onstage, rather than blowing smoke up her ass, I'll press this bad boy up to the microphone and hit play."

While Xavier listens, he folds a cocktail napkin into halves, then quarters.

"What if she doesn't say anything awful at lunch? What if she is perfectly polite?"

Greta takes a sip of vodka.

"Oh, you've never met my mother," she says. "That won't be a problem."

She laughs, mostly to herself, her bruise turning indigo in the bar's low light. Watching her, Xavier remembers the sound of her cheek colliding with the arm of the sofa. It had been a test—another opportunity to see how far he could push her—and the results had surprised him. He had thought, frankly, that he would need to find another way to do it, with either his fist, or a book, or an iron poker; he didn't know if she loved him enough to do it on her own. But then—*bam!*—there she was, stealing a fortifying drag from his cigarette before lowering down to her knees. *And now*, he thinks, *here she is again. Finding solutions to unforeseen problems, coming up with a plan.*

"When will you take your mother to lunch?" he asks.

"Tomorrow." A piece of dirt is lodged beneath one of Greta's fingernails and, using a toothpick, she shovels it out. "She's coming back to Manhattan in the morning."

He scrutinizes her face, searching it for signs of doubt. Reaching out, he runs his thumb along her cheek.

"Anything wrong?" he asks.

"No, nothing."

"You are concerned you will not be able to go through with this?"

Greta doesn't immediately respond, and in the silence Xavier hears a loud crack: someone's angry break shot, echoing from the pool table at the rear of the bar.

She takes hold of his hand, kisses it, then pushes it aside.

"No, of course not," she says. "I'm not concerned about that at all."

FOUR EMPTY BEER BOTTLES SIT on Charlie's coffee table.

"I can't just *leave*," Nick says.

"Why not?" Charlie is drunk. He's still not wearing a shirt. "Who says you can't?"

Nick prepares to respond but stops himself. *Who says he can't?* It's a question that he always thought had an easy answer—his family, namely, but also his job, his friends, his life. Now, with Frank lolling in his lap, he finds himself wondering how true that is; none of those people have ever told him that he *had* to live in New York, no one has ever held a gun to his head; rather, he's chosen to live here because, so far as he could tell, there was nowhere else worth living.

"You said it yourself the other night," Charlie continues.

"What did I say?"

"That you wouldn't mind getting away from your family for a bit. That you thought some distance would do you some good." Charlie curls his lips together. "Those were your words—not mine."

He's right, Nick thinks, *they were*.

"What would I do?" he asks.

Charlie sets his feet on the coffee table. "They've got colleges out there, loads of them. You could teach at UCLA."

"What if it doesn't work out? What if we get out there and within two days we're ready to murder each other?"

"We're talking about a move—not open heart surgery. This will work, Nick, I really believe that. But if it doesn't work out, or if you, like, suddenly decide to hate the sun, then you could come back." He shrugs. "It's not like New York is going anywhere."

Nick nods, slowly, and glances toward the kitchen. There, taped to the refrigerator, are a handful of photographs that, until now, he hadn't spent the time to notice: Charlie with his parents on a crowded pier; the moon over the Pacific at dusk. Looking at them, Nick allows himself a moment to imagine the silkiness of sand creeping between his toes. Instead of tracking down lost sisters or conspiring with scheming mothers, he is sprawled out on a beach towel, an open book in his hand. He scratches beneath Frank's chin and, finishing his beer, taps the bottle against his teeth. *How easy it would be to love his family*, he thinks, *from three thousand miles away.*

Good Work

"Play it again."

"Seriously?"

Tom rips the last scrap of meat away from a chicken wing and tosses the bone on his plate.

"Seriously," he says. "But this time do it backward."

They're watching a video on Cate's phone—one that, in the last five minutes, they've seen fourteen times. Carmichael, wreaking havoc with his blue sledgehammer, in real time, in slow motion, at twice the speed, three times the speed, five times the speed, and—now—in reverse. The tool starts on the ground, and as Cate drags her finger along the phone's screen, she retraces its chaotic path. It rises into the air, through a downpour of shattered glass, before somersaulting twice and falling back into Carmichael's outstretched hand.

She and Tom laugh—they can't stop laughing—and they watch it again, this time (the fifteenth) in the correct order: a scarecrow's swing, an unsure grip, twenty pounds of wood and high-carbon steel careening like a shot put into a glass sign welcoming visitors to the Erie Canal. In the background there is gasping, crashing, screaming. Carmichael grunts and gurgles as he steps aside to let Nancy take a swing. Thanking him—"a helluva try, Chip"—she pushes up the sleeves of her blazer, spits on her palms, and grips the hammer's handle like it was a Louisville slugger. She cocks it behind her shoulder, slices it through the air, and slams its head into the wall, where she leaves a perfect, cantaloupe-sized crater.

The video ends (again) and, folding his hands behind his head, Tom lets out a happy sigh.

He says, "These are the moments that remind me why I do what I do."

ON THE CEILING ABOVE THEM two lights flicker, threatening to quit; at the other end of the office a ringing phone goes unanswered. It's eight o'clock at night and, as far as Cate knows, she and Tom are the only ones left in the office. The staffers have gone back to their share houses; the interns have gone back to their parents'; Nancy has gone back to her hotel. She'll be in her room, on her bed, politely laughing her way through an interview. Last night it was WWKB, and the night before that, a call-in to Maddow. *Tonight,* Cate thinks, *it's WHLD. Newstalk 1270: The Voice of Reason.* A mountain of papers rises from the table between her and Tom. Polling reports and media strategies from the campaign's consultants, the corners of which are stained with traces of tonight's takeout. A six-pack of beer—Heineken, because that's all there was—is on the floor next to Tom's feet. Three bottles are left, and now Tom reaches for one of them. When he leans past her, Cate catches a whiff of something that's now become familiar: Tom's new cologne.

"Buffalo isn't a lot to look at, is it." He tries opening the beer against the table's edge, but his fist misses and ends up slicing through the air. Blushing, he resorts to prying the cap off with a key. Doing her best to hide her grin, Cate follows his gaze to the office window, where she can see the purple outlines of buildings, the reflection of streetlights. "A ghost town where someone forgot to turn off the lights."

"It's not so bad," she says.

The beer fizzes, sloshing out of the bottle. Tom sticks out his tongue and catches as many drops as he can.

"You're right, it could be worse," he says. "It could be Poughkeepsie."

One final bite of sandwich sits alone on Cate's plate, and even though she's full she eats it. She thinks of the list of towns that, until two months ago, she had never heard of, but with which she now considers herself intimate: Dansville, Canisteo, Avoca; Mount Morris, Warsaw, Perry. Geneseo, where there's a fountain with a bear hugging a streetlamp, and

Canandaigua, which she still can't quite pronounce. Pittsford, which had good pizza, and Clifton Springs, which did not. In Attica she ran over a rabbit; in Albion she spilled coffee on her blouse; in Batavia she watched Nancy, mid–stump speech, unknowingly swallow a fly. Nowheres become somewheres when they're matched with memories. These, Cate figures, are hers.

Another phone rings, this time in her pocket.

"Who is it?" Tom asks. And then: "Whoever it is, tell them you can't talk—we've got two beers to finish."

"It's Nancy." Cate knocks the bottle against the table's edge and the cap goes flying off. She winks at Tom. "Good thing I can talk and drink."

When she returns, two televisions show two different worlds: CNN's on one, Fox News is on the other. Mouths move, chyrons flash, images parade across the screens. A riot in Paris for Fox, an oil spill in the Gulf of Mexico for CNN. The sound is muted; the apocalypse is silent. Cate puts her phone away and returns to the table, this time sitting in a chair directly next to Tom's.

"So, what did our fearless leader want?" he asks.

"The email blast that's going out to our lists tomorrow, she wants us to come up with a new subject line."

"The one that's supposed to be from Bette Midler?"

"It's not *supposed* to be from Bette Midler—it *is* from Bette Midler. Her people signed off on it."

"Yeah, yeah, you know what I mean." Tom rolls up his sleeves an inch further, and Cate glances at the thin hairs sweeping across his forearms. "What is it now?"

"The sender is *Bette's iPhone*, and the subject line is 'Nancy needs us ASAP.'"

Tom taps his chin.

"That's bad. That doesn't sound like Bette."

"I know. An intern wrote it. I don't think he even knows who Bette Midler is."

On one of the TV screens, seagulls slick with oil languish on the Texan shore; on the other, a blonde in a pussycat bow is scandalized by French hoodlums and thugs. The images are soft, fuzzy: Cate is getting a little tipsy.

"What about 'Let me tell you why I'm belting for Nancy Harrison'?" she says.

"It's too long. It'll get cut off at 'I'm,' and besides, Bette Midler shouldn't ever have to give a reason to belt." Tom pulls his mouth to one side and thinks. "How about, 'This is urgent'?"

"Too dry. Besides, we used it in an email this afternoon."

"Which one?"

"The Nate Silver update."

"That went out today?"

"Yeah, along with 'Polling Alert' and 'I'll make this quick.'"

"These poor people. They give five bucks and it haunts them forever." Shaking his head, Tom stands up.

"Where are you going?" Cate asks, and is instantly embarrassed. "I'm your boss—you're not allowed to make me do this alone."

"Relax—I'll be right back. This job requires hard alcohol."

Ten minutes and one aggressive pour of bourbon later, Cate says: "'No more hocus-pocus.' We're three days from Halloween, and people fucking love that movie. 'From Bette's iPhone: No more hocus-pocus.'"

Tom rocks his head from side to side.

"Too niche. How about 'It's more fun to fucking win.'"

"Come on, Tom. Don't give up."

She playfully slaps his shoulder, her hand lingering against his shirt for half a second too long. She thinks: *Catalina, what are you doing?*

"I'm not giving up—I'm being serious! Do you know how depressing it is to lose one of these things?"

Google's sleek offices flash briefly in Cate's mind. All those yoga classes and napping pods; all that free food.

She says, "I'm trying not to think about that."

"Well, as someone who's been through it, let me tell you: it's really fucking depressing."

CNN plays a Nissan commercial: a silver car, looping around a precarious bend in the road.

"How many have you lost since you started?" Cate asks.

"Eight."

"*Eight?*"

Tom nods. "Eight."

Cate mouths *wow*. She unscrews the top from the bottle of bourbon and pours another splash into her glass. What is this—her third cup? Her fourth? She can't remember, and also, who cares. Tom's finally found a light he looks good in, and she's well on her way to drunk.

"Well, you win some, you lose some," she says. "Besides, it's about more than winning, right?"

His eyes wide, Tom stares at her.

"Cate," he says. "What else would it possibly be about?"

"Fixing the country's problems? Making people's lives a little bit better?"

"Oh. That."

"Just because America has never lived up to its promises," she says, trying not to slur, "that doesn't mean that it can't start now."

Tom lifts his eyebrows.

"That's a good line."

"Thanks." Winking—no, *trying* to wink—she raises her cup to toast her whiskey. Her cheeks, she is certain, are red. "I wrote it for Greta's speech."

"You think she's gonna give it?"

"I think so. She fucking better. If she doesn't, maybe Bette will."

Tom smiles, a little sadly, and sets his cup on the table.

"I don't know when it became this for me," he says. "I want to say that I saw that all of this was part of something larger. The late nights, the long drives between third-rate towns—I understood how it was all working toward a greater good. But then the winning starts getting in the way. You start worrying less about Americans, and more about whether the other guy will lose. It's miserable, Cate, but winning is so much god-damned fun."

Cate offers a slow, sympathetic nod; she doesn't know what to say, because she wasn't really listening. She imagines him regarding himself in his hotel mirror this morning, dabbing the scent on his neck before he rushes out to meet her. A little here, next to his Adam's apple; a little there, next to his chin. Tom's is a good neck, a sturdy neck—a neck that after another bourbon or two Cate thinks that—*oh my God*—she might like to *kiss*.

Blinking, she tries to regain focus. She is not interested in kissing Tom—it's just an effect of the campaign. One of those weird, bourbon-fueled mirages in which you start imagining what it would be like to spend your life with a man with whom you are, well, *already spending your life*. She needs to remember who she is, the authority she has. Nancy, elections, America, *Bette*. Tonight, Cate and Tom have a job to do, and so help her God, they're going to get it done.

She says, "You smell really nice."

His hand halfway to the bottle, Tom stops.

"Uh, what?"

"Nothing. It was nothing."

"Did you say I smell nice?"

"Maybe."

Tom pours himself a sizable drink, and Cate searches for a smile.

"You could get in trouble for that, you know."

"For saying you *smell nice*?"

"Yes. You're my superior, Catalina. Some people might say that commenting on how I smell is *harassment*."

"Fine, then, I take it back. You smell like shit."

Tom keeps a straight face for a second longer, but then—*there*—his nostrils quiver and his lips begin to twitch. Watching him crumble, Cate thinks: *Thank God*.

Above them the lights flicker again, and this time, when they're done, the room is one-eighth darker: one of them, it seems, has decided to give up.

"It's called l'Orange et Vert," Tom says, sniffing himself. "That means 'orange and green.'"

Cate grins.

"Thanks for that, Tom."

"It's the most expensive cologne I've ever bought. Almost a hundred bucks for some dinky little bottle."

"And who're you wearing it for?"

Tom sets his elbows on the table and leans closer to Cate: now their foreheads are inches apart. On the right side of his mouth, a tiny fleck of red clings to the beginnings of a mustache: buffalo sauce, Cate realizes, glinting in the light.

He says, "Can't a man want to smell nice for himself?"

Cate doesn't answer the question, because Tom isn't actually asking it.

Instead she says, "I'm going to need you to wipe off your face."

"What? Why?"

"Because it's covered in sauce from those disgusting wings," she says, handing him a napkin. "And I refuse to kiss you until it's gone."

Ladies Who Lunch

Nancy's eyes drift around the living room: here is her sofa, her chairs, her sword, her daughter. A moment later the radiator hisses and begins its clanking, a jarring, belligerent sound that both she and Greta ignore.

"Are you sure?" she says. "I don't want you to do anything you're not comfortable doing."

"It will help you, right? Me getting up there and speaking tomorrow?"

Nancy folds her hands and sets them in her lap. Her lips compress.

"Cate and Tom are confident that it will. They think that older voters will—well, they think that they'll like hearing from you."

"Well, then, I'll do it. I think we can both agree that I owe you one. Please make sure they write something for me, though. God knows what I'll say if I have to ad-lib."

Yawning, Greta blinks: she has recently woken up from a nap. Ten minutes ago, when Nancy returned to her apartment from a week on the road, she found Greta asleep on the couch, a book splayed open on her chest. The bruise shading her eye was still there, along with the gash across her cheek, and as Nancy looked at them she could feel a phantom pain creep across her own face. Here was her daughter. *Her daughter!* She placed her keys on the coffee table, followed by her purse, and, despite her attempts to be quiet, the sound woke Greta up.

Now, watching her daughter's yawn become a smile, Nancy feels her heart grow by half. *Oh*, she thinks, *the bewitching power of one's own children! They show you they love you—they smile at you—and in that instant their transgressions are unconditionally forgiven.* The radiator still wailing behind her, she hugs Greta, pulling her in as tightly as she can and pressing her cheek against the top of her head. They stay there for a minute, neither of them saying a word, until, finally, Greta lets out a little squeak and gently squirms away. Her book—the one that was on her chest— falls to the ground and she reaches down to retrieve it. Smoothing down her blouse, Nancy clears her throat. Then she sees, on a small credenza, a vase of fresh yellow freesias. She looks at them for a moment and tries to remember buying them. She can't.

"Those are pretty," she says.

"I asked Nick to go out and get them this morning for me. I know that freesias are your favorite."

"That was very thoughtful of you."

Greta shrugs, and her cheeks go red.

She says, "I was also thinking . . ." but then trails off.

"Yes?"

"Well, I know that you're very busy and everything, but I was *thinking* that it might be fun to have a girls' lunch this afternoon. Just to—I don't know—catch up."

"Where did you have in mind?"

"How about La Goulue?"

"Oh, sweetie. We'd need a reservation, I'm afraid."

"I already made one."

"You did?"

"I used your name, and they offered me whatever time I wanted." Greta tilts her chin and speaks into her shoulder. "I hope that's okay."

Her hair falls in her face—it's not quite long enough to stay put—and, watching her try to fix it, Nancy beams. It's been over a year since her daughter has asked her to do something that didn't involve *fucking off*, and now, here she is, wondering if she has time to *catch up*. Or, no, not simply catch up but rather have *lunch* at *La Goulue*—which, as Greta surely knows, is one of the few things in life that has the power to make

Nancy Harrison happy. To this end, what Greta is offering is more than an invitation—it is an olive branch. An opportunity to wipe their collective history clean and—finally!—start fresh.

Her vision cloudy with tears, Nancy reaches out and takes both of her daughter's hands.

"I'd love that," she says. And then, as she wipes her eyes: "But no wine! I've got calls later."

"Great! And sure—no wine." Greta winks, squeezes her mother's hands, and nearly leaps from the couch. "Just let me go get my shoes."

GRETA CLOSES THE DOOR TO her bedroom, locks it, and exhales.

"Okay," she says. "So far so good."

She takes another breath and pushes her hair out of her face. It's annoying her—she can't get it to stay out of her way. Opening her old desk, she fishes past pens and rubber bands and a Bic lighter until she finds a hair clip, which she uses to hold her bangs in a place where she can forget about them. Her hair temporarily managed, she goes to her closet for some old Vans, thinks twice, and reaches instead for a pair of gold heels. She brushes away some dust, squeezes her feet into the shoes, and then checks herself out in the mirror. She thinks: *Not bad.*

Her old cell phone pokes out from the back pocket of her jeans, and now she uses it to text Xavier.

"Wish me luck," she writes, then records herself saying *Test one, two, three.*

Lowering the device's volume, she plays back the recording: it works perfectly, but still, Greta cringes at the timbre of her own voice. *It's impossible*, she thinks, *that she actually sounds like* that.

NANCY HEARS THE ELEVATOR CHIME: she must have forgotten to close the front door. She leans over to smell the freesias, then goes to the foyer to investigate.

"Mom! You're back."

It's Nick. His cheeks are flushed from the wind, and Nancy watches as he slips out of his coat and hangs it on a peg.

"Where were you," she asks. "I thought we agreed you were going to stay here with her."

"Oh! I—hm. Well, I was picking up some stuff at Zabar's."

"What were you picking up?"

"Some babka."

"Some *babka*?"

"Yeah, and, uh, some duck foie gras."

His hands carry no bags. Also, his shirt is wrinkled and his cheeks are unshaven and there's a faint purple bruise, right at the base of his neck. Nick follows her gaze and, as discreetly as he can, which isn't very discreetly at all, covers the hickey with his collar.

"Where's Greta?" Nick asks.

"She's finishing getting dressed in her room." And now, a small smile: "We're going to have lunch at La Goulue."

"Wow." Nick lifts an eyebrow. "Was that your idea or hers?"

"Hers."

"Does she know she needs a reservation?"

"She called ahead and used my name to make one. You know, your sister is very resourceful when she wants to be."

Taking a step toward him, Nancy now lowers her voice to an excited whisper. "When I got home she was asleep, but then she woke up and we had a very special moment. We *hugged*, Nick. And then *she* asked *me* if I wanted to get lunch!"

"It sounds like you two have really turned a corner."

That's exactly what it feels like. Nancy hasn't allowed herself to think as much in so many words, for fear that articulating it might render it untrue, but her son is right. It does.

"Thank you for getting the freesias, by the way."

"The freesias?"

"The yellow ones that Greta asked you to get this morning. They're lovely."

Nick rubs the back of his neck. He frowns at the floor.

Nancy says, "Honey, you don't eat babka—it has all those carbs. I don't want to know where you got that thing on your neck, but it's fine—I'm not even angry! Everything's *fine*."

"I HAVE AN IDEA."

"What's that, sweetie?"

"I said I have an *idea*." Greta polishes off the last of her wine. "Let's get another bottle."

Five leftover chives from Nancy's lobster cobb form a constellation on her plate. On the other side of the restaurant, behind a long banquette, a large mirror is inlaid on dark, wood-paneled walls. She catches sight of her reflection. When they first sat down they got martinis, then when their food arrived Greta ordered a bottle of Sancerre; now, it seems, she wants to make it two. Nancy's reflection—cheeks ruddy, eyes a little heavy—smiles at her: it knows she's drunk.

"Oh, what the hell," she says. "Why not!"

Greta rises an inch and signals their waiter; sinking back, Nancy drapes her right arm over the back of her chair. Music is playing, the comely voice of Josephine Baker, and listening to it, Nancy closes her eyes. She and her daughter are having fun. It is something that together they rarely experience, and she would be loath to see it stop, particularly over a decision as stupid as a declined bottle of wine. Greta is not sulking, or sniffling, or sneering—Greta is talking. Or, more than talking: Greta is *chatting*, skipping between interests as if they were hopscotch squares. Over the course of lunch, she has shared with Nancy her thoughts on the time she spent in Paris ("*une erreur catastrophique*"); what she gleaned about French trolls ("just as obnoxious as American ones, but they know how to pronounce 'Chablis'"); and Nick ("Who gave him that hickey?" "A boy?" "Who?" "*A boy*"). Twice Greta has apologized to Nancy—once for making a scene at dinner, the other time for making a scene on the Champs-Élysées—and she has as frequently allowed Nancy to apologize to her. She has let Nancy ask questions, and provide commentary, and—on one occasion—suggest a new way for Greta to wear her hair until it "grows back to a more flattering length."

This is another surprise: it seems to Nancy that, at least for now, her daughter likes to hear her talk, even babble. Thirty minutes ago, which was after the martini but before the slippery slope of the Sancerre, Nancy found herself rattling on about a house in Greenport in which she and her children had spent one sweltering August. She became embarrassed—she had been going on and on—though instead of rolling her eyes or checking her phone or deploying any of her other gesticular weapons to which Nancy has become accustomed, Greta leaned her elbows on the table and asked Nancy to keep going. She liked hearing about these memories, she told her mother, all these little snapshots that Nancy could so easily call forth. Greta hadn't done a good job of remembering much of anything, and now she was glad there was someone who did. Nancy—O, nostalgia! O, Sancerre!—obliged her daughter's wishes. She recalled how the three of them all shared one bedroom because at night it was the only place cool enough to sleep. She talked about how Nick fell from a tree and sprained his ankle, and how the neighbors next door had a chocolate Lab named Winston that the Harrisons were instructed not to pet because he was covered with ticks. Finally, poking a finger into Greta's cheek, she reminded her how she'd gotten sick after eating an entire jar of maraschino cherries.

At this point, Greta blushed and finished what was left of her drink.

"I still can't eat them," she said. "I think they taste like fish."

"Like *fish*?"

"Yeah, that's right—like fish. It has something to do with their skins, I think. The way they soak up all that dye."

The new bottle of Sancerre arrives. Josephine Baker sings about her *deux amours*; Nancy rubs her eyes and yawns.

Excusing herself, Greta stands from her chair and wobbles on her heels. She tells her mother that she's in need of the ladies' room.

GRETA BARRICADES HERSELF IN A stall and presses the heels of her palms against her eyes. Maybe her mother isn't feeling well, because even after a martini and a half bottle of wine, Nancy has not said anything remotely controversial or offensive. Instead, she's waxed poetic about Greenport, and chocolate Labs, and too many eaten cherries. Had that actually happened?

Greta doesn't know—after all the booze she's drunk in the past hour, her memories have turned to watercolors, blurry strokes that bleed in and out of focus. She closes her eyes tighter, thinks harder, finally sees it: a jar emptied of its cloying red syrup; a night spent with a twisted stomach. Yes, her mother was right. Unbuttoning her jeans, Greta pulls them down and sits on the toilet. She thinks of that summer in Greenport, smiles, and then, catching herself, frowns. She's enjoying lunch, which is a problem. She shouldn't be having this much fun.

Outside the stall's walls, Greta hears the splash of women washing their hands. Her mouth tastes like Gruyère, onions, and plastic—she's just removed the cap of her lipstick with her teeth. She spits it out into the palm of her hand, pees, and, using a square of toilet paper, wipes a smudge of the city off her shoes. Her toes are squished into their points like ten angry shrimp and, squinting, she tries to remember why she bought them. Before going to Paris she was rarely cursed with the occasion to wear heels. But then—oh, right. Nancy had given them to her, along with a Chanel dress, so she could wear them to dinner. The dinner to which she invited Edward; the dinner where she hauled Greta to the kitchen and slapped her.

With a hand planted on each of the stall's walls, Greta stands. Her phone is still recording, balanced on an Altoids tin near the top of her open purse. So far, what it's captured has been useless—a collection of sentimental memories, along with a few sirens and the noisy background of the restaurant; nostalgia, mixed with the unmanageable din of New York. She needs to take hold of the conversation. Lasso its neck, rein it in, send it careening off in a more spiteful direction. No more talk of the past, and how rosy it appears in retrospect. No more reminiscing about idyllic summers on Long Island or tick-infested dogs.

Sucking in a breath, Greta buttons her jeans.

GRASPING THE BACKS OF CHAIRS as she walks toward the table: her daughter in doubles, and then triples. Nancy widens her eyes, squints them, closes the left one. The replicas are overlaid—now, for the time being, there is only one Greta.

"D'jou wash your hands?" she asks once her daughter has sat back down.

"Course I did—they have fancy soap." Greta flutters her fingers beneath Nancy's nostrils, and then sets her purse on the table. "Wow—you drank that fast."

Picking up her empty glass, Nancy presses her tongue against her cheek and pours herself some more Sancerre. "You were taking too long and I was thirsty."

Their waiter has not yet cleared their basket of bread. Greta grabs a piece and shoves it in her mouth.

Chewing, she says, "I was thinking—"

"Yes?"

"I was *thinking* that you could tell me more about your job."

"My job?"

"Yeah, like, what you *do*. It occurred to me when I was in the bathroom that during your entire campaign I've never asked you what it's like."

A warm rush of pride swells within Nancy—she can't remember the last time her daughter asked her about her work.

"Well," she says, as coolly, and as soberly, as she can, "it's very exhilarating. The opportunity to help people and talk to them—it's all very rewarding."

Greta breaks off another chunk of bread. This one she slathers with butter.

"But it also must be so frustrating?! I mean, you've worked your entire life for this, and now some D-list dipshit might steal it from you because a bunch of old people liked his show."

"You mean Carmichael."

"No. I refuse to say his name." Greta shakes her head; her words bleed together. "I mean, arenchu mad?"

Nancy reaches for the Sancerre and adds another splash. Of course she's mad.

She says, "All voters are entittled to their opinion."

"You mean entitled?"

"What'd I say?"

"Entittled."

"That's funny."

They both giggle. Nancy thinks: *Greta is on her side; Greta is defending her.* After all, here she is, pouring herself another glug of Sancerre.

"Be honest with me," Greta says. "You hate him."

"Now, Greta. I don't hate anyone."

"Oh, come on, Mom."

Nancy doesn't answer—instead she tries to wink, and Greta rolls her eyes.

She says, "This is what I mean! Isn't it hard, keeping all these opinions to yourself? Having to bite your tongue all the time instead of saying what you really think? Being prim and polite and proper?"

"That's politics, honey."

"No, that's the *patriarchy.* Men are allowed to say nasty stuff whenever they want. You're playing by their rules, Mom."

"What would you rather me do?"

"Tell me what you actually think! I'm your daughter, Mom, and this isn't Washington—it's *La Goulue.*"

Nancy again pushes her tongue against the inside of her cheek, wiggles it around a bit, and frowns. She hates feeling as though she's disappointing her daughter, especially now, when they're having such a lovely time.

"Okay," she says. "What do you want to know my real thoughts about?"

Greta scratches her left temple. She nudges her purse an inch closer to Nancy so she can lean her elbows on the table.

"Mitch McConnell," she says.

"A dickless, chinless turtle."

A long pause ensues, after which they both erupt with laughter, their heads tilted back in delight.

"Okay, a good start." Greta nods. "Now do Lindsey Graham."

"Easy: he's camp."

"Chuck Schumer."

"That man would screw a camera if it'd let him."

"Nancy Reagan."

"Now *there's* a woman who was really nasty."

"Nancy *Pelosi.*"

"Off-limits—she'll put a hex on me."

"Okay, then. Angela Merkel."

"The best argument I've ever seen for remembering to tip your hairdresser."

"The Queen of England."

"Bathes in formaldehyde."

Grinning, Greta licks her lips.

"Staten Island," she says.

"Let it sink."

"Buffalo."

"Sell it to Canada."

"Brooklyn."

"*Blech.*"

There's two fingers of Sancerre left in the bottle, and Greta dumps it in Nancy's glass.

She says, "Millennials."

Nancy squints. "Too pink."

"Gen Z."

"Too green!"

"Gen X."

"Who?"

"*Baby boomers.*"

Tossing her head back, Nancy finishes her wine.

"Those goddamned boomers," she says, "would make my job a whole lot easier if they'd hurry up and die."

CORDONED OFF IN ANOTHER BATHROOM stall, Greta stares at her phone's screen, trying to bring it into focus. Once she's got it—once her eyes have uncrossed—she plays back the recording and holds the speaker to her ear.

"Those goddamned boomers would make my job a whole lot easier if they'd hurry up and die," she hears her mother hiss.

In the stall next to Greta's, a woman clears her throat.

"*What* did you just say?"

Greta's head shoots up. She presses her knees together and glares into the light.

"Hey, lady," she calls out. "Mind your own fucking beeswax."

Angry murmurs float out over the bathroom's wooden walls and, moments later, Greta hears a door opening—the eavesdropper, hustling indignantly back to her table. When she's certain she's alone, she listens to the recording again. It's good—clear and crisp and unmistakable. Greta got her mother to call for the demise of an entire generation—the one whose support she most desperately needs—and all it took was two martinis, an awkward hug, and a vat of mediocre Sancerre.

Lurching to her feet, she prepares to go back to the table but stops herself short of opening the stall door. There is an opportunity here, she realizes. Sure, Greta has succeeded, but that hardly seems reason enough to stop—particularly now, when Nancy can barely keep her eyes open or her mouth shut, when Greta has her, dangling like a shit-faced marionette from a string. Yes, she'll keep going: she's already got what she needs, so now she'll aim for what she wants.

She opens a new voice memo, repositions the phone, and kicks the stall's door open with her heel.

Behind her, the toilet flushes on its own.

"I WANT TO TALK ABOUT Dad," Greta says once she's sat back down.

"What do you mean, sweetie?"

"I want to talk about what happened between you two."

"We're having such a good time, though."

"I don't care. I want to know."

"It was so long ago, Greta, and we've done fine, haven't we? You, Nick, and me? I think we've done fine."

Two empty water glasses refract the restaurant's light. A waiter arrives and fills them, spilling a few errant droplets down their sides.

When he leaves, Greta says, "You slept with that man, Edward, didn't you. And Dad found out the night that he died."

Her eyes are stone—two hard dots in a soft, drunk face. Nancy holds their gaze, trying to sift through the past five minutes. They had been laughing, uproariously, and then Greta went to the bathroom and came back changed.

"That's not what happened," she says.

"It is what happened. Eugenia told me."

A woman at the table next to them complains about her salad; on the other side of the restaurant, a wineglass falls and breaks.

"Well, Greta, Eugenia lied." Nancy lifts a finger and swirls it in a loose circle. "It was the other way around."

A phone call came from Howard's chief of staff: this is what Nancy tells Greta. He had something he needed to discuss with her, and he was hoping that she'd meet him for lunch. She was busy—she was litigating a case the next day—but his voice sounded brittle, and he was persistent, and so she said she could give him an hour. Besides, she'd always liked Edward: he was smart, and loyal; he'd gone to law school with Nancy and Howard, and they'd known him for years. One hour turned into two, and then to three—as far as Nancy can remember, she never made it back to the office. The woman whom Howard was sleeping with was Edward's wife.

"Never get married, Greta." Nancy reaches for the wine, realizes it's gone, and instead settles for some water. "It just makes sex more complicated."

She waited a week to confront him—they had plans to spend a week together in Sagaponack, and she didn't want to start a fight with the children in the house. He denied it—he said she was trying to turn him into a political cliché—but as the night wore on, and as the empty bottles piled up, his denials became accusations; he spun up his guilt to blame, which is when Nancy realized that Edward had told her the truth.

"He was slurring his words and stumbling—I should've stopped him from leaving, but I was too fucking angry." She pinches the stem of her glass between two fingers and tilts it right, then left.

It was at the funeral when she realized what Eugenia had seen, when it became clear to Nancy what her mother-in-law thought. She tried to explain herself, to prove otherwise, but it was impossible. People tunnel into their beliefs like ants building farms—Nancy knew this; for the love of God, she worked in politics. They construct lairs, antechambers, and tiny trapdoors to protect themselves from an indifferent and inexplicable world. Eugenia hated Nancy because it was easier than not hating her—because hating Nancy made everything else make sense.

"Why didn't you tell me any of this?" Greta asks. "At dinner this past summer, why didn't you say something? Why didn't you stop me from leaving?"

"I should have. My God, I should have! I suppose I figured that your father breaking my heart was enough, and that the last thing I wanted him to do was break yours, too." A glossy film coats both of Nancy's eyes and her lips quiver. "I'm sorry, I'm very drunk, but do you see what I'm saying? He doesn't have a chance to make all of his mistakes up to you, Greta. I'm here, though, whether you like it or not, and that means that I do."

Boom Town

There's wind. A brisk, autumn breeze that sends ripples over the Hudson and causes a trio of leaves to dance the mazurka around Cate's ankles. Across the river and over New Jersey, big, white clouds shift shapes: a dragon becomes a lamb; an apple becomes a saucer; a troll's squished face folds and eventually implodes on itself. She watches them swell and shrink, and examines their bellies for signs of darkness. She thinks: *I'm really going to be pissed if it rains.*

"So, you want to talk about what happened the other night, or . . ."

It's Tom. He's standing next to her.

"Only if you want to," she says. "But also, we totally don't have to if you don't."

They had kissed—that's what had happened. Or, that is the start of what had happened. Tom wiped the buffalo sauce from his mouth and Cate took hold of his chin and there, in the twenty-four-hour glow of CNN and Fox News, she had kissed him. What followed is more of a blur. She can see glimpses of them clearing the beers and whiskey and takeout containers from the table, and then scrambling to remove certain articles of their clothing. A shoe and a shirt for Tom; underwear and pants for Cate. When they were finished, lying side by side beneath the office's fluorescent lights, she remembers being astonished by how good he had made her feel. This last fact surprises her, though maybe it shouldn't: Tom, for all of his bumbling and complaining and youthful sneakers, is a remarkably gifted lover.

"Is it okay if I want to?" he says.

Cate turns up the collar of her coat: she's starting to blush.

"It's a free country."

Tom clears his throat. With his left foot he scuffs at a piece of gray gum that's plastered to the sidewalk.

"I was thinking that, maybe, when this whole thing is over we could, I don't know, do something. Together."

Cate hears clapping—the head of the city's Department for Aging has finished welcoming the crowd. Reporters scribble in their notepads; mounted policemen redirect traffic; a camera from *Good Morning America* sweeps its lens across the aging crowd. They sit in white folding chairs with free cups of coffee, the shadows of Boom Town falling at their feet. The mayor will speak next, followed by Nancy, and then, finally, Greta. That's the order Cate fought for, and that's the order Cate got. *Greta*. From where Cate is standing, she can see her on the stage, seated quietly next to her mother. Hair blows across her cheek and, tucking it behind her ear, she glances down at the speech Cate has written for her, printed on three pages of thick white paper that are folded in her lap. Watching her, Cate feels a sudden rush of nerves. That speech is the best thing she's ever written. Greta better not fuck it up.

The wind shifts, taking the leaves along with it. In the sky above New Jersey, a horse loses its head.

"Tom," Cate says, "are you asking me out on a date?"

GRETA'S JUMPY, TIRED; SHE NEEDS to focus. Squinting, she searches the crowd for Xavier's face. It takes her a few minutes—there really are a lot of people—but eventually she finds him, standing next to a lamppost on West End Avenue. He's wearing a smart blue jacket and a Mets hat, and when Greta locks eyes with him he offers a wave. Greta smiles—sort of—and then turns to her left. A few feet away, the mayor is saying something about what Nancy has done for healthcare, and how innovation can happen *at any age*. She hears the words—she knows she understands them—but her brain can't seem to bring them into focus. Hanging her head, she stares at her lap: there, on one knee, is the speech that Cate has written for her, and on the other, her phone. *Two grenades*, she thinks, *both with a pin that's itching to be pulled.*

Yesterday, when she and Nancy returned from La Goulue, they kicked off their shoes in the foyer and left their coats on the floor in heaps like two fallen soldiers. Then they promptly passed out. Nancy made her way to her office, where she collapsed in her chair and laid her cheek on her desk. Greta got no farther than the living room couch. Four hours later when she awoke, the light outside had gone purple and she found her mother in the kitchen, groggy and repentant. Nick, who was nowhere to be found, had at some point set out a plate of cold chicken, some rice, two large bottles of radioactively blue Gatorade, and a handful of Advil. At the corner of the table, next to an empty saltshaker, he had also left them a message, written on a pad of paper that someone, at some point, had taken from the Sherry-Netherland Hotel. *Seems like you two had fun,* it said, in tight, caviling letters. *I hope this helps the hangover.*

Leaning over Nancy's shoulder, Greta scratched her nose, licked her lips, and read the note.

"Whatever," she said. "He's jealous we didn't invite him."

She went to her room and, locking the door behind her, exhaled, emptying her lungs for what felt like the first time all day. She recalled what Nancy had told her at the restaurant, of how her chin shook when she spoke: Greta trusted her, and then just as quickly, she didn't. She imagined a bit of green thread, dangling from the end of a spool—she imagined herself pulling it, and pulling it, only to find out the thread was never green but blue. Sitting down at her desk, she popped an Adderall, got to work: she opened the recording on her phone, isolated the moment she wanted, and then, using her forefinger, snipped it out on its own. Her eyes blurry, she squinted at the screen—all she would have to do is press play.

Now there's a tickle in her throat. The mayor finishes speaking, and as Greta glances at Nancy, she lets out a little cough. This is the problem with having a politician as a mother. You never know what to believe.

———

XAVIER'S PHONE BUZZES IN HIS coat pocket: it's Colette, calling for the fifth time today. He ignores her—he's been ignoring her since Wednesday— and instead gives Greta a small, conspiratorial wave. Soon she will walk up to the microphone and play the recording that she made of her mother. Jaws will drop open, and the audience will gasp—Xavier's been picturing it all morning. Greta's mother will stumble and stutter; she will try to take back the microphone as, in the rows of seats in front of her, small phones with even smaller cameras record the spectacle of her fall. Before she has time to realize what has happened, the video (as videos are wont to do) will have begun its ubiquitous spread, leaking like water from a tub, finding cracks and divots and eyes and minds that have until now gone untouched. Within the hour, news stations will be clamoring for explanations, interviews—with Greta, yes, but also with the genius who put her up to the task.

His phone rings again, and Xavier smiles: he's about to become a very famous man.

"AND YOU'RE SURE SHE SAW it?" Lisa asks Nick.

They're in their office at NYU, watching a livestream of Nancy speaking on Nick's computer. The picture stalls, then picks up again; for an instant Nancy is frozen, with Boom Town looming in the background and both of her arms in the air.

Pulling his collar back an inch, Nick points to the bruise on his neck.

He says, "It's the size of a silver dollar, Lisa, of course she saw it. Christ, I'm a full-grown man and I'm hiding hickeys from my mother."

"Good for you."

"Do you think my students noticed?"

A red water bottle covered with ACLU stickers sits at Lisa's feet. She reaches for it and unscrews its top.

"Oh, absolutely. They notice everything. But, hey, at least it's a pretty color."

Fixing his shirt, Nick returns to his screen, trying not to imagine the gossip that a group of pock-faced eighteen-year-olds are presently spreading about him. From his computer's speakers comes the tinny echo of his mother saying *responsibility*. He rests his chin on his fist.

"She looks good," Lisa says from behind him. "*Coiffed.*"

"She's actually wildly hungover."

"Well, you wouldn't know it." Smacking her lips, Lisa takes a sip of water and rolls her chair closer to Nick's. "What's the deal, anyway? She speaks, and then your sister goes?"

"That's the plan, from what I gather."

"Are you mad you aren't there? Do you feel like you're missing out?"

Nick shakes his head.

"I've gone to enough of these things to last a lifetime," he says. "And besides, I have class."

A podium and a small stage have been set up in front of Boom Town's entrance, and now the camera pans across it, sweeping from left to right. As it moves, it collects a trio of bodies—first the mayor, and then Nancy, and, finally, Greta, seated with her ankles crossed. Nick watches her as she shifts and fidgets. He thinks of yesterday morning when, after spying his hickey, his mother thanked him for a bunch of yellow freesias that he had never bought.

"Do you think she'll be good?" Lisa asks. "Like, do you think this will help your mom?"

For a moment Greta glances up, and then, upon seeing the camera, quickly lowers her head again.

There is, Nick realizes, something in her lap.

Tom sniffles once.

"Yeah, I guess that is what I'm doing. I guess I'm asking you out on a date," he says.

The wind picks up, blowing a crimson leaf into his chest. Cate brushes it away.

"That's a bold move," she says. "Asking your boss out on a date."

"Well, I'm a bold guy."

Cate smiles. High above her, an American flag chases its tail.

"Are you, though?" she asks. "Are you really bold?"

Tom considers the question, frowning at the ground.

"No, I guess not. But that doesn't change the fact that I'd like to take you to dinner."

Onstage, Nancy's speech barrels toward its end; she cracks a joke, something just short of funny, and a hundred baby boomers laugh. Soon, in a matter of seconds, she will introduce her daughter. Among flashing cameras and polite applause, Greta will walk to the podium.

Cate says, "I'll make a deal with you, Tom Cooper. If we win this thing, I'll let you take me wherever you want."

GRETA OPENS HER HANDS AND stares at her palms. Moisture glistens in their creases.

She thinks: *What if Nancy hadn't been lying, but rather protecting Greta from the truth? And what if Greta had simply done the thing that children do and mistaken her mother's love for cruelty?* She closes her eyes and slaps her palms shut. Somewhere in the back of her mind she can feel one domino tip over, and then a hundred more. They tumble around corners and collapse in elaborate spirals, and in the blur of black and white she sees the glimmer of an explanation. She had desperately wanted to feel like she belonged to someone, which had led her to believe in something preposterous. It's a theory that's not outside the realm of possibility—in fact, it's squarely within it. After all, people are convinced of lies all the time. Children by Santa Claus, idiots by the internet, and—now—Greta by Eugenia. Her pulse quickens and she worries she'll vomit—who decided to make trust such a fragile thing?

The dominoes continue to fall, one into another, and somewhere within the din of all their crashing she hears her mother, calling her name. At first she thinks she's imagining things, but then the world rushes back to her, flooding her eyes and filling her ears: Nancy is *actually* calling her name. She's staring at her from the podium from where she's been speaking, and she's saying *Greta* over and over again. A nervous smile creeps across Nancy's face, and her eye twitches; along her hairline hang tiny beads of sweat.

Blinking, Greta slips her phone into her pocket and feels herself rising from her seat. It's her turn, she realizes. She's on.

XAVIER STANDS UP STRAIGHTER AND readies the camera on his phone—twenty yards in front of him, Greta is walking across the stage. She moves slowly, and when she hugs her mother, he notices that her arms are shaking. Smiling wanly, she steadies herself at the podium, her fingers wrapped around its edges. She coughs once and wets her lips; Xavier zooms in. On his phone's screen, he sees Greta's pixelated hand unfold three sheets of pixelated paper. He hears her say, "I'm here today to talk about forgiveness," and, ever so slightly, he frowns.

This is not what was supposed to happen.

"Wow," LISA SAYS, "SHE'S LIKE Eva Perón."

Nick grins. For the first time since Greta began speaking five minutes ago, he takes a proper breath.

"Eva Perón was a fascist, Lisa."

"You know what I mean. She's, like, *really* good."

Nick offers no response—not because he disagrees but because he's speechless. On this shitty, NYU-issued laptop, he has watched his sister transform. The change wasn't instantaneous; on the contrary, the beginning was mildly concerning. Greta stumbled over her words and often lost her place. She couldn't land on a rhythm. About a minute in, though, something clicked. Her spine straightened and her shoulders pulled back and her voice—where did it come from, that golden voice!—developed an orator's cadence. Nick was spellbound: here was his younger sister, speaking so eloquently about sacrifice and unity and affordable prescription drugs that, for an instant, he was sure he'd weep.

"I want to learn how to talk like that." Leaning forward on her elbows, Lisa sighs. "Like, when I'm explaining how to use a semicolon to my freshmen, I want to sound like Greta Harrison."

Nick scratches the back of his head. Surprised, and more than a little proud, he laughs.

He says, "Yeah. Me too."

THE CROWD'S CLAPPING IS A wall of thunder, and the world spins at a dizzying pace. Greta gazes out at the hundreds of smiling faces and feels herself smiling back. Then she leans over to her mother and says that she's going to be sick.

"You and me both, pal," Nancy whispers. "I can still taste that Sancerre."

"No, Mom, I'm serious. I think I—"

"Okay, okay." Nancy is still smiling, still waving. "You've done your duty. Go home and get yourself an Alka-Seltzer."

Greta begins to walk away, then spins on her heels and throws her arms around Nancy's neck. This startles Nancy—Greta can feel her shoulders tense, and then with each successive breath relax. Greta holds her for another few moments—long enough to hear another round of applause, to give the photographers time to get their pictures. Once she's released her, she smiles at the crowd again. She gives a shallow curtsy and turns toward home.

La Vie en Rose

The city returns to Greta in bursts: grease-soaked air outside Gray's Papaya; the brownstones set aflame in the brassy October light. On the corner of Seventy-Fourth and Columbus, a driver spills coffee on the hood of his cab. One block north, a cyclist gives the finger to a double-parked van. Here, outside of Zucker's Bagels, is where she smoked her first cigarette, and there, on the steps of the New-York Historical Society, is where she sat when she broke her ankle. She was chasing something—a ball? No, that's right, a Frisbee—when her foot got caught in a divot and down she went. She'd cried and looped her arm around her brother's shoulder, and together they hobbled to the Historical Society. He ran home, and when he returned he had Nancy, her glasses set on her head, a cardigan half on. There was the hospital, a doctor, a cast. Pink? No—red. A boot the color of summer that all her friends took a turn to sign.

A siren echoes down Amsterdam Avenue, and Greta feels it rattling her soul. She laughs, a little nervously: what the *fuck* had she been thinking? She had allowed a lie, told by a bitter old woman, to explain away her loneliness; she had cast herself as a victim because it was easier than the truth. A few feet away, a pigeon inspects the underside of a leaf and abandons it as Greta approaches; across the street, a woman with a scythe-shaped back admonishes her Maltese. It's her mother's neighbor Mrs. Branovich and her awful dog, Helen. Greta watches them for a moment, considers waving, and then turns away. The park is in front of her; the

Hudson is behind her. In the sky over Manhattan, chimeric clouds swell and contract.

From the sliver left between two lace curtains a cat peers at her. Greta stares back and comes up with a plan. She'll destroy the recordings on her phone and tell Xavier that they're through. She had a nice time with him—mostly—but the fact is that hearts can change, and Greta's, as of about seventeen minutes ago, has done just that. Her next boyfriend might not have an apartment on the Seine, or luscious brown hair, but he will believe in climate change and basic human decency, and for Greta, that will be more than enough. She will love him because she loves him—not because she hates her mother—and when she looks into his eyes, she won't be reminded of the terrible thing she almost did.

And how *did* she almost do it? The only explanation is that the girl in Paris was someone else, someone who was not really her. A lost two months whose existence can only be explained by a simulacrum, or sickness. Yes—that's it. *Sickness.* A year ago she had believed the conspiracies her grandmother had told her, which had primed her for this—a virus that had infected Greta's body and filled her with nothing but contempt. It seeped into her blood and dripped into her lungs and bored tiny, hate-filled holes through her brain. But now she is on the rebound, she is recovering. Her breathing is steady and those little hate-filled holes are scabbing over with reason and rationality. And in the meantime, she has concluded that the fate of the country should not be a casualty in her exercise of petty revenge.

Seventy-Fourth Street collides with Central Park West. On the other side of the street is a thicket of half-naked trees, their branches cutting away swaths of sky. Greta turns north, toward the entrance of the San Marino. One step, two steps, three steps. The first drops of rain pelt the tips of her ears, and a hand reaches out to grab her shoulder.

"Xavier," Greta says. "You scared me."

"What is this bullshit!"

His cheeks are shaking and sweat shines on his forehead. He's still wearing his blue wool coat and the Mets hat, and his free hand—the one that is not squeezing Greta's shoulder—is curled into a fist.

She frees herself. All across New York, black umbrellas bloom.

"What bullshit? Were you following me? And Jesus Christ, stop yelling. I'm right here."

"The bullshit that has happened with your mother! Greta, what have you done!"

"Nothing. I've done nothing, and that's the point. I don't want to do this anymore."

"I do not understand."

The wind shifts; the rain lashes. Greta reaches down to button her coat.

"I'm saying that I don't want to be part of this anymore, okay? I'm out."

"You cannot do that to me. That is not how this works."

"What do you mean I *cannot do that to you*? I just did. Thanks for letting me crash in Paris, and et cetera, but *c'est terminé*. It's over."

A taxi speeds up Central Park West and waves curl beneath its tires. Shadows evaporate; leaves disintegrate; Xavier wipes his forehead with the back of his wrist.

"You don't mean that," he says. "You love me too deeply. And I have shown you too much."

"Yes, that is correct. You have shown me how to blame other people and not take responsibility for myself. And in the hands of a white girl from the Upper West Side who doesn't have student debt, that's an ideology that I think we can both agree has proven itself to be particularly destructive. Now, if you'll excuse me, I'm getting wet."

Xavier reaches down and clasps his hand around her wrist.

"What am I supposed to do, Greta?"

His eyes are saucers, the irises shrunken to cruel, blue dots. Is he asking her a question, or baiting her with a threat?

She says: "Let go of me."

"*What am I supposed to do?*"

"Fuck, Xavier, why are you asking me? Go make France fascist. Brainwash some other needy idiot. Bake a loaf of sourdough. Whatever it is, leave me out of it."

Greta rips her hand away and looks down: his nails have left red tracks across her skin.

XAVIER WATCHES HER, JOGGING THROUGH the rain toward the San Marino. She pulls her coat over her head and—without so much as a glance back—disappears inside. His anger spins cyclones, right between his eyes; also, he is soaking wet. His shoes, his trousers, his belt. His shirt, his coat, his hair. *His hair.* A swell that was once perpetually cresting now crashes (limp, lifeless) under his hat.

Clouds sink down, hiding the city's spires, and rain continues making wreckage of the morning. From behind him, Xavier hears three sharp *tsk*s and turns to see a woman walking a Maltese. It's an ornery dog, with white, matted hair: when it passes Xavier it nips at his ankles and then it turns up its nose to bark at the sky. The woman is oblivious. She lets the beast dart across the sidewalk while she struggles with two bags of groceries. Ten yards from the San Marino, she is spotted by the doorman, a grotesquely tall individual with a sloped chin who rushes from his post to unload her of the bags before they tear in two. He is not fast enough: there's a wet ripping sound, and cans of soup roll to the curb. What happens next happens quickly. The dog zooms left, zooms right, then stops dead in its tracks, its eyes glued to a spot across the street, where a squirrel has taken shelter beneath an American elm. They stare at each other: they know what the future holds, and now it's a matter of who makes the first move. The squirrel does—it dashes into the park and the Maltese, jerking its leash free from its owner's hand, takes to the street after it.

The woman screams; an Uber screeches; the valiant doorman abandons a can of New England clam chowder.

Along Central Park West, a crowd gathers and gawks.

Xavier slips into the San Marino, and no one is the wiser.

GRETA'S RIGHT HEEL SLIPS ON the wet floor. Regaining her balance, she strides onward, her footsteps echoing. The lobby is empty; near the elevators an empty settee plays audience for a single white orchid. She presses the up button and looks at her reflection, gilded by the doors. She is feeling good, and light, buoyed by her determination to start her life again. She will get a new job and find a new apartment, one where she can't hear dogs working out their daily dramas, and where her roommate doesn't shave her head in the living room. She will clean herself up: stop smoking, stop drinking, stop gaming, start meditating. Breathe in, breathe out, breathe in. She will become one of those people she sees on the subway: eyes placidly closed, lips curved in a tranquil smile. Instead of resenting everyone around her, she will help them. Doors will be held open, seats will be graciously offered, long-standing injustices will be made right. The world is already burning—it doesn't need Greta Harrison fanning the flames. She will leach out all of her bad blood. She will clear herself of this virus.

A taxi screeches and blares its horn; the elevator chimes and Greta steps into it. She grins and wipes some rain from her cheek, and waits for the doors to close. They do, but too slowly: Xavier slips between them the moment before they touch.

"What the actual fuck, Xavier."

He's soggy, feeble. His cheeks are sallow, and from beneath his hat strands of wet hair are plastered to his forehead. His lips, which three months ago Greta wanted nothing more than to kiss, have been drained of their color. How, she wonders, had she ever found him attractive?

"We are not finished speaking."

"No, but we are, though. We are very much finished speaking."

His eyes dart to Greta's hand, still clutching her phone.

"Then give me that," he says.

"You're insane. You have actually gone insane. There is no way in hell that I am giving you my phone."

"If you do not have the courage to go through with this, then I will."

The elevator stops moving: they've arrived on the seventh floor. Greta sprints to her mother's apartment. Her hands are trembling, and her fingers slick with sweat, and for a moment she fumbles with the keys. But then, *there*: the satisfying *thump* of a lock tumbling open; the give of hinges allowed, finally, to flex. The door swings open, just as she feels Xavier's breath, hot and quick against her cheek.

XAVIER CLOSES THE DOOR, LOCKS it, and barricades it with his body. He stares at Greta, his chest heaving, and then follows her into the living room. His eyes consume the apartment, drinking in the vase of yellow freesias, her father's sword, a mantel crowded with framed photos. Nick balanced on Howard's shoulders, his face smeared with ice cream; Greta's cheek pressed against her mother's, the background a blur of red and orange. A half-empty cup of coffee cools on a side table, and piled on one end of the sofa are pages from this morning's *New York Times*. She watches him take it all in and feels the shame of her betrayal: he is in her family's home; he has infected this space.

"You need to leave." Greta slips her phone into the back pocket of her jeans. "Like, right now."

He takes a step toward her. Then he bangs his shin against the coffee table, says *merde*, and reaches down to rub it.

When he rights himself, he takes off his coat and hat and throws them on the sofa. He says, "I don't think you understand what is happening, my little American cabbage. You belong to me. You have belonged to me since you first decided to speak to me. You may think that you can forget about me, Greta, but you can't. Love is a very insidious thing."

"I don't love you anymore, all right? I don't know if I ever did."

"No? Then perhaps you can tell me why we are standing here. Perhaps you can tell me why you threw a champagne bottle in Paris."

"Because I was stupid, and selfish. Because I was angry at Nancy."

"People do not do the things you have done simply because they are angry at their mothers."

"People also do a lot worse because they are angry at their mothers."

This time making sure to avoid the coffee table, Xavier takes another step toward Greta.

"May I tell you what is going to happen?" he says.

"No, actually, you may not."

"You are going to come with me. There will be no more arguments or fights. We will walk out the door, and we will take the elevator to the ground floor, and you will hail us a taxi to take us to Fox News so we can give them that recording."

"Fox News? You are out of your goddamn *mind* if you think I'm going to Midtown."

He continues to move toward Greta, each step slow and deliberate: a tightrope walk, with nowhere left to fall. She backs away from him, traversing the living room until she can feel her spine colliding with a credenza. A picture topples over; the frame cracks. At Greta's feet there is a jagged shard of glass, cutting her brother's face in half.

When Xavier speaks again, his lips brush against her ear. He walks his fingers down Greta's spine and plucks her phone from her pocket.

"Then I will be taking this. I've given you every opportunity to be a part of something important, Greta. I came with you here, to America, a country of very friendly people with very weak minds, so that we could do something together."

"That's bullshit. I don't think you ever cared about me."

Backing away a few inches, Xavier looks at the device and, frowning a little, pouts his lips.

"No," he says. "I suppose you're right. But don't let that bother you, my sardine—you were very useful nonetheless. And your French! I must say, you've improved immensely. You forget the *subjonctif* only sometimes, and your pronunciation of *écureil* is *parfait*. Now, remind me, with this thing, your password is still *G-R-E-T-A*, correct? And once I unlock it, all I have to do is press play? You know me with technology."

He tosses the phone up once, catches it, and taps it on Greta's forehead. She freezes. It's not that she's unable to move, but rather that she can't think clearly enough to decide which move to make. Her limbs have the sensation of being multiplied; instead of two arms she now has four, each of them tingling. Panic swells in her throat; she's unable to swallow. She tries forcing down the reality bearing down on her and focuses instead on the minutiae that surround it. The sound of rain as it pellets the window. The pale blue of a scarf, worn by a woman she passed on West Seventy-Third. Airplanes over Queens; ferries on the East River;

tulips in springtime, coloring the center of Park Avenue. Life exists outside this moment, she just needs to get through this moment to live it. Her nails dig into her palms, and her forearms ache: she didn't realize she'd had them clenched.

Xavier turns and, unfurling her fingers, Greta reaches behind her, grappling blindly around the credenza. Objects collide with her touch: the face of another picture frame, a bowl with nothing in it, and—*there*— the carved ivory hilt of her father's old sword. With a gravelly roar that ends as quickly as it begins, Greta whips it in front of her. The scabbard flies away and sinks between two couch cushions, where it stands erect as a birthday candle. She looks at the steel, the polished edge: she's never been allowed to touch the sword, and it's lighter than she ever could have imagined. This fact surprises her. Once, at a shooting range in New Jersey, she'd fired four rounds from a Glock G17 and was reassured by how heavy the weapon was in her hand; objects that were deadly, like guns, deserved a deadly weight. But the sword feels slight, delicate, even. She'd forget that she was holding it if she weren't staring at its blade.

"Oh, Greta." Xavier clicks his tongue. "Put that toy away."

"Give me back my fucking phone."

Xavier's chin sinks to his chest. He shakes his head.

"Greta, this is not a *movie*, this is real life. Women like you do not go around stabbing men like me with silly little swords. I'm being very serious right now, my shrimp, you need to put that down. It's vulgar, the way you're holding it, and you're embarrassing yourself."

The rain weakens to a silent drizzle. Greta lowers her arms.

"That's what I thought. All the way down. *Alllll* the way, Greta." He nods. His hair is beginning to dry. "*Bon*. Good girl. Now, I'll be leaving, my flea, and I will be taking this phone with me. I suspect that once your mother has found out what you've done and has lost her election I won't be seeing you again; it's a pity, isn't it? I truly feel that had she and I met we would have understood each other. Well, *tant pis*, as they say. That's life." Xavier grins and buttons his coat. The monkeys carved into the sword's hilt gnaw on Greta's fingers. "In the meantime, adieu, my pussycat. Watch for me tomorrow on Fox News, I'll make sure to blow you a kiss."

Above the Empire State Building, the clouds give an inch while the sun takes a mile.

On the seventh floor of the San Marino, Greta sinks her father's sword into Xavier's back.

A jaw opens, a heart stops. A gorgeous gash of blood paints yellow freesias red.

ELECT NANCY HARRISON!

Pulse Check

"Xavier?"

She says his name quietly, her voice a breath above a whisper. On the windows behind her, drying raindrops color the light.

He doesn't answer. He doesn't even move. A red patch thickens on the back of his shirt. Her head woozy, Greta says his name again:

"*Xavier.*"

She looks around her. Two toppled picture frames, a cold cup of coffee, some couch cushions askew. And also: blood. Tainting the sword, polka-dotting the freesias, staining her mother's afghan rug.

Her mother's afghan rug.

"Fuck," Greta says, dropping to her knees. "Fuck, fuck, fuck, fuck, *fuck.*"

She spits on her hands and scrubs, rubbing her fingers against the wool until they feel blistered, raw. Her mother brought the rug back from Kabul—it had cost her a fortune. Should she use baking soda? Seltzer and salt? Carpet cleaner? She's covered in sweat but her skin prickles; she's breathless, though when she inhales she feels like there's no room in her lungs. She scrubs more, she scrubs harder. The rug is red—the same color, nearly, as the blood that's soaking into it. Maybe her mother won't notice. Maybe she'll walk into the apartment, step over the body, pick up the felled picture frame, and ask Greta to find her a broom.

The body. Two arms, two legs, two feet with their toes turned out. A ballerina, in second position, waiting for instructions at the barre. A head—or a face, more like it—smashed into the other side of the carpet.

His hair—wow, it's back to being gorgeous. Shiny, full, dry after the rain. Greta reaches out to touch it and, with her hand two inches from Xavier's neck, she scrambles backward, pressing her shoulders against the credenza.

Is he—? She says his name louder, and then louder. Kneeling down again, she crawls across the carpet and puts two fingers against his neck. His skin is a little cold, and a little clammy, but then it's also a little cold and clammy outside. What she's feeling for is a pulse. Is this how she's supposed to find it? By searching to the left of his Adam's apple? She doesn't know; she's suddenly forgotten everything. She couldn't tell a person how she'd go about finding signs of her own heart, even now, when she can hear it, thumping in her ears. She presses her fingers deeper into his skin. He doesn't move; she doesn't feel anything. On the back of his shirt, the red spot grows.

A car honks its horn on Central Park West, and it's the loudest sound that Greta has ever heard. Leaping to her feet, she grabs the sword off the floor and readies it again. But then—silence. An eerie quiet that is broken when, finally, she raggedly exhales. The room comes into focus, and her thoughts lock together. She killed him. He's dead. And not fake dead. Not he-will-suddenly-suck-in-a-monstrous-breath-and-stagger-to-his-feet dead. But actually dead. Really, really dead. He will stay there, bleeding out on her mother's carpet, until either he has no blood left or someone moves him. Her wrists spasm, the blade trembles. From the hilt the monkeys grins up at her and—gasping—she drops the sword.

Her fingerprints. They're everywhere. Smeared across the ivory hilt like ink. Her eyes dart around the room again: she sees them on doorknobs, on his hat and coat, on picture frames, on elevator buttons. She tries to think, but her mind runs away from her, feral and wild. He had come at her, right? He had threatened her, and charged at her like he wanted her dead, and in that moment she had given herself over entirely to instinct. Adrenaline flooded her veins. Her tongue swelled and her vision softened; colors drained, then coalesced. It seemed like a second, but also like an hour. When she snapped out of it, there Xavier was, sprawled out on the floor, and there the sword was, dripping in her hand. She dropped it, letting it clang against the floor. She cupped both hands against her face and said *shit* into them more times than she could count and then she reached for her phone to call the police. She—

No. She murdered him. That's what happened. Xavier told her that he would blow her a kiss from the news, and that ignited something in her. A fuse—the shortest one in history. She saw, for the first time, that the maze he had led her into had only one escape. He turned away from her, and as he went she saw going with him her future, her family's future, the life that she was an inch away from regaining. Lunging forward, she pierced the blade's tip straight through his back. The sword was sharp; the job was easy. A finger, poking into one of those little plastic cups of Jell-O she used to eat as a kid. He let out a gasp, and Greta pulled the blade out, pleased with herself. But then he fell, and the first plumes of blood appeared on the back of his shirt and formed little pools on her mother's afghan carpet. She looked at the stained freesias and—this part is the same—cupped her hands over her mouth and started saying *shit*.

She has to call someone: there is a dead French fascist lying in her living room. Her fingers find their way to her waist, to her pocket, to her phone. Instinctively, she presses 9-1-1.

But then she catches herself. She dials her mother instead.

"Mom," she says once Nancy picks up. "You need to come home. Like, right now."

"How to Get Rid of a Body"

Tom screams.

Cate stares.

Nancy reaches behind her and quickly locks the door.

She has seen a dead body before—she needs to stop trembling. Howard, after his accident, on a flimsy hospital bed. A white sheet pulled up to shield his broken limbs, a deep red cut traversing his forehead. *Is this your husband? Yes, it is, or technically, it was.* Those moments were anticipated: she had prepared herself for death—she knew, the second the police called her, before they said *Mrs. Harrison, we have some bad news,* she knew—and so she was ready to stare it in the face. The setting helped: in each of those memories, the body was where it was supposed to be, cordoned off by emergency room walls, oak caskets, dirges, grief. This one is different. This one she is not prepared for. The body is in her living room.

Her voice barely a whisper, she says, "Greta, you need to tell me exactly what happened."

"Well—" Greta starts, stops, starts again. Sentences lack nouns, and sometimes verbs; the Frenchman on the floor is reduced to a string of crude adjectives. Sun floods the living room, bright and fresh from the rain, and Nancy steps over a lifeless leg to close the curtains. Tom sits on the couch, then stands again; his face is the color of leeks. Words keep coming, Greta keeps going, and between them Nancy latches onto the thread of a plot. Deceit, black eyes, and a Louis XIV sofa. Salads at La Goulue and the voice memos app on an old iPhone: a Trojan horse, in the form of a repentant daughter and three bottles of Sancerre. The plan is elaborate and well reasoned. Nancy would be impressed were she not its target. Were there not a man bleeding out on a rug she bought in Kabul.

She says, "So you were recording me—"

Greta wipes her nose.

"Yes. At lunch."

"What did I say?"

"That your life would be a lot easier if all those boomers would hurry up and die."

Cate closes her eyes, and Tom begins pacing. The color still hasn't returned to his face.

"He's staring at me, Cate," he says. "Oh my fuck, he's *staring* at me."

"He's dead, Tom. Greta here stabbed him. He's not staring at anyone."

Howard's sword is on the floor. Nancy looks at it, the unstained parts of the steel reflecting slices of the ceiling, but she doesn't pick it up. "Greta, where is this recording now?"

Greta presses the heels of her palms against her eyes. Then, removing them, she blinks. She takes a deep breath.

"It's still on my phone."

Cate says, "Delete it. Immediately."

Greta's fingers move quickly: a screen is unlocked, an application is opened, a thumb resolutely swipes to the left. On the other end of the couch, Tom says *uh-oh* and rushes to the bathroom.

"Good." Nancy takes Greta's phone and slips it into her purse. "Any-where else?"

"No." Greta shakes her head. But then: "Or, yes, actually. I loaded it onto a thumb drive for backup. It's shaped like a ladybug and it's on my desk. I—"

Nancy doesn't wait to hear the rest. She goes to her daughter's room, finds the drive, and takes it to the bathroom. She thinks for a moment, and then she walks to the toilet. She'll flush it, she decides. Send it through the sewers like an unlucky goldfish. Bringing her hand above the bowl, she shakes the drive, prepares to open her fingers, and . . . stops herself. She thinks of a rumor she heard, six years back. A tight race in North

Carolina, where an incumbent's opponent got the upper hand by having her aides sift through the trash. She looks at ladybug again. She pops it in her mouth and swallows it.

Turning on the faucet, she begins washing her hands, scrubbing at her palms and beneath her fingernails with enough soap to coat her skin in a thick lather. She would say that she's surprised, that she didn't know that Greta had it in her, but that would be a lie. Greta has always had it in her—it's only that, until now, Nancy hadn't been sure what *it* was. Her hands are already clean, but she keeps washing them, anyway—she needs something to focus her mind. She thinks of that French boy's face sinking deeper into her carpet. Does—did?—he have a mother? Of course he did. Everyone has a mother, most of all monsters. What would she do, that monster's mother, if the tables were turned? If she came home and found Greta, lifeless, on her floor?

She considers the options in front of her. Concessions, compromises, consequences: she's good at weighing intangibles. It's how her mind works, how she's trained it to function. Never vote on a bill without reading it first, always think through the What Happens Nexts. She could call the police. She could explain what her daughter did, abide by the law that she's sworn to uphold, hope for some approximation of the best.

Her hands burn; her fingers feel raw. Shutting off the faucet, she fixes her hair in the bathroom's mirror. A drop of water hangs from the faucet's edge.

Police, laws, approximations. She won't be doing any of that. She's known what she was going to do the moment she walked in the door. Options—*ha.* What options? Better to focus on the facts. A dead neo-Nazi is on her floor; a hole is in his back; her daughter's fingerprints are on a bloody sword. There's also an election four days away, waiting for Nancy to swoop in and win it. Her hands are dripping—she needs a towel. She searches and, unable to find one, wipes her hands on her pants instead. She thinks: *Sometimes you're granted the luxury of a choice. Other times, you've got to make do with imperatives.*

When she returns to the living room, Tom is seated on the edge of the sofa. His lips are dry, and sweat shines on his forehead.

"Feel better?" she asks.

He wipes something from the corner of his mouth.

"I think we should call the police. Christ, Nancy, you're supposed to be on MSNBC with Andrea Mitchell in two hours and there's a *dead man* in your living room!"

Greta steps forward, tripping over one of Xavier's shoes. She whispers *shit* and steps back again.

"But they'll arrest me," she says. "They'll charge me with murder."

"No." Tom shakes his head, slowly at first, and then with increased vigor. "We'll reason with them. People are *reasonable*. We'll explain the circumstances, and we'll say that you were defending yourself."

"It'll be all over the internet within an hour."

"Maybe, but at least we won't be in *prison*."

Cate looks at Greta; Greta looks at Nancy; Nancy looks at the blood, drying on Xavier's back.

She says, "No one is getting arrested, and no one is calling the police."

Outside, a neighbor's voice ricochets down the hall, and everyone freezes. Clouds inch across the sky, and the freesias wither in their vase. The voice fades. Nancy's shoulders relax.

"What exactly are you proposing then?" Tom whispers.

Nancy doesn't answer him. She pinches her chin and squints at Xavier: he's smaller than she thought he would be. She wonders how much he weighs.

"Cate?" she says, her eyes still on the ground. "I would never ask you to do something to—"

But Cate is already pulling her hair back into a ponytail. Cate is already rolling up her sleeves.

"I know, Nancy," she says. "Give me a second to think."

Tom watches them both with widening eyes.

He says, "Oh my God. Oh my God, oh my God, oh my God."

His cheeks quiver, along with his fingers and his thighs. Every part of him, Nancy sees, convulses with anxious tremors.

"Thomas." She grabs one of his shoulders and gives it a good shake. "I didn't raise two children on my own to see one of them end up in jail for killing a Nazi, do you hear me? And *we* didn't live through the fucking *Trump* administration to come this far and fail."

Tom breathes deeply, closes his eyes, and exhales; Nancy smells the coffee he drank an hour earlier. He begins counting quietly but doesn't quite make it to ten; when he's between seven and eight there's another sound, this one coming from Nancy's purse.

"What was that?" he asks.

"It's my phone."

"*Fuck*. It's Andrea Mitchell, isn't it."

Nancy looks at the screen. "No, Tom. It's my son."

"Shit!"

Greta turns around and walks toward the window, her hands curled at her sides.

"Are you going to tell him," she says. "Are you going to tell him I killed someone?"

The phone continues its ringing, buzzing against Nancy's palm. *Is she going to tell him?* For three decades Nancy has worked in politics, and never before has the line between innocent and complicit seemed so stark. On one side of it is a ruined rug, a dead body, and four terrified faces; on the other, her oblivious son. With a single sentence she could change all that—she could certainly use his help—or she could do her duty as a mother and protect him with a lie.

Her grip tightening on the phone, she tries telling herself that things could be worse. The campaign could still be four points behind.

"No one's going to tell Nick anything. We're going to fix this on our own. Cate, get those freesias out of here, and Tom—you move him to the bathroom." She clears her throat. "And for the love of God, no one google 'how to get rid of a body.'"

Comeback Kids

Nick Harrison stares at his computer, where eight different windows are open on his browser. The first seven contain articles about Greta that have been published in the last hour; the last one has real estate listings for rentals in Los Angeles. He flips between them quickly, seamlessly, his finger dashing across the mouse pad: CNN, then a bungalow in Los Feliz; the *Times*, followed by a one-bedroom in Hancock Park. Behind him a radiator clanks and Nick slips off his blazer: in two minutes, he knows, his office will be ninety degrees.

Swiveling away from the computer, he reaches for his phone and dials his mother. One ring turns into four, and when he's about to give up, Nancy answers.

"Nick. Hello."

She sounds breathless, he thinks. *Excited.*

"Mom! That was incredible."

"Greta did well, didn't she?"

"*Well?* She was a fucking star!" In the background Nick hears a loud thump. The sound of something heavy colliding with the floor. "What was that?" he asks.

"A bag of mulch."

"Mulch?"

"We're in the garden. At Boom Town. They're planting some perennials and Japanese maples. I stayed to help. A little volunteer work."

"Oh. Well, that was nice of you." Nick scratches at a coffee stain on his desk and rotates back around to his computer. "Did you see what they said in the *Post*?"

"No. What was it? Actually, Nick, give me one second."

The line is muted and, with the phone still pressed against his shoulder, Nick takes the opportunity to shuffle through the open tabs until he finds the right window. "Tragedy in Queens," "A Date with Lady Larceny," "Education: Friend or Foe?"—he reads through headlines until he finds his mother's name. He wants to get this right.

"'Comeback Kid Helps Harrison Seal the Deal,'" he reads aloud once Nancy has returned.

"That's perfect."

"It's more than perfect—it's the nail in Carmichael's coffin. You're going to win this thing, Mom. You're going to be a US senator." There's another thud, this one followed by some ambient grunting. "Is everything okay over there?"

"What? Oh, yes. They're having some trouble with this maple." Nancy sneezes. "Actually, I should get back to these folks. They're, uh, knee-deep in soil, and I'm supposed to be on MSNBC with Andrea Mitchell in an hour. But hey—Nick?"

"Yeah?"

"Why don't you take the weekend off. I'll make sure to keep an eye on Greta—you go do something fun."

Nick scratches his neck: fun doesn't sound so bad.

"Are you sure? I mean, I'm happy to come by tonight if—"

"*NO*," his mother shouts, and Nick moves the phone an inch from his ear. "Sorry—no. You've been such an enormous help already. Why don't you spend some time with that boy Greta says you've been seeing? Go to dinner, or the park, or Florida."

The radiator clanks again—*did she say Florida?*—and, with heat spiraling off his neck, Nick feels himself blush: he hadn't known that Nancy knew about Charlie.

"Actually, Mom," he says, "while we're on the subject, there's something I wanted to talk to you about."

"Can it wait? This maple's about to crush someone."

Outside, a student shuffles past Nick's office, the hood of a pink sweatshirt cocooning her face.

"Sure," he says. "How about I come up on Monday night. I'll bring Chinese food. We'll have an election eve dinner and watch the news."

"Lo mein and Wolf Blitzer. Sounds delightful."

"Great, I'll be there around—"

Six. He doesn't get it out, though, because suddenly the line goes dead. His mother is gone, and so are the indistinguishable noises in the background, the grunts and thuds, the buzz of other voices. The phone still cradled in his palm, Nick stares at the darkened screen.

Damned Spots

Xavier had been dripping when they carried him, his body melting tiny red droplets that now mark a path between the couch and the bathroom. *They're like exploding stars,* Greta thinks, *or beetles squashed by a bike: bits of something that used to be but isn't anymore.* In her right hand she holds a rag, and in the left a bucket filled with bleach and a little hydrogen peroxide. Greta had warned her mother that the mixture could be dangerous—once, in high school chemistry, she'd almost lit the lab on fire by sloshing the two substances together. Nancy didn't listen to her; she said bleach wasn't enough to get rid of the DNA, and to move back. Greta stood still. She watched as, with gloves covering her rings, Nancy spooned the peroxide into the bucket. It was like she'd done this before.

Now, lowering to her knees, Greta dips the rag into the solution, listens to it fizz, and starts scrubbing at the first of the red splotches. A moment later she hears a splash: Nancy tossing the contents of her own bucket onto the rug, draining it of its color, bleaching the fibers a jack-o'-lantern orange. Greta listens and scrubs harder.

She killed someone. She keeps thinking about what it feels like, but if someone were to ask her, she doesn't know what she'd tell them. A nightmare, wrapped in a dream, buried in another nightmare—that'd be one place to start. Her thoughts are sluggish, and then wildly alert; her arms will not stop shaking. She's had other indescribable experiences before—

the first time she did mushrooms; losing her father; falling in love—but with each of those she finally found the words. However late, a vocabulary came to her, one that tied the ephemeral to the concrete, the abstract to the real. She suspects this time will be different. She suspects that years from now she will wake up in the middle of the night, surrounded by either bars or windows, trying once again to articulate how it felt. How it feels. Some parts of her life will never be past tense. This is one of them.

Walking on her knees, she moves on to the next spot, and then the next one. The blood's still wet, so it comes up easily; within forty-five minutes she makes it to the bathroom. His body's still there. His right arm hangs over the lip of the bathtub, and his head droops lifeless to his chest. For a moment Greta does nothing, and then she reaches out to squeeze the tips of his fingers. They're cool, and a little too pale; she holds them for longer than she's comfortable. Then she returns to her work and performs it with a single-minded vigor, picking up the rag and rolling up her sleeves. Her nostrils burn and her head hurts. She ignores it. She keeps going.

Her breath becomes uneven and her heart claws at her chest; she is starting to panic. She thinks of the probability of a single life occurring— the infinitesimally small chance that any of us are here. She thinks of all the memories and regrets, the dreams and desires that she has—with a sword—cut short. Her fingers cramp; she scrubs harder. It's hard enough being a sister and a daughter and a friend and unemployed—she can't be a murderer, too. How far does she have to rewind to take it back, what decisions does she have to undo? She tries to focus on that: the parallel chain of events in which her hands are clean. She does not stab Xavier, which means she does not reach for the sword. She does not speak to him on Central Park West, or meet him at a bar downtown, or allow him to convince her to come back to New York. Her eye is free from self-inflicted bruises; her passport has no recent French stamps. When Nancy asks her to behave herself at dinner she does as she's told, and she doesn't squander her rent money building a digitized, nostalgic world. Also: she doesn't listen to her grandmother. She's able to see the truth for what it is.

Sitting back for a moment, she takes a break and cracks her neck. From the living room her mother calls—she says, *Greta, get in here*—and at first, Greta does nothing. Then she drops the rag into the bucket, stands, and cracks her knuckles. Imagining other lives is pointless. Fate is inescapable when she considers it in retrospect.

Good Housekeeping

The trash room's walls are eggshell and still smell like wet paint. Opening the door to the chute, Nancy takes the apple core she brought with her and tosses it inside. She closes her eyes and holds a finger to her lips, listening as the fruit bounces off the new, steel walls. Seconds later it collides with the bottom. Silence follows, and then a gentle growl: the dutiful cranking of the compactor's gears.

"So." She turns to Greta, Tom, and Cate. "What do you think?"

Stepping forward, Greta peers into the chute. Her bruise is translucent in the light.

"You really think it's strong enough?"

"Absolutely." Nancy gives a single, resolute nod. "It can crush an oven."

"It's true," Cate says, "I've seen the video."

Greta blinks at her. "Who would throw an oven down there?"

"Who would throw a body?"

The light flickers, the gears quiet. Greta leans an inch further into the chute, and then peels herself back. She frowns and stares at the floor, and then abruptly leaves the trash room. Nancy follows, beckoning Tom and Cate along. Once they're all inside the apartment, she closes and locks the door. Inside, the rug is gone; the living room is spotless. Pillows sit fluffed on the sofa and a cashmere blanket hangs on the back of a nearby chair. There's no broken picture frames, no freesias, no blood—only Louis Armstrong, playing on a speaker in the corner. Nancy lifts her chin and sniffs: she smells bleach, along with air freshener. Lilacs and lavender scrubbed chemically clean.

"Tom and Cate are going to get his things out of the apartment," she says.

"His things?"

"His clothes. His phone. The evidence."

Tom says nothing. He is wearing Xavier's blue coat, his Mets hat. Beneath its brim, his face is white.

"We'll take care of it," Cate says. "We have a plan."

"Good." Nancy tries to smile. "You and I, Greta, will handle the body, and then I'll head over to MSNBC to talk to Andrea."

There is a long pause. Louis sings about trees of green, red roses, too. Greta's gaze moves from the credenza to the window to the kitchen.

"There's got to be another way," she says.

"There isn't."

"What about lye? I mean, he's already in the bathtub."

"You happen to have some sitting around?"

"We could buy some."

"That wouldn't look at all suspicious."

Greta scratches her wrist. She walks to the couch, sits on its edge, and thinks.

"Bury him in New Jersey," she says finally.

Nancy shakes her head. She glances at her watch.

"We're not the Sopranos."

Outside, the sky darkens. Clouds that were once retreating launch a new offense.

Greta says, "Okay, let's do it."

"We can throw the sword down, too."

"No." Greta hitches her sleeves up above her elbows. "I have another plan for that."

Separately, and over the course of thirty minutes, Cate and Tom leave. With them they take the contents of Xavier's pockets, his phone, and the rest of his clothes, which Cate folds into tight, perfect squares and shoves into her shoulder bag. Once they're gone, Nancy and Greta head to the bathroom. There, they wrap Xavier's body in two thick sheets

("Frette—it's a real shame") and drag him on his belly through the hall and into the foyer.

"I don't mean to point out the obvious," Nancy says as they're passing the guest room, "but Ethan was much taller."

Greta stops and falls backward on her ass. From the ground she says, "He isn't *that* short. And how much do I have to pay you to never mention Ethan again?"

Reaching down, Nancy helps her daughter up, and as she does she thinks, not for the first time today, of what else she has done in the name of family. The meals she's cooked, the lies she's told, the murder that—now—she's abetted. Would Howard have done all that? It's a hard question for her to answer; she can never quite extract the person he was from the person she wants him to have been. She suspects not, though. In her experience, mothers are the ones who get their hands dirty.

At the front door she closes one eye and presses the other against the peephole.

"We can't drag him," she whispers. "If we get blood on the carpet I'll never hear the end of it from the co-op board."

Nodding, Greta tightens her grip on the sheets, and together she and Nancy prepare to lift Xavier. A sound stops them: a dog barking, followed by a high, cooing voice.

Lowering Xavier's head, Nancy returns to the peephole.

"It's Mrs. Branovich," she says. "And that goddamned Maltese."

She waits, watching as the woman waddles to the elevator, her dog zigzagging behind her. Twenty seconds later the car arrives, and Mrs. Branovich totters into it. The dog barks; the doors close. The coast—at least for now—is clear.

"All right—*go time.*"

They heave, they lift, they shuffle. Nancy's back aches and her knees scream but she doesn't tell Greta to stop—instead, she mouths *hurry up.* Greta does, shifting from a walk to a panicked trot that carries them to the trash room. Balancing Xavier's head against her thigh, Nancy frees a hand and opens it. The three of them tumble inside.

"What now?" Greta asks once they've caught their breath.

"We dump him."

"Headfirst?"

Nancy frowns: it's a question she hadn't thought of.

"Feetfirst."

The sheets they unwrap as if Xavier were a mummy, pulling them off in spirals to reveal his naked, pale body.

"I'll hold the door open," Nancy says. "Remember: lift from your knees—not your back."

A burst of air rushes up the shaft and causes Nancy's eyes to water. Through tears she watches as her daughter strains to lift one leg and then the other to the lip of the chute.

"Okay," Nancy says, "now *push.*"

Greta does, her mouth contorting to a determined, angry snarl. The body gives and jerks forward—and then stops.

"What's wrong?" she whispers.

Past Xavier's belly button, the brush of hair on his groin, Nancy sees his legs, pressed against the opposite wall of the chute.

"He's stuck against the side!"

Halfway down the hall, the elevator door slides open, and moments later Nancy hears the familiar jingling of a leash and collar. Greta freezes and stares at her mother, her fingers pressing into Xavier's shoulders. They say nothing—they hold their breath. Then the dog starts barking, a wild, hyena-like snarl that gets louder by the second. Mrs. Branovich tries to calm her—she says, *Hush now, Helen*—but it doesn't work. Her footsteps fall closer.

Nancy spits to get Greta's attention.

Go! she mouths.

What!?

Go distract her!

But what about him!—Greta nods at Xavier.

Helen starts sniffing: Nancy can hear her nose, getting busy right outside.

I'll handle it!

Greta glances down at Xavier for the final time. She lets him go, wipes her hands on her pants, and violently flings open the door.

"Mrs. Braaaaanovich!" Nancy hears her say. "Oh, dear. Did I just hit your dog?"

"Greta Harrison? I thought you were burning buildings in Berlin."

"Paris! But that was weeks ago. I'm back now! In the flesh! It's been years since we've seen each other, hasn't it?"

"How did you—what were you doing in there? Also, you look sickly. *Wan.*"

"That's sweet of you to say! My mother's been telling me *all about* the new state-of-the-art refuse system that was installed, and I thought I'd check it out. You know, I think it's wonderful that the building is finally taking climate change seriously and moving into the twenty-first century and—gosh, Mrs. Branovich, is Helen okay? I knocked her head pretty hard with that door. In fact—oh, no, she's bleeding. Look, right there on her little head. Let's take her back to your place, Mrs. Branovich, and I can help you get her on the couch for a little R and R. I had a friend whose Pekingese died from a concussion, and I don't think I'd be able to live with myself if that happened to *Helen.*"

Her eyes shut, Nancy waits as the voices fade, seeping into the San Marino's walls until they become as brittle as shells. Once they're gone completely, she positions herself so she's directly behind Xavier, and she shoves him as hard as she can. He doesn't move—his legs are still blocking his fall—and so she shoves him again, leaning into him with all of her weight. This time, she hears something crack and feels something shift. His feet dislodge, and Nancy stumbles forward. The door closes, and on the other side of it she listens to a sound that, for the rest of her life, she will never quite forget: a body, falling seven stories to the floor.

On Morality

At a flea market in Brooklyn, tattooed vendors hawk their wares in the shadow of the Manhattan Bridge. Purses woven from the second lives of plastic water bottles; scrap metal earrings for a hundred dollars a pair. They line them all up at stalls, erected on a swath of cobblestone, where women in leggings browse two feet ahead of their hungover boyfriends. It's Saturday morning—the neighborhood smells of coffee, and sunlight gilds apartment windows. Nearby, through the brick crevices formed by buildings, Cate can see a park. Long stretches of green beside the East River, where the virtuous set out on five-mile jogs and clusters of strollers form spontaneous parades. She watches them, and then turns back to the stall where, for the past five minutes, she's been standing—an arrangement of two card tables covered with dinner plates, their surfaces painted with global skylines. Istanbul, Shanghai, Moscow, Pittsburgh. Picking up Berlin, she flips it over, then turns to Tom.

"This one's nice," she says, "and it only costs three hundred dollars."

His face is gray and there are bags beneath his eyes. She hasn't seen him since yesterday—when, after deciding what to do with the body, they left Nancy's apartment. Now, standing next to her in the market, Tom tugs at the sleeves of Xavier's coat: Cate had asked him to wear it again this morning.

"What the hell are we doing here, Cate?" he says. "And why the fuck do I have this thing on?"

"We're shopping for overpriced place settings. And you're wearing that coat because we need to get rid of it." Cate sets the plate back down and picks up another—Berlin swapped for Budapest. "What'd you do last night?"

Behind them, two women in matching scarves pose for a picture beneath a high stone arch. Tom presses his thumbs against his eyes.

"I went to a movie," he says.

"What'd you see?"

"I can't even remember."

"You can't remember what movie you saw?"

"No, Cate, because ten hours earlier—" He lowers his voice and takes a step closer to her. *There it is again*, she thinks: *that cologne.* "Ten hours earlier we were pushing a body down a trash chute."

Cate runs her finger along the Danube, and then over the belfries of St. Stephen's Basilica.

"They did that—not us," she says. And then: "Oh hey, that place has cute clothes."

The stall to which Cate is pointing is bigger than the others and has, in addition to two glass cases holding hats and gloves, four racks of thick wool jackets. She sets Budapest down and begins walking toward it. Tom is right at her heels.

"Do you know where I went before I came here?" he whispers. "The fucking police station."

Hearing the words, Cate stops. She adjusts her sunglasses and swallows, hard.

"Why'd you do that?"

"Because I couldn't sleep last night! Because I can't even remember what fucking movie I sat through!" He's still whispering, but he might as well be screaming. Between sentences his lips curl against his teeth. "I stood there, watching officers go in and out of the precinct. I was there for almost an hour, and I kept thinking, Tom, you have to do this. You have to walk in there and tell them what happened, because a man was stabbed, and that's the right thing to do."

The sun shifts; a cloud disintegrates. A moment later, the cobblestones are bathed in light.

"And did you?" Cate asks. "Did you go in?"

Tom shakes his head. "I'm here, aren't I?"

A breath that Cate hadn't known she'd been holding escapes in a loud burst. Her head feels light, and her knees shake.

"Here, give me his coat," she says.

They are standing between two of the stall's racks, their bodies shielded by all manner of secondhand outerwear. Bombers, ponchos, parkas, mackintoshes, each with a handwritten price safety-pinned to its hem.

"What? Why?"

"Just do it, Tom."

He pauses, fingering a plastic button, then slips it off his shoulders. Cate looks around her in all directions. When she's certain they aren't being watched, she removes a herringbone trench from a hanger and replaces it with Xavier's coat. Straightening it out, she brushes off its lapel and fixes it with a price tag (*forty-five dollars*) that she takes from a nearby anorak. Then she pays a girl with a bar through her nose for the herringbone trench and, together with Tom, leaves.

"A VERY LUCKY PERSON IS going to buy a very nice coat for the cost of a mediocre dinner with no wine," Cate says. The flea market is behind them—now they are in the park. Across the river Manhattan reaches skyward, its towers and spires framed by blue. "Anyway, it's one less thing to worry about."

Tom stops walking.

"Is that how this works for you?" he asks. "Ticking off concerns until there aren't any left? Putting dead men's jackets on hangers and then taking a stroll by the river? Christ, doesn't this bother you at all?"

Cate's chin dips; she searches her purse for a tube of ChapStick that she knows isn't there. Obviously this bothers her. When she left Nancy's apartment yesterday afternoon, it was in a cold sweat. For the next four hours she traveled to all corners of the city, her heart racing as she deposited the rest of Xavier's belongings, one by one, into far-flung trash cans. A sock, buried beneath an empty Doritos bag; silk underwear, next to a sack of dog shit. Each one a scattered puzzle piece, ready to be swept away before anyone thought to collect it. As she went, she intermittently turned on his mobile, hoping its signal would be caught and recorded by nearby towers—she wanted to create a picture, an image of a man, stalking the city before he suddenly disappeared. She did this until the sun was setting and the wind turned biting, at which point she shut off the phone, crushed its SIM card, and threw it—as hard and as far as she possibly could—into the depths of the Hudson.

All of these tasks Cate completed sweaty, and with a terrified single-mindedness. She didn't blink, because when she did she saw dead bodies; she didn't speak, because she was afraid of what she'd say. Her fear was that if she wasn't actively solving the problem, then she would inevitably become the problem; if she stopped long enough to think about what she had done, the consequences would stalk her. They would hunt her throughout the city, buzzing in her ear like ferocious mosquitos, and keeping her awake until morning. During those moments when she thought she would buckle—when, like Tom, she was certain her feet would lead her to a police station's door—she closed her eyes and pictured her mother. She thought of the last twelve months of her life—a year that Nancy had stolen for them, during which they took trips to the beach, and laughed, and drank beers they weren't supposed to; a year that Cate loaded with more memories than any year should have.

None of these thoughts can she relay to Tom. She can't ask Tom for assurance, or show Tom her red and sleepless eyes—it's why, after all, she's wearing sunglasses. Because Cate knows that if she did—that if she dared to whisper *I'm really fucking scared*—then Tom, surely, would crumble. And crumbling, in all of its tempting and guilt-allaying forms, is the last thing that either of them needs.

"We did the right thing," she says. "We're doing the right thing."

"We need to go to the police. We are aiding and abetting a murder."

"He was a bad man, Tom. He was basically a Nazi."

"So, what, that means he deserved to die?"

"No, that's not what I'm saying. I'm saying that I'm making a moral calculation."

Tom says nothing. He sits on an empty bench and lifts his gaze toward two twirling gulls.

Sitting next to him, Cate asks, "What's the thing you care about the most?"

"Not going to prison."

"Okay." Cate smiles—she can't help it. "But aside from that. Why did you start working in politics to begin with?"

On the East River, a tugboat fights its way upstream, its bow plowing through blue-gray waves.

"The Marshall Islands," he says.

"Wait, literally?"

"Yes. I mean, figuratively, too, I guess." Resting his cheek on his fist, Tom stares down at his feet. "I went there to teach for two years after college. It was the best time of my life. I fell in love, got my heart broken, only wore T-shirts—it was heaven. Anyway, while I was there, I started noticing that more and more people I knew—the Marshallese, especially—were leaving, moving away to places like Australia and the United States. Climate change was making their futures there basically unimaginable. Where would they live? What would they eat? Our inability—or unwillingness—to confront an existential threat had turned all of these people into refugees, and that pissed me off. So, when I got back to the States, I said I was going to do something about it. Twenty years later, here I am."

When he's finished, Cate turns to face the river. The tugboat is gone and the wind has calmed; now all that's there is a placid, sunlit blue.

"I want you to imagine a scale," she says. "On one side is everything you just told me, along with whatever control women still have over their own bodies, the right of black people to vote, and the promise of healthcare for those who can't afford it. If we lose this election, Tom—if we go to jail and Carmichael wins—then all of those things are potentially in jeopardy."

A pigeon alights on the edge of the bench. Tom brushes it away.

"And what's on the other side?" he asks. "Of the scale, I mean."

Cate crosses her legs.

She says, "The life of Xavier de la Marinière."

One moment stretches into another—for a long time, neither Cate nor Tom speaks. In the silence Cate hears the sounds of the park: children laughing at a nearby playground; water sloshing beneath a pier. She thinks of the image she described—a scale, with lofty ideals piled on one end and a monster's death on the other. She isn't sure if she believes herself, or if this is how morality is meant to work. The word itself, which she once thought clear, now strikes her as elusive and undefined. When does the price of Good outweigh its benefits? And at what point does that which is wrong become—suddenly—right? Reaching down, Cate takes hold of Tom's hand: the fact is, she doesn't have the answers to those questions, and she suspects she never will. What she does know is that, sometimes, you do the things you do because you have to, and because the only option life has given you is to protect what you love.

Tom says, "When I talked about wanting to win the other night, I didn't think that it'd feel like this."

Squeezing his hand, Cate raises it to her lips.

"I know." She kisses his knuckles. "But winning never really feels like it's supposed to, does it."

Appel d'Urgence

How colossally shitty is Agent Angie DiFiori's Monday going? Let her count the ways. Number one: the first conversation she had this morning was with her mother, calling from Yonkers to ask her why she wasn't married; the second was with her ex-husband, calling from Hoboken to beg Angie—again—to take him back. Both of those calls began before she'd lifted her head from the pillow; neither of them ended with civility. When she finally got out of bed—and here is number three—she felt a hair ball sticking to the sole of her foot. It wasn't alone, but rather part of a pair—two furry dots forming a regurgitated colon on her bedroom carpet. A gift, of sorts, from her cat, Frederick, an ancient tabby rescue who, despite gut obstructions and feline AIDS and one messy divorce, refuses to die. With her nose scrunched in disgust, Angie reached over to flip on the lights. Her vision was blurry, though—she was still waking up—and so her hand, flaying about wildly in the dark, ended up careening into a lamp. It teetered around the edge of her bedside table, taunting her, before shattering (voilà, number four) with a pointedly pathetic crash on the ground.

Burnt toast, a cold shower, milkless coffee: those were numbers five, six, and seven. A missed C train clocked in at number eight; pigeon shit on her shoulder ticked off number nine; and—now—an order from her boss, Lawrence, to take a call from a blubbering Frenchwoman rounds things out to a fat, even ten.

"Why do I have to talk to her?" Angie folds her arms. On all sides of her, the FBI's New York field office buzzes to life. "I haven't even sat down at my desk yet."

"Because I'm an assistant director of the Federal Bureau of Investigation," Lawrence says. Light bounces off his bulbous nose. "And because when you took this job you swore to protect the Constitution of the United States from all enemies foreign and domestic."

"Yeah, well, I was lying."

"Just take the call, Angie."

Swallowing a bitter sip of coffee, she grimaces.

"What's she even want?"

"She claims her boyfriend's gone missing. Apparently, he got to New York last week and no one's heard from him since, including the front desk at the Marriott Marquis, where he's been staying. They're saying his room hasn't been touched since Friday."

"Maybe he's trying to get away from her. Telling yourself your boyfriend's gone missing is a lot easier than admitting he doesn't love you." Another sip of unsippable coffee. "Also, why doesn't she call the NYPD?"

"She did. They got their hands on the flight manifests and saw that he flew into Newark, so they kicked her over to us."

Angie rolls her eyes.

"Shit like this," she says, "is why we still don't know who killed Jimmy Hoffa."

Lawrence ignores the comment and begins walking back toward his office.

"She's waiting for you on hold," he calls out. "Her name's Colette Legard."

Her shoulders slumped, Angie sits down at her desk. There, a tower of paperwork nearly six inches high is stacked next to her computer. Given her track record this morning, she'd been looking forward to disappearing into the bureaucratic void. She figured she'd put on some old J.Lo, slip off her shoes, and escape whatever dangers were waiting for her in the wings. Errant asteroids and overbearing mothers. Former lovers insisting that finally, and for real this time, they've changed.

She thinks, *Fat chance*, then picks up the phone.

Two hours later, Angie rests a hip on Lawrence's desk, next to a snow globe containing an approximated, miniature version of New York. His glasses are caught on the end of his nose, and now, leaning back in his chair, he removes them.

"Did you say Greta Harrison?" he says. "As in—"

"Yes." Angie nods. "As in that Greta Harrison. Colette says that she's the only person Xavier knew in New York. In fact, she said he came here *with* her."

"Are you sure you heard her right? That accent—it was strong."

"I asked her to repeat herself, like, four times. She says they were living together in Paris, then he followed her here."

"But Colette said *she* was his girlfriend."

Twisting to the right, Angie cracks her spine.

"Well," she says, "I guess he had two."

Lawrence snorts.

"In my next life, I better be French." He taps his knuckles against his desk. "And this Xavier guy, you say he's some sort of internet troll?"

Angie nods. "That's right. A nasty one."

Lawrence leans back further, lifting the chair's two front legs from the ground; for a second Angie worries that he's going to topple over. That doesn't happen, though, and soon he rights himself. Closing his eyes, he rubs a hand over his face.

"What a mess." He picks up the snow globe and gives it a shake. "Any idea where the Harrison girl is now?"

"I found an address for her in Bushwick, north of Irving Avenue. She hasn't been living there since she got back from Paris, though. About an hour ago I went over and asked around, and some coked-out bald girl told me she's been staying with her mother at the San Marino."

"Her mother being Congresswoman Nancy Harrison, who is currently running for Senate."

Angie shrugs and shows her boss her palms.

"That'd be my guess."

"It's neck and neck between her and Carmichael. It's the most watched race in the entire fucking country right now."

"I'm aware of that, too."

"And now you're telling me that her daughter might be involved in the disappearance of a French Nazi."

"I didn't write the news, sir. I'm just reporting it."

Pushing himself away from the desk, Lawrence walks to the window and looks out over Foley Square. His slacks are wrinkled, and what's left of his hair needs a brush: it's the beginning of the day, and still he seems tired. Angie watches him as he clasps and unclasps his hands behind his back. Then he lowers the window's blinds and sits back down.

"There's something about this that doesn't add up," he says.

"I felt the same way, sir."

"Greta Harrison goes to Paris, throws a champagne bottle through a window, then comes back to New York with a French boyfriend who suddenly vanishes?"

"A piece is missing, I agree."

Light creeps through the blinds, throwing daggers across the floor.

"Go up to the San Marino, and see what you can find out." Lawrence rubs his bald spot, thinking. He adds: "And take Liu with you. We need someone with a good bedside manner, a charmer."

"I'd like to think that I'm a charmer, sir."

"You're a lot of things, DiFiori, but a charmer ain't one of them."

Angie looks out onto the field office's floor, where her colleague Charlie Liu taps away at his computer. In two months he'll be leaving, transferring to the bureau's Los Angeles office to be closer to his parents, which for Angie is a bummer—he's funny, and a good sport about things; he always asks Angie if she wants a sandwich when he heads out for lunch. In fact, when it comes down to it, Charlie is one of the few people around here she genuinely likes.

"All right," she says, "I'll grab him on my way out."

Lawrence nods and gives his snow globe another tepid shake. Tiny white flakes swirl around the base of the Chrysler Building.

"Be discreet, DiFiori," he says. "The election's tomorrow, and if it gets out that anyone from this office even breathed on Nancy Harrison, then I'm going to go down in history as the next James Comey."

A GEYSER—THICK AND GURGLING AND five feet high—erupts from the belly of West Broadway. Streets flood, sirens whine, traffic stops; Angie drums her fingers on her Taurus's steering wheel, craning her neck out the window to get a better look. They've been sitting here, stuck on the same block of Reade Street, for nearly half an hour. In front of them is a Maserati with New Jersey license plates; in back of them is a yellow cab with a dented hood. Its driver has kicked its door open, and in her rear-view mirror Angie watches as he steps outside to light a cigarette. Next to her, Charlie rolls down his window, then rolls it back up a second later. Running both hands through his hair, he clicks his tongue.

"Stop that," Angie says.

"Stop what?"

"That thing you're doing with your tongue. The clicking thing."

Charlie closes his mouth, keeps his jaw firm.

"Sorry—I didn't realize I was doing it."

The Maserati inches forward, even though there's nowhere to go. On the sidewalk, a girl with pink hair uses her phone to film surges of gray water, making rapids of gutters. For the third time in as many minutes, Charlie lowers the window.

"And that, too. Either the window is down, or the window is up—decide."

Slouching down in his seat, Charlie folds his hands in his lap. The window stays down.

Over the rim of her sunglasses, Angie glances at him. She opens the center console and searches for gum.

"What's wrong with you?" she asks.

"What do you mean?"

"I mean you've been fussing around like a toddler since we left the office." Beneath an expired parking pass, the foil from a piece of Trident glints in the light. "So, what's wrong with you?"

Charlie sinks deeper into his seat. He reaches for the window, then stops himself, his hand hovering an inch above the button.

"I've got to tell you something, Ange," he says.

The gum is stale, brittle; she wonders how long it's been in there. "Okay—what?"

"I can't go up there—to the San Marino, I mean."

Angie tries—and fails—to blow a bubble. Spit dots the steering wheel.

"Sure, you can. You've dealt with scarier people than Nancy Harrison."

A fireman jogs down Reade Street, an orange traffic cone gripped in his hand. The pink-haired girl giggles and gawks.

"That's not what I mean." Charlie leans forward, resting his elbows on the dashboard. "It's more that—well, the thing is, I'm dating her son."

For a moment Angie stops chewing, the gum stuck between her molars. In front of her, brake lights flash in succession and tires crunch against the pavement: a line of cars, moving like an accordion. Then she hears a door slam and an engine start. The cabbie has finished his cigarette.

"For how long?"

"A month? But Ange, it's serious. He's coming with me to LA. Christ, what if we end up getting married, and I have to tell people at the rehearsal dinner that the first time I met my mother-in-law was when I was interrogating her? It's a conflict of interest, Ange, and I mean that on *literally* every level. I just"—Charlie rolls up the window—"I can't do it."

The cabbie honks his horn, and, dislodging the gum with her tongue, Angie takes her foot off the brake. *What if we end up getting married?* Her first instinct is to shout *Don't do it*, and to tell Charlie to run for the hills; in Angie's experience, the only thing that a husband's good for is fucking a twenty-two-year-old named Crystal in the parking lot of a Costco in Bayonne, and then calling you at six o'clock in the morning when his new lease on life didn't work out. Soon, though, that passes, and the reality of the situation lays itself bare. *Charlie Liu is dating Nancy Harrison's son*: is Angie surprised? Yes, obviously, though also sort of not; given the way her day has been going, this latest wrinkle actually feels right on track. She could, she supposes, force him to go through with the interrogation, anyway. She is, technically, his superior, and having him there might work to her advantage—Charlie's a charmer, that much is true; he could lull the Harrisons into a false sense of complacency in which they reveal whatever it is they may be hiding. On the other hand, he's right about the conflict of interest. Regardless of what they find, if the press gets word that Nick Harrison's boyfriend was the one doing the questioning, then their investigation—their *careers*—are fucked. There will be indictments, subpoenas, hearings; Lawrence will serve their severed heads on a plate.

The Maserati revs its engine, and at the end of the block, traffic begins to move. Angie swallows her gum.

"Okay—stay with the car, then," she says. "But if I get a fucking parking ticket, Liu, you're paying for it."

Goodbye to All That

"Los Angeles!"

Lifting both his eyebrows, Nick nods.

He says, "That's right."

Slowly, Lisa turns the news over, tilting her head from side to side, as if she's trying to peer around it, on top of it, under it. On the other side of Washington Square, a saxophone blares a minor note; a bit closer to where Nick and Lisa are sitting, a man with outstretched arms offers a roost for a flock of shit-gray pigeons. Bodies are splayed out on patches of grass—undergraduates, determined to catch the last bit of sun before it disappears for winter. They light cigarettes and pretend to read books as, at the center of the square, children splash beneath a gushing fountain. Lisa ignores all of it—instead she closes her eyes, licks her lips, and smiles. Bits of chewed-up onions, Nick notices, are lodged between her teeth.

"Wow," she says. "*El Ay.*"

It's a little after one o'clock, and balanced on their knees are small plastic containers from Me, Myself, and Thai, the takeout joint below their office where they met to grab lunch before coming to the park. Nick's is filled with an algae-colored curry, whereas Lisa's has spilling from its edges the ends of flat, greasy noodles. Crossing his feet at the ankles, he watches as she catches one with her fork before adding it to a heaping bite.

"You think I'm crazy," he says.

"No." The noodle slithers through her lips. With her fork she points to the man with the pigeons. "*That* guy is crazy. Yesterday, I watched a bird peck at his scapula for a full ten minutes while he went on and on about Jesus staging a comeback in a UFO. You—you're just in love."

The words settle on Nick like silk, and as he stares out into the lattice of changing leaves, his lips curl into a grin. It's the first time he's heard someone else acknowledge what has become, to him, the most indisputable of facts. Lisa is right—he's just in love.

"Remind me, how long have you known Charlie?" she asks.

"Let's see . . ." Nick scratches his chin, thinks, and adds on a week. "A month."

Using her thumb and forefinger, Lisa fishes out a cube of tofu from her container, then tosses it to a squirrel.

She says, "That's a perfectly acceptable amount of time. I once moved to Taos with a woman I'd known for five days."

"You lived in Taos with a woman?"

"Correct. *Jane.* We rode her motorcycle there and got married on the way. I moved back, obviously, because here I am. New Mexico has too much turquoise for my taste."

For a second Nick imagines Lisa in an adobe hacienda, her wild hair falling to her waist, her bare toes curling against cool orange tile. Waiting for her in bed is a woman—*Jane*—with a cigarette clenched between her lips. Outside, wind whips across red plateaus. A Harley-Davidson bakes in the sun.

He takes a bite of curry. "So, what happened?"

"Oh, I divorced her a week later and got the hell out of Dodge. She insisted on calling me *baby*—that was the ultimate deal breaker. Also, she was a poet. And addicted to nitrous oxide. Anyway, you're leaving! How do you feel?"

A pigeon alights on the bench next to Nick. Securing his curry with one hand, he uses the other to shoo it away. *How does he feel?* A few days ago, the answer would have been *like I'm out of my goddamned mind.* When he left Charlie's last Thursday—after the idea of upending his life was first proposed—he wandered around the city in a nervous daze. He desperately wanted this to work; he was also afraid of the types of unfortunate discoveries that Lisa had described. Being called *baby* and other minor injustices; hidden addictions dragged into light. What would happen, for example, if he got to Los Angeles and learned that Charlie snored, or shot heroin, or liked CBS sitcoms? Under different circumstances, those revelations would have the benefit of being dulled by time—the snoring wouldn't matter, because buffering it would be four months, or years, or decades of daytime bliss; the snoring would have *context*. To this end, Nick figured, being in a relationship—a long one, at least—was not so different from being a lobster, slowly steaming in a pot: you hardly noticed that the water was getting hotter, because mostly you were just happy to be wet. What would happen, though, if you jumped in and it was already boiling? What would happen if the pot was on Hollywood and Vine?

These anxieties did not last long. He saw Charlie on Friday. Saturday and Sunday, too. He listened to his perfect laugh and saw himself in his kind eyes; he let Frank the Dog drool, asleep and happy, in his lap. He considered the possibility that perhaps living was about having as many lives as possible, and this was how his next one was meant to begin. Since then, what he's felt has been your standard stuff: excitement, fear, flashes of self-doubt. Meteorologically, he's thrilled that soon he will have a better relationship with the sun, one in which he isn't bitching about its presence or its absence, but rather appreciating that it's, well, *always there*. On the flip side, there are certain changes for which he is bound to be less enthusiastic. Traffic, for one. Actors, too. Beneath all of that anticipatory static, though, he feels a surprising sense of calm. He was born in New York, he has lived in New York, and now, finally, he is leaving New York. He had always thought that would happen with his body in a casket, or his ashes in an urn, but as it turns out, he was wrong. Instead, he'll be doing it with the man he loves, and on a westbound 757.

Inevitably, he will return—for holidays, because his mother will murder him if he doesn't, and in October, because he likes the city in the fall. He'll rush to all the places that he used to go, the dive bars and restaurants and bagel shops, and feel a tinge of melancholy when he realizes they're no longer his. He'll welcome it, though; he's even excited for it. Because as sad as it is to lose a place, it's even lovelier to know that you left it at exactly the right time.

"I feel good," he says. "No, sorry, I feel *great*."

"Well, that's nice to hear. What will happen to your classes?"

"I'll finish out the semester. Charlie's transfer doesn't go into effect until January. We'll head out right after the New Year."

"That's good. You've still got a buffer to change your mind."

"I'm not changing my mind, Lisa."

"No, of course not. I only meant if things don't work out."

"Have I ever told you how much I appreciate your confidence in my love life?"

"Oh, come on. I'm *kidding*. Your situation is very different from mine. I mean, Jane was a poet. No one, under any circumstances, should ever live with a poet." Another squirrel approaches, and to this one Lisa gives a slice of green pepper. "Have you told your mother?"

He has not. Nancy has been busy—so busy that since last Friday she and Nick have only spoken twice, two quick phone calls during which she told him, more or less, that she didn't have time to talk. It didn't bother him—he knew how elections worked, the ways in which they sucked away spare seconds the closer and closer they loomed. Besides, the distance gave him time to think about how he would eventually tell her, the delicate speech he'd give to announce he was fleeing. Or, no—that's not fair. Nick is not *fleeing*. Nick is *moving on*—that, at least, is how he plans to put it. Last year he switched jobs, this year he's switching time zones. There will be no more favors to be done, or daughters to be rescued, or flights to Paris to catch. Finally, he will be free.

"I'm heading up there this afternoon," he says. "I'll be wearing my bulletproof vest."

The man with the pigeons shakes his arms and birds erupt into the sky. Lisa tracks them, their wings beating the air, their meager talons outstretched.

"And what about Joan?" she asks.

"What about her?"

"Are you ditching the musical? Are you saying—ha!—*goodbye to all that*?"

Far overhead, a plane passes behind a cloud. Nick smiles.

"No," he says. "I've got to do something to keep myself busy out there. Hell, Lisa, maybe I'll even try to make it a *movie*."

She blinks, rubs something from her eye, then stares at Nick's mouth. A hemp bag the size of a koala sits in a heap on the bench next to her. Reaching into it, she fishes out a student's essay and a bright green pen.

"You should call my cousin," she says.

"That's sweet." Nick rubs her knee. "But I know people in LA. It's a pretty gay place."

"No, I meant for your project. She's a producer."

"Your cousin?"

"Yeah. She's done all sorts of stuff. She has a GOTE."

"I have no idea what you're talking about."

"Yes, you do." Lisa rolls her eyes. "She's won all those awards."

"You mean an EGOT."

"Yes. One of those. Anyway, she told me at Passover that she's desperate for new projects."

She rips a page from the student's essay, scribbles something on the back of it, and hands the paper to Nick. Looking down, he sees a name— *Julia*—along with a phone number, written in Lisa's eerily childish script.

"Your cousin has an EGOT," he says.

"That's a big deal, right?"

"Lisa, why did you never tell me this before?"

"Because you never asked." Nick's hand is still there, resting on Lisa's knee, and now she sets her own on top of it. "Also, I guess I was worried that if I told you, you'd go ahead and do something like this."

"Do something like what?"

"Oh, you know, this." Small, silver tears moisten the corners of Lisa's eyes. Laughing, she shrugs her shoulders to wipe them away. "Leave."

Don't Bring Around a Cloud

Greta has a skull in her right hand. An egg-shaped cranium with a flat snout and a long, capable jaw. It belonged, once, to a ferret, or maybe a minx—the sort of woodland vermin that people keep as pets in Russia and West Virginia and certain corners of Alphabet City. She has one finger through the hole where its nose used to be, and another through its left eye. Its teeth are chipped and the color of boiled corn: they need to be brushed.

She turns to put the skull back on the shelf where she found it, and, as she does so, the lower half of its mandible slips from her fingers and falls to the floor.

"Shit," she whispers, and reaches down to pick it up.

She's in a basement the size of a suburban Starbucks, surrounded by all species of collected miscellanea. Old dentist chairs, locked steamer trunks, a fainting couch nabbed from a burning funeral home. Standing to her left is a larger-than-life statue of a Comanche chief; to her right a lion carved from wood. There are buttons, patches, fedoras, bones; pots, lamps, bayonets, wagon wheels. The objects are arranged with no discernible order. They are scattered among armoires that are also for sale and strewn wildly across the floor. *Picking a path through them*, Greta thinks, *is akin to navigating the detritus of a shipwreck—one wrong step and you're liable to crush someone's femur or find a dagger, sinking into your foot.* It smells, generally, of leather and old vinyl records. In addition to two feeble floor lamps (seven hundred and fifty dollars for the pair), light comes from a single window, a slot of blue abutting the ceiling on the other side of the room, through which one can see the antique store's sign—ODDS & ENDS & WONDERS & CURIOSITIES—hanging from a low iron fence.

Her toes knock against something—an ancient globe, its continents the color of a late-summer tan. She picks it up, spins it, sets a finger on Czechoslovakia. Then, from the shop's back office, she hears her old roommate Carl calling her name.

"Okay," he says, and holds out her father's sword, tucked inside its scabbard. "All done."

Setting the globe down, Greta walks toward him, past three loose carousel horses, leaning against a four-poster bed.

"You polished it and everything?" she asks.

Carl nods. A cigarette—half-smoked but extinguished—is tucked behind his ear.

"Did someone use Windex on it recently?"

At the center of her chest, Greta's pulse briefly quickens.

"My mother, maybe," she says. "She likes to keep it shiny."

"Well, the next time she feels like tidying up, tell her to bring it here. That thing's worth a fortune, and Windex'll corrode the blade."

Beneath the window's light, Greta gives a curt nod and shoves the sword into an L.L.Bean duffel bag. Reaching into her pocket, she produces a thick wad of cash.

"Will do," she says.

Dust motes swirl above Carl's head as he licks his finger and counts the money, flipping through the bills like he's dealing a deck of cards. When he's satisfied it's all there—he counts it twice—he gives Greta an awkward, one-armed hug and a quick kiss on the cheek.

"Come home one of these days—Zsófia misses you," he says. "Oh, and also, you still owe me two months' rent."

Outside, sunlight makes fireworks of fallen leaves. Blinking, Greta makes her way east to Third Avenue, where she dodges a man on an electric scooter and lifts a hand into the air. A minute later she's settling into the back of a taxi, the bag, the sword, and the scabbard all set squarely on her knees.

"Where to?" the driver asks. His eyes glance at her in the rearview mirror.

"Uptown, please." Greta rolls down the window. "Seventy-Fourth and Fifth."

THREE CHERUBS RECLINE ON A cloud, their fat thighs propped up on celestial pillows. A vine is strung between them, green and meandering and dripping with purple grapes. One of the angels—the fattest one, with stumpy wings—reaches for a handful as his friends watch and laugh. He'll never actually get them, though—this is a painting—and as Greta leans closer to the canvas, she feels a dreary melancholy. *What a fate,* she thinks, *to always be reaching but never touching. To have your pink, wanting fingers forever an inch away.*

"That one's new. Late Renaissance."

She hears her grandmother's voice, rattling a few inches behind her, and she takes a step back.

"Yeah," Greta says, "I thought so."

Eugenia gives her a toothy smile, and they continue their slow walk down the hall to the second-floor salon. At one point, this room had been Greta's favorite in the house; now it feels stuffy, and oppressively dark, and seems to have as its singular goal making its guests feel small. On a low chinoiserie coffee table, Cora, Eugenia's housekeeper, has set a tray containing a teapot, two small cups, and precisely zero food. This last fact doesn't surprise Greta: there is hardly ever any food.

"You look well." Eugenia lowers herself into a chair across from the sofa and sets her cane across her knees. "Skinny."

She nods her chin to the tea, and Greta pours it. The room fills with bergamot: Eugenia only drinks Earl Grey.

"Oh, thanks," Greta says. "I actually gained like three pounds in Paris."

Lowering her glasses an inch on her nose, Eugenia appraises Greta's arms, her waist. Then she nods, as if she's located the added weight.

"Well, make sure to lose them," she says. And then: "How was Paris? Did you make your mother furious?"

"I've certainly seen her happier."

"Good girl. And the man you went there to see?"

"Oh, him." Greta sips her tea and burns her tongue. "That didn't really work out."

Eugenia nods, and then begins to cough—a violent, wet hack that Greta politely ignores. Her ancient body shakes; her eyes begin to water. She looks old, and frail, but then, she's always looked old and frail—she reached that point, and never progressed past it. Eugenia is a woman of a certain age in the most specific sense: she became old while she was young, and then refused to get any older. She raced to stand at Death's door, and then she refused to knock.

The coughing stops. Eugenia dabs at the corners of her mouth.

"I'm sorry to hear that—you're not getting any younger. But oh, Greta, it *is* so lovely to see you again."

"I'm sorry I didn't come right when I got back."

"I was worried that I had done something to upset you." She folds her hands in her lap. "That was silly of me, though. I taught you better than that."

I taught you better than that: the phrase hangs in the air, then finds its way to Greta's gut. She hates her grandmother—it's a realization that comes to her clearly, cleanly: the pealing of church bells on a silent afternoon. For Eugenia, Greta has a new and untarnished disgust. How did she ever trust this woman? For her entire life, her grandmother has lied to her, and not because she loves Greta, or wanted to protect her, but simply because she could—because she needed someone else to hate Nancy, and there Greta was. Her teacup burns her palms, and she sees her reflection in its amber pool. What she'd really like to do is throw it in her grandmother's face. She'd like to stand up, knock the cane from her lap, and tell her the truth. She won't, though, because she knows that it would be pointless: Eugenia believes what Eugenia believes because it's easier than risking disappointment. She's doggedly avoided it and has lived entirely on spite—*to take that away from her now*, Greta thinks, *would be to kill her, and she's done quite enough killing as it is.*

"Nancy has her last rally tonight. A big party at the Javits Center with over a thousand people. She's going to win, you know."

Eugenia sighs—her shoulders collapse in on themselves.

"It is looking that way, isn't it?"

Sunlight finds its way through thick, red curtains, and Greta hauls the L.L.Bean bag onto her lap. She's done making small talk; she's already been here for over an hour. She's walked through the garden, toured the new art, and—now—burned herself on a cup of too-hot tea. She used to look forward to visiting Eugenia's house, and now she can't wait to never come again. She doesn't like the way the angels were staring at her. It's time to get rid of a murder weapon.

"I brought you something."

Greta unzips the bag and pulls out the sword. On the other side of the coffee table, Eugenia's eyes go wide.

"Is that—"

"It is."

Pulling the scabbard off an inch, Greta shows her grandmother a bit of the blade.

"But your mother—how did you . . ."

"I convinced her, I guess." Greta shrugs. "I know how much you've always wanted it, and it seemed silly to keep fighting over it."

Eugenia reaches out her hands: she wants to touch it. Greta looks at them—the ten skeletal fingers, the two waxy palms—and decides to hold on a little longer.

"This might sound funny," she says. "But throwing a champagne bottle through a window in Paris can really help you put things in perspective."

But Eugenia is not listening. Her head is lowered, and her arms are still stretched out. For a moment Greta wonders if she's dead—if, finally, she pushed herself to take that one last step, and that this is how her body will forever stay. The cherub reaching for his grape; Eugenia grasping for her sword. Then her fingers move, as if beckoning the blade closer; greedily, they curl and wiggle. Greta hands it over.

"Thank you, Greta." Eugenia pulls the scabbard to her fragile chest. "Thank you, thank you, thank you."

Her eyes well up and, moments later, tears spill down Eugenia's cheeks. Turning away, Greta scratches at a scab on her elbow. The whole scene strikes her as silly, and more than a little pathetic, until she realizes that this was never really about a sword, but rather about escaping the truth—that unbearable need to be held, for just a bit longer, by the safe embrace of a lie. And when that happens, Greta holds her breath, closes her eyes, and kisses her grandmother on the cheek—she has, after all, felt that terrible need, as well. Eugenia's skin is dry, and fragile, and is made to taste bitter by a spritzing of perfume. Still, Greta keeps her lips there. She listens to Eugenia's quiet weeping and feels her shoulders shiver and she makes a decision: from now on, she will think for herself. No one—not mothers or grandmothers or handsome French trolls—will tell Greta Harrison what, or whom, to believe.

"WHAT DO YOU THINK SHE'LL do with it?" Greta asks. "The sword, I mean."

Nancy takes a container of red pepper flakes and shakes a few of them onto a slice of pizza. After leaving her grandmother's apartment, Greta was hungry, made inexplicably ravenous by all of Eugenia's crying, so she picked up a pie ("sausage, olives, *be liberal with the cheese*") on her walk back across town. When she arrived at the San Marino, the bottom of the box was hot and wet, and her mother was in the kitchen, listening to Barbra Streisand. She was in full makeup, and her hair was freshly coiffed; she had been on the *Today* show this morning. Standing next to the sink, Greta watched, unseen, as she hummed along to the music and pulled from the cupboards the ingredients to make cookies: flour, sugar, a bag of chocolate chips. None of this was a surprise to Greta—the election is tomorrow, and Nancy is a notorious stress-baker; in the fall of 2014, when she thought she was going to get primaried, she spent two weeks pounding sheets of butter for three hundred croissants, her phone pinned against her shoulder as she cold-called voters. To make herself known, Greta called out *hello!*—she didn't want to give her mother a heart attack—and then set the pizza box down on the table. There, she noticed a thoroughly dissected copy of today's *Post*, alongside a half-finished boulevardier. Instantly, Greta knew, or at least suspected, what her mother was so diligently searching for among its pages. Some mention, however brief, of a missing Frenchman. The dust of human bones, discovered among the trash.

Nancy lifts her slice of pizza, and its point sags toward her plate.

"Probably sneak in here and slit my throat." She takes a bite, and Greta winces. "I'm sorry—it's a little too soon for those kinds of jokes."

"Yes. A little too soon."

The smell of baking dough wafts from the oven while, on a speaker next to the toaster, Barbra sings. *Eye on the target and wham / one shot one gun shot and bam!*

"Her dream was always to donate it to the Met," Nancy says, swallowing. "So, I imagine she'll finally go ahead and do it. She never actually liked the damn thing; she just didn't want me to have something that was hers."

She finishes the slice and reaches for a second one but is stopped, an inch from the crust, by two competing sounds: the first, a timer, buzzing on the kitchen counter; the second, a telephone, ringing in the living room.

Nancy wipes the grease from her fingers with a paper towel, then tosses a pot holder to Greta—one that's yellow, and quilted, and has a large charred hole where it once caught fire.

"That'll be Cate with the new AP poll," she says. "Meantime, take care of that timer, will you? There's nothing worse than a burnt cookie."

Hot air blasts Greta's face as, one by one, she transfers the cookies to a paper towel to cool. Scoop, lift, lower; scoop, lift, lower. It's a simple action, meditative in its repetition, and as she listens to her mother's footsteps clop down the hall, her mind suddenly shuts off. For an instant she forgets everything. She never fought with her mother, or stabbed a French lover dead, or lived—*for a whole entire year*—in Bushwick. But then those memories return: the recent afternoons spent scrubbing the bathroom, the lingering stench of someone else's blood. The weight of them is crushing—when it lands on her she drops the spatula, which lands with a *clang* on the floor. Still, as she crouches down to retrieve it, Greta allows herself to consider that, maybe, this is how normalcy returns for a person—not in a flood but in dribbles. One day you're standing in the kitchen and you realize that you've managed to forget—first for a short stretch, but then a longer one—all the mistakes that you have made. With it come other changes, little bits of peace that you once took for granted but have since thought lost. Sirens wail outside your window and, no matter how close they get, or how threatening, you learn to simply ignore them; strangers glance in your direction, and you trust they're looking at someone else.

In the living room, she hears the muted hum of Nancy's voice, and then the *click* of the phone being returned to its cradle. Footsteps follow—slow at first, but then they quicken; a moment later, Nancy is clearing her throat at the entrance to the kitchen.

"So, how much are we going to beat Carmichael by?" Greta asks when she sees her. A bit of melted chocolate coats her thumb and—happily—she licks it away.

"That wasn't Cate."

"Oh? Who was it, then?"

"It was the doorman."

"What'd he want?"

"It seems as though we have a guest."

"What?" Two cookies remain on the baking sheet. Greta sets the spatula down. "Who is it?"

Swallowing, Nancy lifts her chin and strains her neck.

She says, "It's the FBI."

The Harrison Guide to Entertaining

"Please, have one," Nancy says, gesturing to a plate piled high with cookies.

Agent DiFiori looks around the living room, scrutinizing its corners. Then, careful not to knock the heap over, she takes a cookie and gingerly breaks it in half. Steam rises from the crease.

"These are delicious," she says, taking one bite and then another. "Truly."

Delighted, Nancy clasps her pearls. She leans forward in her chair and winks.

She says, "The secret is to barely beat the egg."

DiFiori lifts an eyebrow and reaches for a second helping. She's a slim brunette with a no-nonsense bun, and on her lap rests a blank notepad and a black Bic pen. She chews slowly and with her eyes gently closed, her jaw working in deliberate circles. Nancy seizes on the opportunity to steal a glance at Greta, who is leaning a hip against the credenza where Howard's sword once stood. Her arms are folded across her chest, and methodically she cracks each of her knuckles with her thumb, pressing against the folds in her skin until the joint clicks. Nancy smiles and crosses her legs: she wants to scream at her daughter to stop. She wants to stand up, walk over to her, and pin her thin arms against her side until she holds perfectly and inconspicuously still.

"Sweetheart," she says, "why don't you go get Agent DiFiori a glass of milk?"

Greta unfolds her arms. Sweat reflects off her forehead.

"Seriously?"

"She must be thirsty."

Agent DiFiori shakes her head. Using the back of her hand, she dabs at her lips.

"Oh, thank you, but I'm fine."

Her gaze still set on her daughter, Nancy smiles and nods toward the kitchen.

"Well, just in case, then," she says.

Greta frowns for a moment, then blinks twice; pushing herself away from the credenza, she walks, her fingers still clenched and fidgeting, toward the kitchen. A moment later, Nancy hears the refrigerator open.

Agent DiFiori says, "I know this must be a busy day for you—"

"Why would you ever think that?"

"—so I'll try to make this as quick and as painless as possible."

Nancy lifts a hand, quieting her.

She says, "Please, take all the time you need. I can't imagine what on earth this is all about."

DiFiori tilts forward and reaches for a third cookie. "We've received a phone call about a missing person. A man by the name of—"

"Is that *Charlie Liu* down there?"

Greta appears in the kitchen doorway, a tall glass of milk in her hand.

"Pardon?" The notepad falls from DiFiori's knees, taking the pen with it. Reaching a hand down, she scoops them both up.

"There's a man leaning against a black car, parked on the other side of Central Park West." Walking to the window, Greta peers down. Milk sloshes over the glass's lip. "And I swear to God it's Charlie Liu."

Nancy folds her hands in her lap. "I'm sorry, but *who*?"

"He's the one Nick's been seeing." Greta sets the glass on the coffee table and sits next to her mother. With her free hand she taps a spot on her neck. "The one who gave him the, well, *you know*."

On the couch, DiFiori straightens her spine and clears her throat. She brushes a crumb from her knee.

"Agent Liu is my colleague," she says. "Given that he, um, knows your son, we both thought it would be best if he recused himself from this investigation, lest there be a conflict of interest."

"So, you're saying there *is* an investigation happening."

"That's my job, Congresswoman—I work for the Federal Bureau of *Investigation*."

"Of course." Nancy concedes with a solemn dip of her chin. Outside, a helicopter thumps against the clouds. "Investigate away."

DiFiori smiles unevenly. She angles her chair toward Greta.

"Have you ever met someone named Xavier de la Marinière," she asks.

In the San Marino's hallway, Mrs. Branovich's dog barks twice. Greta eyes her mother.

"It's okay," Nancy whispers. "You can tell the truth."

There's a pause, at the end of which Greta emits a pained sigh.

"I made a mistake. A horrendous, unforgivable mistake. I do know Xavier—I met him in June. I was playing some stupid game online, and there he was. I should have never spoken to him, but I was lonely, and angry, and generally fucked up. I'm sorry—that's crass." She shakes her head. "I had broken up with my boyfriend, Ethan, and I was *not in a good place.* Anyway, he convinced me to visit him in France, and like a total *imbecile*, I did. I lived with him in his apartment, and believed in all the terrible lies that he was telling me, and when he told me to throw that champagne bottle I didn't think twice about it. I wanted to feel like I belonged to something, you know? I felt like I was turning invisible, like my skin was actually turning translucent and people—strangers, friends, my own family—were staring straight through me. Xavier made me feel special, like I was somehow necessary."

As DiFiori scribbles in her notepad, Greta's eyes well up and tears stream down her cheeks. Scooting her chair a few inches to the right, Nancy rubs her daughter's back.

"It was all a lie, of course—Xavier is a monster. Nick helped me see that when he found me in Paris, and then when I told Xavier that I was leaving him he gave me *this*."

Greta points to her bruise, which has faded to a faint lilac. She buries her face in her hands.

"I realize this is difficult, but I have a few more questions." Agent DiFiori moves to the edge of the couch. "When you were in Paris, did you happen to meet a woman named Colette Legard?"

"No." A heave erupts, followed by two shuddering sobs. "Who's that?"

"It's Mr. de la Marinière's girlfriend."

Greta lifts her head.

She says, "His *what?*" as Nancy digs her fingernails into her daughter's spine.

"Oh, yes," Greta whimpers, and continues, "*Colette.* I'm sorry, I forgot. Xavier had so many of them. Girlfriends, I mean, these little playthings that he slept with. I was one of many. You know how French men are."

"I don't, but I can imagine." DiFiori props her elbows on her knees. "I'm here because Mr. de la Marinière has gone missing. Records show that he arrived in New York on Wednesday of last week, and no one—including the hotel where he's staying—has heard from him or seen him since Friday. According to Miss Legard, you're the only person he knows in the city. I'm hoping you might be able to provide some insights into his whereabouts."

A long, slanted shadow stretches across the wall. Outside, the dog barks again.

"I have no idea. I haven't seen him since—"

Nancy interrupts her.

"Greta." She sets her hand on her daughter's thigh. "Agent DiFiori is just doing her job. Please, dear, tell her the truth."

Closing her eyes, Greta pinches the bridge of her nose.

"I saw him on Friday morning," she says after a protracted pause. "He showed up here, after I spoke at my mother's rally."

Agent DiFiori glances up from her notes.

"I saw that speech," she says. "It was very good."

"Thank you." Demurely, Greta tucks her chin to her chest. "I appreciate that."

"And then what happened?"

"He screamed at me. He told me that he was in love with me, and that if I didn't come back to Paris with him he was going to do something awful."

"Like what?"

Again Greta cries, this time running her fingers through her hair.

"I don't know! Oh God, do you think he would kill himself? Over *me*?"

DiFiori shakes her head.

"Let's not jump to any conclusions. After he said these things to you—after he made these threats—then what happened?"

"I showed up." Nancy smiles and twirls her rings. "And I told him to get the hell out of my house."

Across the coffee table, DiFiori's fingers pinch the tip of her ballpoint pen.

"And what time did this occur?" she asks.

"Oh, I don't know. Noon? Twelve thirty?"

After making a note of the time, DiFiori flips her notepad shut. The pen she slips into the breast pocket of her blazer.

"We can verify that with security footage, certainly," she says.

Condensation fogs the untouched glass of milk. Beside her, Nancy feels Greta's shoulders tense.

"We don't have cameras in the hallways, I'm afraid," she says. "It's a very particular building, and the residents are concerned with their privacy. *Demi Moore* once lived here, you know. I'm sure you understand."

DiFiori runs her tongue across her teeth and turns to face the window. A vein pulses on her neck.

"How about the elevators, then?"

"The elevators?"

"There are cameras in the elevators. I saw them on my ride up."

Rising from the couch, DiFiori buttons her coat. Left on the coffee table is the uneaten half of a cookie, which—after eyeing it for a moment—she pops in her mouth.

"If you'd be so kind, Congresswoman, how about we take a look at those."

THE OFFICE OF THE SUPERINTENDENT of the San Marino occupies a space the size of two parked Subarus, carved out from the southern side of the building's first floor. There's one window—a single pane of dust-streaked glass, which, were the blinds not drawn, would offer views of the sidewalk on Seventy-Fourth Street. Set against one wall is a steel rack of cleaning supplies, and against the other a desk with a computer. There, sitting in the screen's blue-gray glow, Besnik, the building's super, scrolls through security footage from the elevators. A ring of keys hangs from his belt; cords dangle from the office's low ceilings. Nancy leans against a free spot on the wall and smiles at Agent DiFiori.

"So," she says, "the Eff Bee *Eye*. That must be fascinating work."

DiFiori straightens out her blazer.

"I take pride in my work, ma'am."

On Besnik's computer, a parade of the San Marino's residents file into its elevators, their bodies and faces blurred. Here is a film star who sold a tell-all; here is a banker and the woman with whom he's having his third affair. Nancy watches them and wonders if she's able to tell who they are because she knows their stories—if, in other words, the sum of their histories informs the shape they cut. She hopes that's the case—prays for it, actually. Because otherwise, she's fucked.

"There." Nancy taps Besnik on the shoulder. "That's him, right next to my daughter."

Leaning forward, DiFiori scrutinizes the screen. On it, a man in a thick coat talks intensely to Greta, a Mets cap obscuring his face. His fists clench, his arms shake—Greta stares forward, undeterred. The footage is short. Eight seconds at most. The elevator's doors open and, together, they leave.

"Can we see him leaving now?" DiFiori asks.

Besnik grumbles, then gives a curt nod. The chewed-up stub of a pencil is tucked behind his ear. Nancy's pulse quickens—she can feel it in her wrists.

She says, "You know, I've sat on the permanent select committee on intelligence for about eight years now."

DiFiori sneezes, burying her nose in the crook of her arm.

"Yes," she says, wiping her eyes. "I—we, the bureau, I mean—are well aware of that."

"Which is simply to point out that you'll be hard-pressed to find someone who is *as appreciative* of everything you do."

The tips of the agent's ears turn crimson. Her neck strains.

"Thank you, Congresswoman."

"Oh, please, Agent DiFiori. Call me Nancy."

His spine curved to a shallow crescent, Besnik scrolls through more footage. To prevent herself from squirming, Nancy clasps her hands, pressing her fingers into each other until her knuckles are tense and pale. Dust clings to the light, swirling in the air all around her. She watches it for a moment, before turning her sights to the window. She waits.

Then, an interminable minute later, DiFiori says, "*Stop.*" Glancing over, Nancy sees that her nose is six inches from Besnik's computer, and she's scrutinizing a freeze-framed image of a man. He has Xavier's loose posture, and he's roughly Xavier's width; he is also wearing Xavier's blue coat and Xavier's hat.

"Zoom in," DiFiori says, and Nancy watches her eyes. The way they search the screen for clues, abnormalities, details, lies. She thinks: *For the love of God, Tom, keep your head down.*

After a long pause, the agent stands up straight and faces Nancy.

"Nice try, ma'am," she says.

Nancy's breath stops—a boulder in her chest.

"I—"

"He left at one o'clock—not twelve thirty." DiFiori squints at the toes of her shoes. "I wonder where he could have gone."

Nancy exhales and shrugs. Never before have her shoulders felt so light.

"To terrorize someone else's daughter, I imagine."

DiFiori laughs—a little—as Nancy leads her into the San Marino's lobby. It's bright, certainly brighter than it was in Besnik's office, and the sudden change momentarily blinds her. Still, she keeps walking, taking long strides across the marble floor as she blinks away stars; behind her she can hear DiFiori struggling to keep up. At the building's entrance, she stops next to a table containing a single white orchid, where she runs her finger in a long, straight line to check for dust.

"Please let me know if there's anything else you need," she says once they've stepped outside. "It's a mother's worst fear, you know, having her child go missing like that."

From her pocket DiFiori fishes out a set of keys.

"We will, ma'am. And thank you again for taking the time on such a busy day."

"Nonsense—justice always comes first."

Nancy looks toward DiFiori's car, a black Ford Taurus in front of which stands Charlie Liu, his hands clasped at his waist. Shielding her gaze from the sun, Nancy appraises him: kind eyes, attentive ears, a strong, capable chin. Bowing his head slightly, he gives a small wave.

"I hear you've been seeing something of my son," she calls out to him.

A bus lumbers up Central Park West, its horn a frightening bay.

Once it's passed, Charlie says, "I've enjoyed getting to know him, ma'am." His voice cracks; his toes turn inward. "And my dog likes him, too."

Nancy smiles.

"A dog," she says. "How nice."

IN THE LIVING ROOM GRETA picks the milk up off the coffee table and begins drinking it, her eyes pressed shut and her head tilted back. Soon she feels herself in need of air, but still she keeps going, coating her throat in a slimy, viscous film as her lungs burn. It's only when she's finished the milk, and when she has returned the glass to the table, that—finally— she allows herself a breath. Opening her eyes and staring at the ceiling, she gasps, "Holy *shit.*"

She has been here, alone in the apartment, for the past fifteen minutes, ever since Nancy and the FBI agent left to check the security footage from the elevators. In that time she has sat in a chair, curled up on her bed, and lain—flat, like a corpse—on the kitchen's cool, tiled floor. She has paced, stood still, and held her face in her hands; she has pictured her mug shot, splashed across *Page Six.* At alternating moments, she has also felt within her a sort of Hail Mary indignation, a survivalism fueled by nerves and despair. Didn't DiFiori need a warrant, or something? She tried to recall the hundreds of police procedurals she'd watched, the hours and hours of *SVU.* Couldn't she and Nancy kick her out? Tell her to get lost until she had a letter from a judge? She could—she thought she had that right—but then, that never worked out well when it happened on television, did it. The letter is always obtained, the search is always conducted; in the end, all the suspect manages to do is look more suspicious.

And anyway, by that point it was too late; when Greta thought to push back, DiFiori was already downstairs, scrutinizing footage of Tom, wearing Xavier's hat and coat. *Tom, wearing Xavier's hat and coat*—a plan that once struck her as genius was now plainly and nauseatingly absurd, the sort of detail that would be recounted in a podcast about her crime, long after she had been locked up. Frantically she began casing the apartment, sweeping it for any evidence of Xavier. Lowering to her hands and knees, she searched beneath the sofa for strands of dark hair, flakes of perfect skin; then, rising, she jogged to the bathroom where, two days earlier, she had spent hours scrubbing away a dead man's blood. It was then, during this race down the hallway, that she happened to glance out the window to see her mother and Agent DiFiori standing on the sidewalk. They were talking—amicably, it seemed—and around DiFiori's finger swung a ring of keys. Greta exhaled and watched them for a bit longer; Charlie waved at Nancy, and Greta's pulse, which seconds ago had been a jackhammer, slowed in her chest. Her mouth tasted suddenly like mothballs—she realized she was parched. Remembering the glass of milk on the coffee table, she jogged to the living room.

Now, her thirst quenched, she shuffles over to her mother's stereo to play some music—a little Julie London, she figures, to lighten the apartment's mood. Then she stares at the glass, its sides coated in white, a half ring of pink lipstick crowning its rim. She thinks: *could she, Greta Harrison, possibly be this lucky?* Stuffing a cookie into her mouth, she tries to account for every time that she stepped over a crack on the sidewalk or avoided a black cat's path. She tallies the mirrors that haven't been broken and umbrellas that haven't been opened; the fingers crossed, the clovers found, the horseshoes kept. Have all those little omens, those signs in which she's never quite believed, added up to—well—*this*? She reaches for another cookie and eats it as quickly as she did the first; she doesn't know, but also, she doesn't care. She's just happy that she can finally breathe.

In the hallway outside, she hears the chime of the elevator, followed by the sound of her mother's footsteps, making their way assuredly across the carpet. The song that's playing changes—"Perfidia" to "Blue Moon"—and as Greta chews, she wanders back to the window, where she feels the sun warm her face. Once again she peeks down, now with a pair of her mother's old opera glasses and with half her body shielded by thick, linen curtains. The black Taurus is still there, parked on the other side of the street, and Charlie is still standing alongside its hood. He's speaking to someone, though the angle from which Greta is spying makes it impossible for her to make out whom. Her fingertips buzzing, she pushes the curtains aside an inch further and steps to the center of the window's frame. Standing on her tiptoes, she refocuses the glasses, and that's when Greta sees him: Nick—her brother—staring up at her face.

A cyclist yells on the street below, and Nancy returns from the foyer. She's walking briskly, and when she says "Well, *that* was exciting," Greta hisses and raises a finger to her lips. Confused, Nancy mouths *what?* but Greta offers no response; instead, she keeps her chin tilted downward, straining to listen. Annoyed, Nancy walks to the stereo to turn off the music. It's then, once Julie London is gone, done singing about the End of the World, that she hears it, too: another set of footsteps jogging toward them from the elevator.

Greta uses both of her hands to cover her mouth. She says, "Oh, *no*," repeating it over and over, until the words find a rhythm, become a mantra. A moment later keys jingle in the front door, and Nick appears in the living room. He stands there, at first saying nothing, a bag of Chinese takeout swinging back and forth from a hooked finger. He looks around; his eyes narrow. When Greta peeks at his face, she sees that it's a concerning shade of white.

"Why did I run into Charlie outside, and why did he ask me about Xavier?" His gaze darts all around, lingering for a second too long on the rug-less floor and the empty credenza. "And where is Dad's sword?"

Nancy doesn't answer him, and neither does Greta. Instead, she focuses on a pear-shaped shadow on the wall, willing it to consume her whole. Then she hears a loud, wet crash. Looking down, she sees that Nick has thrown the food to his feet. Lo mein lies in heaps next to open cardboard boxes. Rice coats the floor like freshly fallen snow.

"Someone needs to tell me what's happening," he yells. "And it better be the fucking truth."

Crouching down, Nancy sighs and begins collecting pieces of steamed broccoli, dropping them one by one into her open palm.

She says, "Nick, let's take a walk."

The Good Son

The Bethesda Fountain stands, more or less a bull's-eye, in the middle of Central Park. To the north of it is the lake, a spoked body of water dotted with rented rowboats; to the south, a terrace with a tiled arcade. On top of the fountain presides a statue, an angel with her wings spanned wide. In the palm of one hand she holds a lily; with the other she blesses the water at her feet. When it's running, which it is today, that water wets the faces of four cherubs (Temperance, Purity, Health, Peace) before splashing into an upper basin, and then, finally, the pool below. It's not deep, the pool, but it's not necessarily shallow, either: Nick knows because he fell into it, facedown and arms outstretched—an angel, as it were, of a different sort—when he was eight years old.

According to Nancy's retelling of the story, he tripped. She was pre-occupied with Greta, who was two and had spilled the better part of a Mister Softee cone down the front of her shirt, when, from behind her, Nancy heard a loud splash. Spinning around, she searched for Nick ("He had been there, right *there*, walking on the edge of the fountain!") and found him, nearly twenty seconds later, floating unconscious in the pool. It wasn't a big deal—this is a point she has stressed during the story's innumerable recitals, too. While at the time she was *obviously* panicked, as soon as she yanked him out of the fountain he opened his eyes and started coughing, and on his forehead there was only the smallest trickle of blood. *Really*, she thinks, *he was probably just stunned*.

Nick remembers it differently—namely, in his version he was pushed.

It happened fast—he hardly had time to blink—but the image is none-theless there, codified in his memory: his mother, knocking him in the cheek as she turned to help Greta; the sky suddenly gone as water filled his ears. Over the years he tried to reconcile this discrepancy. They would be at dinner parties, or with friends during the holidays, and because Nancy enjoys telling stories, particularly those in which she is the hero, the Incident at Bethesda Fountain would inevitably surface. During these occasions, Nick waited patiently for the climax, the moment where the mother saves the son from a certain, soggy death, and upon its arrival, he cleared his throat to say, "Actually, it happened a little differently." The look that Nancy gave him each time was the same—a combination of bemusement, irritation, and betrayal; an expression that seemed to ask why, or how, Nick could do such a thing. In those moments, as the con-versation around him barreled forward, he would find himself wonder-ing if, perhaps, he *had* gotten it wrong. After all, there were only so many facts a mind could hold on to. The more often a person tells himself a story, the farther it gets from the truth.

Now, seated on the edge of the fountain with his mother, he thinks of what she has finished confessing to him: a man murdered, the blood on his sister's hands. The shock has dissipated—not entirely, but enough for his mind to process the sounds, the smells around him. Running his hand an inch above its water, Nick slowly shakes his head. *He should have run as soon as she hauled him out of it,* he thinks, all those years ago. *He should have packed a suitcase with clothes and crackers, hailed a cab, and booked it west.*

"Say something," Nancy says. She's wearing black sunglasses and a camel hair coat. Her hands rest in her lap.

"What do you want me to say?"

"I don't know." She dips her chin. "Anything."

Under the arches of the arcade, a man strums an out-of-tune guitar, its open case dotted with dollars at his feet. Watching him, Nick says nothing. He waits for the space between words to become intolerably long, and once that happens, Nancy coughs. She's never been good at silences. It's caused her trouble in interviews, and it's causing her trouble now.

She says, "My first priority has always been to make life better for you and Greta."

"You pushed a body down a trash chute, Mom, and then you lied about it to the FBI."

"I'm not saying I've done it *perfectly*, but Nick, sweetie, I've tried."

A woman glides by on Rollerblades. On the lake, two teenagers shift their weight to rock a wooden boat, their laughter reaching up to half-bare branches.

Nancy removes her sunglasses.

"You can't imagine what it's like," she says. "And I don't mean that condescendingly, but factually: you simply can't imagine. One day, you have no one to take care of except yourself. The world isn't a place of danger but of possibility, the future something to be conquered, as opposed to feared. But then, the next day, you have these two faces looking up at you. You love them so much that it's painful—you think on some days that that love may actually destroy you—and everything shifts. When you take a walk, you start noticing all the trash on the street, and you wonder if any of it's toxic. Cars are suddenly going too fast, and men are suddenly standing too close. You go to bed at night thinking about guns in schools and rising sea levels and evil French fascists seducing your daughter, and you decide 'Well, *fuck* it.' The only option is to fix things, because you're sure as hell not going to leave them for your children looking like this."

Nick waits. Then, when he's convinced she's finished, he says, "I wrote you that line about cars going too fast—it was for a speech you gave at Lincoln Center. And also, not every mother helps her daughter get away with murder."

Nancy blushes and nods: this is a point she is willing to concede.

"No, you're right about that," she says. "But parents are people, and politicians are, too. I've spent thirty years as the former and twenty as the latter, and in that time, I've only disposed of a single body. When you have children of your own, Nick, you'll realize those numbers aren't so bad."

The woman on the Rollerblades spins twice, her arms pinwheeling through the air, before taking off backward toward the terrace.

"I should have known you would do this," Nick says. "When you told me that flying to Paris was the last thing you'd ever ask me to do, I should have known there would be one more thing. Because there always is, Mom. There's always one more thing."

"To be clear: I didn't ask your sister to stab that man. She did that all on her own."

A breeze disrupts the fountain's pool. Shivering, Nick shoves his fists into the pockets of his coat.

He says, "I was about to get out of here. That's what I was trying to tell you on the phone on Friday—that I decided to move to California."

Nancy flinches at the news. She pulls her coat tighter across her chest.

"That will be nice. Warmer, at the very least."

"I had these dumb visions of, like, taking the freeway everywhere and watching the sunset on the beach."

"No one goes to the beach in Los Angeles. It's right there, and unless they live right on top of it, they never go."

Nick doesn't look at her—he can't. Instead he focuses on two pigeons, pecking at a slice of bread.

He says, "Whatever. There's not going to be any of that now. No traffic, no sunsets over the Pacific, no not going to the beach. I'm staying here. I'm not moving to Los Angeles."

"Because of all this?"

"Yes!" Startled, the pigeons abandon the bread and take flight. Nick lowers his voice. "And because of Charlie. He's going, and the plan was for me to go with him, but—well, it appears that he and I now have a conflict of interest."

Nick waits as Nancy considers what he has told her. The sun shifts, and she closes her eyes.

"You poor thing—do you love him?"

He swallows, and his throat feels tight. He begins to cry.

"Yeah, I think I might."

High overhead, a plane banks east. Nancy slips on her sunglasses and watches it, the contrail a streak of white against the reddening sky.

"Well, then, you need to go," she says. "If you love him, you have to."

"I can't."

"Why not?"

"Are you kidding? Because I *can't*, Mom." The tears increase their velocity, and the world around Nick turns blurry. His breaths shorten, his hands shake, his heart pounds: he feels anger throbbing in his chest. "This was my opportunity, don't you see? My entire life I've spent picking up the pieces, cleaning up messes for you and for Greta, because that's what I thought being a good son meant. I thought that being loved by you meant making myself useful to you—no, please don't interrupt me, please don't say that I *misunderstood*. This was my chance to escape that, Mom. For the first time I was going to feel free, and like I was living on my own terms. But I can't do that now, can I? Because once again my family has managed to create some clusterfuck from which I am categorically inextricable. Once again, you've found a way to ensure that I'll stay."

"I'm not asking you to stay, Nicholas."

"But I have to, don't I?" A leaf lies at Nick's feet. He crushes it beneath his heel. "You know I can't keep this to myself, Mom. She killed a man, she murdered him. And I'm supposed to not say anything? Even if I manage to do that, someone is going to find out about it, because that's what happens with things like this—*someone always finds out*. And when they do, I'll lose my sister, and I'll lose Charlie. Worst of all, I'll lose you." Nick sees it: the trial, the empty apartment, the holidays spent grieving alone. A future he has spent the better part of his adulthood trying to prevent and that now, at last, has caught up with him. "Christ, Mom, how could you be so stupid?"

Water splashes behind his mother's head, a fine mist that catches the fading light. Birds circle over treetops; squirrels play tag on flimsy branches; a child unspools a heart-shaped kite. Angling herself toward him, Nancy rests her hands atop Nick's knees.

She says, "I wish we weren't here, Nick. I wish we weren't sitting on the edge of this fountain, trying to figure out what to do as our backs get soaking wet and our ears bleed from that awful guitar. I wish your sister never went to Paris. She did, though, and now a man—a monster—is dead. Was she right to kill him? My head tells me no—I think of laws, and rules; I think of all that I've spent my career defending—and I say, of course not. My heart, though . . . well, my heart is telling me that sometimes things are more complicated than my head would like them to be. I don't know which one is right, but also, it doesn't matter. Because I'm her mother, Nick, and what that means is that I'm never going to stop fighting for her, or you."

Crouching, the guitarist takes a break to count his cash. The breeze stops, the water settles; the fountain returns to its ambivalent trickle.

"I'm not going to tell you what choice to make. Ultimately, that's something you'll need to decide on your own. You're right that if you say something—that if anyone says anything—you'll lose me. Greta also, for that matter." Here, Nancy reaches up and slowly scratches at her ear. "And while I can see how, at this present moment, that outcome might hold some appeal, all I'm asking is that you stop and think. Life's a fucking mess, Nicholas, and family is, too. One of these days, though, you're going to look around and be glad we're there."

His back aching, Nick shifts his weight from side to side. He thinks of the pictures on Charlie's refrigerator, the sensation of sand between his toes. He tries to conjure the taste of salt.

"I was going to have a new beginning," he says.

Nancy sighs. "There's no such thing."

"What's that supposed to mean?"

"Just what it sounds like, I'm afraid. Clean slates, new beginnings—there's none of that, not in real life, anyway. There's making sense of yesterday so you can do it better tomorrow. And in my experience, sometimes that requires you to hide something from a person you care about in order to protect them." She stares forward, into the thicket of dying leaves. "There are plenty of things in life that I wish I'd never been told, and a hundred more that I regret having said. Do you understand what I'm getting at, Nick? Yes, you have a duty to be honest. You also have a duty to love."

For a long while they say nothing, and instead allow the world to fill the space between them: the guitarist, plucking out "Blackbird"; the shouts of the teenagers, rocking their boat. After a few minutes Nancy lifts an arm to wave and, following her gaze, Nick sees his sister, standing atop the staircase that leads from the fountain to the terrace. She's shielding her eyes from the sun, searching the crowd for her family, and when, finally, she sees them, she waves, too. From this distance she appears small, fragile; he can't imagine her doing what she's done, let alone having the wherewithal to get away with it. Leaning forward, he props his elbows on his knees. He thinks: *look at this awful mess they've made*, and then considers his mother's proposition. *What happens to a secret when you hide it from someone you love? Does it, like everything else, become dulled by the incessant pounding of life? That is*, Nick thinks, *a possibility*. After a month, a year, a decade, it's conceivable that faces erode and edges soften; that this thing, which is now unfathomably large, becomes small enough to get buried beneath all the other unspoken grievances, the necessary, daily fabrications. The opposite is equally as likely, though. He imagines the weight of what isn't said slowly suffocating him, pressing against his chest as he tries to sleep at night. He imagines lying in bed and hearing it, echoing in that wild western darkness. The howl of so many coyotes, stalking him in the canyon.

Greta descends the stairs while, on the ledge beside him, Nick's phone begins to rattle. He looks at Charlie's name on its screen, then up at his mother. He winces.

"You're telling me to lie to him," he says.

Nancy shakes her head. Reaching down, she brushes her son's hair away from his eyes.

"No." She picks up the phone and places it in Nick's hand. "For the sake of everyone, I'm asking you not to tell the truth."

Epilogue

Five Years Later

Four knights ride on four armored horses, wooden lances positioned in their iron-clad hands. In one of the room's corners, two golden helmets glare at each other; in another, a pistol sets its sights on an iron shield. Between them are scattered crossbows, spears, axes; the incommodious battle dress of Emperor Ferdinand I. There is also a woman—not outfitted in chain mail or a dented breast plate, but rather a sleeveless black dress. Her hair, which is long, and not-quite-blond, is tied up and off her neck. Leaning over, she casually inspects a musket encased in a glass box. Its barrel is steel and its flintlock gold, and on its handle there's a stag, carved from yellow bone. Brushing some hair away from her face, the woman straightens her spine and cracks her neck. From behind, Nancy Harrison taps her shoulder.

"You left me in there," Nancy says, "with those decrepit, Upper East Side vultures."

Greta wipes the side of her mouth with the back of her hand. A purse hangs from her shoulder and she shrugs to readjust it.

"I was getting hot. And the food sucked."

"It really did. All those soggy canapés."

Voices echo from the other end of the gallery, the central corridor of the Metropolitan Museum of Art's Arms and Armor collection. Three kids play tag around an ax as their parents, trying to corral them, consult a museum map. Greta looks over her shoulder.

She says, "Besides, I wanted to see it."

"It?"

With her chin, Greta gestures to a small display case on the other side of the room, where her father's sword rests beneath soft yellow light. Among the mounted knights and six-foot spears, the weapon looks small and unremarkable: a toothpick retrieved from a shirt's pocket before it's tossed into the wash.

"Oh," Nancy says, "that." She looks around the gallery. "Where's your brother?"

"The last time I saw him was in Medieval Art. Charlie called during the reception, and he used it as an excuse to escape some chicken satays."

"Did he seem nervous?"

Greta keeps her eyes on the sword. She says, "It's a big day."

Nancy doesn't respond. Instead she hands Greta a folded paper program, on the cover of which is a pen-and-ink drawing of a patrician woman, along with the words EUGENIA HARRISON: A CELEBRATION OF A LIFE.

"I got you one of these," she says, "in case you missed the stack of them on your way out."

Greta looks at the program for a moment, then shoves it into the depths of her purse.

She says, "I can't believe they closed off the Temple of Dendur, just so everyone could pretend to be sad and eat a bunch of toast squares. If I were a tourist, I'd be pissed."

Three weeks ago, one month short of her ninety-second birthday, Eugenia died. A stroke was what finally killed her—an errant blood clot the size of a marble that hightailed it to her brain and left her facedown in a bowl of soup. Greta called Nancy to give her the news and then, two days later, Nancy read about it herself in the paper. After flipping through the Metro section, she glanced at the obituaries, and there, taking up a half-page above the fold, was Eugenia's face. A *philanthropist of unparalleled generosity*, the paper called her, noting that she'd left the entirety of her estate—every last cent of it—to the Met. A *loving, devoted mother* was there, too. Reading the words, Nancy was struck at first with a sudden, unexpected grief, right at the base of her throat; her knees buckled and her head went light and, reaching down, she steadied herself on the kitchen table. Soon enough that passed; whatever remorse Nancy was feeling gave way to ambivalence. Eugenia had been there, making Nancy's life hell, and now Eugenia was gone. Seeing a smudge on the kitchen window, she found a bottle of Windex and used the obituary to wipe it away. Then she phoned Nick and Greta and asked them to mark the funeral on their calendars. They would put on a good face and do the right thing, she told them. After all, she was running for reelection.

In the gallery, the parents close their map and quiet their children, ushering them into an adjoining room. Nancy makes use of the silence to replay the past four hours: a service at St. Bart's; a car ride uptown; a reception in the shadow of some gray, ancient Egyptian ruins. Early summer light shone through a wall of windows and onto portraits of Eugenia. Here she was as a young ballerina; here she was cradling Howard in her arms. In front of this last photograph Nancy stopped for nearly ten minutes, politely declining offers of smoked shrimp and deviled eggs. But then, from a few feet away, she heard one woman whispering about her, followed by a second. Turning, she looked for Greta and Nick; unable to find them, she left.

Now a crumb lingers on the waist of her daughter's dress. Reaching out a finger, Nancy flicks it away.

"Eugenia was always good at pissing people off," she says. "Why should dying get in the way of that? Your speech at the church was lovely, by the way."

"You couldn't tell I was gagging?"

Nancy shakes her head. "Not at all. You had the two women sitting in front of me sobbing into their handbags."

Grinning, Greta turns and crosses the gallery to examine a case adjacent to her father's sword. There, next to a gold sheath, is a dagger, its handle encrusted in rubies.

"I deserve a raise," she says. "Hey—where's Cate?"

"Morning sickness. She texted me when we were in the car. Tom's mother is in town, too. Neither of them could get away."

Greta looks down at the dagger, the jewels sparkling like snake eyes, set in a silver sun.

"I still think it's weird they're married. Don't you?"

Nancy smiles.

She says, "No. Not really."

The wedding had been small. Twenty people at a restaurant in a quiet part of Brooklyn, with Cate's father acting as the officiant. A few votive candles were set along a curved wooden bar, and between them were white flowers, bunched in glass vases. Peonies, tulips, baby's breath—Cate was fine with whatever, she told Nancy, so long as it didn't include freesias, which, in light of semirecent events, held for her a few (one?) problematic associations. When the ceremony was finished, and Tom had stopped crying, they stuffed themselves with plates of lasagna and carafes of Barolo, then cleared the tables away so people could dance. It was at this point that Nancy chose to discreetly take her leave; her hips didn't move like they used to, and besides, she had a train to catch at six o'clock the next morning. Rising from the corner where she'd been sitting, she hugged Cate, kissed her on the cheek, and asked her where to find Tom.

"He's getting some air," Cate told her. A lily with half its petals missing was tucked behind her ear. "He was telling the chef how happy he was, so I told him to take a break."

Nancy nodded. She said, "Good move," and then, after hugging Cate a second time, made her way outside. There, she found Tom sitting alone on a bench, an unlit cigarette pinched between two fingers in his right hand. He was leaning back with his legs stretched out, his glossy eyes gazing up into the night.

"Marriage looks good on you, Mr. Cooper," Nancy said, and reached down to rub his shoulder.

Startled, Tom shook himself to attention. Then he smiled and stood.

"Yeah." His breath smelled like bolognese and champagne. "I think so, too."

The collar of his shirt had turned up, revealing an inch of his tie, and Nancy spent a moment to fix it.

"Let the chef do her job, okay?" she said.

"I was just glad she could share this night with me."

"We all are, Tom."

A car passed on the street before them, its wheels bouncing over cobblestones, its headlights cutting through the humid night. Tom threw his arms around Nancy, leaning the entirety of his weight into her.

Resting his head on her shoulder, he said, "I wanted to tell you that I quit."

Nancy steadied him on his feet.

"How about we talk about it in the morning."

"No—there's no need to. I love you, Nancy. And I'm thankful. But I can't do this anymore. Winning isn't worth it." He shook his head, then looked into the restaurant's window, where Cate's head was thrown back with laughter. "Not when I have all that."

Nancy didn't ask what *it* was. There was no need to. While the world had moved on from Xavier de la Marinière—no one had much interest in finding a missing monster—she understood the weight on Tom's shoulders. An unwieldy burden that threatened to reveal itself during the most inopportune of moments: a committee hearing in Washington, a press breakfast in Midtown, a wedding in Brooklyn. *If I open my mouth, I'll say it, because those are the only words I know.* Inhale, exhale, close your eyes. Let the moment pass.

Crouching down, Nancy picked up Tom's cigarette, which had fallen to the concrete. She offered it to him, but Tom shook his head; instead, he hugged her again and went back inside. From the curb, Nancy watched as he lifted Cate from behind and spun them both in a circle, her legs kicking as she screamed and laughed. Overhead, a thin cloud coated the moon in gossamer and stars struggled to be seen. Nancy looked up, counting the brightest among them, before hailing a cab to take her home. She would get Tom a new job, she thought as she crossed the bridge into Manhattan, something at the EPA or the Nature Conservancy—he had always had a thing for oceans. Then, once that was done, she'd go about finding his replacement. It wouldn't be hard—in fact, she already had someone in mind

"Oh, by the way, I'm booking you on Maddow." A foot above the ruby-hilted dagger, Greta's fingers fly across her phone. "That lawyer from Port Washington is talking like he wants to get in on the primary, and we're going to shut that shit down right now."

"Good idea. It can't be tonight, though. It'll have to be tomorrow."

Nancy tucks her hair behind her ears. "Speaking of which, where the hell is your brother?"

"What?" Greta glances up from her phone. "Oh, he's over there."

"Where?"

"*There*, by that giant shield with the lion on it."

Standing on her toes, Nancy finally sees Nick, hanging up his phone. He's tan, in that way that New Yorkers who have decamped to California always seem to be, and his hair has been cropped close to his ears. He's wearing a black blazer over a pressed black T-shirt, and when he makes eye contact with Nancy he nods. The first year that he was gone, they hardly spoke. She called, probably too frequently, though more often than not her attempts rolled over to voicemail. Listening to his recorded greeting, Nancy found herself worrying that she had made a dreadful mistake—that in asking her son to share a secret with her, she had suc-ceeded only in pushing him away. Slowly, that began to shift. At Greta's behest, doors that were shut began to creak open, and phone calls were eventually returned. His demeanor was chilly at first, untrusting and detached, though lately she's noticed a warmth finding space between his words. On her most optimistic days, when the sun is high and the train on time, she tells herself that he has forgiven her, even though she knows forgiveness is something for which she can never ask. Rather, like all mothers, the best Nancy can do is hope that, one day, her children will understand.

"Is everything okay?" she asks once he's standing beside her.

"Everything's fine. Charlie called. He's going to meet us at the theater. We should get going, though—curtain's in an hour."

Behind them a docent leads a group of seniors past a case of iron spears. Greta crosses her arms.

"My big brother, having his very own musical open on Broadway."

"Previews, Greta. We're in *previews*." Nick knocks her gently with his shoulder. "You thought it'd never happen, though, did you."

"*What?*" Greta shakes her head adamantly. "That is *not* true. I always knew it was a genius idea."

"Oh my God. That is such bullshit. When I told you I was writing something about—"

"It was what you were calling it, Nick. It was just what you were *calling* it that I had a problem with. *Where She's From* is a much better title!"

"You are *actually* insane. Because if I remember correctly, you said the whole enterprise was—"

"Okay, *enough*." Nancy lifts a hand to silence her children. Then she uses it to rub her son's back. "I'm proud of you, Nick. We both are."

Voices ricochet in the adjoining galleries, and shoes squeak against marble floors. Nick looks at Nancy, his expression blank, and in the instant before he smiles she sees it: all the other bargains that life will ask them to make, the hundreds of thousands of times they'll be forced to redefine what's right. Then Nancy watches as his attention shifts to the glass case before them. He scans it slowly, his eyes gliding over the weapon's steel until they reach a small, white plaque placed directly below it. HUNTING SWORD WITH SCABBARD, it reads, GIFT OF EUGENIA HARRISON IN MEMORY OF HER SON HOWARD.

His voice hovering an inch above a whisper, Nick says, "Before we leave, I'd like to ask a favor."

Greta shifts her weight from one heel to the other; her left shoulder slumps.

"Oh yeah? What's that?"

"The next time I ask either of you to tell me the truth—*don't.*"

Nancy says nothing, but rather looks down and smiles. Ivory monkeys laugh back from the sword's worn handle. Six eyes reflect in fragments off a polished, silver blade.

ACKNOWLEDGMENTS

I first owe an endless amount of gratitude to my editor, James Melia, who has an uncanny ability to hear the stories that I'm trying to tell before I can hear them myself. James's dedication to this novel has been tireless and invaluable, and it's a privilege to work with him each and every day. There is also no one else with whom I'd rather spend an entire night talking about Joan Didion or Diane Keaton.

At Holt, I am also indebted to Amy Einhorn, Marian Brown, Lori Kusatzky, Pat Eisemann, Christopher O'Connell, Jane Elias, Gregg Kulick, and Chris Sergio. This book would not exist without their patience and hard work, and I'm thankful to be part of such a capable team.

For nearly fourteen years, Richard Pine has been my advocate, agent, mentor, and friend, and if I have anything to say about it, he'll be all of those things for fourteen more. At Inkwell, he is joined by Eliza Rothstein and Dave Forrer, both of whom were crucial in bringing the Harrisons to life. My gratitude is also due to Howie Sanders at Anonymous Content. Thank you, Howie, for believing in this book.

Kimberly Burns is a magician, and her guidance is priceless. Thank you, KB, for telling me what—and what not—to say.

While writing this book, I was fortunate enough to have early readers provide their insight on half-baked drafts and ideas, and they deserve recognition here. Molly Zakoor, in particular, was instrumental in giving shape to both the plot and the characters of this novel. Gerold Schroeder, Chris Rovzar, David Ebershoff, Eddy Chevalier, and Elizabeth Dunn were also wildly generous with their time and thoughts. I'm lucky to count them all as friends.

Thanks, also, to Mac Hawkins, Rakesh Satyal, Jason Richman, Peter Schottenfels, Tim Stack, Marine Nikola, Kristine Johnson, Clare O'Connor, Jillian Medoff, Ali Bujnowski, and Beth Machlan. Your guidance, patience, and wine have kept me (mostly) sane.

My family reads everything that I write, whether I like it or not. I love them all fiercely, and would throw a body down a trash chute for any one of them.

Finally, to my husband, Mac McCarty: thank you for sharing your life with me, and for inspiring all that I do.

ABOUT THE AUTHOR

GRANT GINDER's novels include *This Is How It Starts*, *Driver's Education*, *The People We Hate at the Wedding*, and *Honestly, We Meant Well*. He received his MFA from New York University, where he teaches writing. He lives in Brooklyn.